WARFARE, DIPLOMACY and POLITICS

WARFARE DIPLOMACY and POLITICS

Essays in Honour of *A. J. P. TAYLOR*

edited by Chris Wrigley

HAMISH HAMILTON : LONDON

First published in Great Britain 1986
by Hamish Hamilton Ltd
Garden House 57–59 Long Acre London WC2E 9JZ

British Library Cataloguing in Publication Data

Warfare, diplomacy and politics: essays in honour of A. J. P. Taylor.
1. Great Britain – Politics and government – 19th century
2. Great Britain – Politics and government – 20th century
I. Wrigley, Chris II. Taylor, A. J. P.
320.941 JN216

ISBN 0-241-11789-5

Typeset by Computape (Pickering) Ltd, North Yorkshire
Printed in Great Britain by
St. Edmundsbury Press, Bury St Edmunds, Suffolk

CONTRIBUTORS

Kathleen Burk is Lecturer in History and Politics at Imperial College, London University.

John Erickson is Professor and Director of Defence Studies, University of Edinburgh.

Michael Foot is M.P. for Blaenau Gwent, former Leader of the Labour Party, and author.

Éva Haraszti is Emeritus Senior Fellow of the Hungarian Institute for Historical Research.

Eric Hobsbawm is Professor Emeritus of Economic History at Birkbeck College, London University.

John Keegan is Senior Lecturer in War Studies at the Royal Military Academy, Sandhurst.

Paul Kennedy is J. Richardson Dilworth Professor of History, Yale University.

Wm. Roger Louis is Kerr Professor of English History and Culture, University of Texas, Austin.

Margaret Morris is Principal Lecturer in history at the Central London Polytechnic.

Brian Holden Reid is Editor of the Royal United Services Institute *Journal* and lectures in War Studies at King's College, London.

Keith Robbins is Professor of Modern History, Glasgow University.

Charles Townshend is Senior Lecturer in History at the University of Keele.

Chris Wrigley is Reader in Economic History at Loughborough University.

CONTENTS

FOREWORD

The essays in this volume are a tribute to Alan Taylor on his eightieth birthday. He is unique among British historians of the modern period in that he is both popular with general readers and much respected by academic historians. He is also unique in that this is the third *festschrift* in his honour.

There was no difficulty whatsoever in finding historians associated with Alan Taylor and his areas of research who had not contributed to the other collections and who were delighted at the opportunity to pay a tribute to him now. Those were the essays in honour of his sixtieth birthday, *A Century of Conflict 1850–1950* (Hamish Hamilton, 1966), edited by Martin Gilbert, and those in honour of his seventieth birthday, *Crisis and Controversy* (Macmillan, 1976), edited by Alan Sked and Chris Cook. As well as these, Alan himself edited a set of essays stemming from his early seminars at the Beaverbrook Library, a book entitled *Lloyd George: Twelve Essays* (Hamish Hamilton, 1971), which also included many leading historians writing on twentieth-century history.

Several contributors to this volume came into contact with Alan Taylor when he was Honorary Director of the Beaverbrook Library. This housed three major collections of papers central to twentieth-century British history: those of Lloyd George, Bonar Law and Beaverbrook; as well as numerous lesser collections. The Library itself had a unique atmosphere. It had a feel of high politics of the early twentieth century, just as the Round Room at the Public Records Office in Chancery Lane is redolent of medieval history. The Beaverbrook Library was housed in the *Express* building at 33 St Bride Street, just off Fleet Street. One heard printing machinery and saw huge rolls of paper as one went up the stairs of the building. Once in the library one was greeted by former *Express* staff and saw splendid display cases of photographs and documents of leading politicians of the early twentieth century. On the walls there were framed cartoons by Low, and the large room was dominated by a portrait of Beaverbrook by Sickert. As Alan Taylor wrote of it, it was 'an agreeable place to work in – quiet, spacious, air-conditioned.'

For the young researcher it was a memorable place in which to work. It accommodated conveniently six to eight researchers. One could find oneself sitting by people whose correspondence might be in the archive; people such as Richard Law and Dingle Foot. I was also fascinated to hear anecdotes of the period from the staff. Thus I recall the late Rosemary Brooks, who was the archivist for part of the Library's existence, saying that when her father, Collin Brooks, asked Balfour why Austen Chamberlain (the subject of the sixth essay in this book) never reached the top, Balfour bluntly replied, 'Because he was a bore.' Above all, the Beaverbrook Library was memorable because of Alan Taylor's real interest in what researchers were doing and the shrewd comments he often made on their topics.

Alan Taylor developed this interest in what was being done in the Beaverbrook Library by organising a research seminar. The Beaverbrook Library was opened, three years after Beaverbrook's death, on 25 May, 1967, his birthday. Eighteen months later, in December 1968, the research seminar began with papers by Michael Dockrill on 'Lloyd George, Grey and Foreign Policy 1908–1914' and by Alan Taylor on 'Lord Beaverbrook as Historian'. From then, until the Library closed in March 1975, the seminar attracted nearly all the already eminent, plus the coming, British and American scholars of twentieth-century British history.

Of course the Beaverbrook Library phase of Alan Taylor's life is but one small aspect of his immense impact on the study of modern history. For more than half a century he has been publishing books which, in their originality and insight, have made scholars sit up and think again about matters which previously had not been questioned. As Lord Beaverbrook wrote in the collection of essays to mark Alan Taylor's sixtieth birthday, 'The opinions which he freely expresses are combative and disconcerting to those who like a safe and quiet intellectual life.' Beaverbrook added, 'He likes to stir things up.' The contributors to this volume are delighted that at eighty Alan Taylor still does.

CHRIS WRIGLEY

Alan Taylor

Michael Foot

Alan Taylor, the teacher, must first be extolled; no one ever knew better how to stir the excitement of history. The great question – the word 'great', by the way, is one of his favourites which I eagerly purloin – is how he did it or still does it, for this power has never shown any sign of fading. I never attended those notorious, crowded morning lectures at Oxford when, without a note or a moment of hesitation or doubt, he would hold in the palm of his hand the whole audience, including a substantial proportion of the new historians in the rising generation. I did listen, with millions of others, when, against all the odds, this feat was repeated, word-perfect, theme-perfect, on the television screen. But before most others, I believe, I had the most exclusive showing, when for years on end, in the 1950s, we both appeared together almost every week on the same television show *In the News* on the B.B.C. or *Free Speech* on I.T.V. Much the most thrilling part of those occasions was to hear Alan Taylor, the teacher, away from the cameras.

Over the years, he instructed us, first and foremost, on the greatness of the great historians. It was not so much that his choice was original; it wasn't. But he chose of course the great English narrative historians, and somehow he elbowed all the others out of the way into a lesser category. Number One, Macaulay: he could always say something new about Macaulay, and I see he was saying it again in one of his last diary pieces, written at the age of seventy-eight: 'I have just read Macaulay's *History*, all five volumes of it. I am sometimes hailed as his successor. I only wish I were. In my opinion he was the best narrative historian there has ever been, and I am proud to follow in his footsteps. I know that his consuming interest was in political affairs, which he understood from first-hand experience. Political history is frowned on nowadays except by me. But Macaulay was also the wittiest and most penetrating social historian when he wanted to be. He is one of the few historians who make the reader laugh. Gibbon also has his comic passages, but Gibbon's laughter is intellectual, Macaulay's is pure fun. Macaulay was often carried away by his own advocacy. Churchill alleged that he was a persistent liar, which is to get him all wrong. Macaulay was monstrously unfair to William Penn, though it is easy to see why. He was also dishonest in his dealings with Marlborough, but maybe that is less culpable than hero-worship. Indeed, Macaulay's own hero-worship of William III is more at fault than his denigration of Marlborough. No one else would have ventured on the phrase William the Deliverer. Few historians now sing the praises of the Glorious Revolution. Here, I am on Macaulay's side. For me the Glorious Revolution remains the foundation of our liberty. All the more reason to praise it when the basic principles of parliamentary government are threatened as much from the Left as from the Right. However, this does not help my own problem: where am I to find intellectual and literary pleasure now that I have reached the final magical words, "a lock of the hair of Mary"?'

Let us return to Mary's lock and Alan's loving perception of it in a moment. Even granting Macaulay's preeminence, a few others, a very few, are not far behind, Gibbon himself, for example. In another mood or breath he will reinstate Gibbon as 'the greatest of English historians . . . – even though he hardly passes any of the present-day tests. He never looked at a single manuscript text. He did not know that the past is different from the present.' (Quite an indictment, for sure.) Yet Alan continued: 'He captures the reader with his wit rather than his scholarship, though that is pretty good as well.' How rare indeed that wit must have been to have made good for all other deficiencies. And so it was, allied with the will to tell the story in his own way, the indispensable Taylor requirement. And then the third of the great triumvirate, never to be displaced from their pedestals, Thomas Carlyle's *French Revolution*, 'the most powerful re-creation ever written'. Nothing but the most extreme superlative has a chance of proving suitable here, and always Alan would return to it: 'Carlyle sensed the masses as no other writer has done. He expressed their outlook against his own conscious convictions.'

But then again also I should recall that these private Te Deums were sung not only in praise of the safe and the established, even when, as always, he had his own peculiar reasons for allotting them their place in his Pantheon. He would guide us, even more eagerly, to some neglected masterpiece. I recall, for instance, how it was on his recommendation that I turned to Lady Gwendolen Cecil's *Life of Robert Marquis of Salisbury*, 'a work of art, a great biography', as Alan called it. It is indeed, and no one in his or her senses should ever miss it. But I still suspect Alan's motives. He was an admirer of Salisbury's foreign policy, and he detested Disraeli and all his works. I had dared say a good word for Disraeli the novelist, not Disraeli the Tory leader and political mountebank. For Alan, this was going too far. No good word about Disraeli should be tolerated in any circumstances; that was part of his Cobdenite, Gladstonian, Manchester School upbringing. However, even at this date, I must retort that the reference to Lady Gwendolen's work of art had a counter-productive effect. It showed how the old high Tory malice against the Jew-boy who saved them still rankled forty years after his death. Not to be missed, I assure you: no venom to equal the English aristocrat challenged in his own citadel.

However, leaving Gladstone and Disraeli aside for a moment, it was quickly apparent that we shared the same real heroes and that Alan could speak of them or write of them in a way no one had excelled before: for example, Thomas Paine: 'his *Rights of Man* is the greatest political disquisition written by an Englishman', or William Cobbett 'the greatest Englishman', or at least the runner-up for the title (sometimes Alan puts forward Dr Johnson's claim for that title, but this unpardonable lapse must be forgotten), or Charles James Fox.

Reared in a true liberal home and captivated at an early age by Trevelyan's classic *Early History*, I was naturally outraged by the scurvy Namier denigration of Fox and comparably encouraged when so flaming a radical as Alan rallied to his defence. Almost always in those early tutorial classes in which he gave me private inspiration, we were on the same side, and our differences were rare and insignificant. I did sometimes wonder why he would accord such honour to Cobden and Bright, and then withhold it from the Chartist leaders who seemed to me greater men still, made from a different mould. I had an occasional, daring suspicion: would not Feargus O'Connor and William Lovett or Julian Harney have been given their due more readily if they had come from the north, had been born in Manchester, Salford or even Southport? Cobden and Bright and Alan Taylor were splendid theoretical internationalists; but they would insist on speaking in a strong Lancashire accent.

Sometimes too those behind-the-scenes disputations would turn to the lofty question: what is history? And here, as all his pupils know, Alan's invective was more powerful than ever. He could denounce the historical system-makers, Toynbeeism, Burkhardtism, Actonism and every other ism almost with a special, splendid scorn. But what of Marxism? He once called himself a Marxist, and the Marxists, at least the most intelligent of them such as E. J. Hobsbawm, always treated him in turn with a wary, critical reverence. He never attempted to disguise his adoration for the *Communist Manifesto* and *The Eighteenth Brumaire of Louis Napoleon*, while the materialist conception of history could still be treated as a Toynbeeite absurdity. He was the sworn enemy of every theory but his own, yet he always retained a short, sharp answer to the inscrutable question. History, he wrote (in what he called his favourite book), 'is distinguished from other social studies by the fact that in it things happen one after another'.

No bones could be barer, could they? Not a speck of flesh anywhere. Facts, facts, facts. Reality stripped of all sentiment, sentences without verbs; slap them down on the table, like a card player with a fistful of trumps. And never suppose that politicians apply principles, plans, systems, ideologies. Only Taylor's fellow historians are fat-headed enough to imagine that. Oh no! The leaders of men, the best and the worst, live from hand to mouth, from hour to hour, pursue nothing but their own noses, and the people follow, usually with much too much obedience. Such was the Taylor non-theory, which he illustrated afresh, for instance, and magnificently in a spectacular television series called *The War Lords*. We learnt how Hitler stumbled into war; how Stalin stumbled to victory; how Roosevelt picked his way by the most devious means to his liberal pedestal from which the liberal realists so fatuously sought to dislodge him; how Churchill, having achieved power on the ashes of his own Churchill-contrived Norwegian fiasco, stumbled thereafter with the best and the worst, snatching victories from defeats, and defeats from victories.

Let us acknowledge at once: the Taylor non-theory offers many attractions in practice. Taylorite originality is inexhaustible and unfailing. At his best he was always searching for the muddled, inconvenient, disconcerting truth, and stating it in succinct, down-to-earth language. The language indeed is very much part of the man; the staccato style bullies the reader into submission, as if he were perpetually having a pistol stuck in his ribs. And these qualities of simplicity and directness, he implies, are the necessary talents for a historian. He once called this his Bren-gun style, and said he got it from Macaulay.

Alas, most of his fellow historians, or at least those who had the disposition of academic offices at their command, never saw matters in this light. Right from his earliest academic days he showed a marvellous ability to fill Oxford lecture rooms at breakfast time and seduce young minds away from the chaste rut of orthodoxy. He gave them history lessons they had never heard before, and his fellow dons shook their heads gravely. Then he became a television star, and wrote scandalous and highly paid articles for Sunday newspapers, and they shook their heads more gravely than ever. The result was that the most popular of modern historians, truly the Macaulay of this century, was never recognised in his own university.

The first Alan Taylor book I read displayed these qualities in a peculiar setting. It was called *The Struggle for Mastery in Europe, 1848–1914*, and it dealt with established opinions in just about the best-documented period in our history. I started to read it in the belief that even Taylor would have to control his iconoclasms as he marched along those well-beaten tracks. But within a few pages it was evident that all orthodoxies, including Socialist orthodoxies, were to be overturned. That was supposed to be the era *par excellence* of imperialism, when the quest for markets in Asia and Africa transformed the contest in Europe. That was the age which H. N. Brailsford had described in his *The War of Steel and Gold: A Study of the Armed Peace*. That was the age which J. A. Hobson had forecast in his prophetic book on imperialism, which even Lenin himself had adapted for his world-shattering designs. But along came Taylor and knocked all those theories through the ropes. He showed, with staggering simplicity, how the statesmen before 1914 kept their eye on the ball – on the balance of power on the European continent. They did then what statesmen did again in the 1960s and thereafter. They pursued power for its own sake, failed to define coherently their own purposes, chased their own tails. Strategy, not economics, governed diplomacy.

The Introduction to that same 'old-fashioned' diplomatic history, by the way, contained a few paragraphs which illustrated the Taylor genius at its peak, the combination of breath-taking generalisation worthy of Marx himself with detailed incident, worthy, shall we say, of Pepys, another of Alan's unlikely heroes: 'In the last resort the First World War was brought about by the coincidence of two opposite beliefs. The rulers of Austria–Hungary believed that there would be revolution if they did not launch a war; the rulers of Germany were confident that there would not be a revolution if they did.' 'Both beliefs,' added Taylor, 'would have astonished Metternich.' And then he added, even more astonishingly, the best story ever told: 'When Victor Adler objected to Berchtold, foreign minister of Austria–Hungary, that war would provoke revolution in Russia, even if not in the Hapsburg monarchy, he replied: "And who will lead this revolution? Perhaps Mr Bronstein sitting over there at the Café Central?"' Mr Bronstein was, of course, Leon Trotsky, and thus Alan Taylor, the anti-theory historian, quoted an historical accident to upset the theorists.

And perhaps this is the moment to take that fresh, promised glance at the lock of hair. Macaulay made a hero out of the William III whom modern scholars have reduced to a dour, calculating homosexual. Such a tale is impossible to believe when one reads the last few pages of Macaulay's history, when the king was dying, which do indeed reveal how short, sharp sentences, every one immediately, palpably intelligible, can produce the effect, and 'when the most rigid Pharisee of the Society for the Reformation of Manners could hardly deny that it was lawful to save the state, even on the Sabbath . . . He closed his eyes, and gasped for breath. The bishops knelt down and read the commendatory prayer. When it ended William was no more. When his remains were laid out, it was found that he wore next to his skin a small piece of black silk riband. The lords in waiting ordered it to be taken off. It contained a gold ring and a lock of the hair of Mary.'

Every Taylor book, fat or slim, contains a wealth of similar treasures. I can count some twenty or thirty of them on my shelves, produced while his honours-laden competitors have been content with much more meagre tomes. I have picked out one at random. It is *The Trouble Makers*, and I see that Alan has written his own judgment in it for me: 'My best book.' I opened it again at random and read on page 100: 'It was no mean achievement for Hobson [the J. A. Hobson quoted above] to anticipate Keynesian economics with one flick of the wrist and to lay the foundations for Soviet policy with another. No wonder that he never received academic acknowledgement nor held a university chair.'

I turned over the pages again with endless curiosity and fascination. 'Today's realism will appear tomorrow as short-sighted blundering. Today's idealism is the realism of the future.' And if you are reaching for a pinch of salt, to couple with that dose of not-so-frequent Taylorite Socialist dreaming, let me tell you that what he offers on page after page is something approaching *proof*, and patriotic proof at that. 'The dissenters,' Taylor insists, 'have been deeply English in blood and temperament – often far more so than their respectable critics. Paine, Cobbett, Bright, Hobson, Trevelyan – what names could be more redolent of our English past? One of the dissenters found better words than mine: "How indeed, can I, any more than any of you, be un-English and anti-national? Was I not born upon the same soil? Do I not come of the same English stock? Are not my family committed irrevocably to the fortunes of this country? Is not whatever property I may have depending as much as yours is depending upon the good government of our common fatherland? Then how shall any man dare to say to one of his countrymen, because he happens to hold a different opinion on questions of great public policy, that therefore he is un-English, and is to be condemned as anti-national?"'

Alan would describe how he recited those words with peculiar affection. The first advice on European history he was given on arrival at Oxford University was to read that speech of John Bright. Bright was one in Alan Taylor's gallery of Manchester heroes, but Richard Cobden was the favourite. Often, as I have indicated before, I would challenge Alan on his allegiance to these bourgeois figures; why would he not accord his accolade to the Chartists? Surely they were even more deserving of Socialist sustenance than this middle-class Manchester crew, but he would have none of it. Richard Cobden remained for him the most immaculate of great men. My impression is that his prejudice was influenced not solely by Cobden's Manchester connections, but also by the manner in which he argued. 'Our political past,' he wrote, again in that book *The Trouble Makers*, 'was shaped by the clash of argument as well as by family connections and systems of land tenure.' This was a sentence primarily designed to dismiss the Namiers and the Trevor-Ropers. It also serves the purpose of indicating why history, as told by Taylor, retained its perpetual modern inflection. While pretending to search only for the facts, he was also looking for the ideas and the arguments, in nooks and crannies, where most of the orthodox historians were never inquisitive enough to poke their noses. And that, perhaps, is the way in which he established his famous or infamous friendship with Lord Beaverbrook.

Taylor read Beaverbrook's books on politics with fresh eyes. The style, in any case, had a kinship with his own; the taste of the two men for brevity and clarity was similar. But Taylor also set aside the preconceived assumption that Beaverbrook must be a second-rate journalist writing for the hour or the day or for the immediate sensation. He wrote a review in the *Observer* in which, incredibly in the light of all previous academic judgements, he compared Beaverbrook with Tacitus.

I was present in the room when Beaverbrook read that review, and his life was transformed. He had indeed always been most modest about his own writings, never expecting to be regarded as anything more than a chronicler, the good teller of a tale which he knew himself to be and had every right to accept as a fair assessment. As for the comparison with Tacitus, utterly flattering as he believed it to be, it meant that a new world and a new friendship had opened before him. Alan Taylor became his intimate confidant on all these questions, his biographer, and perhaps his truest friend. Certainly the public judgement on Beaverbrook's writings was transformed by that single verdict. Not all his writings, of course, are in any sense in the same class. Most of them *were* sheer journalism. But the three or four main books on politics *are* masterpieces of political writing, and it took Alan Taylor's discernment – and his courage – to make the discovery in full measure.

Few of his other fellow historians are ever treated with such sympathy; instead, they are more often the victims of the Taylor contrariness. He upsets every orthodox apple-cart in sight and fouls his own academic nest with aquiline droppings. To change the metaphor hastily, his whole performance resembles more a Guy Fawkes night in which rockets, squibs, Catherine wheels and Roman candles crackle and flare in endless profusion.

Carlyle himself once said: 'How inferior for *seeing* with is your brightest train of fireworks to the humble farthing candle.' True, no doubt, but fortunately Carlyle never felt it necessary to abide by his own precept, and fortunately too Alan Taylor has never suffered from these pious inhibitions. Both love paradox; both know the art of overstatement. What Macaulay and Carlyle and Taylor all have in common, and the reason why they are great narrative historians, is that they are ready to risk making judgements in every paragraph, almost every sentence. They write with simple, reckless passion, like poets or pamphleteers. It is not an easy style to acquire, which is why so few survive from one century to another. Study those Taylor epigrams and paragraphs more carefully, and one can see how elaborate their interlocking architecture may be; how he had devised for himself a style which could be turned to every purpose and would never lose its appeal. The reader's attention is never lost for a single second. Such a purpose could never have been pursued if it had not been serious. And, of course, he is at his most serious in facing the greatest peril for all mankind.

He knows more about the cause of the two world wars of this century than anyone else on the planet. This does not mean that we must accept as irrefutable his explanation of the likeliest cause of the Third World War. But at least his opinion should not be just pushed aside. He knows much more about the whole subject than, say – to put the claim as modestly as possible – our Secretary of State for Defence, Michael Heseltine.

Alan Taylor has expounded his view on these matters in defiance of orthodox opinion and, more especially, left-wing orthodox opinion. He showed how the origins of the First World War were to be traced much more to upsets of the balance of power in Europe than to the struggle for markets in Africa. He brought fury on his head from all quarters, Left, Right and Centre, when, some thirty years after most experts had pronounced all debate about the origins of the Second

World War dead and buried, he carried out a brilliantly successful exhumation.

In some respects, particularly in its timing, the volume which caused all the trouble on this occasion – *The Origins of the Second World War* – was the bravest or, if you wish, the most reckless he ever wrote. His purpose was to apply the Taylor doctrine or non-doctrine of history to the 1930s, to Hitler and his opponents and his appeasers, to illustrate how accidents, miscalculations, short-term expectations could produce the mightiest convulsions, how all men, even power-crazed dictators, could never impose their rigid wills according to some fancied destiny; much more probably they too would be caught in traps which they had never envisaged. Of course, his aim was not to exonerate Hitler, to excuse those who had fawned on him, although he did declare his wish to restore some of its ancient credit to the old word *appeasement*. The manner of his statement was not in the fashionable idiom of the time (the one which had become fashionable only after 1939 or even 1940). He looked at this historical period, as he did at all others, as one in which the choices were still open. Even the Hitler war could have been avoided if other possibilities had been explored, by the politicians and nations who should have been ranged against the dictators, no less than the dictators themselves. It was a brave and brilliant attempt to tell the truth.

But his enemies pounced from all sides. Some jaundiced academic authorities had been waiting to catch him in the coils of his own paradoxes. Political opponents had even stronger incentives. Just at that moment he was at the peak of his notoriety as a leading campaigner for nuclear disarmament, and had he not exposed himself in his true colours as a lily-livered appeaser, the only man who dared utter the dirtiest word in the political dictionary? How they all set upon him, led by his old sparring partner who had beaten him to the Oxford history chair, Hugh Trevor-Roper, not yet disguised as a Cambridge Head of College, a Conservative Peer of the Realm and our chief exposer of Hitler forgeries, a more profitable vein in Sunday journalism that even Alan had ever dared to open!

It was the moment when he showed most intrepidly his combined devotion to his political faith and his craft as a historian. Others might have been crushed by such an assault, but how little his assailants knew their man. In pursuit of historical truth, the old Cobdenite had been ready to pay proper honour to Palmerston. And nothing then or thereafter would prevent him from uttering, in language so simple that everyone could understand, what new crimes the human race might be contemplating, and who might be the criminals, and his knowledge of history should teach us all not to confuse the lessons of different epochs, not to debase for ever such honourable words as appeasement, not to imagine so cosily that the challenge of world-wide extermination had ever been presented in the same form before. He expressed some of these truths more simply than anyone else. Perhaps that was his real offence; the people *could* understand. Thomas Paine had once been found guilty of high treason for the same reason.

So what does this brave voice, quite accustomed to the wilderness for a platform, say about our present predicament and our future? He said it most bluntly in his Romanes Lecture for 1981. The sentences are uttered with Macaulayesque assurance, Johnsonian finality: 'The prime cause of the war lay in the precautions that had been taken to ensure that there would be no war. The deterrent dominated strategical planning before 1914 . . . The deterrent did not prevent war: it made war inevitable.' Then, later, he concludes, rising to an unscripted, inspired climax: 'I deplore the historians who, against all past experience, declare that this time the deterrent in the shape of nuclear weapons will preserve peace for ever. The deterrent starts off only as a threat, but the record shows that there comes a time when its reality has to be demonstrated – which can only be done by using it. So it was in August 1914 and so it will be again. So far we have done very well. We have lived under nuclear terror for forty years and are still here. The danger increases every day. Without the abolition of nuclear weapons the fate of mankind is certain.

'Can nothing be done to avert this fate? We can expect nothing from the nuclear scientists, the political experts, and, least of all, the statesmen. But for ordinary people there still remain standards of right and wrong. One of these is that no country, no political system, is entitled to employ mass murder in order to maintain itself. We are often told that the renunciation of nuclear weapons by a single country – I hope our country – would expose it to nuclear destruction once it could not retaliate. I believe that the reverse is the truth: if we do not possess nuclear weapons there is no point in destroying us. In any case, is it not morally better to face, perhaps to experience, nuclear obliteration than to inflict this obliteration on others?

'These weapons of mass destruction are designed and manufactured by human beings. Politicians and military leaders may initiate the preparations for nuclear warfare but the actual manufacture is in the hands of scientists whose devotion should be to the future of mankind. For that matter, every citizen of a free country has a responsibility to help in ridding the world of nuclear weapons. This will not be easy, but it must be done.'

This is the note of warning which, in our most perilous age, made Alan's voice more effective than any other. The philosophers led by Bertrand Russell, the writers led by J. B. Priestley, the scientists led by Solly Zuckerman, the journalists led by James Cameron, the astronomers led by Martin Ryle, the churchmen too, as we atheists must acknowledge, led by Donald Soper and Canon Collins and Bruce Kent, all put their case for nuclear disarmament with great force. No one did it with stronger authority than Alan Taylor; no one has answered his Romanes lecture.

One reason why he did it so effectively derives from another quality which so far I have not attempted to indicate in these pages. Despite all his own assertions to the contrary, he has a theme, a flag to wag, a sentimental cause, a hero, apart even from Cobden. He is a great little Englander, and at the end of his own book on England he typically squeezed a purple passage into an aphorism: 'The British Empire declined; the condition of the people improved. Few now sang "Land of Hope and Glory". Few even sang "England Arise!" England had risen, all the same.'

That tribute was provoked by the conduct of the British people – his English, with the others allowed in to share the glory – in the war of 1939–1945. And Taylor loves the facts and the English, and, for all his aggressive scepticism, he could never quite disentangle one from the other. The peace-loving Cobdenite believed it was abundantly right to fight and win the most legitimate war in history, right for the English people he loved, and right for the democratic Socialist cause in which he had always set his faith. All the more does he deserve an audience when he tells us that the new weapons transform the scene and that deterrence will not work any more than it did before.

Curiously, the Alan Taylor who was often taunted for his cynicism, who prided himself on his realism, returned to his old Dissenter's doctrine: 'Conformity may give you a quiet life; it may even bring you a University Chair. But all change in history, all advance comes from nonconformity. If there had been no trouble-makers, no Dissenters, we should still be living in caves.'

And what was the Dissenters' chosen weapon? 'It is a question of morals. Sooner or later we shall have to win the younger generation back to morality. I wonder where they learnt that it was buncombe. Was it from contemporary philosophers or from the day-to-day behaviour of statesmen? This country of ours fought two world wars mainly for high principle; and the only lesson drawn from this by the young is that might is right. It now seems unbearably priggish to say that the country which went to war for the sake of Belgium and Poland must not, in any circumstances, drop the H-bomb. But it is true.'

A. J. P. Taylor and 'Profound Forces' in History[1]

Paul Kennedy

> Of course historians must explore the profound forces. But I am sometimes tempted to think that they talk so much about these profound forces in order to avoid doing the detailed work. I prefer detail to generalisations . . .
>
> Taylor, 'War Origins Again'[2]

> The first World War left 'the German problem' unsolved, indeed it made it ultimately more acute . . . If events followed their course in the old 'free' way, nothing could prevent the Germans from overshadowing Europe, even if they did not plan to do so.
>
> Taylor, *Origins* . . .[3]

> . . . it seems from the record that [Hitler] became involved in war through launching on 29 August [1939] a diplomatic manoeuvre which he ought to have launched on 28 August.
>
> Taylor, *Origins* . . .[4]

The three quotations with which this essay begins reflect, in an all too obvious way, the problems which confront every scholar who grapples with motive 'forces' in History, and especially with the analysis of short-term events *versus* long-term trends, and with the general *versus* the particular. It is an intellectual challenge which was set in one's schooldays ('Distinguish between the short-term and the long-term causes of the French Revolution'), and it does not become the easier to handle as one studies more and more History. On the contrary, the greater the evidence which is available about an event as complex as, say, the origins of the Reformation or the Second World War, the more likely historians are to differ as to the interpretation of the mass of data which confronts them. Do the 'general trends' of the period appear so overwhelming as to carry all before them? Do the particular actions of idiosyncratic leaders affect the decisions of states? What is the role of accident, and coincidence?

These are questions about causality which have divided historians since time immemorial, and the quite different interpretations advanced by the various schools of thought have often revealed more about the political ideology and the personal prejudices of the writers themselves than about the topic under dispute. It is not a coincidence that the importance of long-term historical forces making for 'change' and 'reform' has usually been stressed by writers of a progressive bent, whether it be the Whig historians of the nineteenth century or the Marxist, 'New Left' and radical-Liberal authors of the twentieth; for them, the political and social transformations of their age can be regarded both as personally welcome, and as historically inevitable and natural. It is also no coincidence that many of the scholars who have called attention to the particular happening in History, to the role of chance and accident, to the critical importance of individual personalities and unique events, to the 'ups and downs' of political affairs rather than their teleological character, have been ideologically conservative; from Namier in the 1930s to the so-called 'Peterhouse' school at Cambridge today, such investigations have been very quickly seen as having a subtle (or less-than-subtle) political message, as well as being important contributions to historical research.

Because of this larger background, and the philosophical and methodological dimensions to the topic, there can be no prospect in the present brief essay of fully discussing causation in History. The purpose instead will be to focus more narrowly upon Mr Taylor's discussion of the 'profound' and the 'less profound' forces which affected European diplomatic relations and the origins of the two world wars of this century. These topics are of considerable importance and interest to the general public, and they are ones which have been discussed in a large number of Mr Taylor's books; but the approach proposed in this essay may be the more interesting, methodologically, since his writings have been remarkable in pointing to *both* the profound *and* the particular/accidental aspects of historical causation – without, however, an explicit reconciliation of the two.

Because of the theme chosen in this essay, certain of Mr Taylor's better-known books will not be discussed, simply because they do not lend themselves so easily to analysis: *English History 1914–1945*, for example, as the final volume in the textbook 'Oxford History of England' series, has been ignored; *The Trouble Makers* is also not discussed; and the various collections of essays will not be analysed. On the whole, the section which follows will concentrate upon Taylor's handling of the 'German problem' and the two world wars. But that alone is a large enough field.

An early example of Mr Taylor's emphasis upon the short-term and unexpected elements in international relations came in his 1938 publication *Germany's First Bid for Colonies 1884–1885: A Move in Bismarck's European Diplomacy*. Challenging an earlier historiography which had explained that 'bid' as being the outcome of a steady growth of German commercial interests overseas since 1871, and the increase in public enthusiasm for empire, Taylor argued instead that the creation of German colonies was really the result of a clever diplomatic manoeuvre by the Chancellor. By picking a series of quarrels with a bewildered British government over African and Pacific territories in 1884, Bismarck was hoping to persuade the French that Paris and Berlin had similar concerns in the tropics and should stand together against London; with the deeper consequence of this Franco-German colonial *entente* being a lessening of their rivalry in Europe, to the benefit of Germany's national security. This cunning diplomacy, of inventing a new rival (Britain) in order to ameliorate tensions with an old one (France), lasted only a year. With an unexpected crisis arising in the Balkans in 1885, and a change of government occurring in France, Bismarck felt that he had to reverse course and improve relations with Britain. Such tactical shifts were characteristic of the man, and perhaps of the 'old diplomacy' in general; the interesting feature in this case was that this short-term policy had produced, as a side effect, the longer-term German presence in Africa and the Pacific.[5]

Diplomatic manoeuvrings, short-term bids for advantage, and the all-too-frequent misunderstandings and miscalculations of statesmen are also at the heart of one of Taylor's most famous books, *The Struggle for Mastery in Europe 1848–1918*.[6] Although this brilliant survey is now over thirty years old, it still serves as one of the major texts of international history in the modern period. For scholars already versed in the background details, Taylor's account is a joy to read; but his penchant for noting the implicit contradictions, the unrealised hopes, and the unexpected outcomes of so many diplomatic policies, make this hard going for the novice:

> The balance which Bismarck had created at the beginning of 1888 was a curious one. Russia received diplomatic support at Con-

stantinople from France and Germany, and was opposed there by the three Powers of the Mediterranean entente; on the other hand, Salisbury, not Bismarck, restrained this entente from turning against France. The outcome was more curious still. The French, much against their will, were driven to support Russia more closely; Germany, much against Bismarck's will, ceased to support Russia at all. The French recognized that support for Russia contradicted their traditional policy in the Near East and threatened their investments in the Ottoman empire; they would have preferred to resurrect the Crimean coalition with England and Italy – 'the only rational and fruitful policy'. Egypt stood in the way, and here Salisbury refused the slightest concession. The French tried to approach England, as Austria–Hungary had done, through the Italian back-door; but instead of seeking to cajole Italy they chose the method of threats – patronage of the pope and the launching of a tariff war – weapons which made Crispi more hostile than ever. Their only practical result was to stimulate Anglo-Italian naval cooperation, culminating in a demonstrative visit to Genoa by the British fleet. The French were driven back to Russia . . .[7]

Nonetheless, as we shall see below, this book does also try to grapple with 'profound forces', albeit in an episodic way. It is certainly much less one-sided in focusing upon the role of the accident and the particular event than two later works of his upon the origins of the First World War. The first of these, admittedly a slim one, is *War by Timetable*, whose title gives away its argument:

When cut down to essentials, the sole cause for the outbreak of war in 1914 was the Schlieffen Plan – product of the belief in speed and the offensive ... Yet the Germans had no deliberate aim of subverting the liberties of Europe. No one had time for a deliberate aim or time to think. All were trapped by the ingenuity of their military preparations, the Germans most of all.[8]

And although this book makes references to the European alliance system, to the mood of the times, and even to 'the deeper problem of Germany', it also contains one of Mr Taylor's most sceptical comments ever about profound causes:

It is the fashion nowadays to seek profound causes for great events. But perhaps the war which broke out in 1914 had no profound causes. For thirty years past, international diplomacy, the balance of power, the alliances, and the accumulation of armed might produced peace. Suddenly the situation was turned round, and the

> very forces which had produced the long peace now produced a great war. In much the same way, a motorist who for thirty years has been doing the right thing to avoid accidents makes a mistake one day and has a crash. In July 1914 things went wrong. The only safe explanation is that things happen because they happen.[9]

Nor has such iconoclasm left him in more recent publications. In his collected scripts to the 1977 television series *How Wars Begin*, Mr Taylor briefly refers to the 'long background' or 'profound causes' of the seven modern wars which he surveys; but very swiftly changes gear, when declaring

> All these explanations have some validity. But there is also another more prosaic origin of war: the precise moment when a statesman sets his name to the declaration of it. The statesman is no doubt a creature of his time and shares its outlook. But the actual act of signing his name has often little relation to the profound causes, as I discovered to my surprise when developing my theme.[10]

Finally, there is his most controversial book of all, *The Origins of the Second World War* (first published, 1961; with 'Second Thoughts', 1963), a path-breaking survey of European diplomatic relations between 1919 and 1939 which, through its presentation of the evidence, assaulted all sorts of sacred cows. In particular, it argued that the documentary record showed that Hitler did not have a preconceived plan which unfolded stage by stage through the 1930s; that he was as often reacting to unforeseen contingencies as he was forcing events on; that the erratic diplomacy of the 'appeasers' who governed Britain and France, together with hard-to-control occurrences in eastern Europe and the volatility of British public opinion (as strongly for 'standing up' to Hitler in 1939 as it had been for 'appeasing' him in 1938), pushed the rulers of both sides towards, and into, a conflict which no one had wanted. Thus

> The War of 1939, far from being premeditated was a mistake, the result on both sides of diplomatic blunders.[11]

It is scarcely surprising that this book involved Mr Taylor in more heated controversy than any other during his career. *The Origins of the Second World War* was praised, attacked, cheered and denounced as reviewers rushed to interpret its direct and indirect meanings: on its contemporary implications for the Cold War; on its revision of the picture of the 'appeasers'; on its use of evidence, and the status given to the published diplomatic documents; on its treatment of Hitler's aims and actions; and, perhaps above all, on what it *excluded* from the story of the causes of the war.

And this latter point brings us back, of course, to the handling of 'profound causes'. Leaving aside, therefore, Mr Taylor's use of the documents and his quotations from them – disputed by scholars such as P. A. Reynolds, F. H. Hinsley, H. R. Trevor-Roper and others at the time, and by Professor Weinberg in his great tomes later[12] – there lies the question of what aspects of historical causality may be missing, or at least downplayed, in *Origins*. There is little, for example, on National-Socialist thought, on its obsessions about Germany's place in the world and the need to deal with internal and external foes.[13] And while some economic statistics are employed in the book – to demonstrate the relatively low level of German armaments spending in the 1930s, and hence the absence of preparing for a world war – their reliability is disputed by other scholars, especially T. W. Mason, who has re-interpreted Germany's economic problems to argue that by 1937/38

> . . . The only 'solution' open to this regime of the structural tensions and crises produced by dictatorships and rearmament was more dictatorship and more rearmament, then expansion, then war and terror, then plunder and enslavement . . . A war for the plunder of manpower and materials lay square in the dreadful logic of German economic development under National Socialist rule.[14]

It was in response to Mr Mason's criticisms that Taylor admitted, 'I fear I may not have emphasised the profound forces', although he also went on (see the introductory quotation to this essay) to reiterate the importance of doing the 'detailed work' and of 'adding up the trivialities'. And, while making concessions that certain parts of *Origins* might now need to be altered, the author's later reflections on the controversy show that he remains convinced of the essential validity of his argument that the 'war of 1939' was an accident.[15]

How is one to respond to the challenge which Mr Taylor has thrown out to scholars by this almost impish knocking-down of cherished assumptions? It is unsatsifactory, as even his arch-critic H. R. Trevor-Roper noted, to ascribe this all to 'mere characteristic *gaminerie*, the love of firing squibs and laying banana-skins to disconcert the gravity and upset the balance of the orthodox'.[16] To begin with, it is proper to note that Taylor's reminder of the importance of the short-term, the tactical, and the immediate *is* a vital point, whether it concerns the general methodology of History or the interpretation of specific episodes. For example, Bismarck's colonial bid is nowadays seen by many historians as having been caused by a variety of factors, including domestic-political and economic causes which might well be described as deep-rooted and 'profound'; but the short-term conjuncture of diplomatic circumstances prevailing in the summer of 1884 is also acknowledged as part of the whole story.[17] In the same way – and much more significantly – it would now be admitted by Mr Taylor's strongest critics that the story of the origins of the Second World War could never be looked at from the older perspective after the appearance of his book in 1961. The calculating element in Hitler as well as the irrational fanatic; the opportunist as well as the dreamer of a thousand-year *Reich*; the role of chance, and of the unforeseen opportunity; the dialectic between longer-term ambitions *and* tactical flexibility – these are the problems which historians of this period now grapple with, in direct consequence of Taylor's thesis. When these contrary elements are intelligently synthesised, the results are satisfying indeed.[18] But would that synthesis have come about without Taylor's assault on the older orthodoxies? One doubts it.

If the story could be halted at this point, with the establishment of Taylor's role as the sceptical critic of 'profound causes', our analysis would be a simple one. After all, the writing of History must be, despite the best efforts of scholars, an exercise in selectivity and thus (to a greater or lesser degree) in subjectivity. According to the historical theme being pursued, as well as political and ideological preferences, writers will tend towards the general or the particular, towards the broad changes or the specific events. To use J. H. Hexter's terminology, most historians incline to be either 'splitters' or 'lumpers'. Each approach has its merits – and its dangers. Each side is in constant tension with the other, both correcting, and being corrected by, its opposite. What we have in Mr Taylor, therefore, may simply seem to be one of those scholars who successfully remind us of the importance of the particular in History.

But the remarkable thing about this writer is that he has also, at so many other times, reminded us of the importance of the long-term trends and general forces in History. In some ways, of course, this is hardly surprising. After all, even the most specific monographs need to say a little about the larger context within which their study is to be placed; and given the array of broad-ranging books which have come from Mr Taylor's hand – *The Course of German History*, *The Habsburg Monarchy*, *From Sarajevo to Potsdam*, etc. – generalisations are unavoidable. Indeed, given his epigrammatic style and fondness for proposing a new way of looking at old topics, Mr Taylor offers sweeping generalisations in all of his works, to the delight of admirers and to the annoyance of 'professionals' in particular fields. And many of them do indeed seem to come from a puckish enjoyment of pointing out life's foibles, or of using analogies: thus, the readers of *The Course of German History* were informed that 'it was no more a mistake for the German people to end up with Hitler than it is an accident when a river flows into the sea . . .' More recently, he startled a London audience by suggesting that Operation 'Barbarossa' in 1941 was caused (partly? largely? It is not clear) by the German Army being 'bored' and needing employment.[19]

Those sorts of generalised *obiter dicta* will not be discussed here. What seems to this writer much more important are the instances in which Mr Taylor has offered an analysis of the larger structures in international affairs, and of the changes which occurred in them over the longer term. Again, for the purposes of brevity, our concentration will be upon the European scene and the deeper causes of the two world wars; but that, again, is a large enough field for a discussion of this point. For example, in the 'Introduction' to his book *The Struggle for Mastery in Europe*, Taylor offered his readers one of the most decisive and penetrating analyses of 'what it took to be a Great Power', and what significant alterations occurred between 1848 and 1918 in the population, military and industrial balances which would – in the event of great, modern wars – largely determine their outcome. Here, at least, there is no hesitation at all about the importance of 'profound forces':

> We must now translate these economic figures into political terms. In 1850 Prussia and Austria, the Powers of central Europe, had still some reason, though not much, to fear the domination of France. They would be supported against it by Great Britain; and this support was decisive. The Russian bogy, though still apprehended, was in reality out of date. It rested solely on manpower and could not be effective, once coal and railways came into their own. Between 1850 and 1870 economic forces worked in line with political tendencies. The Balance of Power was strengthened; and the Bismarckian system after 1871 corresponded to the reality of a number of Great Powers in Europe. After 1890 this Balance began to crumble. Germany towered above all the other continental states; and the Balance was hardly redressed when British power was thrown into the scale against her. But this situation, too, was precarious. The United States could challenge Germany, even if she dominated the continent of Europe; and at the end Russia was developing more rapidly than any other country in the world. The Germans had an opportunity, but it was not one that would last.
>
> There was thus some sense in most of the calculations that the statesmen of Europe stumbled on in their process of muddle and improvised decision.[20]

All these were seminal and important points, and it is proper to note just how many later writers have accepted Mr Taylor's basic framework in their own studies of international relations in this period, and in explaining the background to Germany's challenge to the 'system' in 1914.[21]

Moreover, at the end of the same impressive work, whilst surveying the international order of 1918, Mr Taylor again pointed to the most significant features of the new power balances:

> Though Germany's bid for the mastery of Europe was defeated, the European Balance could not be restored. Defeat could not destroy German predominance of the Continent. Only her dismemberment could have done it; and, in the age of national states, this was impossible. France was exhausted by the First World War; Great Britain, though less exhausted, was reduced no less decisively in the long run. Their victory was achieved only with American backing and could not be lasting without it. On the other side, old Russia was gone for good.[22]

It is from this starting-point, moreover, that Taylor took up the story again in the early chapters of *The Origins of the Second World War*. As he pointed out there, 'In November 1918 Germany was decisively defeated by the Western Powers on the Western Front; but before that Germany had decisively defeated Russia in the East, and this had a profound effect on the pattern of the inter-war years.'[23] In the place of a Great Power on Germany's eastern border, there was now a plethora of small, uncertain, rivalling states. And while Germany had to pay greatly for her defeat (in terms of large reparations, border concessions, and very restricted armed forces), as well as to accept sweeping constitutional and political changes internally, her *core* as a formidable nation-state was much less affected:

> However democratic and pacific Germany might become, she remained by far the greatest Power on the continent of Europe; with the disappearance of Russia, more so than before. She was greatest in population – sixty-five million against forty million in France, the only other substantial Power. Her preponderance was greater still in the economic resources of coal and steel which in modern times together made up power. At the moment in 1919, Germany was down-and-out. The immediate problem was German weakness; but given a few years of 'normal' life, it would again become the problem of German strength. More than this, the old balance of power, which formerly did something to restrain Germany, had broken down. Russia had withdrawn; Austria–

> Hungary had vanished. Only France and Italy remained, both inferior in man-power and still more in economic resources, both exhausted by the war. If events followed their course in the old 'free' way, nothing could prevent the Germans from overshadowing Europe, even if they did not plan to do so.[24]

By these statements alone, therefore, Taylor has anticipated, and essentially explained, the Second World War in Europe; as he remarks elsewhere, 'The first war explains the second and, in fact, caused it, in so far as one event causes another.'[25] The whole story of the diplomacy of the 1920s and 1930s is, in a nutshell, one of Germany seeking to re-assume its natural place as the leading European power, and of its neighbours to the East and West reacting to that fact with a variety of policies. In this sense, Hitler was being traditional in desiring that which every other German also desired; the French were being natural in worrying about such changes; and it was perfectly understandable for the British to seek to ensure that the artificial order of Versailles was readjusted by peaceful means, that is, by a strategy of the 'appeasement of Europe'. That his problem was not solved peacefully was due, in Taylor's view, to the appeasers' failures to keep their diplomacy in line with these larger realities:

> Such were the origins of the second World war, or rather of the war between the three Western Powers over the settlement of Versailles; a war which had been implicit since the moment when the first war ended. Men will long debate whether this renewed war could have been averted by greater firmness or by greater conciliation; and no answer will be found to these hypothetical speculations. Maybe either would have succeeded, if consistently followed; the mixture of the two, practised by the British government, was the most likely to fail.[26]

The fact of the matter is, therefore, that, despite Mr Taylor's sceptical remarks about 'profound causes', he himself does not ignore them – or all of them. It is true that, like his old chief, Namier, he has little time for the role of ideas, for public opinion ('I do not know how to handle public opinion'[27]), and for what one might term larger social forces: things which – rightly in this author's view – other historians have seen as vital for a fuller understanding of German imperialism in the 1880s and 1890s, and of Nazi expansionism in the 1930s. Yet in respect of the workings of the international system – and of the breakdowns in that system – it is clear that Taylor believes both in specific circumstances *and* in profound causes. In the bibliographical essay (but not in the main text) of *The Struggle for Mastery in Europe*, he writes that 'Policy springs from deep social and economic sources; it is not crudely manufactured in foreign offices.'[28] And, in one of his more notable, sustained analogies in *The Origins of the Second World War*, he proposed a valuable way of relating the profound causes to the specific events:

> Wars are much like road accidents. They have a general cause and particular causes at the same time. Every road accident is caused, in the last resort, by the invention of the internal combustion engine and by men's desire to get from one place to another. In this sense, the 'cure' for road accidents is to forbid motor-cars. But a motorist, charged with dangerous driving, would be ill-advised if he pleaded the existence of motor-cars as his sole defence. The police and the courts do not weigh profound causes. They seek a specific cause for each accident – error on the part of the driver; excessive speed; drunkenness; faulty brakes; bad road surface. So it is with wars. 'International anarchy' makes war possible; it does not make war certain. After 1918 more than one writer made his name by demonstrating the profound causes of the first World war; and, though the demonstrations were often correct, they thus diverted attention from the question why that particular war happened at that particular time. Both enquiries make sense on different levels. They are complementary; they do not exclude each other.[29]

Yet, however useful this 'road accident' analogy in theory, the connection between the two levels is never fully made in practice, leaving many a reader with the impression that he has encountered two different historians at work: one who points to the longer-term shifts in the balance of power as the key to understanding great-power diplomacy; and another who is deeply sceptical of 'profound causes', who feels that politics is as full of misunderstandings and accidents as anything else in life, and who frequently asserts that 'statesmen are too absorbed by events to follow a preconceived plan'. So how should we understand this contradiction?

In the first place, it is important to concede again that the tension between the profound and the particular is inevitable in every historical writing, and the more so in those which cover great and much-researched themes. If historians of early-seventeenth-century England, for example, are still hotly debating over whether there is an easily-detectable 'high road' to the English Civil War, or whether that conflict was simply the result of short-term, largely unconnected and unpremeditated events, we should not be surprised that more recent historical happenings also produce greater differences of opinion about evidence and causality. Very often, historians will incline one way or the other depending upon the nature of their book. Thus, those tracing the broad sweep of modern history, such as Geoffrey Barraclough's *An Introduction to Contemporary History* or W. H. McNeill's *The Pursuit of Power*, inevitably focus upon 'profound causes', using specific details merely for illustrative purposes.[30] Those whose chief focus is socio-economic history also incline in that general direction, and are often impatient of scholars who cannot see the larger picture. 'Political historians', Eric Hobsbawm wrote tartly, 'have professed to find no economic reasons for this virtual division of the world between a handful of West European powers (plus the USA) in the last decades of the nineteenth century. Economic historians have had no such difficulty.'[31] Yet the political and diplomatic historians will answer, for their part, that, when they examine the records of the decision-makers, they find little evidence of economic arguments for colonies; instead, there is a primacy of strategical and political calculations made by the 'Official Mind', which despite attempts at coherence and planning often reveals the vagaries of accident, individual personalities, and the need to respond to quite unexpected external crises in the tropics.[32]

This leads us to a second, related point: that the very nature of diplomatic documents, upon which such works as *The Struggle for Mastery in Europe* and *The Origins of the Second World War* are heavily based, is not especially helpful in making the 'link' between a particular day's diplomacy and profound causes. On the contrary, a diplomatic despatch (and especially a telegram) is much more likely to emphasise the immediate, the tactical, the particular; while the euphemistic and often stilted language of foreign offices can reinforce this sense that non-diplomatic calculations are of little import. If there are 'unspoken assumptions' behind many of the decisions of statesmen, it is not easy to detect them from a swift reading of a diplomatic despatch.[33] Methodologically, therefore, the level of broad balance-of-power shifts which Taylor covers in the early sections of his books, remain separate from the dazzling diplomatic narrative which occupies most of the text; the day-to-day events become an autotelic process, to be understood and read on their own terms; and occasional references to background developments do not suffice to close the 'gap' between the various levels.

But, in addition to these general explanations, there is surely one final, very private reason for the discrepancy: it lies in the idiosyncratic and engaging personage of Mr Taylor himself. Ideologically, he has always been on the radical Left in British politics, whether in the ILP, or more briefly in the Communist Party, or more ambivalently in the Labour Party. The major developments in domestic and in global politics which were central to so many of the 'trouble makers' – those critics of the existing order whom he captured in his favourite book[34] – were also his own concerns: the rise of the working classes, the coming of the welfare state, the end of the imperialist system, the creation of a social revolution in Russia. These are among the major 'profound forces' of the twentieth century, as are those other broad developments (the Fascist counter-offensive, the rise of the USA) with which Mr Taylor has had little or no sympathy.

It would be all too easy for him, therefore, to write books which both elaborated on these trends and reflected his own sympathies; but that would have suppressed and concealed *another* Mr Taylor: the nonconformist, the fighter for unpopular causes, the Quaker-educated youth who had no religion, the socialist who wrote for the Beaverbrook Press, the maverick historian who insists on upsetting our traditional views of the past – in other words, the convinced individualist who believes that man makes his own history and can do what he chooses, against the tide and if need be against the 'profound forces'. Delighting as he does to be found going in the opposite direction to everyone else on most matters, it is not surprising that he also gets pleasure in showing how much of History was unplanned, accidental and idiosyncratic. 'For me writing history has been Fun on a high academic level,' Taylor notes at the end of his autobiography.[35] One wonders if it would have been such fun if his writings had always featured the *inevitable* consequences of *inexorable* profound forces. There would no doubt have been much more of a connection between the general and the particular; but such an obvious and predictable form of explaining causality in History would not have sat easily on a man who for eighty years now has relished kicking over the traces. Annoying the professionals, delighting the vicarious, and forcing almost all his colleagues to look at certain historical problems in a new light, Mr Taylor has certainly had his fun – and made History a somewhat less serious business than it otherwise would have been.

Notes

1 What follows is a modest essay in historical methodology. While it may seem curious to offer this critique of Mr Taylor's method in a *Festschrft*, the fact is that all historians grapple with the tensions which arise between the general and the particular, and his writings simply offer a more spectacular case. Furthermore, the last person to complain about another's criticisms is the iconoclast from Birkdale.

2 A. J. P. Taylor, 'War Origins Again', reprinted in E. M. Robertson (ed.), *The Origins of the Second World War* (London, 1971), p. 140.

3 Taylor, *The Origins of the Second World War* (Harmondsworth, Mddsx., 1964 edn.), p. 48.

4 Ibid., p. 336.

5 Idem., *Germany's First Bid for Colonies 1884–1885: A Move in Bismarck's European Diplomacy* (London, 1938), passim.

6 Oxford, 1954.

7 Op. cit., p. 325.

8 Taylor, *War by Time-Table. How the First World War began* (London, 1969), p. 121.

9 Ibid., p. 45.

10 Taylor, *How Wars Begin* (New York, 1979), p. 14.

11 Idem., *Origins*, p. 269.

12 The controversy is best followed in two edited works: Robertson (ed.), op. cit., passim; and W. R. Louis (ed.), *The Origins of the Second World War: A. J. P. Taylor and His Critics* (London, 1972), passim. In addition, see G. L. Weinberg, *The Foreign Policy of Hitler's Germany*, 2 vols. (Chicago. Ill., 1970 and 1980).

13 On which one might consult, *inter alia*, K. Hildebrand, *The Foreign Policy of the Third Reich* (London, 1973); W. Carr, *Arms, Autarky and Aggression: A Study in German Foreign Policy, 1933–1939* (London, 1972); M. Hauner, 'Did Hitler Want a World Dominion?', *Journal of Contemporary History* (1978), pp. 15–32.

14 T. W. Mason, 'Some Origins of the Second World War', reprinted in Robertson (ed.), op. cit., pp. 124–25.

15 Taylor, 'War Origins Again', loc. cit., pp. 136–141; and especially '1939 Revisited' (The 1981 Annual Lecture, German Historical Institute, London, 1982), passim. One should note in this debate Taylor's careful phraseology 'The war of 1939', *not* 'The Second World War' – an obvious modification of the title of the 1961 first edition of his *Origins* book.

16 H. R. Trevor-Roper, 'A. J. P. Taylor, Hitler and the War', reprinted in Robertson (ed.), p. 98.

17 H. Pogge von Strandmann, 'Domestic Origins of Germany's Colonial Expansion under Bismarck', *Past and Present*, 42 (1969), pp. 140–59; P. M. Kennedy, *The Rise of the Anglo-German Antagonism 1860–1914* (London, 1980), chapter 10.

18 See, for example, Alan Bullock's British Academy lecture, 'Hitler and the Origins

of the Second World War', reprinted in Robertson (ed.), pp. 189–224; C. Thorne, *The Approach of War 1938–39* (London, 1967); A. Adamthwaite, *The Making of the Second World War* (London, 1977).

19 Taylor, *The Course of German History* (London, 1961 edn.), p. vii; idem., '1939 Revisited', p. 15.

20 Taylor, *Struggle for Mastery in Europe*, pp. xxxi–xxxii.

21 A few examples might include R. Langhorne, *The Collapse of the Concert of Europe: International Politics, 1890–1914* (London, 1981); L. L. Farrar, *Arrogance and Anxiety: The Ambivalence of German Power, 1848–1914* (Iowa City, Iowa, 1981); A. W. DePorte, *Europe between the Superpowers* (New Haven, Conn., 1979); P. M. Kennedy, 'The First World War and the International Power System', *International Security*, vol. 9 (Summer 1984).

22 Taylor, *Struggle for Mastery in Europe*, p. 567.

23 Idem., *Origins*, p. 43.

24 Ibid., p. 48.

25 Ibid., p. 42.

26 Ibid., p. 336.

27 Idem., '1939 Revisited', p. 13.

28 Idem., *Struggle for Mastery in Europe*, p. 575.

29 Idem., *Origins*, pp. 135–36. This point is ably discussed in F. H. Hinsley's review, 'The Origins of the Second World War', reprinted in Louis (ed.), op. cit., pp. 69–80.

30 G. Barraclough, *An Introduction to Contemporary History* (Harmondsworth, Mddsx., 1967 edn.); W. H. McNeill, *The Pursuit of Power: Technology, Armed Force, and Society since 1000 A.D.* (Oxford, 1983).

31 E. J. Hobsbawm, *Industry and Empire* (Harmondworth, Mddsx., 1969 edn.), P. 131.

32 For a famous example of this, see R. Robinson and J. A. Gallagher, with A. Denny, *Africa and the Victorians: The Official Mind of Imperialism* (London, 1961); and their essay 'The Partition of Africa', in *The New Cambridge Modern History*, vol. xi (Cambridge, 1962).

33 For a successful example, see J. Joll, '1914: The Unspoken Assumptions' (Inaugural Lecture, London, 1968).

34 Taylor, *The Trouble Makers: Dissent over Foreign Policy, 1792–1939* (London, 1969 edn.).

35 Taylor, *A Personal History* (London, 1983), p. 274. Also worth reading in this connection is E. B. Segal, 'A. J. P. Taylor and History', reprinted in Louis (ed.), op. cit., pp. 11–25.

John Bright and William Gladstone

Keith Robbins

The main pieces of furniture in the sitting-room of his Wesleyan grandparents, Lord Wolfenden recalls, were a grand piano and two murky oleographs, one on each side of the massive fireplace. They represented John Bright and William Ewart Gladstone. Such a partnership, however, would not always have been congenial to either man. In his tribute in the House of Commons on 29 March, 1889 Gladstone had to admit that their views had by no means invariably coincided but argued that the 'supreme eulogy' which was Bright's due was that he had lifted political life to a higher elevation and a loftier standard. John Bright was a man to be held in 'reverential contemplation'. This paper sketches their relationship and reveals that there were moments when they contemplated each other with less than reverence.

'All that I can remember,' Gladstone recollected many years later concerning a deputation received at the Board of Trade, probably in 1842, 'is the figure of a person in black or dark Quaker costume, seemingly the youngest of the band.' This youthful figure sat a little forward on the bench and intervened in the discussion. Gladstone was 'greatly struck by him'. He seemed rather fierce, but very strong and very earnest. The young man was John Bright. There is no matching account of this first meeting. Naturally enough, neither man had any inkling of the circumstances that were to bring them together in the future. Gladstone, too, might have made a strong impression on an observer, but might have seemed otherwise very dissimilar. They were on opposite sides, not only in the long room at the Board of

Trade, but in every major political question of the day. Gladstone seemed an 'insider', a man of the Establishment, while Bright was an 'outsider' and a Dissenter. Whatever his commercial background, Gladstone was moulded by Eton and Christ Church, Oxford. Painstakingly and methodically he had worked his way through the classical curriculum but at the same time was a man of Christian Europe. If not a 'pure' scholar, or 'independent' spirit, the range of his reading and knowledge was formidable. He had, moreover, so disciplined himself that he had acquired the habit of steady application and retained a puritan concern for strict economy in the use of time. Bright's formal education had, in contrast, been rudimentary. The Society of Friends was well-endowed with schools but Bright had not greatly benefited from any of them. Beginning at a small academy near Warrington, he moved to the more famous school at Ackworth. While not dissatisfied with the instruction there, the amount of meat provided was inadeqaute and he moved on to York. 'Bootham School' was little better. Unlike in the later days of Mr Taylor, it then inhabited inadequate buildings on low-lying ground. His final school, high upon the border of Lancashire and Yorkshire, had fresh air as its chief recommendation. To his intense relief, or so he publicly professed later, his schooling had enabled him to escape the classical heritage which meant so much to Gladstone. He did not have Latin or Greek, and claimed that the English language was quite sufficient for any man, since it embraced the best prose and best poetry in the world. Even if he had entertained the wish for a university education, his father would not have paid for it and the Universities of Oxford and Cambridge would not have welcomed him.

As a young man, what would immediately have struck the observer was the handsome plainness of his Quaker attire. It had lingered in Gladstone's memory. John Bright sprang from a long line of English Friends and felt no affection for the Church of England. He abhorred the principle of establishment. His objections to the Church Rate had brought about his first excursion into local Rochdale politics. It was in public vituperation against the Vicar of Rochdale that he matured as an orator. Before his connexion with the Anti-Corn Law League, his milieu had been that of small town Dissenting politics. His blunt language, not to mention the 'sit-ins' he organized in Rochdale Parish Church, indicated a tone and temper far removed from the Gladstonian wrestling with abstract issues of Church and State. Their intellectual worlds were far apart and if their political worlds should ever coincide it could only be in circumstances of conflict. Both men agreed, however, that such issues were serious and not to be trifled with. An avid and early reader of Miall's *Nonconformist*, Bright looked for the day when the state church would be dethroned and full equality for the Dissenters established. Gladstone was moving away from the initial formulation of his views on church and state, but remained a profound churchman.

This fundamental ecclesiastical difference also seemed to be matched by general political disagreement. The reform crisis of 1830–32 had been the first major political event in the lives of both young men. While Gladstone, in enlightened Oxford, had miserably observed the advance of reform, in the North of England Bright was exultant about the prospects which it opened up. A first dent had been made in the power of the aristocracy. Gladstone, however, slipped sedately into the House of Commons in 1832 through the good offices of Lord Lincoln. A few years later, Bright was deeply involved in the novel problems of constituency organization in newly-enfranchised Rochdale. Inevitably, their perspectives on political life were different. Gladstone started his political career in the House of Commons, feeling his way at an early age, but doing so at the political centre of the country. He observed the great men of his time at close quarters, eventually placing himself at the feet of Sir Robert Peel. This relationship stimulated his awareness of what it entailed to hold office and possess power. He saw at close quarters the demands which administration placed upon a minister, or at least as Peel chose to interpret responsibility. Such a prospect did not cause him to tremble. Gladstone felt he possessed both the physical stamina and the intellectual resilience for such a life. At thirty-three, public life in the world of high politics was proving both demanding and congenial. The House of Commons was an agreeable institution and, not without some inner tension, the pattern of his time and the distribution of his energies were becoming settled between parliament, family and his country estate.

Bright, by comparison, had no such early acquaintance with the ante-rooms of parliamentary power. He was a working man with a business to worry about. The family home at Rochdale stood directly opposite the mill. John was sent by his father to learn the trade from bottom to top. Like many men of his stamp locally, Bright senior had no wish to see his children corrupted by an academic varnish which would destroy their willingness to work in the mill. Yet, however we explain it, it is clear that very early in his life John Bright did not wish to be confined to industrial Lancashire. He had paid a youthful visit to Westminster to see Parliament in operation for himself. But, if he were even to contemplate a parliamentary career, it would not only be the problem of his business (though there were brothers who could assist) but also the tradition of the religious society to which he belonged both by birth and conviction. Yet, despite strong pockets of resistance, an apolitical quietism amongst Friends was steadily yielding to a more dynamic conception of political responsibility. Certainly, politics held many perils, but perhaps it was not necessary for a Quaker in parliament to compromise his principles. Bright himself endorsed this latter view, though his would-be parents-in-law required a good deal of explanation from him before they willingly entrusted their daughter to his charge. For his part, he was at this point able to claim that reports of his political activity had been greatly exaggerated. His zeal to root out injustice went beyond what was normal in a small-town politician in the North of England.

By 1842, Bright was in the process of achieving a national reputation stemming from his role in the Anti-Corn Law League. While he had not played a major part in its foundation, his capacity as an orator soon brought him into prominence. His fame derived from his speaking tours up and down the country. His robust, even reckless, attacks on the defenders of the Corn Laws greatly appealed to his audiences. Bright himself once remarked that the printed page never does justice to the capacity of an orator and we can only dimly grasp the excitement aroused by his language and style. Bright was in his element on these public occasions, far more so than he was subsequently to be in the more formal arena of the House of Commons. These exhausting trips gave Bright a 'popular' constituency which Gladstone as yet neither desired nor knew how to address. Yet, peripatetic though his existence was in the early 1840s, Bright also remained a man with a local base. He remained rooted in Rochdale, and liked to think that his continuing residence there gave him an appreciation of local sentiments denied to 'London politicians'.

It would, however, be misleading to think of Bright simply as a 'provincial'. He could compete with Gladstone in the extent of his European and Levantine travels. Although his father had been somewhat dubious about the value of youthful continental expeditions, he had consented both to a trip through Northern France and Belgium and, in 1835, to a lengthy voyage through the Mediterranean to Smyrna, Constantinople, Alexandria and Jerusalem. His experiences gave a rather different perspective on the world. He took on his journey both his bible and the poems of Byron, and came dangerously near to succumbing to the latter in the exotic Levantine climate. He came back to England through Italy and France. While the sight of St Peter's in Rome did not cause him to reflect sadly on the divisions of Christendom, as Gladstone had done, he was prepared to accept that St Peter's was a building of spectacular splendour.

One other difference is worth noting. Gladstone was a married man, though not without his problems, but Bright was already a widower and had responsibility for his child. Gladstone's marriage had brought him into the Glynne connexion, and removed him further from his Liverpool past. Bright had married a fellow member of the Society of Friends, whose social origins and lack of social aspiration seemed to accord with his own expressed lack of interest in such matters. It may be, however, that Bright took up his campaigning career with such intensity as a way of overcoming his remorse at the early death of his wife. His public belligerency, therefore, hid a sadness and obscured a private inner lack of direction which was to have a bearing on his future career.

That career began, on a wider stage, with Bright's rather unexpected and somewhat fortuitous election to the Commons as member for Durham City at a by-election in 1843. In the House, he immediately harried the ministry on the predictable topic of the Corn Laws but his vigour on this matter was matched by his assault on the Game Laws. He quarrelled publicly and conspicuously with Lord Shaftesbury on the subject of factory legislation. Neither a Whig nor a Tory, Bright felt himself detached from the existing parliamentary groupings and carved a name for himself as the terror of the squires and shires. He was inclined to the view that the repeal of the Corn Laws owed something to his efforts.

After 1846, Bright and Cobden saw their triumph, or so they conceived it, as the prelude to a major 'middle-class' assault on the aristocratic supremacy – on the land, in parliament, the army, the Foreign Office or wherever it might be found. Their dissatisfaction was chiefly with the Whigs. Bright repeatedly warned that they could not expect his support indefinitely if, as seemed to be the case, they ignored his opinions. Yet he did not lead a 'party', and his relations with other 'Radicals' were frequently cool. It was as though he preferred the satisfaction of 'principled' aloofness, to the compromises and personal arrangements of day-to-day politics. There were, however, changes in his style of life. Quaker dress and Quaker language were abandoned, though he remained a Friend who regularly attended meetings for worship. He had also married again, to a Quaker lady, but one who came from a wealthier and more socially ambitious family. The tedium of his London existence was only relieved by his willingness to dine out, though such social proclivities did not bring him into contact with Gladstone in any intimate fashion. Gladstone's own parliamentary position in the late 1840s and early 1850s, though he had reached it by a different route, was almost as awkward and anomalous as Bright's, but there seemed no basis for common action. A 'shabby and undecided lot' was Bright's description of the Peelites in November 1852, though individual speeches by Gladstone gained his approval. Bright described Gladstone's speech on the 1851 Ecclesiastical Titles Bill as 'great' and he likewise admired his demolition of Disraeli's 1852 budget, but these were the diary jottings of a connoisseur of oratory, not the opening moves in a parliamentary alliance.

On the whole, Bright felt that the Aberdeen government formed in December 1852 was at least better than what had gone before. Nevertheless, in the process of its construction, he overestimated the degree to which 'the Radicals' would be able to press their influence, although he did not expect office for himself. It was difficult enough to squeeze in six Peelites. At the Exchequer, Gladstone's performance seemed in general to receive Bright's approval. The administration as a whole, however, did not excite his enthusiasm. His attention at this time was chiefly engaged in the politics of 'causes' – Ireland and India in particular – and it was inconceivable that his well-informed views would bring ministerial approval, even supposing that Bright was interested in any such thing.

The outbreak of the Crimean War changed the picture. Bright's approach to the government's policy does not require elaboration. The way Gladstone spoke about this period in his 1889 encomium is itself revealing. Bright's oratory had made him well-known but 'we had not till then known how high the moral tone of those popular leaders had been pitched . . . and with what readiness they could part with popular sympathy'. Gladstone certainly did not see himself at the time as a 'popular leader' but he did remark to his brother Robertson in November 1854 that Bright's letter on the war was 'an able and manly one' though he could not fully associate himself with its sentiments. When Gladstone did resign from the government in February 1855, he wrote what is his first surviving letter to Bright asking to be allowed to make his resignation explanation to the House from the seat which the 'Manchester men' normally occupied. There was, however, no indication that Gladstone intended to take up a more permanent residence among the Manchester school. That 'school' was in any event in grave difficulty. Bright himself suffered the double blow of a comprehensive nervous breakdown and the loss of his Manchester seat. His political career seemed in ruins and he was strongly urged by members of his family not to attempt to resume it. It was, however, only a short time before he returned to the Commons, still with a zest for politics, but with some awareness of his limitations.

These years had also been difficult for Gladstone and there were many guesses about his future direction, though he had Homer to console him. The finishing touches to that great work coincided in February 1858 with a letter from Bright. It urged him not to throw in his lot with Derby and the Tories. If he did so, Bright wrote, he would be linking his fortunes 'with a constant minority, and with a party in the country which is every day lessening in numbers and in power'. Gladstone returned an appreciative reply, expressing his gratitude for Bright's concern: perhaps it confirmed him in his nervous intention to refuse Derby and Disraeli. The path to his post-Palmerstonian destiny was beginning to clear, but not fast enough for Bright, who expressed the view in September 1858 that Gladstone did have courage, but it was spasmodic. His conclusion was that Gladstone dared not 'accept the lead of a popular party – Oxford and tradition seem to hold him fast'.

Gladstone's acceptance of his old office under Palmerston in 1859 might be taken as confirmation of this fact. Thereafter, the two men seem to have seen a little more of each other, but were not intimate. Indeed, they watched each other warily. For example, the following year Gladstone declined to attend the proposed banquet for Cobden to be held in Bradford, giving as explanation that he did not want in anyway to divert attention from Cobden. Bright wrote to Cobden interpreting this to mean that 'he does not want to be more clearly allied to outside and unorthodox politicians such as you and I are'. However, Lord Clarendon, an outside observer, suspected Gladstone of being 'a far more sincere Republican than Bright'. In the light of Gladstone's equivocations on reform and the paper duty, Bright would have found that hard to believe. Nevertheless, his language both about and to Gladstone was becoming both more elevated and direct. 'There is a fine conscientiousness in Gladstone' he told his wife 'and a reverence which touches everything sacred with beauty'. He wrote to Gladstone himself of the prevalent feeling that the Chancellor was to be the man to show the country a wiser policy and teach a higher morality. Even so, he was not prepared to cut defence expenditure as savagely as Bright wished. In March 1861 he told Cobden that he would publicly declare that Gladstone had an undue love of office if he consented to any lessening of Income Tax whilst the Paper Duty was kept on by the will of the Lords. Lady Waldegrave was telling Gladstone in the summer that most of his Cabinet colleagues were predicting that he would 'lead the Bright party'.

The American Civil War seemed to make such a development unlikely. In August 1861 Bright thought it would be wrong to expect too much of Gladstone. He would not make much of a fight for his views in Cabinet and would not endanger the government. By early 1862, Bright wrote to Cobden agitatedly urging him to keep writing to Gladstone about the United States, concluding, a little despairingly, 'You *must* do what you can to prevent Gladstone from going wrong.' Gladstone had indeed been showing no anxiety to ingratiate himself with the Bright faction. His concern seemed more to mend his fences with Palmerston. Even so, the speech at Newcastle in October when, amongst other things, Gladstone declared that Jefferson Davis and the other leaders of the South had made a nation, came as a shock to the North-supporting Bright. He concluded that Gladstone's mind was too unstable for him to be a successful leader of party or nation. He was born of a slave-holding family and the taint was ineradicable. A coolness descended. Bright's own popularity seemed to be reviving and with it some renewed confidence in his own capacities.

In conversation with Gladstone in February 1864 he lamented that nothing could be done on such matters as armaments, extravagance and Income Tax while the old man was at the head of affairs. Palmerston's longevity was indeed disconcerting. Bright was already beginning to revive the cry of franchise reform. Gladstone must have had one eye on that fact when he committed himself in May 1864 to his impressive but enigmatic declaration that 'every man who is not presumably incapacitated by some consideration of personal unfitness or of political danger is morally entitled to come within the pale of the constitution'. Bright wrote at once to his wife detecting 'a new era in the Reform question'. It showed that Gladstone was looking outwards and made him more than ever 'the dread of the Aristocratic mob of the West End of London'. Gladstone's unmuzzled descent upon South Lancashire Bright deemed 'a national gain'. His connection with Oxford had done something to drag the old university on, but that effort was not worthwhile. The Liberal Party would either settle the Reform question or be broken up. At this juncture, both men went out of their way to praise each other's wisdom, though they did not prove too precise about what 'reform' entailed. By the summer of 1866, Bright was urging 'A General Election for Reform and for a Reform Government'. It would bring 'an immense force of popular feeling into the field' and Gladstone would carry the day.

Advice of this sweeping character was frequently filtered through, but the relationship between the two men was not exactly intimate. Bright saw his role as that of the out of doors politician who generated the demand for Reform, but could not deliver it: 'pariah' or 'outsider' among politicians, was how he put it. It is not surprising, therefore, that his relationship with Gladstone in the critical years 1866/67 was not without its complications. Bright's public campaigning may have helped persuade Derby that the Tories might themselves introduce a Reform measure. 'The great meetings are telling on the fools and rascals' was Bright's objective verdict. Gladstone, somewhat disturbed at the immense force of popular feeling, had deemed himself 'better out of the way of politics during the recess' and departed for Italy. From there he noted Bright's oratorical triumphs with apprehension and wrote that the Reform question was 'separating Bright from us'. He was not pleased by what he read of Bright's speeches and consoled himself with the reflection: 'We have no claim upon him . . . and I imagine he will part company the moment he sees his way to more than we would give him.'

If Bright were to contemplate 'parting company' perhaps the moment had arrived. He was at the height of his fame as a speaker. His reputation for Radicalism had revived with his attacks on the aristocracy. He had established a somewhat shaky relationship with respectable working men – though it did not take them long to discover that Bright's enthusiasm for the extension of the franchise excluded a considerable 'residium'. Bright did indeed allow himself to be seen in the lobbies talking to Disraeli, but it is unlikely that there was much possibility of an independent role. In a letter to Richard Congreve, the positivist, he ruled out the possibility of leadership. He was outside the class – Crown, Parliament, Church, Universities, Army, Navy, Land and Society – which formed a citadel, and he had no wish to join it. Everything depended, he wrote, on whether Gladstone or Russell would take the lead.

For his part, Gladstone was so uncertain of Bright's status and intentions that he refused to give the customary opening of session dinner in 1867. He dared not invite Bright to attend, and he dared not omit him. When Disraeli introduced his hastily concocted measure at the end of February, Bright denounced it as a 'wretched proposition'. Further inconclusive private exchanges with Disraeli took place, and Bright may have been playing a waiting game. If so, he had some success, for a reluctant Gladstone increasingly felt obliged to seek his advice in connection with the franchise. At the same time, he had to be wary of those disaffected members of his own party who thought that the existing government was preferable to one in which Bright himself might well turn out to be a disastrous Cabinet minister. When the 'Tea Room' did achieve Gladstone's humiliation, Bright was at first despairing. He slept badly, coughed frequently, and buried himself in Milton in the hope of regaining paradise. He then became afraid that, after this 'smash perhaps without example' as Gladstone modestly called it, William Ewart would withdraw from public life. Bright decided that, for all his shortcomings, Gladstone could not be allowed to take this course. On 7 April he went down to Birmingham and there delivered his well-known panegyric. There was no one who could add grandeur or dignity to the stature of Mr Gladstone.

While this action cemented the link between the two men, the Reform crisis itself had still to be settled. While Bright kept on contrasting the 'subtle wickedness' of Disraeli with the 'honest courage' of Gladstone, what chiefly concerned him was the behaviour of Russell in the Lords in supporting the provision that in contested three-member constituencies the voters were to have but two votes.

He had no patience with what he termed 'peculiar crotchets' whether they came from Mill, Lowe or the Lords. Gladstone was favoured with this opinion and it was not the only subject on Bright's mind and which a future Gladstonian government might care to attend to. He now dined frequently with the 'Opposition Cabinet' and was in general more freely and easily accepted in Society and political circles than at any time in the past. He was invited to the Royal Academy dinner, and the Prince of Wales confessed to great nervousness at having to speak in his presence. Bright's usefulness to the nascent Liberal party at this juncture chiefly lay in his connexions with the Irish and the Dissenters. He could be vitally important in preventing Protestant feeling from getting the better of Anti-State Church feeling on the Irish question. Both in England and Ireland Bright suddenly found himself 'quite a lion everywhere'.

When Gladstone achieved his majority in 1868 and could form his first government, it was inevitable that Bright should receive an invitation to join the Cabinet. Throughout the election campaign, he had been assiduous in informing Gladstone on the content of his speeches. While suggesting that the Irish Church, education and the reduction of service expenditure constituted the government's priorities, he revealed his own 'moderate' stance by commenting, in a letter to Thorold Rogers, that Gladstone might encounter difficulties in future 'as much from the unreasonableness of the Radicals as from the timidity of the Whigs'. In accepting office, he warned Gladstone that he would prove a disappointment. The Prime Minister responded by putting a man with 'special training' under Bright at the Board of Trade. Despite this assistance, it did indeed turn out to be the case that Bright was not made to be a Cabinet minister. By February 1870, illness had again overtaken him and in December he resigned. During this short period of office, he had frequently made his views known to the Prime Minister on the Irish Church and Land questions. Gladstone treated Bright's contributions with respect, but felt under no obligation to adopt them completely. Bright's resignation, however, marks a fixed point both in his career and in his relations with Gladstone. Until the breakdown, he could still be considered a strong political figure who could, conceivably, have destroyed party unity; if, for example, he had pushed his views on Irish Land to an extreme. So Granville, at least, considered. After his resignation he could never be considered again by informed circles as a contender for effective power, whatever public impression he might still make. Perhaps it is not too fanciful to suggest that Bright crumbled because of his own inability to reconcile the conflicting personal, social and intellectual pressures which crowded in upon him. After 1870, although only fifty-nine, Bright became an increasingly ill-tempered elder statesman, devoting more time to billiards and country houses. Even so, he could not resist the temptation to favour Gladstone with his views on the Pope, the Fenians, relations with France, and other matters. No doubt conscious that a potential rival had faded away, Gladstone treated these submissions with elaborate respect and an element of affection crept into their correspondence.

When Bright's health did improve, he could still be useful. He accepted invitations to Hawarden and the Prime Minister consulted him quite frequently, pressing him to return to the Cabinet. In August 1873, a highpoint was reached. Gladstone took the initiative in suggesting that they should 'bid farewell to Misters' in addressing each other. Bright reiterated that 'official life is not natural to me as it seems to be to you', but he agreed to rejoin the Cabinet in September 1873. He stated that he would not separate himself from his Nonconformist friends, but would try to alleviate their feelings: therein lay his usefulness. His sympathy with Gladstone in these months of 'minsterial embarrassments' was complete, and he deplored the 'constant humiliations'. Gladstone announced his retirement after his defeat in the 1874 election and Bright wrote expressing his regret, but comprehending the reasons. 'For myself,' he added, 'if I could have foreseen either the result of the Election of last year, or your retirement from the conduct of the party, I should certainly have withdrawn from Parlt.' He concluded with expressions of friendship.

Their relationship, however, was not to terminate in occasional meetings and exchanges of letters. Bright did not withdraw from the scene. He dined out as assiduously as ever, finding himself more at home in the company of the aristocracy than of the new school of Radicals in the Commons – men like Dilke or Fawcett. He saw Gladstone from time to time, but was in no sense acting in concert with him. When the Eastern crisis first broke, Bright was playing bowls on his brother's lawn and he continued to regard its unfolding with Drakean detachment until he was forced to make a limited number of public utterances on the subject. While deploring Turkish atrocities, he feared that the logic of Gladstone's position led to war. He gave no encouragement to notions that Gladstone should return to the active leadership of the party, stating that he had chaired the meeting which had chosen Hartington as his successor and would not act to unseat him. He evaded Gladstone's attempts to involve him in the agitation. The veteran orator now maintained that he lacked confidence in 'public fervour in a matter of this kind' and returned to North Wales for as long as he could. The South of France gave him an even more secure retreat a few months later.

Throughout 1876, Bright found Gladstone's conduct somewhat

worrying and was consulted on the matter by Granville and Hartington. After listening to him on 23 March Bright recorded that he spoke 'at length, but occasionally under unusual excitement'. In late April, Bright was deeply involved in the anxious party discussions concerning Gladstone's resolutions on the war. He agreed to act as spokesman for the leadership in persuading Gladstone to amend their content. In the event, Bright was satisfied with Gladstone's speech. His view throughout the Eastern crisis was that Gladstone was burdened with a sense of responsibility connected with the Crimean War. In May 1877, however, he was very cautious in his comments to a Birmingham friend about Gladstone's return to the party leadership. If Chamberlain, Dale, or anyone else sought to urge Gladstone to return 'they will place him in much difficulty and will compel him entirely to repudiate it and they will show how little they are able to estimate his character.' The following day Gladstone was to address the inaugural meeting of the National Liberal Federation in Birmingham. In general, Bright does not seem to have been very enthusiastic about Gladstone's return though, as he wrote to his wife in February 1878 'there is a noble earnestness about him which the Tory party and insincere men among us cannot bear'.

Two years later, however, Bright again accepted Gladstone's invitation to join a Liberal Cabinet. This time, no attempt was made to give him any executive responsibility. Bright had discussed Cabinet-making at Hawarden and there was no inkling of the impending disagreements. In July 1882, true to his record as a short-stay minister, Bright again resigned. This time, however, it was not the customary fuzziness in the head which afflicted him but a strong disagreement with the government's Egyptian policy as it had culminated in the bombardment of Alexandria. Gladstone had tried hard to prevent Bright from taking this step, urging, so Bright recorded, that the government's policy was correct and in the best interests of peace. There is, in this remark, a note of asperity, which no doubt lingered on despite the professions of mutual regard which accompanied the resignation.

That asperity culminated in their open disagreement concerning Home Rule for Ireland. While in the Cabinet, Bright had made his impatience with the Irish increasingly plain. The maintenance of the United Kingdom seemed to him supremely important. In October 1881, for example, he wrote strongly against Parnell and urged that he should be 'denounced'. As he watched events in 1884–5 he was more and more unhappy with the government's course. Once again, what he had detected as the wayward element in Gladstone's character was asserting itself. 'The chaos continues', he wrote to his daughter in March 1886 'and I see no way out of it. The Leader brought us into it and can only get us out – but I fear he is not magnanimous enough to make the sacrifice. He will throw the country into confusion and will break up the party in his effort to force them to accept what they in a vast majority of their hearts condemn and what he knows they condemn.' He wrote to Gladstone in May 1886 stating that his personal regard for the Prime Minister had made him silent hitherto in the House of Commons, but he stressed that he profoundly disagreed with what was being proposed. Gladstone's policy of surrender would only place more power in the hands of Parnell and his men to war against the unity of the Three Kingdoms without increase of good to the people of Ireland. Partly because he did not completely agree with Chamberlain or Hartington either, Bright did not attack Gladstone in public. In private, however, he was scathing in his comments and his criticism was the consuming passion of the remaining years of his life. When the two men met in the street they did stop and shake hands, but there was now a deep division between them.

At the close, therefore, the notion of Bright and Gladstone as the twin heroes of the nineteenth-century Liberal party, enshrined in those oleographs, was not the complete truth. The two men were never close partners and, paradoxically, in their old age it was Gladstone who seemed 'radical' and Bright 'conservative'. The fulsomeness of Gladstone's tribute obscures the extent to which he had come to regard Bright as a broken reed when it was a matter of 'action not words'. For his part, Bright admired Gladstone's remarkable capacities but had grown wary of what he termed his waywardness. In his prime, Bright was a great man of the platform. Gladstone, who had been led to 'the people', in part by that example, was nonetheless pre-eminently a man of government, in a way Bright never could be. Sometimes rivals, sometimes colleagues, sometimes friends, the complementary abilities of the grand old Dissenter and the grand old Churchman were nevertheless vital to the maturing of the mid-Victorian Liberal party.

British Military Intellectuals and the American Civil War: F. B. MAURICE, J. F. C. FULLER AND B. H. LIDDELL HART[1]

Brian Holden Reid

The 'lessons' of military history have never ceased to exert an irresistible fascination over generations of military thinkers. In a previous *festschrift* presented to A. J. P. Taylor, Captain Sir Basil Liddell Hart, after reflecting on H. M. Tomlinson's remark that 'the war the Generals always get ready for is the previous one', concluded that 'He was wrong. The war for which they prepare is often the one before last'.[2] The purpose of this essay is to assess the writings of British military intellectuals on the American Civil War, in a way not considered by Liddell Hart's sweeping generalisation. As the writers under consideration, Major-General Sir Frederick Maurice, Major-General J. F. C. Fuller and Liddell Hart himself, were heavily influenced by the experience of the First World War, the conclusions they drew from the 'war before last' and their stress on the 'lessons' that had been ignored by the generals who prepared for war in 1914, had a direct bearing on the development of their military thought.

The American Civil War, the only great war waged between the end of the Napoleonic Wars and the opening of the First World War, had long been considered a source of valuable instruction for British officers. Indeed the British Army had taken an interest in the conduct of the American Civil War since the bombardment of Fort Sumter. Sir Garnet Wolseley had accompanied General Robert E. Lee's Army of Northern Virginia at the height of its success. Early British writings were pro-Confederate and this partisan spirit reached an apogee with the publication of Colonel G. F. R. Henderson's *Stonewall Jackson* (1898), a romantic and engagingly written book which had a profound influence on the education of successive generations of British officers.[3] After the First World War perspectives on the Civil War changed. The unprecedented scale and cost of 1914–18 offered up new 'lessons' to be studied by staff officers, for as Jay Luvaas rightly points out, the Great War revealed completely novel standards by which to judge generalship.[4] This new wave of writing had an influence on Civil War historiography no less profound than Henderson's and helped shift the focus of studies away from the Confederate to the Union cause and sought to reassess military developments in the mid-nineteenth century in relation to the conduct of war in the twentieth century.

The books of Maurice, Fuller and Liddell Hart covered a wide range of issues posed by the Civil War. The campaigns of 1861–65 had thrown up a large number of arresting personalities of varying military skill who had made a lasting mark (for good or ill) on the war. Each of these three writers was greatly concerned with the impact of the personal factor on generalship. Maurice's *Robert E. Lee, The Soldier* (1925), Fuller's *The Generalship of Ulysses S. Grant* (1929), and *Grant and Lee* (1933), and Liddell Hart's *Sherman: Soldier, Realist, American* (1930), were all biographical in scope though they were not true biographies. They were philosophical treatises on the conduct of war shaped to fit biographical form; they also elevated the 'great captain' at a time when British generals of the First World War were increasingly criticised for personal shortcomings.

As far as the conduct of operations was concerned, Maurice, Fuller and Liddell Hart examined the novel tactical and technological features of the Civil War with far greater insight and imagination than their pre-1914 predecessors – especially the tactical dilemmas arising from the spread of trench warfare. The stalemate of 1861–65, the tension between the initial expectations of a 'March on Richmond' and the reality of a series of inconclusive battles of attrition fought in Virginia and Tennessee, clearly foreshadowed the almost identical experience of 1914–18, in which the 'War would be over by Christmas' optimism was replaced by the bloody reality of the Battles of Verdun, Somme and Third Ypres (Passchendaele). In both wars disappointments and crises arising from initial military failures and unexpectedly heavy casualties led to a clash between the civil and the military power, so that Lincoln's relations with General George B. McClellan revealed some comparable features to Lloyd George's tussles with Robertson and Haig.[5] In the light of these developments, all three of these writers (especially Fuller and Liddell Hart) examined the way in which the strategical problems of 1861–65 had been solved and used their interpretations as platforms for proselytising their own views about the conduct of the next great war in Europe.[6]

Major-General Sir Frederick Maurice is the least well known. His writing is elegant and scholarly and less tendentious than that of either Fuller or Liddell Hart, though it is also more cautious, less enlightening or stimulating. Reliable and solid, Maurice's books are worthy of serious study, though he is simply not in the same league as Fuller and Liddell Hart, two of the most widely read and influential military writers of the twentieth century. Widely regarded as a future CIGS, Maurice sacrificed his career in 1918 when, as Director of Military Operations, he publicly accused Lloyd George of lying over the issue of the strength of the British Armies in France. Thereafter working as a journalist, Maurice published his *Lee, The Soldier* (which was conceived as early as 1902 during his student days at the Staff College). Its success led to an invitation to give the Lees Knowles Lectures 1925–26, on which he based another book, *Governments and War* (1926), a study of civil-military relations North and South 1861–65. In 1929 Maurice was appointed Professor of Military Studies, King's College, London.[7]

By choosing Lee as his model, Maurice sought to vindicate the British Army's pre-1914 teaching on generalship, with its heavy pro-Confederate bias and stress on the rapid manoeuvrability of small columns as exemplified by Stonewall Jackson's campaign in the Shenandoah Valley in 1862. Maurice did not claim that this was entirely correct, as he thought the stress on Stonewall Jackson exaggerated, but he held that the fundamental Confederate model was sound. It is also fair to add that his view of Lee was still influenced by Henderson's romantic approach. In Maurice's opinion, a British staff officer 'could not do better' if he wished to understand the scope of future planning problems, than to make a detailed study of General Lee's dispositions during the Seven Days Battles and the campaign of Chancellorsville. Lee also received lavish praise for grasping that the Civil War would be a long war that could not be waged by volunteers only. Moreover he had successfully urged the Confederate President, Jefferson Davis, to pass a Conscription Act despite fierce opposition from Congress.[8]

It was, however, the economy of Lee's strategy that most impressed Maurice, as the prodigal casualty lists of 1914–18 had brought home to British military thinkers the overriding importance of avoiding heavy losses which had been either ignored or glossed over in pre-1914 teaching. The manoeuvre that brought Stonewall Jackson to Richmond before the opening of the Seven Days Battles in June 1862 transformed an overall numerical inferiority of 3:4 to a local superiority of 12:7 at the decisive point. This interpretation would now be disputed by historians of the Civil War who insist that Lee was profligate rather than prudent in his use of the South's resources.

But Maurice's views serve to underline an important characteristic of British writing about the Civil War: it exaggerated the modernity of prominent American commanders. Maurice, Fuller and Liddell Hart were all guilty of interpreting the Civil War from back to front. As the stalemate of 1914–18 had a precedent in the past, they started out with views as to how this should have been broken and worked back into history to secure their justification. The overwhelming odds that Lee faced after 1863 forced him, so Maurice claimed, to adopt new methods: 'if his campaigns of 1862 are models of what may be accomplished by bold manoeuvre against superior numbers,' he wrote, 'the campaigns of 1864 are not less remarkable examples of how to hold a strong active and skilful enemy in check.' Lee's use of entrenchments was 'fifty years ahead of its time'; 'if the Allies in August 1914, had applied Lee's tactical methods . . . then the course of the World War would have been changed.'[9]

Lee had forced Grant to face the obstacles that had perplexed the generals of 1914–18: 'the problem before him [Grant],' Maurice wrote, 'was not how to carry the first lines of the enemy, but how to beat the reserves behind those lines.' As Lee had no reserve in the 1864 campaign this comment is misleading. Lee was not the 'modern' general of Maurice's imagination. His interpretation illustrates how the post-1918 generation of British writers twisted the record of the Civil War to fit their preconceptions of how the First World War should have been conducted. Modern historians no longer view Lee as a modern general.[10] Nevertheless they continue to accept the fundamental model by which the conduct of the Civil War is treated by some measure of 'modernity' which conforms to future conflict, not to the 1860s. Grant and Sherman have now replaced Lee as the example of 'modern' generalship which is praised by historians. For United States historians there is an element of special pleading involved, as Americans are proud of their Civil War and the 'modernity' which is the source of such special praise.[11] To better understand the Civil War and gauge more precisely its place in the evolution of warfare, the kind of analysis which is now exclusively deployed against Lee should also be turned towards Grant and Sherman. They should be judged by the standards of the nineteenth century, and not those of the twentieth, and this can only result in a more informed understanding of their generalship.[12]

Though his arguments are not in themselves novel, the book most responsible for the improvement in Grant's military reputation was General Fuller's *The Generalship of Ulysses S. Grant*. A critical reading of this book reveals that Fuller relied heavily on Adam Badeau, *The Military History of U.S. Grant* (1881), a book written by Grant's military secretary and verging on the 'official status'. But, in British writing on the war, Fuller's eloquent and magisterial book represents a landmark. Whereas Maurice had only slightly adapted the Confederate model and switched his attention from Jackson to Lee, Fuller brushed it aside contemptuously as unworthy of serious study. Among the very last students to pass through the Staff College before the outbreak of war in 1914, by the mid-1920s Fuller no longer believed that Confederate generalship had the slightest relevance to the education of Staff officers. 'Lee and Jackson [were] certainly not much more than third degree,' he complained to Liddell Hart in 1923. 'Jackson has certainly been overrated.'[13]

The main burden of Fuller's complaint was that Henderson's *Stonewall Jackson* had completely neglected the problem of scale in modern warfare. Henderson had provided a satisfactory model for a small, semi-professional army, but this had little relevance to wars fought in the Age of the Industrial Revolution which were won by numbers and industrial capacity. Siege warfare and a strategy of attrition predominated because technological improvements in weaponry resulted in the domination of the rifle bullet and the supremacy of the defensive. Every general engagement was to some degree an experiment, 'an uncertainty generated by the tactics he [the general] had been taught and the tactics the rifle bullet was compelling him to adopt . . . the tactics of the rifle bullet had to be discovered'.[14]

Fuller judged the Civil War to be the first great conflict of the Industrial Revolution and the wars of 1861–65 and 1914–18 stood in close relationship. Although one was based on steam power and the other oil power, Fuller concluded that 'their influence on the means of waging war is similar; for, both in 1865 and 1918, war is brought to an end by the collapse of the industrially and financially weaker side'. Fuller's close analysis of the ramifications of these changes on the strategy and tactics of the war casts great credit on his ability as an historian. It has had an influence on the writing of scholarly history which extended far beyond professional military circles. In Fuller's writing it is impossible to separate the professional pundit from the serious historian. Modern scholars have merely filled out the details or extended the parameters of his discussion. Fuller showed convincingly how shoulder-to-shoulder charges were rendered obsolete and that men had to be deployed in short rushes covered by skirmishers. The defender was entrenched and held his fire until the attacker broke cover, whereupon he was driven back in confusion. Fuller also stressed how the novelty of these conditions probably excused Grant and Lee from entirely coming to terms with them. He found it much less easy to excuse the failure of British generals to understand them half a century later. The yardstick he chose to judge generals of the Civil War (while recalling their tactical failures) was:

which general most clearly grasped the strategic potential of attrition? By this criterion Grant scored decisively over Lee.[15]

Fuller argued that Grant was a great general and a greater strategist than Lee, because he understood the need to apply the resources of the North to wear down the South with remorseless tenacity. After his appointment as General-in-Chief in April 1864, Grant was the model coordinating generalissimo, subordinating himself to the wishes of his political masters while organising the operations of all theatres as well as Virginia, which Fuller contended, obsessed Lee to the exclusion of all else. Grant exerted all the economic, moral and military pressures of attrition to mount an overwhelming assault on the territorial integrity of the Confederacy in 1864, hinged around a strategic rear attack launched by Sherman so as 'to strike the enemy at the decisive (most profitable) point – his [the enemy's] back'. Thus it suited Fuller to follow Adam Badeau, who had argued forcefully that the inspiration behind the March to the Sea had been Grant. In Fuller's account the grand strategy of the Union in the closing months of the Civil War unfolds like a grand, unified conception.[16]

Grant took the field against Lee and pinned him down. Sherman marched to Savannah. Once this port had fallen he was instructed to march northwards destroying the South's food supplies and morale. It mattered little that Lee seemed to elude Grant in Virginia for, argued Fuller, 'if he cannot destroy Lee, then he will destroy his communications; if he cannot destroy his communications, then he will invest Petersburg. Though means vary, his idea remains constant; he holds fast to Lee, so that Sherman's manoeuvre may continue'.[17]

Fuller magnified excessively Grant's stature as a strategist. The victories of 1864–65 though they followed in sequence were certainly not the result of some far-seeing grand design. The lines of advance were dictated by the lines of communication and supply rather than by strategic inspiration. On strategic questions Grant was not a visionary but an opportunist. When Sherman advocated a march through Georgia, Grant was at first sceptical. Once Thomas was strengthened at Nashville securing Sherman's rear, the Army of the Tennessee was given virtually *carte blanche*. There was little coordination involved – in a modern sense. Once Sherman began his March through Georgia, he lost contact with Grant, and the government in Washington was even uncertain as to the point at which he would emerge on the Atlantic coast. Liddell Hart, who had begun his own study of Sherman's generalship, observed that: 'It is easy to show that Grant had a vague idea of pushing ultimately to the Atlantic coast. But there is no originality in this "idea" which had long been mooted by Halleck, even by McClellan and hundreds of others.'[18]

Liddell Hart was hardly an unprejudiced observer as he thought that he had discovered the first true modern general in Sherman. Unlike either Maurice (who had risen to DMO) or Fuller (who had become GSO 1 of the Tank Corps), Liddell Hart's experience of the First World War was limited to that of an enthusiastic subaltern who had been gassed on the Somme. Nevertheless his outlook was profoundly influenced by the Great War: arguably *the* influence on his career. He became convinced that the great battles of the First World War had been a ghastly mistake. Skill and manoeuvre must return to the battlefield to restore the decisiveness of warfare and reduce its social and economic cost: in the next war great battles of attrition would have to be avoided. During the 1920s Liddell Hart refined his basic ideas into a formula termed the Indirect Approach. Though T. E. Lawrence was more significant in developing the philosophical dimensions of the Indirect Approach, Sherman was important in nourishing the development of his tactical and strategic theories in the 1920s.[19]

The clarity and persuasiveness of Liddell Hart's *Sherman* place it at the forefront of his works on strategy. Arguing that direct assaults were unjustified, Liddell Hart actually went so far as to suggest that not only was the Civil War won in the West, but that final victory had actually been delayed 'by the direct battle-lusting strategy which had governed the campaign in Virginia', which had been 'faithfully imitated with even greater lavishness and ineffectiveness on the battlefields of France from 1914–1918'. Sherman understood that economic factors supported military power. If decisive battles could not be won over the enemy's armed forces by a direct approach, then the main assault should be a strategic indirect approach which avoided battle and sought to destroy instead the basis of war production which had become more vulnerable 'as civilisation has become more complex and the distribution of conflict more general'.[20]

How valid is Liddell Hart's interpretation of Sherman as a distinctive and modern strategist? His book has been rather less influential than Fuller's *Generalship of Ulysses S. Grant*, though it has certainly contributed to a recent emphasis on military operations in the West, especially among scholars of Confederate strategy.[21] As an individual, Sherman has inspired less interest than Grant. Apart from Lloyd Lewis's biography, Liddell Hart's *Sherman* remains the only detailed study of his generalship notwithstanding the didactic intrusions of the Indirect Approach – though this could be put down to the neglect of other historians rather than to the book's intrinsic merits as history. Liddell Hart's view of Sherman's development of the Indirect Approach determined the book's structure. Liddell Hart contended that after Grant's departure to Washington and Sherman's promotion to command the Military Division of the Mississippi, his planned advance towards Atlanta was designed 'not itself to crush the enemy but to unhinge his morale and dispositions so that his dislocation renders the subsequent delivery of a decisive blow practicable and easy'. This is an important distinction. The Indirect Approach did not rule out battle as a theoretical possibility but underlined that the manoeuvres which prefaced battle should be so bewildering that the enemy would be in no position to resist once the attack was launched. 'To move along the natural line of expectation,' Liddell Hart wrote, 'is to consolidate the opponent's equilibrium, and by stiffening it to augment his resisting power;' a direct attack, he concluded, 'even if at the outset successful ... rolls the enemy back snowball fashion, towards his reserves, supplies and reinforcements'.[22]

The means that Sherman supposedly used to secure this distraction were what Liddell Hart called the 'baited gambit'. Sherman's army advanced 'in a wide, loose grouping or net, which could be quickly drawn in round the point of contact with the enemy'. This was designed to tempt the Confederates to attack while widely dispersed, but as soon as they moved into the open the columns joined to inflict a defeat on the defensive. This concept of the offensive-defensive, by forcing his opponent on to a 'series of tactical offensives and at the same time to maintain an almost continuous progress, was a triumph of strategic activity which of its kind is almost without parallel in history'. Liddell Hart had to explain away the Battle of Kenesaw Mountain – a costly repulse. This was easily achieved by blaming Grant, who had 'impressed upon Sherman the need of gripping [General Joseph E.] Johnston' and thus forced him to undertake an operation against his better judgement and true strategic instincts.[23]

But the core of Liddell Hart's case rests on the operations undertaken after the fall of Atlanta, when Sherman had escaped the clutches of Grant's 'orthodox strategy' and when it is clear that 'the bareness of Grant's orders is significant of the co-operation between the two men'. Plunging into the Confederate heartland, Sherman disregarded the Confederate Army of the Tennessee which actually advanced northwards. Liddell Hart characterised Sherman's army charitably as a 'huge "flying column" of light infantry', as all transport and unnecessary baggage had been left behind. His view of Sherman's 'bummers' was rather romantic and he sidestepped the moral issue raised by their slack discipline and marauding encouraged by Sherman's general order that the Army of the Tennessee should 'forage liberally on the country'. Though it is true that Sherman's form of punitive warfare pales by comparison with many far worse atrocities committed since 1865, Liddell Hart's special pleading needs to be further analysed because it conceals an ambivalence in the Strategy of the Indirect Approach. Sherman himself declared that he aimed to show 'the vulnerability of the South and make its inhabitants feel that war and industrial ruin are synonymous terms'. Liddell Hart sought to find a way to reduce the dislocation caused by modern warfare and yet promoted a method which involved an attack on the social and economic foundations of military power. His only way out of this dilemma was to argue the case for Sherman within operational terms. He portrayed the 'bummers', for instance, as operating within the norms of regular warfare, when they did not. 'However careless of the forms of discipline,' he remarked on their behaviour during the March through Georgia, 'they were imbued with the essential fighting discipline and developed such dashing team-work that they would clear the front of the enemy cavalry quicker and better than the proper cavalry had done in previous campaigns.' If indeed Liddell Hart was correct in suggesting that Sherman's campaigns in Georgia and the Carolinas were examples of the Indirect Approach, he never faced up to the possibility that it would transfer the horrors of great battles of attrition away from armies and unleash them upon the civil population.[24]

There remains nevertheless some doubt as to whether Sherman's campaigns were quite the exact examples of the Indirect Approach represented by Liddell Hart. Like Fuller's analysis of Grant's strategy, Liddell Hart conveyed a neatness and imposed a framework on Sherman's operations which was exaggerated. It is unlikely that Sherman was quite the distinctive, consistent and original strategist that he portrayed with such skill. There were undoubtedly some elements of the Indirect Approach in Sherman's generalship, but it is significant that in Sherman's own *Memoirs*, which were hardly muted or self-deprecating, he made no reference to any major difference of opinion about the nature of strategy with Grant. Quite the contrary, some chapters indicated clearly that he believed, like Grant, that geographical objectives were subsidiary to seeking out the enemy's army in battle. 'I was strongly inspired by the feeling,' Sherman wrote, 'that the movement on our part [through Georgia] was a direct attack upon the rebel army;' and he readily conceded that General Thomas's victory at Nashville in December 1864 was necessary to secure his seizure of Savannah. He actually downplayed the strategic importance of the Marches in a revealing passage:

> I only regarded the march from Atlanta to Savannah as a 'shift of base' as the transfer of a strong army, which had no opponent, and had finished its then work, from the interior to a point on the sea-coast, from which it could achieve other important results. I

considered this march as a means to an end, and not as an essential act of war.

This and other references confirm that Sherman had not completely broken with what Liddell Hart called 'conventional strategy'.[25]

Although a more conventional biography than Fuller's *Generalship of Ulysses S. Grant*, Liddell Hart's *Sherman* is a less impressive achievement. Though the social, economic and psychological factors are crucial to his argument, Liddell Hart only paid lip service to them in his book, which is fundamentally a campaign narrative of the highest quality. The compass of *Sherman* rarely sweeps beyond the area of operations to embrace the war as a whole. Liddell Hart's brief discussion of the effects of industrialisation on war and the related tactical changes is derived (without acknowledgement) from Fuller's work. Despite his many assertions about the great importance of social and economic factors, Liddell Hart envisaged war as a clash of armed forces. Fuller gave more attention to the way in which political factors shaped the strategy of the war. But it was Maurice who was most alert to the real political significance of the American Civil War and how problems of civil–military relations in 1861–65 foreshadowed so many of the difficulties encountered during the First World War.[26]

In writing *Governments and War* it was hardly likely that Maurice would ignore his own experience as DMO or that of his superior, the Chief of the Imperial General Staff, General (later Field-Marshal) Sir William Robertson. Maurice argued that civil–military relations should be *balanced*. He disapproved of the United States constitution in principle because the war powers drew an insufficiently clear distinction between the command and *control* of armed forces. Thus 'on such occasions as either President was tempted to exercise the military functions of Commander-in-Chief he was usually unsuccessful'. As Maurice deplored all political interference in operational matters, he argued that policy should be clearly formulated in writing by the political head of the nation at the outbreak of war. Then commanders knew 'the objects for which they are to fight and the military policy for which they are to follow'. As any ambiguity would rebound on the war's conduct, Maurice suggested that these should be resolved at the earliest opportunity.[27]

The Civil War provided Maurice with an abundance of raw material with which to make his case *vis-à-vis* the First World War without actually engaging in any controversy over the conduct of 1914–18. Military professionalism had been quickly checkmated in both wars. McClellan in one and Haig and Robertson in the other then demanded greater authority to fight their wars. When their efforts achieved little, civilian leaders concluded that they were just as able as soldiers to frame military plans. Though political imperatives might demand a place in military considerations, Maurice nevertheless concluded 'that advice and plans framed at a distance are usually either mischievous or inapplicable when they reach the front'. Maurice's prescriptions sound sensible and balanced. But like his chief, Robertson, he failed to consider that in both wars political pressures were as complex as military requirements and that inevitably they would interact on one another. They could not be separated as tidily as he seemed to think.[28]

Governments and War forms two parts. The first two chapters discussed Confederate civil–military relations. Here President Davis and General Joseph E. Johnston were criticised for their feud. 'There is little prospect,' Maurice warned, 'of harmony between policy and strategy, when there is discord between soldier and statesman.' Lee was praised for his excellent relations with Davis but his diffidence nevertheless led to distortions in their relationship: 'ultimately Lee's modesty (and caution) worked against him.'[29]

Maurice found the civil–military relations of the Lincoln Administration far more instructive. He traced Lincoln's efforts to find a workable system for the conduct of war, trying one general after another until the arrival of Grant when the proper balance between soldiers and statesmen was at last established – a pervasive theme of American historical writing on the Civil War since 1945. Maurice was critical of both McClellan's hostility to his political chiefs and of Lincoln's usurpation of command functions, but his sympathies were largely with Lincoln. There is perhaps an unconscious echo of Robertson's own downfall when Maurice concluded that the root cause of McClellan's dismissal was 'his incapacity to establish relations of trust and confidence with Lincoln'. Intrigues against McClellan 'tended to harden him in his opinion that all the politicians in Washington were dishonest schemers and all the administrators incompetents'.[30]

Lincoln's relations with Grant, by contrast, were so cordial that Maurice concluded that Lincoln was only 'searching' for a general able to take military responsibility from his shoulders. Like Fuller, Maurice believed that Grant's combination of patience and respect, added to a quiet determination not to permit any political interference in military planning, were ideal qualities for a commanding general. 'Soldier and statesman set about their business without interfering with each other, and consequently the work of both prospered.' Maurice judged that Grant and Lincoln evolved a modern command system more advanced than anything created in Europe 'until von Moltke in 1866 and 1870 displayed the Prussian methods to an astonished military world'. That the office of Chief of Staff, created to shift Halleck sideways in 1864, had no permanence and was not revived until 1903 was not remarked upon by Maurice. On the issue of command the Civil War had fewer 'lessons' to teach than he believed: the system created by Lincoln was merely a brief but happy conjunction of compatible personalities.[31] Lord Charnwood, Lincoln's English biographer, wrote in 1927 that 'the chief point is that I am sure you have got A. Lincoln and the process of his growth and the size he obtained as exactly as a historian can get anything'. Later historians have not disagreed with Charnwood, for Maurice laid down the framework within which later narrative historians, notably T. Harry Williams and Kenneth P. Williams, while not accepting every point of his interpretation, have filled out the detail.[32]

Despite certain differences of perspective, Maurice, Fuller and Liddell Hart shared some basic attitudes towards their chosen area of study. All three of these writers were busy working journalists – only Fuller remained in the Army until 1933. They were not scholars in the conventional sense. Fuller had to study volumes of the *Official Records*, the basic primary source on the Civil War, in between postings and on the train.[33] Their work was incorrigibly didactic: there were clear 'lessons' that had to be learnt. The past provided signposts to the future and historical writing had to have *utility*. This approach had its strengths as well as its limitations. Their books have had an enduring value not only because of their trenchant analysis and readable style but because their didactic intent demanded a more extended theoretical discussion which has adequately served the needs of a great number of historians and biographers who, for whatever reasons, found that it suited their purpose not to alter the basic structure but only varied their arguments.[34] Maurice, Fuller and Liddell Hart are also firmly within the overwhelmingly *biographical* tradition of so much Civil War writing, however much they may have abused it by their didactic distortions. As Fuller and Liddell Hart used their books as vehicles to attack the established heroes of the British Army – Lee and Jackson – the result was books imbued with passion and commitment.

On the debit side, it is possible that the legacy of this kind of didactic history is less happy. Maurice, Fuller and Liddell Hart were writing when scholarly military history lacked prestige or even experienced practitioners in both Britain and the United States. They dominated the field often because there were so few qualified scholars who could assess their interpretations and comment authoritatively on them. In the field of Civil War history, British writing has a unique prestige in the United States. Though didacticism in military history is less influential, the authority lent by their names (for instance,

Maurice is singled out for special praise in Douglas Southall Freeman's *R. E. Lee*) has reinforced a form of military history which has often been rather narrow in focus: the comparison of the talents of individuals in the most partisan spirit, with usually some vague yardstick of 'modernity' as the gauge of genius.[35] The American Civil War should be considered on its own terms, and its military history treated in relation to the mid-nineteenth century, not the twentieth, with full cognisance taken of the political, social and economic pressures weighing on the peculiar conditions of a *civil* war, without one eye necessarily being focused on later developments or wars quite different in character and aim – such as the two World Wars. These critical comments should not suggest, however, that Maurice, Fuller and Liddell Hart themselves did not produce some of the most challenging and thought-provoking interpretations of the Civil War.

Notes

1 An earlier draft of this essay was much improved by the comments of two distinguished historians, Mr Brian Bond and Professor Peter J. Parish. For their constant advice and help, I am deeply grateful. I am also obliged to the Trustees of the Liddell Hart Centre for Military Archives, King's College, London, for permission to quote from copyright material.

2 Sir Basil Liddell Hart, 'French Military Ideas Before the First World War', *A Century of Conflict: Essays in Honour of A. J. P. Taylor* (ed.) Martin Gilbert (London, 1966), 135–6.

3 Education is, of course, relative. General Fuller recalled in connection with Jackson's victory at Cross Keys in 1862, 'a major recommending Henderson's *Stonewall Jackson* to a brother officer, and then, a few minutes later, when this book was being discussed, committing the error of supposing that "Cross Keys" was a public house in Odiham and Jackson the name of the man who ran it'. *The Army in My Time* (London, 1935), 53–4. Likewise Duff Cooper in 1918 overheard two British officers in France 'discussing the American Civil War . . . as to which side Washington fought on or whether he was only President at the time'. *Old Men Forget* (London, 1953), 209.

4 Jay Luvaas, *The Military Legacy of the Civil War* (Chicago, 1959), 209.

5 There are differences: Lincoln was less concerned about casualty figures than Lloyd George. Lincoln thought the generals were fighting too little; Lloyd George that they were fighting too much. But their views of their respective commanders were broadly similar: Lincoln thought McClellan 'an admirable engineer but he seems to have a special talent for a stationary engine'. Lloyd George wrote of Haig that 'I have never met a man in a high position who seemed to me so utterly devoid of imagination'. See T. Harry Williams, *Lincoln and his Generals* (New York, 1952), 178; David Lloyd George, *War Memoirs* (London, 1937), II, 1366.

6 A. J. Trythall, *'Boney' Fuller* (London, 1977) is valuable for the background; also see my forthcoming *J. F. C. Fuller*, chapter 5.

7 There is no biography of Maurice. See John Gooch, 'The Maurice Case', *The Prospect of War* (London, 1981), 146–63, and Nancy Maurice, *The Maurice Case* (London, 1972). General Sir Horace Smith-Dorrien to Maurice, 26 April, 1925: 'You would have been CIGS some day I am sure – I admired you for it.' Maurice Papers 3/5/155.

8 F. B. Maurice, *Robert E. Lee – The Soldier* (London, 1925), v, 66–7, 113; also see his romantic comparison with the Duke of Wellington, ibid., 289–92.

9 Ibid., 98, 112, 116, 119–20, 217; also see Maurice's *British Strategy* (London, 1929), 116–17. Douglas Southall Freeman, *R. E. Lee: A Biography* (New York, 1934–6), IV, 177; also see Freeman's Review of *Lee – The Soldier* in the *Virginia Quarterly Review*, copy in Maurice Papers 3/4/15.

10 Maurice, *Lee 233–4*. For modern scholars critical of Lee's strategy, see Grady

McWhiney, 'Who Whipped Whom?', *Civil War History*, XI (1965), 5–26, Thomas L. Connelly and Archer Jones, *The Politics of Command* (Baton Rouge, 1973), Grady McWhiney and Perry D. Jamieston, *Attack and Die* (University of Alabama Press, 1982).

11 Marcus Cunliffe pointed this out in 'Recent Writing on the American Civil War', *History*, 50 (1965), 33–4.

12 Russell F. Weigley, with an eye on the First World War, compares Lee unfavourably with Grant because the latter ignored the mirage of the Napoleonic decisive battle that so hypnotised Lee. He cites no contemporary evidence that Grant foresaw the great battles of attrition of 1864, when battles continued for weeks without respite and his analysis resembles a rationalisation after the fact. *American Way of War* (Bloomington, 1977 edition), 140, 142–3.

13 Fuller to Liddell Hart, 2 March, 1923, Liddell Hart Papers 1/302/32. *Grant and Lee* (London, 1933), 12. See Liddell Hart's complaint that Fuller drew 'so largely upon Badeau's book . . .' Footnotes to History, The American Civil War, 4, 8, Liddell Hart Papers 10/1929/138b. The importance of their writings is attested by Edward Hagerman, 'Looking for the American Civil War: Myth and Culture', *Armed Forces and Society*, 9 (1983), 344–45, 'the perspective of modern military analysis, initiated in the 1920s and 1930s by Fuller and Liddell Hart, provides a component crucial to understanding Lee the general'.

14 J. F. C. Fuller, *The Generalship of Ulysses S. Grant* (London, 1929), 26–8, 56, 62–6, 200, 256.

15 Ibid., 28, 62–6, 380; *Grant and Lee*, 252–8; also see John Buechler, '"Give 'em the Bayonet" – A Note on Civil War Mythology', *Civil War History*, VII (1961), 129–31.

16 Fuller, *Generalship of Ulysses S. Grant*, 122, 142.

17 Ibid., 211–13, 244, 265, 295.

18 Liddell Hart to Fuller, 9 July 1929, Liddell Hart Papers 1/302/175.

19 Brian Bond, *Liddell Hart* (London, 1977), 47–9; Brian Holden Reid, 'T. E. Lawrence and Liddell Hart', *History*, 70 (1985), 218–31; Jay Luvaas, *The Education of an Army* (London, 1964), 398–400; Liddell Hart, *Memoirs* (London, 1965), I, 168–71.

20 Liddell Hart, *Sherman: Soldier, Realist, American* (New York, 1930). The British edition had the sub-title, *The Genius of the Civil War*. All quotations are from the second British edition (1933), vii–viii, 74, 430.

21 See Archer Jones, *Confederate Strategy: From Shiloh to Vicksburg* (Baton Rouge, 1961).

22 Liddell Hart, *Sherman*, 243, 108.

23 Ibid., 253–4, 264–5, 277.

24 Ibid., 231, 331, 336, 346.

25 William T. Sherman, *Memoirs* (New York, 1875), II, 170, 218–19, 220; Weigley, *American Way of War*, 500-ln52.

26 Bond, *Liddell Hart*, 167–8; Liddell Hart, *Sherman*, 273; Liddell Hart made no reference to Sherman's detestation of newspaper correspondents, for example – hardly a 'modern' trait.

27 Maurice, *Governments and War* (London, 1926), 21, 76–7. The US edition was called *Statesmen and Soldiers of the Civil War* (Boston, 1926).

28 Ibid., 15, 21, 76–7. The echo of Robertson's experience is clear. In April 1918 he

complained, 'Everyone who advises should also be the executor, then there is no doubt where the responsibility rests or where the guidance comes from.' Robertson to Major-General Sir R. Bannatine-Allason, 26 April, 1918, Edmonds Papers II/1.

29 Maurice, *Governments and War*, 37, 43–6, 60–5.

30 Ibid., 93.

31 Ibid., 98–9, 100, 102–3. Ludwell H. Johnson, 'Civil War Military History: A Few Revisions in Need of Revising', *Civil War History*, XVII (1971), 122–4.

32 Lord Charnwood to Maurice, 7 February 1927, Maurice Papers 3/5/163. These ideas have influenced Williams, *Lincoln and his Generals* and Kenneth P. Williams, *Lincoln Finds a General* (New York, 1949–54), 5 vols.

33 Fuller to Liddell Hart, 19 April, 1929, Liddell Hart Papers 1/302/165/166, reveals some of the difficulties confronting the soldier–author by a military career. It is also perhaps important to note that Fuller and Liddell Hart, and presumably Maurice also, were interested in books that would *sell*. It was therefore in their interests to reach a conclusion that would provoke controversy and gain notice. When Liddell Hart insisted that Fuller should alter his interpretation otherwise his 'mistakes' would amuse American historians, he replied: 'I . . . am ready to amuse the American historians, though they will never amuse me.' Fuller to Liddell Hart, 12 July, 1929, Liddell Hart Papers 1/302/176.

34 Bruce Catton's two volumes, *Grant Moves South* (Boston, 1960) and *Grant Takes Command* (London, 1970), have not altered the basic interpretation adumbrated by Fuller.

35 See especially Thomas L. Connelly, 'Robert E. Lee and the Western Confederacy', *Civil War History*, XV (1969), and Albert Castel, 'The Historian and the General', *Ibid.*, XVI (1970); Williams, *Lincoln and his Generals*; and Charles P. Roland, 'The Generalship of Robert E. Lee', *Grant, Lee, Lincoln and the Radicals* (Evanston, 1964), for typical examples of judgements on Civil War generalship.

Inventing Military Traditions

John Keegan

The visitor from Sandhurst to *Ecole spéciale militaire de St.-Cyr*, in its new buildings at Coëtquidan in Brittany, cannot fail to be struck, if he spends more than a few days in the sister academy, by the remarkable difference in ethos between the two institutions. His own is characterised by informality. Cadets wear civilian clothes for much of the day; little importance is attached to seniority, seniors treating juniors as equals from after their arrival; formal ceremonies are few. The only one of real importance is the Sovereign's Parade, which celebrates the seniors' departure. And it is appropriate that this should be so, for the British officer is encouraged to think of his real military life beginning at the moment when he joins his regiment and enters its rich world of living military tradition. At St.-Cyr almost the reverse is true. It is there that he is immersed in the traditions of French officerhood which he will be expected to carry with him from regiment to regiment during his peripatetic career. Thus the St.-Cyr year is spangled with days of initiation, commemoration, and organised pranks: *Bahutage*, *Amphiarmes*, *Gala*, *Voyage d'études*, the *Demi-tour* of 30 June, the *Remise des Casoars*, *Baptême* and *Triomphe* of the year's end and the re-enactment of Austerlitz (*'la Sainte Austerlitz'*) on 2 December. The ten letters of AUSTERLITZ are themselves used to signify the ten working months of the year[1] (A for October, Z for June, OO for the summer holiday), by which calendar 2 December itself becomes 2S. This private system of dating is easily mastered; less so is the *Spéciale's* argot:[2] *pompe* (non-military studies – studies are *colles*) which include *chien vert* and *chien jaune* (administration and military law), *gogo* (geography) and *tapir* (topography); *mili* (military studies) which include *barbette* (fortification) and *bronze* (gunnery); and *crapahut* (physical training) which includes *pique-boyau* (fencing), *pete-sec* (gymnastics) and *zèbre* (equitation). The juniors (*bazars* or *melons*) are rehearsed by the seniors (*anciens* or *officiers*) in this argot until they are word perfect; they must become word perfect too in the Cyrard songs, particularly *La Galette* and *Pekin de Bahut*, for these are sung at the *Baptême*. At that solemn torchlight ceremony of transition from the junior to the senior year ('qui se déroulait à l'origine dans l'allegresse générale . . . mais de nos jours est devenu une cérémonie de caractère religieux'), each junior kneels before 'his' senior to be crowned with his shako, decorated for the first time by the *casoar*, the plume of red and white feathers which – tradition has it – Queen Victoria presented to the school in 1855. When baptised, the junior intake (*promotion*) is summoned to rise by the master of ceremonies (*Père Système*) of the senior intake, who addresses it for the first time by its *titre de promotion*.

The *titre* will have been chosen only after much thought and by a strictly regulated procedure. The *Père Système* – formerly the cadet lowest in the order of merit but latterly elected – canvasses the *promotion* (or *promo* – St.-Cyr makes a fetish of abbrevation*) through his circle of assistants (*Cour des Fines*) and submits the three most popular choices to the Minister of Defence. He selects, occasionally amending, that which he prefers. Thus the *promotion* of 1968–70 submitted *Souvenir de l'Empereur*, in honour of the bicentenary, and got back *Souvenir de Napoleon*. The care taken in, and political scrutiny given to, the *titres* can be explained in two ways: first, the *titre* is that by which the members (among whom thereafter 'le tutoiement est obligatoire . . . quelle que soit la différence de grade') will identify themselves throughout their lives and it cannot therefore be taken for some flippant or transitory reason; second, it encapsulates the spirit in which the *promotion* enters on its military life. This was not originally so: the significance of the first *titre* (*Firmament*, 1830–32) has been forgotten; *Comète* (1835–36) commemorated the reappearance of Halley's comet, *Ibrahim* (1835–36) the visit of Mehemet Ali's son to the school in the latter year. By that date, however, *promotions* had already begun to take contemporary French victories as *titres* (*l'Isly*, 1843–4) and the trend was to become more marked thereafter. The promotion of 1854–55 took *Sébastopol*, 1859–60 *Nice et Savoie*, 1860–61 *Puebla*. Promotions next began to take not only French victories but also French heroes (notably in the twentieth century

* thus foreign cadets are *crocos* (crocodiles), classmates are *cocos* or *cos* (co-conscripts), casoar is *caso*.

young St.-Cyriens recently killed in action, like *Pol Lapeyre*, 1926, and *Bournazel*, 1932, both killed in the Rif war, and *Jeanpierre*, 1961, killed in Algeria). French alliances (*Drapeau et l'Amitié Américaine*, 1916–17 – one suspects a hasty conflation – and *Amitié Franco-Brittanique*, 1939–40) or phrases expressive of hope or resolve for the future: in 1871, *Revanche*, in 1939 *La Plus Grande France*, in 1942 *Veille au Drapeau* (Vigil before the Flag, chosen by the unsummoned *promotion* of 1943–44), in 1954, the French empire's year of agony, *Union Française*, in 1958, the crisis of the Algerian war, *Terre d'Afrique*.

Such was the significance which the *titre de promotion* had attained among French officers by 1939 that both the Gaullist *Ecole des Cadets de la France libre*, organised in England in 1942, and the *Ecole Militaire Inter-Armes*, established at Cherchell in Algeria after Operation Torch, conferred *titres* on their *promotions*, much abbreviated though their training was. The *Ecole des Cadets* chose successively *Libération*, *Bir Hakeim*, *Fezzan-Tunisie*, *Corse et Savoie* et *18 Juin* (the latter the date of de Gaulle's appeal to the French people in 1940), while the E.M.I.A. chose *Weygand*, *Tunisie*, *Libération*, *Marche au Rhin*, *Rhin Français*, a neat catalogue of French military history between 1942–45. Moreover, as soon as was possible, steps were taken to attach these non-Cyrard *promotions* to the tail of the regular sequence. On 20 May, 1945, those Cyrards of *Croix de Provence* (1942) who had been sent after the liberation of the Métropole to complete their interrupted training at the E.M.I.A., presented the St.-Cyr colour, which had been hidden by the last commandant on the school's dissolution, to the representatives of their junior promotion, *Veille au Drapeau*. They in their turn presented it a week later to their juniors, the Cyrards of *Rome et Strasbourg* (1944). All three groups belonged to the fifth *promotion* of the E.M.I.A., *Marche au Rhin*. But the sixth, *Victoire*, and seventh, *Indochine*, also contained representatives of *Croix de Provence*, *Veille au Drapeau* and *Rome et Strasbourg*, were thus legitimised and, on the repatriation of the E.M.I.A. in July 1945, formed the nucleus of the reborn St.-Cyr in its new location at Coëtquidan. 'Ainsi donc, la tradition était renouée et la continuité de St.-Cyr assurée.'

Attempts were made, nonetheless, to stifle the rebirth, on the one hand by military radicals, who suspected that *la Tradition* had done much to form *la mentalité Maginot*, on the other by *résistants* among the new politicians of the Fourth Republic who hoped to overcome the political inertia of *La grande muette* with the progressive dynamic of the *maquis*. The destruction, by American bombing in 1944, of the original buildings at St.-Cyr l'Ecole and the existence of the traditionless E.M.I.A., gave them their opportunity, on which they capitalised by abolishing the old 'G.U.' (*Grande uniforme* of madder red trousers, blue tunics, shako *bleu-ciel*, the St.-Cyr colour, and red and white *casoar*), substituting new colours on which '*Honneur et Patrie*', replaced Napoleon's own '*Ils s'intruisent pour vaincre*' and denying official recognition to the *rites de passage* – *Remise des Casoars*, *Baptême* and *Triomphe*. But in vain. The first post-war promotion (1945–46), calling itself *Nouveau Bahut* (*Bahut* is Cyrard for the school buildings), appointed its *Père Système* and *Cour des Fines*. Little by little they and their successors claimed back the essential Cyrard totems and traditions: in 1947 the designation *spéciale* and the colour with the Napoleonic inscription, in 1948 the public celebration of the *Baptême* and *Triomphe*, in 1949 the *Grande uniforme*. Finally, in 1952, they achieved the separation of St.-Cyr from the *Ecole Speciale Militaire Inter-Armes* (as Coëtquidan had been known since 1947). Henceforth there were to be two schools at the same location: the E.M.I.A., for cadets recruited from the ranks, and once again the *Ecole spéciale militaire de St.-Cyr*, for the *lycéens* who had survived the traditional *corniche* (year of preparatory study) and succeeded at the *concours*.

This perhaps over-lengthy account of the St.-Cyr *Système* has seemed worthwhile for four reasons: first, because of its inherent interest, almost as great for the outsider as for Cyrards themselves; second, because it helps to illuminate the self-image of the French officer corps – truly a corps in the way that the British officer body is not – and so to understand the central role which the corps has played in the life of the nation in the last hundred years; third, because, denials to the contrary, the *Système* does much more than 'maintain' the school's traditions. Not only are those traditions constantly embroidered and added to, though that is certainly the case.* But the *Système* is also an institution for the outright invention of tradition, annually in the case of the *titre*[3] and the *promo*'s insignia, intermittently, but no less unequivocally, when a break in tradition requires repair. It is, after all, only by a feat of imagination that the 'continuity' (in the sense of the 'apostolic succession', which the school seeks to

* The *Triomphe* dates in present form only from 1889, the *Remise des Casoars*, only from 1890. It was then known as the *Benédiction*, was quite facetious in character, and was held in the barrack room on the eve of the juniors' first day of leave, usually the Sunday before Christmas. Each *melon* knelt at the foot of his bed, holding his shako, while 'une fine galette, officier très bahuté' (versed in Cyrard customs) passe devant chacun lui ordonnant de baiser son caso, puis de coiffer le shako. La courte cérémonie se termine par un defilé dans la chambre en riant et sans aucune mise en scène'. The mise-en-scène today requires flaring torches, military bands, the use of an open-air amphitheatre, the presence of generals and parents, the solemn chanting of verses ('Noble galette, que ton nom/Soit immortel en notre histoire/Qu'il soit ennobli par la Gloire/D'une vaillante promotion') and the evocation of a quasi-religious atmosphere.

establish) of post- with pre-war St.-Cyr can be discerned.* Fourth, and finally the *Système* is concerned with what a little enquiry quickly reveals to be the main staff of military tradition (and so the staple of the inventor): the dress of the soldier (at St.-Cyr the G.U.) and the name and pedigree of his unit (at St.-Cyr the *promotion*).[4]

It might be expected that invention would work powerfully on other elements of the military life; that, for example, given the organic character of military society, the eternal family rituals of marriage and burial would stimulate the creative and the theatrical in masters of military ceremonies. Military funerals, however, conform to a remarkable international stereotype, at their grandest requiring a gun-carriage cortège and a fusillade over the grave, and appear to remain stereotyped for fear of affronting the principal mourners with any departure from precedent.[5] Military weddings usually seem to conform to a stereotype, though the observant British spectator may have noticed that in recent years the Household regiments' practice of leaving the lining of the exit from the church to their NCOs is catching on with less grand regiments, whose officers would previously have done it themselves, holding their swords to form an arch over the heads of the bridal couple. They are also following the Guards' habit of marrying in morning coats instead of uniform. Snobbery is a powerful solvent of tradition.

Military baptism, meaning – like the Cyrard *Baptême* – the induction of recruits, appears almost as stereotyped as funerals and weddings. It is true that the Israeli armoured corps has devised a particularly dramatic form of induction for its members, staged by night on the summit of Masada, the national shrine where the last Zealot rebels committed mass suicide rather than surrender to the Tenth Legion. But its ingredients, the burning of torches and the swearing of an oath, are common to similar ceremonies in other armies. Regiments of the Soviet army, for example, take 'all the new recruits before the personnel and the unit banner. Generally the ceremony is conducted at a historical site of revolutionary or combat glory. As each recruit's name is read out, he leaves the ranks and reads

* The representatives of *Charles de Foucauld* and *Croix de Provence* who baptised *Veille au Drapeau* at Cherchell in May 1945 had never themselves crossed the portals of the *Maison-Mère* (the conventual term is authentically Cyrard) at St.-Cyr l'Ecole but had received what training they had in a dreary infantry barracks, the Caserne Miollis, at Aix-en-Provence. The promotion baptised a week later, *Rome et Strasbourg*, had not even been enlisted; in 1943 its members were schoolboys who had sat a '*concours camouflé*', under the noses of the Germans, allegedly for admission to *Ecole des hautes études commerciales*. And all, of course, were destined in 1943 not for the *Armées – du métropole, d'Afrique*, or *coloniale* – but for Pétain's pathetic armistice army.

the text of the oath, after which he signs a special roster and returns to the ranks. After the oath has been taken, the band plays the national anthem and the unit then passes in review. The day is a holiday.' The ceremony, however, is a revival of a Czarist one, from which it differs only in that it is the commissar rather than the regimental chaplain who instructs the recruits in the significance of the oath.[6] And it in turn derives from Frederick the Great's army: 'They conducted us into a hall, which seemed as big as a church, and brought up several badly-holed colours and ordered each of us to take hold of a corner. An adjutant, or whoever he was, read us a whole screed of articles of war and pronounced a few formulae, which the others murmured after him . . . Lastly, he swung a colour over our heads and dismissed us.'[7] Braker, the recruit, does not tell us that the recruit's free hand had to be held aloft, with the thumb and third and fourth fingers joined, but so it had, and the Bundeswehr, who have revived the Prussian ceremony, insist that it is. The eighteenth century Habsburg salute required the fingers to be arranged in the same way, a custom perpetuated in modern Poland, where it must have been revived by Pilsudski.

Military meals are notoriously an occasion for ritual. The most enjoyable element of the *jour de Camerone*, the Foreign Legion's commemoration of Danjou's last stand in 1863, is the memorial dinner, at which the youngest legionnaire present reads an account of the battle, *Tiens, voilà du boudin* is sung and large portions of the redoubtable sausage are eaten. Some was parachuted to the defenders of *Isabelle* at Dien Bien Phu on 30 April, 1954. In British regiments, tradition largely attaches to the form in which the loyal toast is drunk, or to the reasons for it not being drunk at all. The King's Shropshire Light Infantry, for example, claim that they were exempted from the obligation[8] in 1822 at Brighton, when they had protected the Prince Regent from a hostile theatre crowd. Other regiments drink seated, citing sea service, during which they adopted the naval habit, itself said to derive either from royal command or from the lack of headroom in men o' war. The Royal Sussex Regiment formerly drank the loyal toast seated, claiming naval service, but that of their honorary colonel, the head of the House of Orange, whom they had served as mercenaries in the sixteenth century, standing. In 1953 Queen Juliana, when dining with the regiment, insisted that her health be drunk seated also, and that has now become the regimental tradition.

Such identifications of outright invention are rare, for reasons which anyone who has ever dined in company, military or civilian, will readily understand. Port makes for dim memories, so that tonight's spontaneous gesture becomes next year's unalterable tradition. What can certainly be said of all British mess customs is that any claiming to antedate the nineteenth century are certainly younger, messes themselves dating only from the Peninsular War, and that those claiming to antedate 1871 are probably not as old, since it was the abolition of purchase in that year, and the consequent anchoring of the officer to his regiment, which turned the mess into the time-hallowed club of modern times. As for Camerone day, sacrosanct though it has become, it was certainly not celebrated before 1890.

This short review of the styles of military funerals, weddings, 'baptisms' and meals, encrusted with ritual though they appear to be, ought to demonstrate that they provide unsatisfactory material for the study of the 'invention' of tradition. Dates are vague, forms are procrustean, nothing is written down. It is therefore to pedigree and uniform that one must return, for there the inventor leaves traces of his handiwork, in the form of fudged genealogies and borrowed finery.

No historian needs explaining to him the difficulties of inventing convincing pedigrees or, for the individual or family, the attractions. British historians, aware of the long and genuine pedigrees of their own national regiments, may, however, feel surprise that regimental pedigrees need to be invented. The need has nevertheless been felt in many armies, both in those of recent foundation and in others of older date where military catastrophe or political upheaval have broken a valued line of descent. It is indeed a general rule that in dealing with the regiments of any army except the British, and its imperial siblings, the greatest caution should be observed in accepting any pedigree, for careful examination will almost always reveal exactly the same pattern of illegitimate births or bigamous marriages which invalidate the cases of human claimants to name or fortune the world over.

It is name, of course, rather than fortune which military genealogists covet, for though a new unit may make a reputation for itself overnight by the capture or defence of some nodal strategic point or political totem – as the 'Jerusalem Brigade' did in 1967 – or by the demonstration of some novel or spectacular military function – as Hermann Goering's parachutists did in 1940 – the effect is usually achieved by the careful orchestration of publicity and tends, therefore, to be transient. Real military reputations are in general won only slowly and painfully, by a combination of select recruitment, which automatically ensures the concentration of public concern, genuine risk-taking and heavy casualties. Reputations, too, are usually only borne by regiments (rather than divisions or corps), partly because regiments are the oldest of permanent military formations (and so have had the time to acquire them), partly because as groups they conform to the laws of human scale and are thus the largest units which can easily be invested with a comprehensible identity, partly because divisions and corps are too cumbersome and expensive for even the most affluent state to maintain permanently in being.[9]

'Good' regiments are thus desirable properties.[10] How are their deeds trafficked in? The French have a particularly brisk approach to the business. They simply decree that a newly-formed regiment *is* an historic one, by virtue of the fact that it has been given a previously-used number. Thus, for example, their modern 41st Regiment is deemed to be the *Régiment de Monsieur*, founded 1634, though that regiment, transformed into the 41st Demi-brigade at the revolution, was disbanded in 1803, the next 41st (1820) disbanded between 1923–28, the next dissolved in the rout of 1940, and the present 41st not raised until 1944. Now stationed at Rennes in Brittany, it parades with a Breton bagpipe band, or *Bagade*, which is claimed to be 'traditional' and helps to make the day hideous at local *fêtes folkloriques*.[11] An even more extreme example of the French Army's way with a pedigree is that claimed for the modern 94th *Régiment d'Infanterie de Marine*. It is deemed to be the *Royal Hesse-Darmstadt*, raised as a foreign regiment in 1709, disbanded in 1815 (after changes of title both with revolution and Empire), re-raised in 1855, dissolved in 1940, re-raised after the liberation, 1944–45, re-raised for Algeria, 1956–62, and re-raised 1967, when furthermore it was given the suffix *de Marine* to help preserve the identity of one of the regiments of *Infanterie coloniale* then undergoing disbandment.[12]

Some French regiments can do better than that. The 1st, *Picardie*, '*le premier régiment de la Chrétianté*'[13] claims descent from *les bandes de Picardie*, brought into royal service in the 1470s, and can indeed show an almost uninterrupted existence from the beginning of the sixteenth century. 'Almost' is, however, the catch. Like all but one French regiment, its pedigree is fatally broken in the period 1815–20 when Louis XVIII, who had a thoroughly rational suspicion of the loyalty of his regiments, following their behaviour at the beginning of the Hundred Days, deliberately disbanded all of them and remustered their manpower into *légions départmentales*, which shared neither name, colonel, garrison nor complement with any pre-existing unit. The sole exception was the 2nd Dragoons, whose colonel was able to re-enlist his men the day after he had discharged them and which therefore preserved its identity in fact if not in law. By a remarkable coincidence, the 2nd Dragoons also survived the other great regimental débâcle, that of June 1940. Reconstituted after the rout as part of the Armistice Army of 100,000 (arithmetical tit-for-tat by the Germans) allowed by the conquerors to Vichy, the regiment remained in being until November 1942 when its commanding officer, Schlesser, escaped to North Africa with the standard. It was there reconstituted, took part in the liberation and survives to this day, the only French regiment with an authentic seventeenth-century pedigree (for comparison, the tally in Britain is eight cavalry and twenty-two infantry regiments). The next time, therefore, that any reader of this paper meets a French soldier wearing on the right breast pocket of his tunic a little pendant badge identifying him as a member of *Picardie* (even if they should meet in Cambrai, the regimental depot), or *Walsh* (a flight of Wild Geese come to roost among the tyre factories of Clermont-Ferrand), or Royal-Vaisseaux (do they drink M. Giscard d'Estaing's health seated?), he should express interest but reserve judgement.

The Germans have shown the same readiness to fake regimental pedigrees as the French, though their methods have been more circumspect. Some careful cross-posting of personnel after the catastrophe of Jena in 1806 allowed the Hohenzollerns to 'preserve' the existence of 1st Foot Guards (another self-proclaimed 'First Regiment of Christendom', nominally founded in 1688, and into which the heir apparent was commissioned at the age of ten) and they later also resurrected Frederick the Great's *Gardes du Corps*. Later in the century, Wilhelm II's tinkering with the pedigrees of some of the regiments of the X Corps brought about a slightly eerie encounter, on the battlefield of Le Cateau on 26 August, 1914, between some of their dead and some live scouts of the Suffolk Regiment. The latter, wearing in their caps the arms and motto of Gibraltar, *Montis Insignia Calpe*, were puzzled to find that the German uniforms bore a cuff band also inscribed Gibraltar, a coincidence which became one of the minor mysteries of the First World War. It was not definitively cleared up until 1954.[15] What then appeared was that, in 1899, the Kaiser had issued an order for the regiments of the X Corps, which was recruited in Hanover, to assume the battle honours formerly borne by the Hanoverian regiments of the independent kingdom. These had, however, fought on the wrong side in 1866 and, unlike those of the Kingdoms of Saxony or Baden, had not been incorporated intact into the new German army. The whole of the Hanoverian army had in fact been disbanded in 1867 and new regiments created from the Hanoverian *Wehrkreis* (as it became), formed of drafts from Prussian regiments. The Kaiser undoubtedly hoped that this *caesura* would have been forgotten in the ensuing thirty years, for he proceeded to allot to them not only the honours of the old Hanoverian army of the eighteenth century (hence the Gibraltar cuff title, given to the 73rd Infantry and 10th Jäger) but also those of the King's German Legion, George III's corps of Hanoverian exiles who had made their way to England after the dissolution of the Hanoverian army by Napoleon in 1803. The 13th Uhlans, which he deemed to be the 1st Dragoons of the K.G.L., thus acquired 'Garcia Hernandez', perhaps the most prized of all Napoleonic battle honours, since it was on that field that Major Bock of that regiment achieved the feat, unique in the Napoleonic wars, of breaking a French infantry square. Others were given 'El Bodon' and 'Barossa', as well, of course, as 'Peninsula' and 'Waterloo'. Only at the old Hanoverian regimental colour inscription, 'MIT ELIOT ZUM RUHM UND SIEG' (Eliot had commanded the Anglo-Hanoverian garrison of Gibraltar during the great siege of 1780–83), did the Kaiser's acquisitiveness stop short. He ought to have denied himself all, for his claim lay across two, if not three, clear breaks in the line: between the X Corps and the Hanoverian army, 1867, between the reformed Hanoverian army and the King's German Legion, 1816, and between the K.G.L. and the old Hanoverian army, 1803. The whole episode is redolent of his notorious anglophilia/phobia.

The 'Gibraltar' trail might be expected to have petered out at Le Cateau. But it does not. For, on the creation of the 100,000-man army after 1918, Seeckt, its guiding star, decided that one way to outwit the restrictions laid by the Allies on its future expansion would be to make each of the very many fewer regiments of the *Reichswehr* the *Traditionsträger* of several of the *Kaiserheer*'s, which, when fortune favoured, he intended should re-emerge from the chrysalis. Thus, for example, the 9th Regiment became *Traditionsträger* of the 1st Foot Guard's (and acquired the nickname *Graf Neun* because of its attraction for aristocratic officers). The traditions of the 73rd Hanoverian Infantry passed to 5th Company of the 16th Infantry and the Hanoverian Jäger to the 9th and 12th Companies of the 17th Regiment. When the time came for re-birth, in 1935, however, Hitler showed no enthusiasm for Seeckt's long-laid plan. His wish was for an army which would look to him, rather than to its imperial past, and so, though the *Reichswehr* regiments remained theoretically *Traditionsträger*, the new regiments he raised assumed completely fresh identities.

A fresh identity, separate and distinct from those of the *Wehrmacht*, *Reichswehr* and *Kaiserheer*, was also what the *Bundeswehr* sought – or had sought for it – at its inception in 1956. The Baudissin Committee believed it could be found in the concept of the *bürgerliche Heer*, the 'army of the citizen in uniform' which would be built on and informed by the spirit of *innere Führung*. A school of *innere Führung* exists to this day and a good deal of lip service is paid to its teaching. But as much, if not more, of the *Bundeswehr*'s spiritual energies is devoted to the search for roots. Though the practice is not approved (but equally, in Colonel Bertold von Stauffenburg's acute caveat, not forbidden either), many regiments have deemed themselves to be *Traditionsträger* of those from the past, either because they share a common number, or garrison, or officers from the same family. Colonel Stauffenburg's *Panzeraufklärungbataillon 11* has taken on the traditions of his father's 17th Cavalry Regiment of the *Reichswehr*, itself the *Traditionsträger* of the 2nd Prussian Dragoons from Schwedt-am-Oder, and it is as the *Schwedterdragoner* that the battalion is known to itself today. The officers of the 1st *Panzergrenadierdivision* at Hanover have breathed on the embers of the King's German Legion's traditions and talk both knowledgeably and wistfully of '*Gibraltar*'. And the ceremonial *Wachbataillon* at Bonn regards itself as the *Traditionsträger* of the 1st Foot Guards and so presumably, in its dowdy not-quite-fieldgrey and NATO helmets, as both *Graf Neun* and the 'First Regiment of Christendom'.[17]

Mildly comical though this search for roots can be made to appear, the alternatives – such as making up regimental 'traditions' completely new – often appear funnier still. One cannot believe for example that even the most committed East German communist can take the following regimental history completely *au sérieux: '1956: the ZEH Regiment* (of the Nationale Volksarmee) takes part in its first exercise as an organised unit; 1958: A great movement to strengthen the young people's army is under way. The factories are sending volunteers into the garrison. Thus a company of the ZEH regiment will bear the name Karl Liebknecht from now on. This is shown by a flag presented by the People's Own Enterprise Heavy Machine Industry Karl Liebknecht at Magdeburg; 1961: on 13 August the regiment completed their mission to secure the national frontier (i.e. at the time of the building of the Berlin Wall). The Central Committee of the Free German Youth bestowed the Free German Youth honour banner on regimental personnel for their unsurpassed performance of duty in combat along the national frontier; 1963: the regiment's personnel fulfil their national commitment in Hagenow county by bringing in the potato harvest; 1968: the ZEH Regiment is endowed with the honourable name Arthur Ladwig, which will be carried on the pennant of the regimental colours;' and so on.[18] Invention failed, however, when it came to choosing an appropriate uniform for the East German army. Its original Soviet styles proved so embarrassingly unpopular after the Berlin rising of 1953 that the leadership performed a complete volte-face and reintroduced the dress of the Wehrmacht, down to such details as identical collar patches and arm-of-service piping colours (*Waffenfarbe*) and, of course, jackboots.

That a communist régime found itself obliged to choose between only two styles, that of a conquering power resented by the population, and that of a national past to which its own ideology was inimical, tells us a great deal about the second principal method of instant tradition-making, the sartorial. It has long been recognised that uniforms are almost as important to armies as weapons or tactical doctrine. What is less readily perceived is that the vocabulary of military fashion is a very limited one, which cannot at all easily be expanded by decree. 'Ruritanian' is a deadly adjective. It killed overnight President Nixon's efforts to outfit the White House police in attire he thought more appropriate to the dignity of their office, and it is a word every clothing committee has on the tip of its tongue when examining fashion sketches. Completely new branches of the armed services have had some success in persuading their members to wear an untraditional garb (Cecil B. de Mille, for example, designed uniforms for the post-war United States Air Force Academy of distinctly cinematic cut, and Royal Air Force officers wore between the wars, apparently without complaint, a full-dress hat modelled on the open-cockpit flying helmet), but soldiers (and, to an almost monomaniac degree, sailors) seem to require clothes which proclaim that they are soldiers (or sailors) and will not allow them to be mistaken for anything else.[19] This in turn determined that, at least until the appearance of completely functional clothing during the Second World War, only a dozen or so items of dress were really popular, a fact attested by their very slow evolution in style and constant reappearance in European military wardrobes between the seventeenth and twentieth centuries. The items I would pick out for notice, roughly in chronological order of appearance, are the Kurtka (the long form-fitting frock coat), the hussar outfit, the grenadier cap (both the mitre and bearskin types), the classical helmet (both with a crest and with a spike – the *pickelhaube*), the wide-awake hat, the Zouave outfit and, right at the end of the period, the British khaki service dress suit, worn with collar, tie and Sam Browne belt.

What invested these items of dress with their desirable qualities was, of course, the military reputation of those who originally wore them. What allows one to include these items in a discussion of 'the invention of tradition' is that they did not remain the property of their original owners, but were widely borrowed by those who coveted their name. Clothes instantly simplified the business of inventing a tradition for a new regiment, or for a new army. Instead of the laborious business of faking a pedigree, new uniforms could be ordered and issued[20] and military neophytes turned in an instant into battle-hardened warriors – French peasant lads into Macedonian hoplites, muzhiks into Roman legionaries, East Anglian ploughboys into pandours from the Habsburg military frontier, West Indian freedmen into mamelukes; banana republic police lieutenants into Grenadier Guards officers – transformations, each one of which actually happened, can be dated to the year, sometimes to the day, and which provide material for endless speculation on the self-image and psyche of military society over several centuries.

Why the borrowing of the oldest items began is more difficult to isolate. The Kurtka, the hussar outfit and the bearskin cap are not western European but come from the eastern border with the Ottoman and Tartar lands. A rough explanation might be that, with the discontinuation of armour in the sixteenth century, itself brought about by the appearance of firearms, soldiers found themselves without an inherently soldierly garb. They made do during the next century by wearing small pieces of armour – gorgets, corselets, gauntlets – with their civilian doublets, until about 1660 when travellers from Poland, Sweden and the Habsburg lands began to appear in a costume which was both handsome in itself and said to be 'correct' for campaigning against the heathens (as it was, because it had been copied from them). This kurtka – the knee-length, sleeved, form-fitting coat *à la Polaque* – caught on so quickly that its eastern origins (it is both the Cossack and Ottoman kaftan and the Mogul alkalak, with an origin somewhere on the Central Asian steppe) have been forgotten in the west, where it is thought of, if thought of at all, simply as a development of the doublet. Fashion experts have shown that that is not so. Less interesting than its provenance, though, is its eventual destination. Having clothed, as the *justaucorps*, all European soldiers during the eighteenth century and later, as the coatee, with its tails buttoned back, all European infantrymen until the mid-nineteenth century, it was re-discovered, as the alkalak, by the British in India after the Mutiny. As the alkalak, it was the common dress of the irregular cavalrymen whom they had brought from the Punjab to hunt down the regular mutineers (who were naturally dressed as Hungarian hussars) and, as a 'loyal' garment, immediately became 'correct' for clothing the Indians (and later the white officers) of the re-formed cavalry. A hundred years later, when independent Ghana wished to find a uniform for its mounted presidential bodyguard, for which the national costume provided no idioms, British designers imported a design copied exactly from the Indian cavalry's.

The journey of the hussar outfit – fur busby, heavily frogged dolman, slung pelisse, tight embroidered trousers – is better charted (as, given the extraordinary effect it produces not least in feminine hearts, it ought to be). Brought westward by the Hungarian light cavalrymen recruited into the French army – which had heard of their success against the Ottomans – at the beginning of the eighteenth century, it was soon judged 'correct' for any light cavalry, Hungarian or not, so that by the beginning of the nineteenth century most armies – including the British and United States – had hussar regiments. By a curious leap, the costume was also judged appropriate for irregular infantry, with the result that the British rifle regiments raised for duty in the Peninsula were given a uniform of dark green (the colour worn by the Prussian and Austrian *Jäger*, and their derivatives, the French *Chasseurs*) but cut and embroidered hussar-style. Two streams of tradition thus met in their outfit. But it was soon to become autonomous, for, in South Africa and Ceylon, the British put Rifles, dressed as hussars, back on horseback, called them Mounted Rifles, and implanted in the minds of the colonials later brought to fight the Boers the idea that 'Mounted Rifles' was the title by which a colonial cavalry regiment should correctly style itself. Most Australian, New Zealand and Anglo-South Africa cavalry regiments therefore called themselves, after 1900, Mounted Rifles, thus completing the return of the hussar idea (less the hussar outfit) to the borders of a different empire two hundred years after its journey had begun.

The grenadier hat, probably also Hungarian in origin, arrived in Western Europe simultaneously with the hussar style but ended by making a quite different statement about the role of its wearer. Adopted initially for functional reasons, since it allowed the grenadier a free-arm swing in throwing his bomb, it acquired with the grenadiers, who soon became élite troops, a special exclusivity, and was by the beginning of the nineteenth century to become the distinctive headgear of bodyguard infantry. For inexplicable reasons the two styles in which it was worn – as the bearskin, and as the mitre of metal or embroidered cloth – were Catholic (Austrian and French) and non-Catholic (Prussian, Russian and British) respectively, but, once it became ceremonial in significance, some interesting cross-postings transpired. The British, for example, had ceased to wear their mitre before the Napoleonic wars broke out. The First Guards re-adopted it after Waterloo as a reminder that they had beaten Napoleon's Grenadiers in that battle, but, of course, chose the French bearskin style in order to make the point. Tsar Nicholas I, when forming his 'inner guard' of Palace Grenadiers in 1827, also gave them the French bearskin, in memory of the defeat of the Imperial Guard in the Moscow Campaign of 1812. The Pavlovski Guards, founded by Tsar Paul in 1796, however, had been given the Prussian mitre, as a mark of his dislike of the ugly Potemkin style (and looser Potemkin discipline) introduced by that great minister into the Russian army in the previous reign. During the period of similar reaction in the Prussian army after the Wars of Liberation, Frederick William borrowed back from the Pavlovski the mitre cap to give to the First Foot Guards (the 'First Regiment of Christendom') and, as a tremendous mark of royal favour, their mitre was passed on to the First Prussian Grenadier Guards by Wilhelm II in 1894. At the same time the First Foot Guards were re-equipped with caps modelled more exactly on those of Frederick the Great's army, which Tsar Paul had copied in the first place (but to which neither the First Foot nor the First Grenadier Guards had themselves belonged).

The practice of borrowing from the eastern frontier persisted into the Napoleonic wars, Napoleon himself bringing Polish lancers in *czapska* and *plastron* into the Grand Army as late as 1807. But the barbaric style had by then found a competitor for favour in an equally military but civilised idiom, that drawn from the warfare of antiquity. The surprise is that classical idioms did not appear earlier than 1743,[22] when Marshal Saxe invented the cavalry helmet *à crinière*, but it perhaps needed a general with passion for the stage to perceive that fancy dress could be translated to the theatre of war. His was an immensely successful translation. Attempts to dress the new armies of the French Revolution forty years later in Roman styles were a ridiculous failure, but the classical helmet caught on at once, was copied by all the enemies of France during the Napoleonic wars, remained the 'correct' dress for heavy cavalry throughout the nineteenth century, continues to top the outfit of ceremonial heavy cavalry uniforms to this day and most recently turned up on the heads of Moise Tshombe's motorocycle bodyguard during his presidency of the short-lived Katanga republic.

Robbed of its crest and surmounted by a spike or grenade emblem – an invention of Tsar Nicholas I and an allusion to the Roman infantry legionary's headgear – the classical helmet became standard in the Prussian and Russian infantry from 1843. Given up by the Russians in the 1880s, from which time onwards their uniforms tended increasingly towards an invented Slavic style,[23] it remained in use in the Prussian (later Imperial) army until 1918 and achieved worldwide popularity after its victories of 1866 and 1870. It was taken into wear by the British infantry in 1878 (the cavalry had worn a version, imported by the Prince Consort, since the 1840s), by the American army in 1881 and by many others, including several South American armies and even the Papal Swiss Guard, before the end of the century. In the process, however, it acquired political as well as military associations, thanks to the severity with which the 2nd Prussian Grenadier Guards ('the Bloodhounds') acted against the Berlin revolutionaries of 1848. That episode made it 'correct' for policemen, on whose heads it appeared throughout much of the world; thus, for example, though never adopted by the Habsburg armies, to which it stood as a symbol of their defeat in 1866, it was worn by the Viennese city police from the end of the nineteenth century until 1918, as, in a suitably liberalised form, it still is by our own.

The nineteenth century also saw the re-appearance of a hat 'liberal' in its own right. This was the 'wideawake', wide-brimmed soft hat, sometimes turned up at one side and decorated with feathers. In the seventeenth century the everyday dress of the soldier, it was borrowed back by the mid-century nationalists and revolutionaries, from the 'Bohemian' world of literary and artistic rebels (Kossuth made it his own) and used to stand as a symbol of anti-Habsburg and anti-Hohenzollern sentiment. (As late as 1853 Liszt drew the attention of the police to himself by wearing a 'democratic' hat in Karlsruhe.) The *Bersagliere*, the Piedmontese light infantry raised by La Marmora in 1836, wore it in their campaigns against the Habsburg armies in 1848 and 1859 (as they do to this day); it was then, in obedience to the familiar principle of imitation, borrowed back by the Habsburg volunteers who went to fight for Maximilian in Mexico, so acquired 'correctness' as dress for colonial campaigning, was chosen as the headgear of the Imperial German *Schutztruppen* in the African colonies (1889) and passed from them to the Orange Free State and Transvaal State Artilleries (1890). It was their hat which the British, Australians and New Zealanders copied during the Boer War, which became the Australian 'slouch' or 'bush' hat, and so outfitted the Fourteenth Army in Burma, thus established itself as 'correct' for jungle warfare, was taken up by the *Corps expéditionnaire* during the Indo-China War and, thus locally domesticated, commended itself to the American Special Forces during the Vietnam Campaign. Kossuth would no doubt have been surprised by its eventual destination and political associations.[24]

Uniform during the nineteenth century became much subject to other Romantic influences, and once again it was the dress of barbaric peoples which recommended itself as right for new regiments or new forms of warfare. The most popular, interesting and mobile of these inventions was the 'Zouave' style – short waistcoat and baggy trousers, cummerbund and fez (or Moorish turban). It is, of course, simply the male costume of the Ottoman empire, was worn as far north as Bosnia and as far west as Morocco, was first seen in western Europe on the backs of the Mamelukes whom Napoleon brought back from Egypt in 1799, was enthusiastically adopted by the Philhellenes in the Greek Wars of Liberation (since it was worn in Greece by Christians and Turks alike)[25] but achieved world-wide popularity after the French conquest of Algiers in 1830. Impressed by the fighting powers of a local tribe, the *Zoaoua*, the conquerors outfitted a new regiment, whom they called the Zouaves, in their style. But they drafted into the regiment not only local native volunteers but numbers of Paris insurrectionists of 1830, whom the new government had found too hot to handle, and so legitimised the mameluke dress both for native and for irregular European wear. It recommended itself in that way first to the Piedmontese *Bersaglieri*, then to several American volunteer regiments (impressed by the performance of the Zouaves in the Crimea) raised for the Civil War, and to many of Maximilian's volunteers who, after his defeat in Mexico, brought it back with them when they enlisted in Pio Nono's Papal Zouaves in 1866. The defenders and attackers of the Porta Pia, stormed by the *Bersaglieri* in 1870, were thus identically clothed. Its immense popularity also helped to solve the expanding colonial empires' difficulties in choosing appropriate clothing for their new native armies, which often lacked a sartorial idiom. The Italians chose it for their Eritrean infantry. The British put their Indian infantry into an adaptation of the style after the Mutiny, and copied it exactly for the West India Regiment, with which they also garrisoned their West African possessions. It was thus still in wear in Ghana at the moment of independence in 1957 and was instantly discontinued, as the garb of servility, in favour of uniforms modelled on those of the British Foot Guards. Almost at the same time, however, independent Morocco, whose Sheriffian troops had worn it before Lyautey's conquest of 1912, was reintroducing it for ceremonial wear in its army as a mark of liberation from colonial rule.

The last style at which one might look, though so unobtrusive is it that 'style' might seem an inappropriate word to describe it, is the British 'service dress', the khaki suit worn with a collar and tie and Sam Browne belt, adopted about 1910. In its infancy, the uniform was thought both undignified and unmilitary by friends and enemies alike. Captain Edward Spears, appearing in uniform at the Ministère de la Guerre on 4 August, 1914, quickly detected that the French thought that 'to go to war in a collar and tie represented an attitude of levity quite out of keeping with the seriousness of the situation'; while Hauptmann Walter Bloem, glimpsing near Mons a few days later a man in 'a grey-brown uniform, no, in a grey brown golfing suit with a flat-topped cap', asked himself, 'Could this be a soldier?'[26] In the decade following the war, the question was to be answered unequivocally by the spread of the Sam Browne belt (by then precisely as useful as the sword it was supposed to support) throughout the military world. It was even accepted by the *Reichswehr*. But its most significant adoption was by the White Russian armies, in which the British tunic (known as the 'French', after Sir John) also became popular and was often made up in black cloth.

The colour black, the khaki shirt and tie and the Sam Browne belt thus acquired an anti-Bolshevik connotation, and hence provided the styles needed by the new para-military right wing parties in Italy and Germany. These parties were, of course, also the inheritors of the traditions and, on a large scale, of the personnel of the 'shock' formations of the First World War, the Italian *arditi* and the German *Stosstruppen*. Black was, as a result, to become a politically tabu colour after the Second World War (retained with some embarrassment even by the Anarchists to whom it had originally belonged) while the Sam Browne belt lost all the popularity it had so suddenly acquired outside Britain. The paramilitarization of wartime uniforms and the politicisation of war-raised shock units – of which that of the French *paras* is the most recent manifestation – has also given established armies cause to think about the ramifications of 'inventing' tradition. Old regiments and old styles have come to seem even more desirable possessions than they looked to Wilhelm II – guarantees of 'bravery in war, obedience in peace'. What more can we want of soldiers?

Notes

1 At the end of the last century the ten letters used were UN OFFICIER. The change is probably due to the institutionalisation of 'tradition' following the move to Coëtquidan.

2 *L'Album d'un Saint-Cyrien* (G. Virencques, Paris, Plon, 1896) records over 300 words of argot, many of which have survived the school's migrations from St.-Cyr l'Ecole.

3 The invention can be completely self-nourishing. In 1964, the fiftieth anniversary of the outbreak of the First World War, the junior *promotion* chose *Serment de '14*, a reference to the hasty baptism of *Croix du Drapeau* by *Montmirail* on 31 July, 1914, after which both left for the front, taking with them their *casoars* with which each newly-commissioned sous-lieutenant had sworn to decorate his service cap at the moment of first meeting the enemy. The evidence is, however, that the oath was sworn only by about thirty of the six hundred present.

4 Most of the information for St.-Cyr comes either from personal knowledge or from *Histoire de l'Ecole spéciale militaire de Saint-Cyr*, Lt.-Col. M. Camus, Les Ecoles de Coëtquidan, mimeographed, 1971. See also Louis Rousselet, *Nos grandes écoles militaires et civiles*, Paris, Hachette, 1888, General R. Desmazes, *Saint-Cyr*, Paris, 1948, and Virencques, op. cit.

5 On the other hand, there were strong traces of invention in the military funeral of President Kennedy. And most of the ceremony of British royal funerals seems to have been invented by Lord Esher (information from Professor Michael Howard), who arranged Queen Victoria's funeral. The now jealously guarded 'tradition' that the gun-carriage should be pulled by sailors arose from an accident with the horses at the foot of Windsor Castle hill, and the rope used by the hastily impressed blue jacket team was the communication cord from the royal funeral train. The tradition that the company colour of the Queen's (or King's) Company of the Grenadier Guards should be interred with the monarch seems to date from Edward VII's funeral and has developed. At his burial, a miniature copy of the colour was laid on the coffin, at George VI's the colour itself was used to pillow the king's head.

The role of bodyguards at royal funerals is instructive. In ancien-régime France the right of accompanying the king's body into the burial vault belonged to the *garde de la manche*, an inner group often of the *garde écossaise*, itself one of the four *gardes du dedans du Louvre* who formed a separate part of the *maison militaire du Roi* from the even more numerous *gardes du dehors*. The idea of conferring such a special right seems to have attracted other, younger, royal houses, for Nicholas I, when he created his Palace Grenadiers in 1827, gave them the right also, and he encouraged Frederick William of Prussia to form a similar bodyguard, the *Schlossgardekompagnie* (1829). The right of guarding a dead pope's body belongs to the Noble Guard, formed by Pius VII in 1801.

The invention of 'inner' guards by nineteenth-century courts became a positive mania. Our own Honourable Corps of Gentlemen-at-Arms was revived as a respectable military body in 1862 and the Royal Company of Archers, previously a private archery club, acquired the title of the King's Bodyguard for Scotland in 1822. The Habsburgs, who already had the Royal Hungarian (1760), Royal Arcieren (1763) and Trabanten (15th century) Lifeguards, raised the *Hofburgwach* in 1802 and the *Leibgardereitereskadron* in 1849. The Pope added the Palatine and Noble Guards (for the Roman bourgeoisie and 'black aristocracy' respectively) and the Papal Gendarmerie to the Swiss Guards during the nineteenth century. Napoleon III's *Cent-Gardes*, raised in imitation of the Bourbon *Cent-Suisses* but dressed like Napoleon I's cuirassiers, became the butt of some of the most scurrilous of contemporary republican journalism.

6 Herbert Goldhamer, *The Soviet Soldier*, Crane Russak, N.Y., and Leo Cooper, London, 1975, p. 192; for the Tsarist ceremony, see Vladimir Littauer, *Russian Hussar*, J. A. Allen, London, 1965, p. 95.

7 Christopher Duffy, *The Army of Frederick the Great*, David and Charles, 1974, p. 57.

8 Traditionally imposed after the '45, and so requiring in some regiments that water glasses and finger bowls be removed from the table, so that Jacobite officers could not pass their port glasses above and drink mentally to the 'king over the water'. Jacobitism was certainly extinct by the time mess life became formalised.

9 The Soviet Army has, however, kept in being all the twenty divisions of the garrison of East Germany (Group of Soviet Forces Germany) since they arrived there in 1945, and carefully preserved their honour titles.

10 The officers of the Grenadier Guards devoted considerable effort during the First World War to arguing against the general use of the term 'grenadier' to denote the new specialists in grenade tactics; as a result of their representations the term 'bombers' was adopted instead. Sir F. Ponsonby, *The Grenadier Guards in the Great War*, Macmillan, 1926, Vol. III, pp. 230–3.

11 The appeal of the bagpipe is erratic. Many colonial volunteer regiments raised in the British Empire in the last century called themselves 'Scottish' or 'Highlanders' and raised pipe bands (a manifestation of 'Balmorality'), but neither in Canada nor Australia have they survived as parts of the regular armies which succeeded the volunteer forces; nor in South Africa, where the army, particularly since 1934, has been deliberately 'Afrikaanerised', with new regiments being given Voortrekker heroes' names. But curiously the pipe bands, raised by the British for the frontier and mountaineer regiments of the Indian Army, became domesticated, are preserved by the successor armies and have taken the fancy of the new Gulf States. The Kuwaiti army has recently hired a Scottish pipe major on a three-year contract at £41,000 to train its pipe band.

12 Before 1897 the *Infanterie coloniale*, which was financed and controlled by the Minister for the Colonies, had been called *de marine*. These *marsouins* latterly achieved a position analagous to that of the Gurkhas in the British army and their patrons in the army high command managed by the revival of the *marine* suffix in 1967 to avoid the total extinction of the *armée coloniale*.

13 The oldest British regiment, the 1st Royal Scots (raised 1633 for service under the King of France), prizes the nickname Pontius Pilate's Bodyguard and facetiously claims descent from the legion whose soldiers diced for Christ's clothes at the foot of the cross. For *Picardie*'s claims see the article by General Adolenko, *Revue historique de l'armée*, 1969, I, pp. 15–22.

14 See D. Devilliers, *L'Etandard evadé. L'Epopée du 2e Dragons*, Paris, 1957, and R. O. Paxton, *Parades and Politics at Vichy*, Princeton U.P., 1966. Schlesser became first commandant of Coëtquidan after the war, was a moving spirit in the

importation of St.-Cyr traditions, and was removed during the anti-traditionalist reaction.

Even after the occupation of the *Zone libre* the Germans allowed Vichy to retain a token military force. It was called the First Regiment of France (an allusion to the *Premier bataillon de France* on the St.-Cyr colour) and consisted of three battalions of horse and bicycle cavalry. Laval thanked Rundstedt for granting permission to raise it. 'The creation of a French Army,' he said, 'even though small, could oppose the viewpoint that the *real* French Army was in North Africa', Paxton, op. cit., p. 398.

15 Journal of the Society for Army Historical Research, Vol. 32 (1954), pp. 93–4.

16 Though in 1943 he presented to the 199th Infantry Regiment, the 'successor' of the 16th Bavarian Reserves Regiment in which he had served in the First World War, a cuff band in commemoration of the association. The 44th Division, raised in Vienna, was also granted the title 'Hoch- und Deutschmeister', the title of the Habsburg 4th Infantry Regiment raised in that city, and named for the head of the Teutonic Order.

Himmler, by contrast, went in for heavy mythologising in the naming of the divisions of his *Waffen SS*: 9th and 10th Panzer Divisions were called *Hohenstaufen* and *Frundsberg*, 17th Panzer Grenadier *Götz von Berlechingen*, 7th, recruited in Austria, *Prinz Eugen*. Foreign SS divisions were given appropriate national titles: 6th (North European) *Wiking*, 22nd (Balkan *Volksdeutsch*) *Maria Theresa*, 21st (Albanian) *Skanderberg*, 23rd (French) *Charlemagne* and 23rd (Yugoslav muslim) *Kama*.

17 For a long look at the *Traditionsträger* idea in action see Gerd Stolz/Ebhard Griesen, *Geschichte des Kavallerie-Regiments 5 Feldmarschall von Mackensen. Geschichte einer Stamm-Regimenter in Abrissen und Erinnerungen, 1741–1945*, Schild Verlag, Munich, 1975. This regiment (the Blücher Hussars) was adopted by the modern Panzerbataillon 2 of the Bundeswehr in 1958.

18 Ullrich Rühmland: *East German Army Dictionary*, Bonner Druck- und Verlagsanstalt, Bonn, 1972, p. 192. Great thought has been given in the East German Army to the question of tradition. Most regiments now bear the names of suitable proletarian heroes, e.g. Bebel, Rosa Luxemburg, Thälmann, but also Scharnhorst and Gneisenau *and* Florian Geyer, whose name Himmler gave to the 8th SS Cavalry Division. Where German names lack, Russian names are supplied. The internal security regiment of the Ministry of the Interior is named after Dzerzhinski, the (Polish) founder of the Cheka.

19 The Royal Air Force also got away with the extremely difficult feat of inventing a new set of officers' rank titles after 1918. But it failed to persuade its non-commissioned members to accept a system derived from the Anglo-Saxon *fyrd* (Vice-reeve for corporal, etc.) and even today it is possible to read in *Times* obituaries that 'Group-Captain ——— preferred on retirement to be known as Major, the rank he had held before he transferred to the new service from the army' (even though it entailed a drop of two steps in the hierarchy).

20 The privileged were able to watch Field Marshal Idi Amin, in conference with a London military tailor, in the full flood of creation during a visit to Sandhurst in 1972. (The field marshal is not a graduate of Sandhurst, though journalistic tradition is well on the way to making him one.)

21 Paul also insisted that recruits for the Pavlovski should all have snub noses, which he thought went best with the mitre, and this tradition was faithfully observed until 1917.

22 Classical military texts were circulating in translation by the sixteenth century. See Michael Mallet, *Mercenaries and their Masters*, Bodley Head, 1974.

23 The 'Trotsky' uniform (of pointed cloth helmet and heavily 'brandenbourged' overcoat), was not a bolshevik invention at all, but the final development of this 'Slavic' trend. The Red Army found the prototype stocks unissued in Moscow in 1917 and appropriated them. The style was nevertheless reverently re-created for the Soviet Army's fiftieth anniversary parade in Red Square in 1968. For this, and most other uniform references, see John Mollo, *Military Fashion*, Barrie and Jenkins, 1972; the book is eminently worth reading as a commentary both on the invention of tradition and the military *Weltanschauung*.

24 It was also 'invented' by the newly-raised United States Cavalry in 1853, perhaps because of its 'cavalier' silhouette, was on Custer's head shortly before it was scalped at the Little Big Horn in 1876, remained in use during the Cuban Campaign of 1898 (it was worn by Roosevelt's Roughriders) but is now only worn by the drill instructors of the United States Marine Corps – again, an odd destiny for the 'liberal' hat.

25 On Prince George of Denmark's accession to the throne of Greece in 1863 he outfitted his guard (the Evzones) in this style, which they wear to this day. The Greek army had previously worn French-style uniforms. The change was probably intended to demonstrate the foreign king's esteem for the 'traditions' of his adopted people.

26 E. L. Spears, *Liaison 1914*, Eyre and Spottiswoode, 1930, p. 14; Walter Bloem, *The Advance from Mons*, Davies, 1930, p. 56.

'Et l'honneur?' Politics and Principles: a Case Study of Austen Chamberlain

Margaret Morris

A. J. P. Taylor has demonstrated how haphazard, unconsidered or lightly considered actions have usually been decisive in bringing about the outbreak of war. In 1914, for example, Archduke Franz Ferdinand's chauffeur took the wrong turning in Sarajevo; William II gave assurances to Austria without consulting his generals because Moltke was on holiday and he, himself, was in a hurry to get away to the North Sea; the Tzar ordered general mobilisation to make a show of boldness in front of his generals, who were dithering about how to make a gesture of support for Serbia; and Germany's attack on France was dictated not only by anxiety to avoid a war on two fronts but also by the inflexibility of railway timetables. Yet British participation in the First World War cannot be seen as yet another link in a chain of almost accidental happenings, because it was preceded by several days of Cabinet discussion, lobbying by Opposition and military leaders, public meetings and resolution mongering of all kinds. Thus it was a considered and not a random decision, and so must be seen as an exception to the general tendency so convincingly argued by Mr Taylor. What, therefore, lay behind it? The advocates of war believed that Britain must intervene on the side of France no matter how the war started so, for them, the German invasion of Belgium was not decisive, although it was a fortuitous circumstance in helping the Government to justify its stand and win over most of the Cabinet. But at the heart of their thinking, alongside their general assessment of British interests, there was the question of honour.

The notion that a nation, like an individual, must at all costs safeguard its honour was frequently voiced by the aristocrats and gentlemen who controlled international relations in the early twentieth century. Thus, when the British Cabinet was still hesitating and Cambon, the French Ambassador, was trying to influence events, he gave vent to the bitter cry, 'Et l'honneur? Est-ce que l'Angleterre comprend ce qui est l'honneur?'[1] Those to whom these words were reported found them utterly compelling, particularly Austen Chamberlain, the Shadow Chancellor of the Exchequer, who will serve as a case study for the purposes of this essay. He took the lead in pressing his Opposition colleagues to take a forthright stand with Asquith. They responded and Bonar Law sent a letter to the Prime Minister on Sunday morning, 2 August, which read as follows:

> Lord Lansdowne and I feel it our duty to inform you that in our opinion as well as that of all the colleagues whom we have been able to consult, any hesitation in now supporting France and Russia would be fatal to the *honour* and to the future security of the United Kingdom, and we offer H.M. Government the assurance of the united support of the opposition in all measures required by England's intervention in the war. (my italics)

Sir Edward Grey, scion of a noble family which had provided Cabinet Ministers for generations, agonised over his own and Britain's obligations. Although formally free, the logic of the Entente and the naval arrangements which accompanied it left him no choice unless he betrayed his principles. He outlined his moral dilemma to the House of Commons:

> How far that friendship [i.e. with France] entails obligations, let every man look into his own heart and his own feelings and construe the extent of the obligation for himself. I construe it myself as I feel it, but I do not wish to urge upon anyone else more than their feelings dictate as to what they should feel about the obligation. My own feeling is that if a foreign fleet . . . bombarded and battered the undefended coast of France, we could not stand aside.[2]

The acceptance of a gentlemanly code of honour as a guide to policy-making did not confer wisdom on Britain's rulers; this hardly needs saying in the context of participation in a war for which the price far outweighed any benefits. Yet without appreciating that truthfulness, straight-dealing, respect for treaties, keeping one's word or one's faith, integrity, unselfishness and loyalty were taken seriously, it is not possible fully to understand the political debates of the early twentieth century. Naturally, the extent to which politicians adhered to the code in practice varied considerably from Austen Chamberlain, once described by Frank Pakenham as 'the perfect British Parliamentarian; a phenomenon inspiring awe',[3] down to those who paid only lip-service to it. Thus, although his extreme uprightness exposed Austen Chamberlain to mockery, he epitomised widely-held values, so that an examination of how he acquired these beliefs and how they influenced his actions may throw some light on the cultural and ideological perceptions of the British statesmen of his time.

Imbued though he was with the attitudes of Britain's traditional ruling class, Austen Chamberlain was not one of them but the son of Joseph Chamberlain; a Unitarian not an Anglican; a Liberal Unionist not a Conservative; and, although a rentier like them, his means were relatively modest and he was frequently worried about money. He was predestined to enter Parliament, however, as surely as if he had been the conscientious elder son of a Cecil, a Derby, a Grey, or any other of the great landed families who dominated British politics in the nineteenth century. He was at preparatory school in Brighton when Joseph Chamberlain became an MP in 1876, and his father entered the Cabinet four years later as President of the Board of Trade while Austen was at Rugby. The talk at the family table in his holidays was dominated by politics, for Joseph made it a practice to talk to his children of everything in which he was involved. At what stage 'Radical Joe' began to nurture an ambition to found a political dynasty is not clear but he certainly brought up his elder son to believe that there could be no finer way to spend his life than to devote it to politics. Joseph also provided him with the appropriate education and training: Rugby was followed by Trinity College, Cambridge, where he read history, and by two years on the Continent – not quite the aristocratic 'tour' but he spent approximately a year each living with families in France and Germany and had the opportunity to meet his father's political contacts (Clemenceau in France and Bismarck in Germany). At the age of twenty-nine he was found a seat and in March 1892 entered the House of Commons, where he remained until his death forty-five years later. He never followed any other trade or profession, but regarded politics as a full-time occupation with its own expertise: as he once wrote, 'Politics are an art, requiring a training and a study of their own.'

Men who enter Parliament because they see it as an honourable calling rather than an opportunity to crusade for a particular cause or underprivileged class are rarely initiators of policy, and Austen was no exception. Although he took part in many political campaigns, initially as his father's lieutenant and later on his own account, he tended to respond to the pressure of events or the leadership of more committed men, rather than initiate policy himself. His approach was generally pragmatic and chiefly concerned with immediate tactics and practicalities. In a letter to his brother in 1917, he wrote, 'Bob Cecil says what shall we conservatives [small 'c'] inscribe on our standard after the war? I don't know. I'm something of an opportunist, as, in the midst of such a struggle, every wise man must be, and I've never been good at the philosophy of politics.'[5] It would be wrong, however, to describe him as lacking direction, because he was committed to the 'good government' of Britain, and to a political stability which transcended party loyalty or personal ambition. He was guided by objectives so basic that they are better termed beliefs or principles. First, he was a patriot, pledged to defend the British Empire and protect its interests. Secondly, he was anxious to protect private capitalist enterprise and maintain the existing social structure against real, potential or imaginary threats from the working class. Thirdly, he venerated Parliament as an institution and was concerned to maintain the principles, correct procedures and dignity of the British constitution. This led him to mount a strong attack on the undue influence of the press in the spring of 1918; later in the same year he protested about the release to the press of a report on the Aliens Question by a group of MPs before it was seen by any member of the Cabinet, 'this procedure was highly improper . . . and made the task of the Cabinet much more difficult'.[6] In the December 1916 crisis, he was clear-headed about what he felt should be the correct arrangement, 'I wanted the War Committee to be the Cabinet and would not sit in a Cabinet with no power under a War Committee with all power.'[7] He saw it as his duty to accept responsibility for the Mesopotamian crisis in 1917 and resign as Secretary of State for India; and in 1919 he was outraged at Lloyd George's proposal that he should be Chancellor of the Exchequer without a seat in the Cabinet. His principled stance on these issues exposed him to disparagement, especially by the Northcliffe press, but a case can be made that his influence held in check Lloyd George's inherent tendency to move towards a presidential style of government. Later, in his tussles with Robert Cecil over the League of Nations, his main concern was that Britain should have only one foreign policy and that it must be determined by the Foreign Secretary.

It is ironic that the son of Joseph Chamberlain should become such a thorough-going conservative (always with a small 'c') and stickler for the formalities, especially as it was his father who was the main formative influence upon him. The force of Joseph's character and his domination over everyone around him at the time when Austen was just reaching adulthood has been well recorded, not least by Beatrice

Potter (later Webb), who visited Highbury in 1884, her perceptions heightened by passionate attraction and an awareness that she was being considered for the role of Joseph's third wife. As she confided to her diary, 'the submission of the whole town to his autocratic rule arises from his power of dealing with different types of men; of enforcing submission by high-handed arbitrariness, attracting devotion by the mesmeric quality of his passion, and manipulating the remainder through a wise presentation of their interests and consideration of their petty weaknesses.'[8] It was inevitable that Austen, 'a big fair-haired youth of handsome feature and open countenance and a sunny sympathetic temperament', should come under his father's spell, the more so as Beatrice conceded that Joseph 'had one great quality – warm devotedness to those who devote themselves body and soul to him'. Had Joseph stayed a radical, Austen would certainly have followed in the same direction, but by the time Austen came back from his continental visits, the breach with Gladstone had hardened. Joseph's marriage to Mary Endicott in November 1888 may have hastened his drift to the right. It was certainly expected to do so by Beatrice Potter, still despite herself obsessed by him: 'This marriage will decide his fate as a politician. He must become a Tory. The tendencies of his life are already set in that direction . . . She will see entirely through his eyes; by her sympathy with his injured feelings against his old party she will intensify the breach; by her attraction to the "good society" she will draw him closer to the aristocratic party.'[9] What Beatrice failed to foresee was that it would be Austen who would be most influenced by the social round and contacts of his father's new life. The conditioning begun at Rugby was continued in the drawing rooms of various Duchesses, and his identification with gentlemanly values was completed.

Temperament and inclination interacted with the influences of his upbringing. Austen was a born conciliator and much preferred matters to be settled by negotiation and compromise rather than by confrontation. He was at the opposite extreme from his father in this respect and when acting independently was usually able to be flexible on policy matters in the interests of good relations with colleagues. Nothing illustrates his approach better than an extract from Lord D'Abernon's diary for 23 November, 1924:

> A long interview with Austen Chamberlain, the new Secretary of State. I found him strongly in favour of the Commercial Treaty with Germany, although a narrower man with his strong protectionist tradition might have seen in it an objectionable tendency. He said: 'while I am a protectionist and you are a Free Trader, I

hope we are neither of us so fanatical as not to realise the great advantage which can be obtained from a judicious mixture'.[10]

Innate courtesy, together with studied correctness in procedural matters, open-mindedness about policy and a willingness to apply himself earnestly to mastering details, made him an excellent chairman, as even the youthfully arrogant Keynes admitted in relation to Austen's chairing of the Royal Commission on Indian Finance and Currency, 1913–14: 'I must say that Austen came out of the ordeal very well, and I believe he may yet be Prime Minister – I don't suppose on the purely intellectual score he is any stupider than Campbell-Bannerman.'[11]

If he had not both misjudged and mishandled the situation in 1922, Austen would indeed have been Prime Minister. Despite this failure he had a very long record at the top, if not the very top, of British politics. For over thirty years he was a Front Bench spokesman (much longer than either his charismatic father or his half-brother, Neville); he was in the Cabinet for a total of fifteen years, and he held many offices and positions, including some of the highest – he was twice Chancellor of the Exchequer (1903–5 and 1919–21), Leader of the Conservative Party (1921–22) and Foreign Secretary (1924–29). Even those who did not rate him very highly found that they could not dispense with his services: Lloyd George recalled him to the War Cabinet after his resignation over Mesopotamia and could find no better candidate for Chancellor of the Exchequer in 1919; and Baldwin felt it worth offering him the Foreign Secretaryship in order to bring him back into the fold in 1924. In 1931 it was his own choice to step down unless invited to return to the Foreign Office and, as late as 1935, he was offered a non-departmental post as 'Minister of State' to give advice on foreign affairs and defence. This offended both his vanity (he still hankered after the Foreign Office) and his concept of what was constitutionally correct, and he rejected it:

> Neither in foreign affairs nor defence should I have had any defined position or authority . . . I could perceive no prospect of public usefulness in the acceptance of an offer so conveyed, and I came to the conclusion that what he wanted was not my advice or experience, but the use of my name to help patch up the damaged prestige of his Government.[12]

Thus Austen Chamberlain was a man of considerable standing over a long period and cannot be said to have been unduly hampered by his rigid adherence to a strict code of honour, despite F. E. Smith's glib and much-quoted gibe that he 'always played the game and he always lost it'. Although sometimes seen by younger men as excessively stuffy, even pompous, his uprightness won him more respect than Lord Birkenhead's laxer ways, and he was able to have at least a limited influence over nearly all the important political events of his forty-five years in Parliament. This is not to deny that Austen's judgement of men, an essential attribute of a successful politician, was not sometimes impaired by his expectation that others would follow the same rules of conduct as himself. Thus he failed to anticipate in 1911 that Bonar Law would go for the leadership rather than back Austen as the senior tariff reformer; and, although Austen stepped down in his favour, he never afterwards had a high regard for him. Similarly, in 1922, he counted on his followers to abide by their obligation to be loyal to the policy determined by the Leader of the Party and to subordinate their judgement to his, as he had so often done to Balfour. He was misguided, also, at this time by expecting that others would share his view that it would not be decent just to ditch Lloyd George. In general, he did not understand that he had used up all his credit by successfully imposing the Irish Treaty on the Party against the opposition of the Diehards, and so needed to tread warily. Nor did he correctly gauge the extent that his attempt to realign party politics to create a permanent anti-Labour national party with the Coalition Liberals, but maybe excluding the Diehards, would trigger off a defensive explosion among Conservatives.

Austen could have been luckier in the period when he was Leader of the Conservative Party: he took office at a time of maximum tension and division over Ireland, and of general uncertainty caused by the breakdown of the old, two-party system. Indeed, during most of his career, the times in which he lived were not auspicious for a man of his temperament and outlook, and he was unfortunate in several respects. First, he preferred harmony over confrontation but became prominent at a period of sharp divisions over policy both between parties and within the Unionist grouping to which he belonged. (The Conservative Party and Liberal Unionist Party were not formally united until 1913.) He was unfortunate also in that for over ten years, from 1903 to 1914, he felt obliged to play two hands: his father's as well as his own. This was both a psychological strain and a handicap to the development of his independent stature. In addition, he was forced to spend what could be regarded as the years of his political prime (his mid- to late-forties and early fifties) in opposition, whereas his talents thrived best when he had the opportunity to be constructive. He enjoyed holding office for, as he disarmingly admitted, 'there was no pleasure in the world like sitting in some big office of administration or in Cabinet, and feeling that you were helping to mould and direct the policy of your country and make her history'.[13]

But he was out of office from January 1906 until May 1915, and was in Parliament for thirty-three years before he had the opportunity to hold the office he found most fulfilling, that of Foreign Secretary. Finally, Neville's entry to Parliament complicated his political role by again introducing family considerations; his ambitions for his brother tied his hands both in 1923–24 and in his last period as an anti-appeasement elder statesman.

Many politicians have to respond to unfavourable circumstances, and many shared Austen's assumptions about morality guiding political as well as personal behaviour, but he was unique in having to operate alongside first his father and then his brother. This affected his actions on many occasions and has influenced the assessments historians have made of his role ever since. He has suffered from being the middle Chamberlain and has tended to be presented as a rather shadowy figure, filling in the space between his controversial father and his more forceful brother. Very often he has been judged by how far he helped them achieve their objectives, rather than by how far he achieved his own goals. This may have been inevitable to some extent because both Joseph and Neville set out to force through change and took hard lines on policy, whereas Austen's perceptions and instincts centred on the maintenance of stability. It is difficult to measure contributions to stability, and this may have led to his being underrated. This is very well illustrated by developments during his first period as Chancellor of the Exchequer.

The circumstances of Austen's appointment were unusual and his promotion has usually been seen in the context of Balfour's need to tame Joseph and prevent him splitting the Party before Balfour had had the time to carry through his foreign and defence policies.[14] Balfour shrewdly realised that Austen, although young and relatively inexperienced for such a senior post, was competent, cautious and hard-working, and would be able to handle it. Sir Michael Hicks-Beach, a former Chancellor under whom Austen had served as Financial Secretary, told his son that he regarded Austen's appointment as Balfour's only good one.[15] By the standards of the time, he proved to be a good Chancellor and produced two budgets which were praised as examples of sound, orthodox finance. Yet, no matter how he rose to the occasion as Chancellor, he has been mainly judged on his relative failure to carry forward his father's crusade for tariff reform. Indeed, at first this was how he saw his own role. He wrote to Joseph on his first evening in residence at 11 Downing Street:

> I do not think there are many fathers who have been and are to their sons all that you have been to me; and my prayer tonight is that the perfect confidence which I have enjoyed so long may continue

unimpaired by our separation; and *that I may do something to help you in the great work which you have undertaken.*[16] (my italics)

A Chancellor of the Exchequer cannot, however, just be someone else's 'Ambassador', Julian Amery's description of his situation.[17] The strain of still trying to serve as Joseph's lieutenant while holding a major office under Balfour was soon causing him anguish, and eventually he was forced to take a decision to go against what he knew were his father's wishes. This was in March 1905, when he decided not to resign when Balfour decided to allow the Conservatives a free vote on a Liberal resolution against a general tariff. His sister understood how difficult it was for him to be independent: 'You have suffered much I know, and in nothing so much, I think, as in feeling that it has prevented you walking absolutely side-by-side with Papa, that by the necessity of the case you were forced to see things at times differently, from inside, from his outside view.'[18] It was a relief to Austen when Balfour finally resigned and freed him from trying to be loyal to two masters. Whether he was right to rely on Balfour's judgement in March 1905, and not on his father's, must be a matter of opinion over whether tariff reform or party unity should have been given priority. Despite his torn feelings, Austen seemed to have a greater self-confidence after being forced to take an independent stand. Certainly, at the time of the Valentine letters (February 1906), he was quite decisive in working to reunite his father and Balfour. But then came Joseph's disabling stroke, which left Austen again acting as his father's substitute both in his own eyes and those of others – a situation which lasted for eight long years until Joseph's death in July 1914.

After Joseph's stroke, the options narrowed, as without him there could be no question of a bid to challenge Balfour. An essential step for the tariff reformers became his conversion, and Austen, compelled by his love for his stricken father, did his best to push him into taking a firm stand. But Balfour had no intention of doing so. This led to several years of frustration for Austen because, no matter how often Balfour disappointed him, he could see no alternative course. His convictions about the benefits of tariff reform may have been less deep than his father's but he believed that the policy could be made electorally popular if argued consistently and whole-heartedly and put at the forefront of Unionist policy. He based this belief on his experience at the reactions of the audiences at the very many public meetings he addressed. In early 1909, for example, he spoke to twelve meetings in six weeks in different parts of the country and came back from Wolverhampton, where he addressed a meeting of 2,000–3,000 and an overflow 'holding twice the number — they were packed like herrings in a barrel', to find five more invitations to speak. In the days before public opionion polls politicians depended on mass meetings for knowledge of public opinion and Austen felt that he could speak with authority. This made Balfour's prevarications harder to bear, especially after the Unionists' failure to dislodge the Liberal Government at either of the 1910 elections.

Austen could not compromise over priority for tariff reform because of his loyalty to his father, although, during the 1910 inter-party Constitutional Conference, he would have liked to see progress towards a rapprochement between the two main parties. Even over Ireland, where he favoured a federal solution, he felt anxious to make an effort to make the Conference succeed. He was prepared to accept the use of a referendum although he did not approve of the device: 'I thought it injurious to the authority of Parliament, very difficult to work so as to obtain a judgement on the real issue and capable of great abuse in times of strong passion and excitement.'[19] He was 'broken-hearted', however, when, after the conference had failed, Balfour offered to submit tariff reform to a referendum. His bitterness may have influenced him to become a 'Diehard' over the 1911 Constitutional Crisis, one of the rare occasions when he took a hard instead of a moderate line. He was influenced by his concern that the country should not be left 'at the mercy' of a House of Commons majority in a single Parliament.

It is interesting to return to Mr Taylor's thesis about the importance of accidental happenings when considering Austen's career during these years. If his father had died in July 1906 instead of being left paralysed, he would have been free to pursue tariff reform at a more leisurely pace, or let it lie until economic pressure brought it back on the agenda or until it was less controversial. The urgency and the pressure came from the need to produce results for the crippled giant in his wheelchair before it was too late. Austen Chamberlain was an extremely sentimental and loving man towards all his immediate family but his filial devotion towards Joseph verged on the obsessive: he would never allow any criticism of him and was always quick to defend him. It may be that his touchiness on his behalf, together with any suggestion that he himself was behaving in a way that could be seen as disloyal or divisive, reflected suppressed awareness that Joseph's role in both 1886 and 1903 was destructive. This is as maybe, what is certain is his feeling of obligation towards his father and his belief that this could best be served by winning the campaign for tariff reform. This was the background to his decision to stand down in favour of Bonar Law in 1911: he was not sure he could win if it came to a contest with Walter Long, especially with Balfour standing aloof and Law in the ring, so he withdrew, although he very much wanted to be Leader at that time. Ironically, his hope that Bonar Law would carry the Party to accept tariff reform proved unfounded and, in any case, it would have given his father greater pleasure than anything else for him to have been chosen as Leader. It is unsound to speculate what would have been the effect on British political life if he had so become, but the tone of the Conservative Party would have certainly been less abrasive than under Law, and he would have taken a more balanced view of the Ulster question. He was deeply shocked both by Asquith's mishandling of the Irish Home Rule Bill and by the Curragh mutiny – 'The fabric of society is loosened. It will take long to repair the rents' – and he would certainly have tried to avoid such outright confrontation had he been at the helm of his party.[20]

In assessing Austen Chamberlain's role inside the Conservative Party it would be misleading to label him 'a wet' in the current use of the term, because his interest in social reform was too insubstantial and his periods at the Treasury left him too cautious about public expenditure, so he had a very limited conception of what was possible. Yet he envied Lloyd George the chance to introduce health insurance, which he felt was on the right lines, and had traditional Tory paternalist attitudes about the poor. His chief 'wet' characteristic, however, was his moderation and preference for conciliation.

It was in international relations that he had most scope for his talents as a negotiator and the Locarno agreement was a considerable achievement, despite its many limitations. It brought Germany back into the fold of international relations and so prepared the way for her admission to the League of Nations. It thus reinforced the League in practice, even if regional treaties could be seen as undermining the principles of the League. Of course it was more 'a symbol' (Mr Taylor's description) than a concrete guarantee and its provisions over the eastern frontiers of Germany were minimal, almost an invitation to press for revision. Yet it provided a framework for proceeding through agreement rather than force and it was not easy to foresee in 1925 that the period of reconciliation the Treaty fostered would be so short-lived.

It may have been idealistic in the inter-war period to hope that peace could be maintained but Austen was under no illusions about the standards of political behaviour which were necessary for international stability. Thus he was one of the earliest anti-appeasers following the accession to power of Hitler. As early as April 1933 he warned the House of Commons against negotiating with his régime:

> What is this new spirit of German nationalism? The worst of the old-Prussian Imperialism, with an added savagery, a racial pride, an exclusiveness which cannot allow to any subject not of 'pure

> Nordic birth' equality of rights and citizenship within the nation to which he belongs. Are you going to discuss revision with a Government like that? Are you going to discuss with such a Government the Polish Corridor? The Polish Corridor is inhabited by Poles; do you dare to put another Pole under the heel of such a Government?
>
> After all, we stand for something in this country. Our traditions count for our own people, for Europe, and for the world. Europe is menaced and Germany is afflicted by this narrow, exclusive, aggressive spirit, by which it is a crime to be in favour of peace and a crime to be a Jew. That is not a Germany to which we can afford to make concessions. That is not a Germany to which Europe can afford to give equality.
>
> I understood that the promise made by the Five Powers was of equality of status, to be reached by stages. Before you can afford to disarm or to urge others to disarm, you must see a Germany whose mind is turned to peace, who will use her equality of status to secure her own safety but not to menace the safety of others; a Germany which has learnt not only how to live herself but how to let others live inside her and beside her.[21]

He was utterly clear, also, even prescient, over Hitler's march into the Rhineland: 'I declare to you my profound conviction that if the League cannot secure redress now . . . it will not be long before Germany violates her new engagements with a much stronger army, and the world is involved in a disastrous war.'[22] Yet Austen was unable to impart his understanding of the military threat implicit in Nazism to Neville. He felt that he had a far better understanding of foreign affairs than his brother but would do nothing to undermine Neville's chance of succeeding to the leadership. This impeded him from playing a more forthright role among the Conservative opponents of appeasement.[23] By this time, also, his style of moderate, reasoned, restrained contribution to Parliamentary life was probably too deeply ingrained for him to organise a rebellion and he had always fought shy of anything smacking of disloyalty or divisiveness. Thus, at the last stage of his life, Austen's codes of honour and correct political behaviour enabled him to see the dangers threatening his country and the peace of the world, but disabled him from taking more than formal action to prevent them. 'Et l'honneur . . . ?'

Notes

1 Austen Chamberlain, *Down the Years* (1935), p. 99.

2 Keith Robbins in *Sir Edward Grey* (1971), p. 297 argues that calculation of British interests was as important as the moral commitment and disputes Professor Joll's assessment that Grey was guided by the ethical code of a 'high principled, slightly priggish Wykehamist'.

3 Frank Pakenham, Lord Longford, *Peace by Ordeal* (1935), p. 106.

4 Letter to Dr L. P. Jacks, 9 January, 1936: AC Papers Birmingham University 41/3/4.

5 Dated 24 September, 1917, Neville Chamberlain Papers 1/27/12.

6 CAB 23/7 War Cab. 443, 10 July, 1918.

7 Letter to Neville Chamberlain, 11 December, 1916, AC Papers 15/3/7.

8 *The Diary of Beatrice Webb*, ed. N. and J. MacKenzie (1982), Vol. I, 1873–92, pp. 104ff.

9 Ibid., p. 265.

10 Lord D'Abernon, *Ambassador of Peace* (1930), Vol. III, p. 115.

11 *Collected works of John Maynard Keynes* (1971), Vol. XV, p. 222.

12 C. Petrie, *Life & Letters of Austen Chamberlain* (1940), Vol. II, p. 406.

13 Austen Chamberlain, *Politics from the Inside* (1935), p. 70.

14 A. Gollin, *Balfour's Burden* (1965), very clearly explains his strategy.

15 Lady Victoria Hicks-Beach, *Life of Sir Michael Hicks-Beach*, vol. II, p. 195.

16 C. Petrie, op. cit., vol. I, p. 126.

17 J. Amery, *Joseph Chamberlain and the Tariff Reform Campaign: Life of Joseph Chamberlain* (1969), Vol. VI, p. 765.

18 Hilda Chamberlain to Austen, 5 December, 1905. Quoted in Petrie, op. cit., Vol. I, p. 166.

19 Austen Chamberlain, *Politics from the Inside*, p. 194.

20 Ibid., pp. 619–32.

21 Quoted in Petrie, op. cit., Vol. II, p. 392.

22 Letter to Gilbert Murray, 16 March, 1936, Austen Chamberlain Papers, Box 41/3/24, Birmingham University Library.

23 This is discussed by N. Thompson, *The Anti-Appeasers* (1971), pp. 25–26.

'In The Excess Of Their Patriotism': The National Party and Threats of Subversion

Chris Wrigley

Alan Taylor has described *The Trouble Makers* as his 'favourite brainchild'. In this, the book of his Ford Lectures of 1956, he studied those who challenged the basis of British foreign policy from the late eighteenth century to the Second World War. 'A man can disagree with a particular line of British foreign policy,' he commented, 'while still accepting its general assumptions. The Dissenter repudiates its aims, its methods, its principles. What is more, he claims to know better and to promote higher causes; he asserts a superiority, moral or intellectual.'[1]

This essay looks at the attitudes of a group which vehemently opposed the 'Trouble Makers' of the First World War, the ultra 'patriots' who formed the National Party in August 1917. The members of the Union of Democratic Control were so many red rags to these John Bulls. In November 1917 when right wingers, both those still in the Unionist Party and those who had broken away in the National Party, attempted to arrange the recall of unrepresentative (i.e. 'unpatriotic') MPs, William Joynson-Hicks declared, when seconding the motion:

> . . . the whole question here is whether those hon. Members whom we desire to send back to their constituents are not here (*sic*), not as delegates of their constituents, but as delegates of outside powers foreign to their constituents, foreign to their country, of some body such as the Union of Democratic Control and bodies of that kind.[2]

The views of the members of the National Party and those who shared their views on the right wing of the Unionist Party were the antithesis of those of the 'Trouble Makers'. Sir Henry Page Croft, the leading light of the National Party, could not have made this clearer than when, in July 1917, he addressed the suggestion that peace discussions with Germany would involve consideration not only of German war crimes but also of British ones. He declared,

> This country can say with truth today, as it said at the beginning of the war, that we have no crimes, that we have a clean sheet from the very day that we entered this war, actuated by the very highest motives that ever actuated any nation, and we have a clean sheet right up to the present moment. Our conduct has been clean and utterly against the atrocities of the German nation . . .
>
> How is the Christian faith going to stand if the war ends as these hon. Gentlemen would have it end? If a man goes berserk and murders women and children and breaks every law of civilisation, is there any single thing which we can find in Christianity or any word in the Bible which tells us that mankind should stand on one side and allow the thing to go on? What would be the inevitable result? Surely it must be that if this crime is not punished it will happen again?[3]

Whilst the seven MPs and seventeen members of the House of Lords of the National Party did not represent in themselves a strong force in the politics of the latter part of the First World War, they were significant as a ginger group when taken in conjunction with the more belligerent Unionist backbenchers. They and their like are shadowy yet powerful groups which never quite come on stage in Alan Taylor's important study, 'Politics in the First World War'.[4] Unlike many groups on the right which were purely anti this and that affront to their values, the National Party did offer positive policies, especially in the area of industry and industrial relations. In this they represented a continuity with the pre-war tariff reformers and those propagating imperialism and social reform.[5]

The National Party was a response in 1917 to what some on the Right saw as a need to revitalise the war effort and stop the crumbling of the social order. In responding, the National Party and others on the Right came forward with policies which they felt would appeal to 'patriotic labour' and the electorate at large.

The formation of the Lloyd George Coalition Government in December 1916 reassured many of the Right for a few months that the war was going to be pursued with greater vigour. Milner, before leaving on his mission to Russia in January 1917, reassured his friend F. S. Oliver,

> There is great drive here, but also great chaos. I hope that it will not be too great for me to introduce some element of order when I get back . . . There has been energy *and purpose* in the work of the last five weeks; *with* some luck you ought to see a difference in results some two or three months hence. If results are much better, much will be forgiven for a time. The almost comic crudeness of the method won't so much matter.[6]

Many right wingers were reassured for a time by the presence of Milner and Carson in the government (even if Milner did grumble frequently about Lloyd George's organisational methods).[7] Both were held in high esteem by the Unionist Right. As Lloyd George later wrote, 'Lord Milner made a special appeal to the young intelligentsia. The Diehard element also trusted him in the essentials of the faith.'[8] Milner appears to have been close to many of the developments on the Right in these years, including, perhaps, via F. S. Oliver, the formulation of the National Party's programme.

However, the Right did not stay reassured long. The putting of the British Army under French orders, as agreed by Lloyd George at the Calais Conference of 26 and 27 February, 1917, brought some close to apoplexy. Those who broke away to form the National Party were strong supporters of Britain's military leadership.

What appears to have triggered off the revolt of some of the Right to form a break-away party was concern over labour, both in terms of manpower for the army and unrest in industry. On the issue of adequate numbers of troops for the Western Front, Henry Page Croft later recalled, when writing of the formation of the National Party,

> The whole question of providing men for the forces was always dealt with from a political rather than a national point of view. Again and again one heard at Westminster the word passed round 'the workers will never stand it', 'conscription is foreign to our national character', 'if you drive the people too hard there will be a revolution' etc. etc.[9]

The need for firm action on manpower, including applying conscription to Ireland, was very much a key issue with National Party members.

What is not so readily recognised is that the issue of labour unrest at home was equally important in triggering off this revolt within the Unionist ranks. The founders of the National Party were scandalised by the failure of the government to deal firmly with it and with the increasingly related anti-war movement; these issues being vividly illustrated by the widespread engineering strikes in May 1917 and the Leeds Convention of June 1917, a convention calling for 'a people's peace' and the establishment of soviets in Britain. Page Croft later grumbled that then the workers 'had only to threaten to strike and immediately wages were raised'.[10] At the time, when sounding out support for a break-away group, Viscount Duncannon wrote to F. S. Oliver,

> From one cause and another labour unrest in the country continues to develop. It may be that a very grave state of affairs is threatening. If the Government realise this, they do not at any rate appear to cope with it.
>
> A few of us, accustomed to work together at the Tariff Reform League feel that we ought to help in trying to combat this unrest. We are anxious to start a movement with that object.

Oliver was invited to meet Lord Leconfield, Page Croft and Duncannon at the offices of the Tariff Reform League.[11]

The family connections between some of the founding figures of the National Party bring to mind those between the ruling élite in Sir Lewis Namier's studies of politics in the 1760s. Lord Leconfield was a member of a family well connected with many leading Unionist figures. His cousin George Wyndham (who died in 1913) had been Chief Secretary for Ireland 1900 to 1905 and a friend of Milner. Leconfield's heir, Hugh Wyndham, had been a member of Milner's kindergarten in South Africa. Leconfield's father-in-law, Colonel R. H. Rawson, was MP for Reigate and was one of the seven Unionist MPs to join the National Party. Rawson had married the second daughter of the second Earl of Lichfield and, like Major Rowland Hunt, was a noted foxhunter. Hunt had served in South Africa with Lovat's Scouts and then become MP for Ludlow from 1903. Another military man in the National Party who had an interesting past was Major Alan Burgoyne, MP for North Kensington and owner of considerable property in Australia. He had been imprisoned by the Russians in 1903 on a charge of spying in Port Arthur and had gone on to write on naval matters and to be editor of *The Navy League Annual*. Major the Hon. Douglas Carnegie, MP for Winchester, like his father the ninth Earl of Northesk, was a member. Another case of a father being a peer and the son an MP was that of the eighth Earl of Bessborough and his son Viscount Duncannon, who had succeeded George Wyndham as MP for Dover.[12] Duncannon had served under Sir Henry Wilson, Chief of the Imperial General Staff, and provided the link between Wilson and the National Party. Indeed Wilson's official biographer wrote later,

Duncannon and others were busy organising a party in the House of Commons to bring pressure on the War Cabinet and to oblige that body to adopt Wilson's ideas concerning the plenary tapping of existing resources of the United Kingdom in manpower, and concerning the vital importance of, by some means or other, eliminating Turkey and Bulgaria from the struggle.[13]

The leading figure in the National Party was Brigadier-General Henry Page Croft, who had an outstanding record on active service in France. He was an energetic campaigner who had been involved in many right wing pressure groups. Before the First World War he had been at the centre of The Confederacy, a group aiming to ensure that all Unionist candidates were pledged to support tariff reform, and later of the Reveille movement, which preached imperial and social reform measures within and without the Unionist Party, as well as being chairman both of the Organisation Committee of the Tariff Reform League and of the Imperial Mission.[14]

Before the National Party had been thought of, Page Croft had been keen to involve F. S. Oliver more in his pressure groups. He had asked him to draw up 'a short brief' on tariffs to help ensure 'that the defenders of nationalism shall have the very best case' at the January 1917 TUC conference. He had also succeeded in getting Oliver co-opted on to the executive of the Tariff Reform League in February 1917.[15] When it came to the forming of the National Party, Page Croft and his circle had ample military and aristocratic connections but less ability to communicate with the electorate.

To put it bluntly, F. S. Oliver had the brains and the skill with words which most of the founders of the National Party lacked. John Buchan later wrote of him, 'For a decade he was the ablest pamphleteer in Britain,' and added, 'Oliver did not write because he liked writing, but because he had causes to plead. A preacher at heart, he testified at all times to the truth that was in him.'[16] His book, *Ordeal By Battle*, published in June 1915, was written 'to establish the *Need* for National Service, in order that the British Empire may maintain itself securely in the present circumstances of the world'. In his book he saw hope for Britain in 'the spirit of the people', to which he felt the politicians had failed to appeal. Like his mentor, Lord Milner, he had a contempt for party politics and *Ordeal By Battle* was scathing on politicians generally. Oliver listed the causes of British weakness as 'our indolence and factiousness; our foolish confidence in cleverness, manoeuvres and debate for overcoming obstacles which lie altogether outside that region of endeavour; our absorption as thrilled spectators in the technical game of British politics . . .'[17] Oliver was the ideal man to write a manifesto for the National Party.

Much of the National Party's programme can be found among the arguments of the pre-war right wing factions. The notion among those of the Right of themselves as the guardians of the national interest, against the divisive party politics of radicals and socialists (who stressed class differences, preached Home Rule and generally undermined the unity of the Empire), was well established and well aired before the First World War. Also some of the ideas concerning industry had been aired by tariff reformers in the decade before 1914.[18]

Several of the Unionist pressure groups of the earlier part of the First World War were also precursors of the National Party. The first of these was the Unionist Business Committee, a group revived by Basil Peto and Ernest Pollock in January 1915, which campaigned not only for increased munitions production but also for a range of other matters deemed to lead to 'the more effective prosecution of the war', including tariffs, rationalisation of industrial resources and tougher action against aliens. There was also the Unionist War Committee, formed in January 1916, which successfully campaigned for conscription and less successfully, later in 1916, for the Nigerian palm kernel and palm oil firms confiscated from Germans to 'be sold only to natural born British subjects or companies wholly British'. The *Morning Post*, in January 1916, expressed the hope that the Unionist War Committee and its Liberal counterpart would form the basis of a new patriotic National Party.[19]

Lord Milner had been busy in orchestrating such pressure groups among the 'titled, landed and official classes' (to use the wording of *Kelly's Directory*). During much of the First World War Milner appears to have acted out that favourite of right wing fantasies – immortalised in the writings of such authors as Arthur Conan Doyle and John Buchan – of the *éminence grise* working to save the nation through his public school, Oxbridge, army and Whitehall contacts. In the early part of the war Milner was much involved in organising the Royal Colonial Institute, the National Service League and the Socialist National Defence Committee to campaign for conscription and to build up support for imperialism and moderate social reform. He was also very much involved in helping to raise financial and political support for the British Workers' League, an organisation of 'patriotic labour'.[20] A Scotland Yard report on it stated,

> This league is open only to British subjects, and the main principle is to pay all attention to British needs and ideals, and to have a Parliament representative of a sane, common sense, practical business element. It is said to be based upon a desire to supply British needs from British lands, by British resources and labour.

> The promoters say that, first and foremost, it is founded on the fact that Parliament with its old political shibboleths of Toryism, Radicalism, and Socialism, which are losing their significance, has as an institution sunk into disrepute.[21]

Milner, like others on the Right, often expressed the hope that a 'National Party' would emerge. Thus, in April 1917, when writing on the efforts of the various reconstruction committees, he observed,

> But all proposals of this kind, which involve dealing with constitutional problems in a more or less rational and scientific way, instead of the hand to mouth method, which all *parties* prefer, brings me back to the fundamental question, how people, who think and look ahead, and are not pure empirics, are to put themselves into a position to exercise effective influences on the course of affairs. They will never get it under our present party system, which is more or less in abeyance, but will revive again, I fear, when the war is over, unless we can get a lot of new men, unpledged to the old parties, *in to the next House of Commons*. We want a group of independent 'Nationalists'. Where are they? Will they stand? Is there any rudimentary organisation for getting them in? They need not be very numerous, but they ought to exist as a coherent nucleus in the Commons.[22]

Milner's description, in this instance, is applicable to what the National Party turned out to be; a small ginger group in the House of Commons. While the National Party was to be something of a vanguard of the Right, what Milner really hoped for was a Party which would appeal to a wider social spectrum.

When the National Party was actually launched, Milner and his followers were sympathetic and discreetly supportive, but did not join it. By August 1917 the Unionist backbenchers might grumble at the government's handling of aspects of the war, but few were in doubt as to its commitment to win the war. Whilst applauding the views in the National Party's manifesto, Dougal Malcolm, another of Milner's associates, wrote to F. S. Oliver,

> . . . I cordially agree with you that this is not the moment for the formation of a new party. If it were, the new party, to do anything effective, would require funds, an organisation, a caucus, the running of candidates – an effort to cast out devils by Beelzebub, the Prince of Devils. And really I don't think that there is matter here for a new party. A new party, I take it, must profess objects which are not the objects of existing parties, and all sane people

must want Reform, Union and Defence in the sense in which the words are used in the draft manifesto. The upshot of which is that the energetic spirits who have been thinking about a new party would do better by trying to reform existing parties from within than by attacking them from without . . .[23]

Edward Wood (the future third Viscount Halifax), who had been interested in the idea of a National Party, saw another major problem; that is, if the initiators of such a party were not to appear 'interested wreckers', 'everything . . . would depend upon the moment and method of announcement'.[24]

Later Page Croft regretted that he had been unable 'to hold back' when he found that his twenty-one sympathetic MPs of early August had dwindled to eight when it came to the actual launch on 30 August. At the time Page Croft and his colleagues, nevertheless, may have been optimistic. They acted then because of the current instability in politics, which centred around Arthur Henderson's resignation from the government and included rumours that Lloyd George was 'working away at forming a National Party'.[25] Also Page Croft may have been unduly hopeful of success because of the support he expected to get from the Press. The National Party did get very vigorous support from H. A. Gwynne and Ian Colvin of the *Morning Post*, which provided daily 'puffs' for the National Party for some weeks after its launch. Other editors who were sympathetic included Leo Maxse of the *National Review*, and Geoffrey Robinson of *The Times* (the latter better known by the name he took in 1917 of Geoffrey Dawson). Robinson was another close associate and a great admirer of Milner. As the National Party derived a large proportion of its ideas from Milner, there was much truth in Lord Northcliffe's response to Page Croft's appeal for support in the 1918 election: 'We do, generally speaking, support your policy – or rather the policy which my staff say you take from my newspapers!!'[26] Page Croft and Duncannon were also over-confident that they could take pressure groups such as the Tariff Reform League and the British Empire Union into the National Party. In the case of the former, when Page Croft and Duncannon tried to bring about its amalgamation with the National Party, they came unstuck; after some acrimony at the Tariff Reform League meeting on 15 September, 1917, Duncannon resigned as President and a motion recommending amalgamation with the National Party was referred back to the executive for further consideration.[27]

The actual launch of the National Party was planned carefully. In the week following the launch, 40,000 copies of the manifesto plus reply slips were posted out 'to all and sundry'. Offices were opened in London, Leeds, Manchester, Birmingham and Bristol to deal with replies and any enquiries. Activists in the British Empire Union and the Tariff Reform League were mobilised. According to Duncannon the immediate result was very good. He wrote, on 31 August, 1917, 'We were flooded out with letters today. All sorts – admirals, sailors, soldiers, working men etc. etc. Local Unionist leaders and *some* local official Liberals.' Page Croft later gave a similar account of the membership: 'A large majority of our recruits were service people, including distinguished admirals and generals.'[28] This membership was in line with the seven (and, for a while, eight) MPs who broke away from the Unionist Party. Other than Page Croft, a member of a brewing family, the only one of these with an obvious industrial background was Sir Richard Cooper, MP for Walsall, a second baronet and a member of a family chemical manufacturing firm. He, with Page Croft, was to be one of the two most active National Party members in the House of Commons.[29] Ambitious young Unionist MPs, however much they agreed with the manifesto, did not secede. This was put very frankly by William Ormsby-Gore (later to be Secretary of State for the Colonies, British High Commissioner in South Africa, and the fourth Lord Harlech):

> I know I am in agreement with your programme, but I should like time to consider before I sever my connection with the Conservative Party. I particularly do not wish to do anything without consulting my chief Lord Milner . . . Wherever Milner leads I shall follow and whatever party he is in, I shall be in.[30]

At the heart of the National Party's thinking was the belief that 'the people' were 'basically sound'; that all would be well if it were not for persons who were, at best, incompetent or, worse, were greedy or, worst of all, were out to subvert the country. Declarations to the effect that 'the people are sound *but* . . .' abound in the writings and speeches of the Right both before the First World War and during it. In the war, party politicians were among those seen as incompetent, profiteers among the greedy, and aliens, pacifists and Bolsheviks among the subversives.

The National Party's manifesto expressed these points clearly.[31] It ascribed wartime discontent and anger to these causes:

> They are due to a deep rooted feeling – to a sort of despair – that something in our present social and political system is at work to prevent men from obeying their natural instinct of co-operation and comradeship. And also they are due partly to the fact that there are influences in operation, set on foot and paid for by the enemy,

to sow suspicion and stir up strife in England, Scotland, Ireland and Wales, no less than in Russia and France.

In the conduct of the war the National Party, like many on the Right, supported the Armed Forces and condemned the politicians. Its manifesto made much of the shortcomings of the politicians both in peace and war. Thus of pre-war politics it commented, 'It was played very much like golf, under pleasant social conditions, and in a leisurely fashion as if time and tide and the German enemy would wait patiently upon the convenience of British statesmen.' In the war Page Croft showed some caution in praising the military. Men such as they, who had been involved in actual fighting, were alert to the fact that the feeling of cameraderie among front line troops often did not extend to the 'staff' behind the lines. He was also aware of 'the fear of militarism' which he felt was 'already abroad in the country'. Hence he advised Oliver to remove from an early draft of the manifesto a quotation to the effect that 'the soldier shall rule us'.

> So many senior officers have proved putrid in this war that even our citizen soldier might hesitate to quite agree. I like the phrase so much in Ruskin's words that I dislike uttering the caution; but can we risk so bold a statement? There is to me a great distinction between 'the man who has fought' and 'the soldier'. The men who have fought and saved must rule us – most of the fighting MP's would however tell you privately that it is the nation in arms that they love and admire – it is so great because it has done such wonderful things in spite of our generals who are commonly known as 'the soldiers' and who were admirable for an army of 50,000 men but have not shone in the army of 2,000,000 in any way except the courage of a mad bull. All this is hateful to say and has nothing to do with the Regular Army which died to save us . . .[32]

The National Party leaders, who had taken a firm line against 'the German menace' before the First World War, were strident on German issues during and after it. The British Empire Union, so closely linked to the National Party leadership, used as letterheading the slogan, 'The British Empire for British Subjects. No German Influences. No German Labour. No German goods that compete with British'. The National Party's manifesto called for 'the eradication of German influence'. It also called for a continuation of the war-time alliances as 'the only condition of safety for the world against Prussian intrigues' but added, 'We have to guard, however, against the folly of a policy of revenge. Such a policy will afford us no real defence but the very reverse.' However, by early 1919 Page Croft, incensed by Lloyd

George's wish that Bolshevik delegates should attend the Peace Conference, was taking an implacable line. He wrote to the Press,

> The P.M. appealed to the country for a mandate to take to the Peace Conference and the country told him in unmistakeable terms that Germany must pay the net cost of the war; that the criminals should be punished; that all Germans should be restored to the land of their birth; and that he was expected to crush any idea of Bolshevism.[33]

The National Party argued not only for the removal of German influences in Britain but for the British Empire to pursue a policy of autarky. At the Party's first annual conferences in March 1919 Page Croft moved 'that the vital needs of the nation should be met by its own soil and factories, and that reciprocal economic advantages should be established for all parts of the British Empire'. In so doing he called for more government backing for agriculture which, he said, 'with the Navy was our first line of defence'.[34]

During the war National Party concern went beyond German industrial penetration to fears of subversion. The early part of the First World War saw widespread exaggerated fears of German spies, especially among those of German background. The National Party speakers on the subject were certainly not guilty of understatement. 'The German spy system, we know today,' Sir Richard Cooper informed the Commons in October 1917, 'is deep, thorough, scientific and more powerful in some cases than armies of millions of men.' He went on to warn that '. . . we have 25,000 enemy aliens in this country who are not at present interned, every one of them owing allegiance to their Kaiser'.[35] The National Party held big public meetings on the issue and presented to the House of Commons a petition with a million signatures which called for action against aliens.

However, Germans were only part of the 'aliens issue' to the National Party. 'Aliens' could be a euphemism for Jews. Numerous Jews in Britain had come from Germany. As William Rubinstein has commented, 'There can be little doubt that the National Party's anti-alien campaign was directed primarily against Jews.' This was another continuation of pre-war attitudes of the Right. Both Cooper and Page Croft had demanded restrictions on immigration before 1914. The National Party leaders frequently made anti-semitic comments in their writings and speeches. Newspapermen, such as Maxse and Colvin, who supported them were notable for anti-semitic writing.[36] The National Party succeeded in appealing to those who chose to see Jews as being behind the failings of the British government and subversion in the country. This attitude is well illustrated in a letter commenting on the formation of the National Party, which was written by a serving officer in France who was the son of a Conservative MP.

> In scanning the personalities of this group I can find no lawyer politician, no international Jew. Lloyd George is not a member, nor is Mr Masterman, nor Sir Frederick Smith. I cannot find the names of a Rothschild, a Samuel, a Sassoon, a Levi, an Isaacs, or a Mond.[37]

The National Party, with misplaced pride, stated that aliens were ineligible to join it. After the First World War Page Croft tried to inflict this attitude on the House of Commons. In 1920 he proposed 'that no one not born a British subject and son of a British father should be eligible for either House of Parliament or any government post whatever, and that for ten years no German should be allowed to live in this country'. Anti-semitism, along with obsessive anti-Bolshevism, continued to be a feature of many on the Right after the First World War.[38] Much later, Page Croft was Under Secretary of State for War in Churchill's Coalition and 'Caretaker' governments of 1940–45. It is not surprising to find Churchill cautioning him during the 1945 general election campaign:

> I see you used an expression in your speech the other day about Laski that he was 'a fine representative of the old British working class' or words to that effect. Pray be careful, whatever the temptation, not to be drawn into any campaign that might be represented as anti-semitism.[39]

Popular unrest during the First World War was seen by the Right as being stirred up, sometimes even created, by pacifists or Bolsheviks, if not by outright German agents. Page Croft condemned the activities of the pacifist MPs for playing on 'the feelings of those tired, patriotic people', the factory workers, 'in order to get them to turn in the direction of an inconclusive peace with its disastrous results in the future'. Later, when supporting calls for the government to take tough measures against peace propaganda, he asked in the Commons, 'Is it not a fact that precisely this same propaganda with leaflets took place in Russia and Italy with the same appalling results . . . ?'[40]

The October Revolution and the ensuing events in Russia provided the National Party and the Right generally with immense scope for creating conspiracy theories. Page Croft took the view that 'the Bolsheviks were the instruments of Germany'.[41] Their actions in Russia scandalised the Right in Britain. Basil Peto, for example, used an Adjournment Debate in the House of Commons in October 1918 to vent his anger over the treatment of one of his constituents. 'Holdcroft was arrested without warning,' he exclaimed to the Commons, 'on the pretext of being a "capitalist"!' Peto went on, summoning up his knowledge of Palmerston's England, to add:

> I remember vaguely reading there was a case . . . of a gentleman – I think Greek by origin – who was called Don Pacifico, for whom, in spite of his name and shadowy claim to British citizenship, the British government threatened to go to war for far less than what has been inflicted on British citizens in Russia.[42]

Earlier in the year Page Croft had written to each member of the War Cabinet urging the need for a 'constitutional tsar' to lead the Allied armies into Russia to deal with the Bolsheviks.[43] After the war, the National Party supported the Lloyd George Coalition Government's activities against Lenin's government and vigorously took up the cause of the White Armies ('The cause was a greater one than the Crusades ever knew').[44]

The Bolsheviks, inevitably, were seen by the Right as being behind industrial unrest in Britain. This fitted in well with the attitudes of the Right to the pre-war industrial unrest. The formula was the usual one: the working class were basically sound *but* they were being led astray (or even intimidated) by agitators, often agitators who had captured the leadership of the trade unions. After 1917 the hand of the Bolshevik could be discerned in almost any strike. In dealing with the Clyde and Belfast strikes of early 1919, the *Morning Post*'s editorial took a line which (albeit a little less crudely expressed) was to be a common one from that day to this in the press of the Right:

> It is not merely an industrial movement: it is an attempt at revolution. The leaders are not recognised trade union leaders; some of them are not even British working men. The bell-wether in the Glasgow upheaval is a Jewish tailor called Shinwell; in the Belfast strike Shinwell's counterpart is one Simon Greenspon, a Jew of Russian descent. These two are the Trotskys of Belfast and Glasgow; they have Trotsky's aims and are using Trotsky's methods, and there is little room for doubt that they have a common source of inspiration. Who, may we ask, is pulling the strings of both these movements? Where are the funds coming from which finance them?[45]

All in all the National Party was near the front of the field in pursuit of 'subversives' of one kind or another.

In the *Dictionary of National Biography*'s entry for Page Croft, the

National Party's programme is simply described as one of 'xenophobic imperialism'. The National Party's policies offered also a certain amount of 'social reform' to the British working class.[46]

Given the continuity of the National Party from the pre-war tariff reform pressure groups, this is not surprising. The social policies followed on, albeit more vaguely, from the constructive policies evolved by the more advanced wing of the tariff reformers in the period from 1907. In 1907 to 1908 those associated with Austen Chamberlain and Milner came forward with a programme which included a broader, but contributory, scheme of old age pensions than that enacted by the Liberal Government and a minimum wage in industries 'in which voluntary and effective organisation of workers has not been found practicable'. The latter proposal was also cautiously aired by Arthur Steel-Maitland, who linked the use of tariffs to keep out goods produced by 'foreign sweated labour' with the possibility of 'the introduction of a Wages Board with power to fix a minimum wage – such a wage to have reference to the minimum standard of decent subsistence'.[47]

In both this programme and that of the Reveille movement, which was launched in October 1910, much emphasis was put on national unity. When the earlier programme was published it proclaimed tariff reform 'as the only means of protecting employment, of increasing production, and of equitably providing additional revenue for national defence and social reform, it is essential to the union of classes'. Similarly, the Reveille movement's programme, also published with accompanying fanfares in the *Morning Post*, proclaimed,

> . . . Tariff Reform is only a means to an end, and that end is the promotion of national security and prosperity . . . the Reveille programme makes no distinction between foreign and home politics. A national policy regards them as inseparable.[48]

These themes resurfaced in the National Party's manifesto, which made much of class unity. It asserted, 'The great hope of recovery after the war lies in working together, in the union of classes, in their mutual forbearance and consideration, understanding, and sympathy. Ruin sits on the other scale.' It also argued that the right internal policies were a key element in defence against external threats: 'Our surest alliance for this purpose is an internal and not a foreign alliance – an alliance of labour and capital, of enterprise and trading ability, of invention and industry, of landlord and tenant.'

The National Party also offered action against immediate working class grievances in the war – 'oppression and "profiteering"'. In drafting this F. S. Oliver had been following Milner's response to the May 1917 engineering strikes. In a revealing letter, Milner wrote,

> My own remedy for labour unrest – which, with you, I consider very serious – is twofold. One is to remove the grievances on which agitators prey. These, as far as I can make out, at the present moment, are principally:
>
> a the bullying and unscrupulousness of certain employers of labour, who are taking advantage of the suspension of trade union restrictions during the war, and
> b the high price of living, coupled as it is, in some instances, with profiteering.
>
> Secondly, to go for the agitators. I do not believe they would be nearly so dangerous without the grievances, but I do not think the removal of the grievances alone will ever disarm them. They are out for mischief and, failing genuine grievances, which of course are most useful to them, they do the best they can with sham ones.[49]

These points were taken up almost verbatim by the National Party MPs. Thus, in July, Page Croft said in the Commons, 'The government would do well . . . to deal very strenuously with any man who may be proved to be a profiteer; it will do well greatly to increase the penalties upon manufacturers who may break their bargains in connection with industrial questions . . .'[50]

Yet the National Party generally was less specific on social reforms than the more advanced tariff reformers had been. Specific reforms scared specific interests. Though on occasion, when apparently pressed in public, Page Croft appears to have been very happy to proclaim as National Party policies some of the pre-war policies of the most advanced tariff reformers, notably the 'standard minimum wage'.[51] Some traditional or 'Radical Right' Unionists had been disconcerted before the First World War by the radical nature of the policies emerging from the more advanced tariff reformers. The National Party was a later mouthpiece for these groups as well as for the Milnerite and more radical tariff reformers. This ensured that its policies were a mass of contradictions (just as had been those of the groups on the Right before the war). In fact they were a mosaic of stock attitudes and prejudices of the Right, regardless of the consistency of the overall design.[52]

More advanced social policies were put forward during the war by a group of Unionist MPs around Arthur Steel-Maitland, who were also much influenced by Milner. These proposals were aired in a series of discussions which took place for over a year, initially between Steel-Maitland, James Hope and Sir Laming Worthington-Evans and two leading figures of the British Workers' National League. The radical nature of the Unionist concessions appears to have been inspired by a speech by Lord Milner at Leeds on 24 January, 1916. In it Milner spoke of the State 'as a third partner, as a controlling and harmonising influence in the relations between capital and labour'. He suggested that it had a right 'to share in exceptional profits', not just war ones, and to 'exercise a certain amount of control' over the investment of capital.[53] The Unionists talked seriously, among other things, of dividing surplus profits between employers, workers and the state, enforcing collective bargaining on all in a trade when two-thirds of employers and employees agreed on terms (including the provision of a minimum wage), providing maintenance grants for children staying at school beyond the legal minimum leaving age as well as various proposals for safeguarding essential industries, toughening up the law on aliens and making 'physical military drill under a cadet system ... compulsory on boys in every class of school'.

The motivation for these talks was declared to be a feeling by 'both the tendencies of thought represented that it would be a deplorable national calamity if peace should bring with it a relapse into the class bitterness, mutual suspicion, and stereotyped habits and traditions of mind which the shock of the conflict had so largely dispelled'.[54] These discussions received the blessing of the Unionist leadership. At the Special Unionist Conference on 30 November, 1917 Bonar Law declared,

> I feel it is our duty to try to get – I will not say on our side but to work with us – the section of Labour which is national and imperialistic ... We have got to get on our side if we can, the section of Labour which recognises that for all classes, employers and employed, production is the one thing to be aimed at ...

Amery wrote in his diary, 'Personally, after all the years I spent at the up-hill task of creating a Unionist Labour Party ... it was a great satisfaction to see the thing bearing fruit at last.'[55]

'Patriotic Labour,' as we have seen, was very much an enthusiasm of Milner's. During the war he devoted much energy to fostering it. He seems to have seen it as much a means of countering trade union militancy as a way of broadening the electoral base of the Unionist Party. In early 1916 he was writing of his hope that it would 'knock out "the Independent Labour Party"' and would make 'Imperial Unity and Citizen Service "planks" on its platform'. As with the

Unionist proposals and the National Party's programme, the policies of the British Workers' League (as it was known from March 1917) drew heavily on Milner's ideas. Its programme included 'a standard living wage' for all workers, municipal or state control of 'national monopolies and vital industries', the revival of agriculture, the development of the Empire's resources, fighting the war to victory and the expropriation of German economic and industrial interests throughout the Empire.[56]

The call of 'class unity' was, indeed, much heard in Britain during 1917 to 1920 when the existing social system was under very strong pressure. As during the pre-war industrial unrest, there was a body of business opinion eager to rally together centre opinion. This outlook received considerable public notice when Neville Chamberlain, as Lord Mayor of Birmingham, called for a new spirit of partnership between capital and labour when welcoming the Trade Union Congress to Birmingham in September 1916. The industrialist Dudley Docker, described by his biographer as 'industry's leading Milnerite', helped to launch Whitley Councils during his Presidency of the Federation of British Industries. The *Morning Post* also welcomed the Whitley scheme for a hierarchy of joint committees (employers and workers) to discuss wages, working conditions and other issues in various industrial sectors. Docker expressed hopes that the respect for each other developed by officers and men at the Western Front could be continued when they returned to industry. 'The men who have fought side by side,' he asserted, 'can live in peace together.'[57] Such sentiments were identical to those expressed by the National Party leadership.

Dudley Docker and other businessmen supported both 'Patriotic Labour' and the National Party. During 1918 and 1919 Docker and his associates pumped large sums of money into the National Democratic Party (as the British Workers' League was then known) and a wide range of anti-socialist endeavours. Much of this was done through the British Commonwealth Union, which had strong but unofficial links with the Federation of British Industries. The British Commonwealth Union's outlook was also similar to that of the National Party; indeed its executive director, Patrick Hannon, informed Page Croft, 'We are both determined to keep out of power in the future the Party trickster and the bolshevik . . .'[58] Docker had long aired views similar to the National Party and he provided it with the backing of his London evening newspaper the *Globe*. In the 1918 election it urged its readers who lived in constituencies where National Party candidates were standing to vote for them.[59]

The National Party, like the Unionist Party, saw 'Patriotic Labour' as a complementary group. The British Workers' League, not surprisingly, was eager not to be identified publicly as a wing of the Unionists. Just before the setting up of the National Party they were embarrassed (at a time when they were involved in discussions with Steel-Maitland) by the Tariff Reform League making public statements 'which would seem to identify their organisation' with it. Hence they decided that Page Croft should be asked to see that this was stopped; though by the time he was contacted the National Party had been set up, and this was deemed by the British Workers' League to have altered the position.[60] In practice, many on the Right came to see the National Party and the British Workers' League as two sides of the same coin. Indeed renegade trade unionists such as Havelock Wilson of the National Seaman's Union were common figures on both organisations' platforms. The *Morning Post*, very much a sponsor of both, observed in an editorial when the National Party was launched:

> What we should like to see would be an alliance between these gentlemen and what is best in the industrial forces of the country. There need not be union, but there might be cordial co-operation. The British Workers' League is also in its different way a possible nucleus of a national party, since it offers to our working men a policy at once democratic and patriotic ... Then there are the organised trades and industries of the country. Hitherto they have looked in vain for a vital understanding of their hopes and needs, their problems and the dangers which confront them. ... What, for example, is the Federation of British Industries doing? They and similar organisations might surely co-operate with a band pledged to Production as a national policy.[61]

After the First World War, with the Labour Movement continuing to threaten the *status quo*, the National Party became more strident against non 'patriotic labour' and its appeal became one of action in class warfare. The National Party became a precursor of the many private strike-breaking organisations set up before the General Strike in 1926 and later. Its real nature is well displayed in an advertisement it put out in February 1919:

> To Fight the Great Bolshevik Menace. Organise! Organise! The National Party calls upon all Law-abiding Citizens – upon the *Great Middle Classes – Discharged Service Men – Patriotic Labour* and all who will resist the present efforts to paralyse the community, to establish an organisation to render attacks against the liberties of the people impossible.
>
> Two things to be done at once!

1 Large funds are required to provide an immediate organisation
2 Volunteers are invited to sign on and hold themselves in readiness to carry on the vital services of the State.

No one joining this movement is necessarily in any way committed to the National Party.[62]

The National Party's significance is that it was one of the responses of sections of the British ruling élite when the fabric of society was under pressure during the latter half of the First World War and its aftermath. It was but one of a whole range of pressure groups which mushroomed up or were revitalised in these years which preached 'the unity of classes' whilst trying to mobilise against labour 'extremism'.[63]

In this it was, in part, an expression of the better-to-do classes' anxieties about the considerable decline in deference and discipline that they felt was taking place then. Such a decline was largely the result of the dramatic changes in the labour market arising from the removal of some five million men to the Armed Forces. Increasing discipline in society had been one of the Right's aspirations before the war. Page Croft, in arguing for two years' compulsory national service in 1908, had asserted 'even the extreme faddists will have to admit that the character of the British race will gain, in that its manhood will learn discipline and acquire steadiness . . .' Before the war, Dudley Docker and other industrialists had felt that military training of the labour force was desirable as the habits of military discipline would carry over to the factory floor.[64] With the wartime and post-war unrest, bodies such as the explicitly named Duty and Discipline Movement gained publicity for their activities in the *Morning Post* and other right-wing newspapers, as well as increased membership. Thus in February 1919 one finds the Earl of Meath, on behalf of the Duty and Discipline Movement's executive, proclaiming at a meeting held in Grosvenor Square, 'It is urged that when all classes, even the poorest, perceive that they have everything to gain from the stability of Crown and Empire, and everything to lose from revolution and anarchy, many of those who at the moment are restless will become the staunchest guardians of national unity and order.'[65]

The National Party was not only a part of these expressions of ruling class anxiety but also, as has been outlined, a continuation of the more advanced tariff reform movement of pre-war years. The tariff reformers argued that their political position was mid-way between Liberal Free Trade and Socialist collectivism.[66] Some historians in more recent times have seen the 'social-imperialists' of pre-war Britain as forerunners of fascism.[67] The National Party was a successor to these pre-war groups. Its leadership often indulged in anti-semitism and suffered from acting 'in an excess of patriotism'.[68] However, apart from its public meetings on the subject of German aliens, its lack of demagogy and its upper-crust nature make it appear rather different from the fascist parties of continental Europe. Nevertheless, it is not surprising to discover that one of its Parliamentary candidates went on to be a founder member of the British Union of Fascists.[69]

If the National Party is judged as a potential rival to the Unionist, Liberal or Labour Parties then one can but agree with John Ramsden's verdict that it was 'a complete fiasco'.[70] If it is judged as a ginger group, then the verdict can be a little less harsh. Certainly, as an expression of the concerns and prejudices of the Right it is of considerable interest. The National Party articulated many of the feelings of the Unionist rank and file. Moreover its prejudices were those expressed in much popular literature of the period. The adventure stories of John Buchan and 'Sapper' (Lt. Col. H. C. McNeile) and, less explicitly, the tales of upper crust life of Dornford Yates, and even the comic portrayals of P. G. Wodehouse, have much that is of the same ethos as was expressed by the National Party.

In the novels of John Buchan and 'Sapper' the heroes are of the leisured class and the villains often include Jewish Bolsheviks. In *Mr. Standfast*, to take an example by Buchan, Richard Hannay, the hero, is a plain, blunt, unread fellow who sees through the follies of book-learned pacifist intellectuals and the naivety of Labour delegates. The arch villain is a cunning German aristocrat disguised as a liberal intellectual, and another villain is a Portuguese Jew. Patriotic labour on the Clyde, in the form of Andrew Amos (David Kirkwood?), is praised; whereas the militant shop stewards, including 'a fierce little rat of a man, who spoke with a cockney accent' (Emanuel Shinwell?), are exposed as rogues or dupes. The moral is not only expressed in the title but expressed in monologues such as,

> What's dooty, if you won't carry it to the other side of hell? What's the use of yapping about your country if you're going to keep anything back when she calls for it? What's the good of meaning to win the war if you don't put every cent you've got on your stake?[71]

With 'Sapper' things are less subtle. In *Bulldog Drummond* (1920) the revolutionaries are described as 'Bolshevists, Anarchists, members of the Do-no-work-and-have-all-the-money Brigade', and the arch-villain tries to co-ordinate industrial unrest, 'using the tub-thumping Bolshies as tools', so that he and other financiers can make fortunes 'if

England became a sort of second Russia'.[72] In the sequel, *The Black Gang* (1922), the hero and his upper crust former military cronies form a vigilante squad; 'the ideals and object of this gang were in every way desirable . . . the . . . object was simply and soley to fight the Red element in England . . . Whenever a man appeared preaching Bolshevism, after a few days he simply disappeared. In short a reign of terror was established amongst the terrorists.'[73]

Probably books of this kind, which sold (and still sell) in large quantities, were more effective than politicians in putting over the values that motivated the National Party. In such books Bolsheviks were turned into almost pantomime demons. Their frenzied activities could be contrasted with 'English values'. 'A decent orderly home, inhabited and maintained according to the means of the owner,' asserted Dornford Yates, 'is a rock upon which a statesman can build, and points a moral which agitators find it hard to refute.' This indeed was a contrast with 'Sapper''s 'Experts of the Red Terror . . . butcherers of women and children whose sole fault was that they washed'.[74]

As John Buchan was Director of the Department of Information during the war, one wonders whether his type-casting of Bolsheviks in the public image of late nineteenth-century anarchists was deliberate propaganda. One wonders this especially, as he was another associate of Milner and a friend of F. S. Oliver (who for a few weeks worked with him).[75] Apparently he became concerned about propaganda within Britain at the time of the engineering strikes in May 1917.[76] Perhaps he, like 'Sapper', was as much a product of this ethos as a populariser of it. Certainly involvement in the British Intelligence Services in this period was not necessarily a mark of great political sagacity. This was shown by the political career of Sir Reginald 'Blinker' Hall, after he resigned from being Director of Naval Intelligence. Hall was to become a Die-Hard Unionist MP in 1919. Archibald Salvidge observed of him,

> He seems to live in a melodramatic world of his own entirely peopled by spies. Everyone who is not a Tory is either a German, a Sinn Feinner or a Bolshevist. Mention any politician of the Left, and 'Blinker' nods and blinks mysteriously and mutters, 'Wait a bit, sir. I'm watching him. I'll have his hide'.[77]

However, whilst writers such as Buchan and 'Sapper' undoubtedly popularised 'ultra patriotic' notions more widely than a body such as the National Party, the National Party did function as an often effective ginger group, rallying support for a number of causes of the Right. When it was set up, it organised opposition to pacifists and aliens. The *Morning Post*, in an editorial, observed, 'It will furnish a balance at least to the small and active group of pacifists who work in the opposite direction to induce betrayal and increase infirmity.' It went on to crusade against Bolsheviks in Russia and in Britain, and to rally opposition to moves to liberalise the administration in India and to achieve a settlement in Ireland. From its start, it campaigned against corruption in politics, focusing on the sale of honours and the use of official posts to make private gain. In the House of Commons Page Croft was persistent in raising the issue of the sale of honours, embarrassing the Unionist leadership as well as Lloyd George, and eventually succeeding in getting the practice curtailed.[78]

In such action the National Party activists, in Parliament and in the country, were in effect a vanguard of the Right against the Coalition Government. By 1920 there is every sign that the Unionist rank and file were no longer enamoured with Lloyd George, and that the National Party's preoccupations were close to their own. In Page Croft's constituency, Bournemouth, his supporters and the orthodox Conservative and Unionist Association came together to form 'a powerful Constitutional Association to resist the Council of Action and movements calculated to undermine the Constitution'. As opposition among grass-roots Unionists grew to the Coalition, 'The National Constitutional Association', according to Page Croft, 'used the old machinery of the National Party to stage most of the Die-Hard meetings'.[79]

The remnants of the National Party were one element in the wider Die-Hard revolt against the Lloyd George Coalition Government. In turn the Die-Hards were a minority of the Unionist MPs who destroyed that government at the Carlton Club meeting of 1922. Yet, whilst Page Croft was not a significant figure in these events, it is suitably symbolic that he should have issued, with no sense of irony, given his role in forming a break-away party five years earlier, a statement warning Unionist MPs that their leaders' continuing involvement in the Coalition Government amounted to an 'attempt . . . to smash their great and historic party'.[80]

With the fall of Lloyd George, many of the views put forward by the National Party and groups like them on the Right had become the orthodoxy of the Tory Party. In a way, this is comparable to what Alan Taylor describes as happening on the Left by 1920: 'The Union of Democratic Control and the Labour movement were one so far as foreign policy was concerned.'[81]

Notes

1 A. J. P. Taylor, *The Trouble Makers* (1956), p. 13.

2 99, *H.C. Debs*, 5s, c.251; 13 November, 1917. The motion was moved by Basil Peto.

3 Debate on the Consolidated Fund. 96, *H.C. Debs*, 5s, c.1549 and c.1556; 26 July, 1917.

4 This was given to the British Academy as the Raleigh Lecture for 1959. In it he recognises the mix of Labour policies and Die-Hard policies as a force in 1917–1918. See A. J. P. Taylor, *Politics In Wartime* (1964), pp. 38–40.

5 The best account is W. D. Rubinstein, 'Henry Page Croft and the National Party 1917–1922', *Journal of Contemporary History*, 9, 1 (1974), pp. 129–48.

6 Milner to F. S. Oliver, 16 January, 1917. F. S. Oliver Papers 7726/86/44–5. National Library of Scotland.

7 For an example of Milner's complaints, see Leo Amery's comments on a dinner party given by F. S. Oliver, 12 March, 1917. J. Barnes and D. Nicholson (ed.), *The Leo Amery Diaries*, Vol. 1 (1980), p. 145.

8 D. Lloyd George, *War Memoirs*, Vol. 3 (1934), p. 1043.

9 Lord Croft, *My Life of Strife* (1948), p. 129.

10 Ibid.

11 Duncannon to F. S. Oliver, 17 July, 1917. Oliver Papers 7726/98/56.

12 *Kelly's Handbook To The Titled, Landed And Official Classes For 1919. Who's Who 1919. Dictionary of National Biography*. It is interesting that the entry in the *D.N.B.* for Duncannon, who was to be Governor-General of Canada 1931–35, makes no mention of his part in the National Party. W. Nimocks, *Milner's Young Men* (1968).

13 Major-General Sir C. E. Callwell, *Field Marshal Sir Henry Wilson*, vol. 2 (1927), p. 6. For Page Croft speaking in favour of detaching Turkey and others from Germany see 96, *H.C. Debs*, c.1549; 26 July, 1917.

14 Croft, op. cit., pp. 43–44 and 53–57. N. Blewett, 'Free Fooders, Balfourites, Whole Hoggers. Factionalism within the Unionist Party 1906–1910', *Historical Journal*, 11, 1 (1968), pp. 95–124. R. A. Rempel, *Unionists Divided* (1972), pp. 176–92. A. Sykes, 'The Confederacy and the Purge of the Unionist Free Traders 1906–1910', *Historical Journal*, 18, 2 (1975), pp. 349–66. A. Sykes, *Tariff Reform In British Politics 1903–1913* (1979).

15 Page Croft to Oliver, 26 December, 1916; Oliver Papers 7726/96/173. G. E. Raine to Oliver, 14 February, 1917; ibid., 7726/97/92.

16 J. Buchan, *Memory Hold-The-Door* (1940), pp. 209 and 211.

17 *Ordeal By Battle* (1916 edition), pp. 313–29. On Oliver earlier see Nimocks, op. cit., pp. 125–30.

18 J. R. Jones, 'England' in H. Rogger and E. Webber, *The European Right* (1965)

especially pp. 32–54. G. R. Searle, 'Critics of Edwardian Society: The Case of the Radical Right' in A. O'Day, *The Edwardian Age* (1979), pp. 79–96.

19 J. O. Stubbs, 'The Impact of the Great War on the Conservative Party' in G. Peele and C. Cook, *The Politics of Reappraisal 1918–1939* (1975), pp. 14–38, especially pp. 23–29. J. Ramsden, *The Age of Balfour and Baldwin 1902–1940* (1978), pp. 112–14.

20 R. Douglas, 'The National Democratic Party and the British Workers' League', *Historical Journal*, 15, 3 (1972), pp. 533–552. J. O. Stubbs, 'Lord Milner and Patriotic Labour 1914–1918', *English Historical Review*, 87, 4 (1972), pp. 717–754.

21 E. N. Henry, Scotland Yard, to A. Steel-Maitland, 5 October 1916, enclosing a Special Branch memorandum by P. Quinn; Steel-Maitland Papers GD/193/99/2/1. Scottish Record Office.

22 Milner to Oliver, 8 April, 1917; Oliver Papers 7726/86/52–53.

23 D. O. Malcolm to Oliver, 27 August, 1917; ibid., 7726/98/91–92. Malcolm was a Director of the British South Africa Company.

24 E. Wood to Oliver, 30 July, 1917; ibid., 7726/98/74–75. Wood did not join it but expressed the hope that a National Party would emerge 'by the co-operation of men of all parties, among the manifold cross divisions that the times are bound to bring forth', rather than by Page Croft's method. E. Wood to Oliver, 29 August, 1917; ibid., 7726/98/98–99.

25 Croft, op. cit., p. 130. Duncannon to Oliver, 16 August, 1917; Oliver Papers 7726/98/83.

26 Northcliffe to Page Croft, 28 November, 1918; Page Croft Papers CRFT 1/17/4/NO/2. Churchill College, Cambridge.

27 Duncannon and Page Croft to Oliver, 25 and 28 July, 1917 respectively; Oliver Papers 7726/98/64–67 and 93. The *Morning Post*, 13, 15 and 17 September, 1917. For Austen Chamberlain assuring Page Croft on 24 October, 1917 that the Tariff Reform League leadership felt 'that there was no occasion for either you or Duncannon to leave the executive of the League', see Page Croft Papers, CRFT 1/6/25/CH8.

28 Duncannon to Oliver, 25 July and 31 August, 1917; Oliver Papers 7726/98/64–67 and 111–12. Croft, op. cit., p. 132.

29 The eighth was Captain the Hon. E. A. Fitzroy, who was unhappy at the National Party contesting by-elections given that it had 'clearly laid down . . . that unswerving support would be given to L.G. in the pursuit of the war to ultimate victory'. Fitzroy to Page Croft 7 October, 1917; Page Croft Papers CRFT/1/11/36/F1/3. He resigned from it on 31 October. See further letters of 31 October and 2 November; ibid., F1/4–6. Fitzroy was the younger son of the third Baron Southampton. He was MP for Northamptonshire South, and he saw active service in France in 1914–1916. He was to be Speaker of the House of Commons from 1928 until his death in 1943.

30 W. Ormsby-Gore to Page Croft, 7 September, 1917; ibid., CRFT 1/17/20/OR/1. He was Parliamentary Private Secretary to Milner and an Assistant Secretary to the War Cabinet.

31 Published in the *Morning Post*, 30 August, 1917.

32 Page Croft to Oliver, 'Friday night'; Oliver Papers 7726/98/116–19. It was written very soon after Duncannon's letter to Oliver, 28 July, 1917; ibid., 98/70–71.

33 Letter to *Morning Post* (dated 29 January), 30 January, 1919.

34 The *Morning Post*, 21 March, 1919.

35 Cooper went on to contrast the failure to do this with the French government's recent action in executing Mata Hari in spite of the French 'deep respect for womankind'. 98, *H.C. Deb*, 5s, c.1573–1579; 31 October, 1917. See also Croft, op. cit., pp. 130 and 139.

36 Rubinstein, op. cit., pp. 144–45. On Maxse and Colvin, as well as anti-semitism during the First World War generally, see C. Holmes, *Anti-Semitism in British Society 1876–1939* (1979), pp. 71–72, 80–82 and 121–40.

37 A copy enclosed in a letter of Duncannon to Oliver, 8 September, 1917; Oliver Papers 7726/98/127–30.

38 Rubinstein, op. cit., p. 144. Professor Rubinstein points to the irony of Page Croft's daughter marrying a German Jewish refugee, who was a socialist, penniless and spoke no English. M. Cowling, *The Impact of Labour 1920–1924* (1971), pp. 81–84. Holmes, op. cit., pp. 141–54. G. S. Lebzelter, *Political Anti-Semitism in England 1918–1939* (1978), pp. 14–29.

39 W. S. Churchill to Page Croft, 20 June, 1945; Croft Papers, CRFT 1/8/42/CH/108.

40 96, *H.C. Debs*, 5s, c.1554; 26 July, 1917. 99, *H.C. Debs*, 5s, c.557; 15 November, 1917.

41 Letter to the *Morning Post*, 30 January, 1919, and elsewhere.

42 110, *H.C. Deb*, 5s, c.1744–1746; 31 October, 1918.

43 I suspect Lloyd George's sense of humour is in evidence in his reply which thanked him for his 'suggestions as to the correct policy to be adopted'. For his reply, 13 May, 1918, and that of A. Chamberlain, 7 May, 1918, see Page Croft Papers CRFT 1/15/45/11 and 1/6/29/CH/12.

44 Rubinstein, op. cit., p. 143.

45 The *Morning Post*, 31 January, 1919. For British born Bolsheviks all being Jewish or Irish, see ibid., 24 February, 1919. On attitudes to the 1910–14 industrial unrest, see Sykes, *Tariff Reform*, pp. 259–60.

46 Entry by M. R. D. Foot, *DNB 1941–1950* (1953), pp. 187–88. On the theme of 'imperialism and social reform', see B. Semmel, *Imperialism and Social Reform* (1960), G. R. Searle, *The Quest For National Efficiency* (1971) and R. J. Scally, *The Origins of the Lloyd George Coalition* (1975).

47 In 'Labour' in a set of essays entitled *The New Order: Studies in Unionist Policy* (1908), p. 376, edited by Lord Malmesbury. Malmesbury was a key figure in Page Croft's constituency party and was in the chair at the dinner which launched the Reveille movement.

48 For these programmes see Sykes, *Tariff Reform*, pp. 195–98 and 226–28.

49 Milner to I. Colvin, 5 June, 1917; Milner Papers, Vol. 144. Bodleian Library.

50 96, *H.C. Debs*, 5s, c.1554; 26 July, 1917.

51 As at the National Party's first annual conference, the *Morning Post*, 21 March, 1919. It is quite possible that he pre-arranged to be 'pressed'. Perhaps his willingness to support radical measures explains why a National Party official told Sanders that it 'was sick of Page Croft and hoped to get rid of him'. Diary entry 3 November 1918, J. Ramsden (ed.), *Real Old Tory Politics* (1984), p. 111.

52 See Sykes, *Tariff Reform*; A. Sykes, 'The Radical Right and the Crisis of Conservatism before the First World War', *The Historical Journal*, 26, 3 (1983),

pp. 661–76; and G. R. Searle, 'The 'Revolt from the Right' in Edwardian Britain' in P. Kennedy and A. Nicholls (eds), *Nationalist And Radical Movements In Britain And Germany Before 1914* (1981), pp. 21–39.

53 *Yorkshire Observer*, 25 January, 1916; copy in Steel-Maitland Papers, GD/193/99/108–110.

54 Draft Memorandum discussed by the five on 19 October, 1916; ibid., 99/2/170. The discussions took place between September 1916 and the political crisis of that December and resumed between April and November 1917. For the minutes of the meetings and related material see ibid., 99/2/6–195.

55 Ramsden, op. cit., p. 118. Barnes and Nicholson, op. cit., p. 178.

56 Milner to Lady Roberts, 25 February, 1916; Milner Papers, Vol. 142. On Milner and 'Patriotic Labour' generally see A. M. Gollin, *Proconsul In Politics* (1964), pp. 538–50; Stubbs, 'Patriotic Labour'; and Douglas, op. cit.

57 D. Dilks, *N. Chamberlain*, Vol. 1 (1984), pp. 181–82. R. P. T. Davenport-Hines, *Dudley Docker* (1984), pp. 4 and 116–17. R. Charles, *The Development Of Industrial Relations In Britain 1911–1939* (1973), p. 116.

58 J. A. Turner, 'The British Commonwealth Union and the General Election of 1918', *English Historical Review*, 93 (1978), pp. 528–59. See also K. Middlemas, *Politics In Industrial Society* (1979), p. 132; J. A. Turner, 'The Politics of "Organised Business" in the First World War' in J. A. Turner (ed.), *Businessmen And Politics* (1980), pp. 46–48; and Davenport-Hines, op. cit., pp. 127–30.

59 Davenport-Hines, op. cit., pp. 69–125.

60 Minutes of the meetings of the Steel-Maitland group with the British Workers' League leaders, 15 August and 26 September, 1917; Steel Maitland Papers, GD 193/99/2/225 and 159.

61 The *Morning Post*, 30 August, 1917.

62 A large advertisement, the *Morning Post*, 10 February, 1919.

63 For a survey of many of these see S. White, 'Ideological Hegemony and Political Control: The Sociology of Anti-Bolshevism in Britain 1918–1920', *Scottish Labour History Society Journal*, 9 (1975), pp. 3–20.

64 H. Page Croft, 'A Citizen Army' in Malmesbury, op. cit., pp. 267–68. Davenport-Hines, op. cit., pp. 40–41.

65 The *Morning Post*, 19 February, 1919. For their general aspirations see Admiral Penrose Fitzgerald on how 'on board a man-of-war . . . dirty, lazy, uncouth, ill-mannered ragamuffins' were transformed 'into smart, well-dressed active, willing seamen'. The Duty and Discipline Movement, *Anarchy Or Order* (1915), pp. 69–70.

66 See, for example, Ronald McNeill, 'Socialism' in Malmesbury, op. cit., pp. 320–21.

67 See Sykes, 'The Radical Right', pp. 674–75.

68 The phrase was actually applied to Basil Peto and W. Joynson-Hicks by the Liberal MP, David Mason, but is very apt for the National Party MPs as well. 99, *H.C. Debs*, 5s, c.251.

69 The candidate was T. D. Pilcher, who stood for Thornbury. For a discussion of it as a proto-fascist party see Rubinstein, op. cit., pp. 146–48. Davenport-Hines, op. cit., p. 123.

70 Ramsden, op. cit., p. 114. Sanders noted in his diary in October 1917 that the National Party 'has been received with derision'. Ramsden (ed.), op. cit., p. 89.

71 *Mr. Standfast* (1919), pp. 23–37, 69–70, 202–3, 233, 237–38, 110–12, 72–75; and 250. It was written between July 1917 and July 1918.

72 *Bulldog Drummond* (1920), pp. 179 and 181.

73 *The Black Gang* (1922), p. 310. The Bolsheviks in the story even include a Polish Jew who bayonetted to death the Russian Royal Family.

74 *Maiden Stakes* (1928), cited in R. Usborne, *Clubland Heroes* (1953), p. 43. *The Black Gang*, p. 267. Other books on the *genre* include A. J. Smithers, *Dornford Yates* (1982) and C. Watson, *Snobbery With Violence* (1971).

75 J. A. Smith, *John Buchan* (1965), pp. 175 and 201.

76 M. L. Sanders, *British Propaganda During The First World War* (1982), pp. 63–67 and 71–72.

77 Diary notes, March 1919. S. Salvidge, *Salvidge of Liverpool* (1934), p. 173. Salvidge was to blame Hall as Conservative Chief Agent for not advising Baldwin against calling an election in 1923 which resulted in the Tories losing and Hall losing his seat. However Hall is always praised for his secret service work, including in Buchan's *Greemantle* (1916). He may have been a key figure in the Zinoviev letter episode. L. Chester, S. Fay, and H. Young, *The Zinoviev Letter* (1967), pp. 98–101.

78 The *Morning Post*, 30 August, 1917. 99, *H.C. Debs*, 5s, c.30–31; 12 November, 1917. Page Croft, op. cit., pp. 142–63.

79 Ibid., pp. 153 and 160.

80 M. Kinnear, *The Fall of Lloyd George* (1973), pp. 74–91. Cowling, op. cit., pp. 70–90. Page Croft, op. cit., p. 165.

81 Taylor, *The Trouble Makers*, p. 165.

Pens versus Swords: A Study of Studying the Russian Civil War, 1917–22

John Erickson

Pray accept, *Glubokouvazhaemyi Professor Teilor,* through this medium and with your name duly transcribed into its Russian form when it is cited – as it frequently is in Soviet sources – with respect to your publication, an introduction to Colonel, latterly Professor and Doctor of Historical Sciences Vasilii Dmitrievich Polikarpov of the Institute of General History, Soviet Academy of Sciences. The introduction may be quite superfluous but the conjunction is not gratuitous, since (military rank apart) there seems to be a certain similarity of approach in dealing with the problem of war, the delineation and identification of wars in terms of their initiation or their termination, though in the case of Professor Polikarpov this has been concentrated upon bringing both ideological order and historical accuracy into the investigation of what is generally termed the Russian 'civil war' – *grazhdanskaya voina* – which is depicted as having followed on the October revolution.

Professor Polikarpov, in spritely but elegant style, would at once take exception to the notion that the civil war just 'followed on' from the October seizure of power by the Bolsheviks. Indeed, the burden of his research and writing over many years, culminating in two original, stylish and penetrating monographs, *Prolog grazhdanskoi voiny v Rossii Oktyabr 1917–fevral' 1918* and *Nachal'nyi etap grazhdanskoi voiny (Istoriya izucheniya)*,[1] is that the failure to understand the nature of events between October 1917 and February 1918 has led not only to a lack of comprehension of the organic and ideological connection between the 'triumphal sweep of the October revolution' and the struggle against armed counter-revolution in these months, but also to a serious misunderstanding or even maltreatment of Lenin's basic tenets on the nature of the revolutionary process. Professor Polikarpov is at pains to point out that it is impossible to understand revolution, without understanding counter-revolution and emphasises that the point has immediate contemporary relevance – witness the destruction of the revolution in Chile.[2] All the more important, therefore, to study and understand the 'Leninist concept of the history of the civil war in Russia' and its underpinning of the Marxist–Leninist theory of socialist revolution.[3] Otherwise, without such recourse to Lenin's precepts and an attempt to understand the significance of the 'armed revolution' fighting armed counter-revolution in the first instance, the result is merely a stylised version of the 'civil war', formally but mistakenly periodised within the three 'Entente offensives' directed against Soviet Russia.[4] In other words, the civil war was not like Topsy and 'just grow'd': the 'triumphal sweep' of the October revolution depended upon the capacity to defend itself, the struggle of armed revolution against armed counter-revolution in a process which requires further understanding and rigorous utilisation not only of Lenin's works but also the publications of the 1920s, including those emanating from the 'counter-revolutionary' camp.

In an earlier essay on the historiography of the civil war, written in a very rigorous style and signed as Colonel and Candidate of Historical Sciences, Vasilii Polikarpov acknowledged the work already done, not least in breaking the Stalinist mould, but castigated the failure to explore in proper fashion 'Lenin's military legacy' – mere popularisation would hardly suffice – and the lack of any 'scientifically based' resolution of the problem of periodising the civil war. For all the profusion of terminology in works written in the 1920s and early 1930s, the importance of the 'initial period' was indubitably recognised and identified more or less as that timespan between October 1917 and the revolt of the Czechoslovak Legion (May 1918). However, with the appearance of the 'Short History', *Istoriya VKP(b). Kratkii kurs* in 1938, heavy-handed Stalinism, this 'initial period' was totally expunged from the historical record and historical recognition, while even at a later stage, free of the Stalinist shackle, historians still stumbled over how and when the civil war 'began' – from the end of October 1917 with the Kerensky-Krasnov push on Petrograd, or the spring of 1918 (the beginning of intervention in the north and the Far East) or yet again the summer of 1918, the Czechoslovak revolt and the onset of 'the intervention')? All this might have carried more weight if the 'end' of the civil war, generally dated with the defeat of Wrangel in the Crimea, had corresponded more closely to the facts, but the struggle continued for some time yet in the Far East and had still to flicker out completely in other areas.[5] Though these strictures have been countered by subsequent publications, Colonel Polikarpov's tart observation on the lack of formation and unit histories is well founded even now and he does quite a service in pointing to the wealth of publication in the 1920s and 1930s.[6]

A decade later, following his own precepts which demanded a rigorous study of Lenin's works – not mere incantation – and an intensive scrutiny of sources, not excluding those derived from the 'enemy camp', Professor Polikarpov produced *Prolog grazhdanskoi voiny v Rossii* in 1976, a work which received due approbation in 1977.[7] The introduction to *Prolog* is an extensive bibliographical essay, illustrating the scope of material available from Soviet archives but also the relevance, indeed the propriety of using not only Soviet items but also those 'petty-bourgeois' and downright 'reactionary' in origin. A case in point is the supplement to G. Lelevich's *Oktyabr' v Stavke* ('Lelevich' being the *nom de plume* of L. G. Kalmanson), published in 1922, which drew heavily on the contemporary press including the *Byulleten*, a dozen copies of which Lelevich attached as an appendix to his book and thereby preserving a 'unique source' on the affairs and activities of the *Stavka*.[8] This is neither the time nor the place in which to dissect *Prolog* but rather to advance to Professor Polikarpov's subsequent work published in 1980, *Nachal'nyi etap grazhdanskoi voiny*, which not only looks anew at the fundamental question of the 'beginning' (or the 'beginnings') of the civil war in Russia but also views this problem through the prism of attempts to garner primary materials, organise research and arrange for formal historical writing, a protracted process which affected historical perspectives as well as political priorities and military realities – who should write and how and why.

In many respects *Nachal'nyi etap* is an expansion of that first bibliographical commentary in *Prolog*. True, the compilations and documentary collections published between 1957–67 represented an advance, a substantial advance, but the importance of the 'military reduction of counter-revolution' was not fully recognised: one major documentary collection could only treat the 'armed struggle' after the most insipid fashion, while going into much greater detail with respect to other aspects of the class struggle, yet here was the class struggle assuming its most acute form.[9] There is a certain paradox here, for though much material was destroyed – deliberately lest it fall into hostile hands, as in the Ukraine and in Siberia – this did not and does not preclude closer investigation of the 'initial period' and the first months after October 1917. Professor Polikarpov cites the value of the records of V. A. Antonov-Ovseenko, People's Commissar for the Struggle with Counter-Revolution, lodged in the Central State Archive of the October Revolution (TsGAOR SSSR), particularly his reports to Lenin at the end of December 1917 and in early January 1918. To these can be added the material available from the journal *Krasnyi Arkhiv*, early documentary collections and, not least, contemporary memoirs.[10]

Thus, though the material bearing on the tumultuous months after October 1917 is relatively sparse compared with the later stages of the civil war, the 'big' civil war, all was and is not lost. In *Nachal'nyi etap* Professor Polikarpov sets out to show why, hence the sub-title the 'history of a study'.

Without recourse to Lenin, the pure, undistilled Lenin as opposed to the concoctions derived by a variety of authors and commentators (many of whom engage Professor Polikarpov's ire),[11] it is impossible to establish the main characteristics and features of this 'initial period' of the civil war. Essentially, as opposed to previous civil wars, the civil war in Russia was expressly a new form of the class struggle, with the armed struggle taking pride of place when viewed against other forms of the class struggle, with political agitation assuming an importance not witnessed in any other war plus the political support for internal counter-revolution on the part of foreign imperialists forming the initial phase of 'anti-Soviet intervention'. Leninist theoretical and historical legacies must perforce be used to lend their aid in undertaking a 'fruitful' study of the civil war, not least in making the right connection between military action and the political revolution.

The turbulent, geographically disparate 'initial period' of the civil war was inevitably enmeshed with attempts, many of them rudely improvised, to provide some kind of military analysis together with political propagandising – as Lenin duly prescribed and in which he himself played a major role – but with the overriding need to build a new revolutionary army, the Workers–Peasants Red Army (RKKA), guide lines of military practice and the codification of military experience were urgently needed. In spite of anarchic preferences for autonomous and unruly 'detachments', *otryady*, or the socialist *sancta simplicitas* of a militia sent out to fight the foe, the survival of the revolution depending on fielding an orthodox regular army with all its impedimenta, including officers, NCOs and trained soldiers.[12] The Imperial Army had died in its tracks, while the Bolsheviks fielded a motley array of Red Guards, worker battalions, sailor squads and multifarious local detachments, all to fight off 'armed counter-revolution', but a Bolshevik command system emerged with the creation, at Lenin's behest of the Revolutionary Field Staff, followed in turn by the Supreme Military Soviet and the All-Russian Supreme Staff (*Vserosglavshtab*). Sundry and select ex-Imperial senior officers had already offered their services to the Bolsheviks, employed and utilised under the euphemistic designation of 'military specialists' (*voenspets*), the precursors of the thousands of ex-Imperial officers about to be marshalled into the Red Army to provide a desperately needed officer corps (and followed in short order by the conscription of ex-Imperial NCOs).

While the revolutionary combatants, such as Antonov-Ovseenko, fought off counter-revolution with their improvised squads and conserved what they could of their papers and their impressions, the tidy-minded 'military specialists' serving with the All-Russian Supreme Staff (*Vserosglavshtab*) had set up a 'military-historical unit' attached to the Operations Administration on 8 May, 1918. But the business of building an army under fire does not go well with military-historical research which is time-consuming in its own right and at a time when 'war' meant the gigantic panorama of the First World War, still raging on. It was left to a very senior 'military specialist', ex-Imperial Lieutenant General M. D. Bonch-Bruevich (brother of V. D. Bonch-Bruevich, intimate of Lenin), serving with the Supreme Military Soviet, to suggest the establishment of a 'military-historical commission', committed to and commissioned for the preparation of 'a short strategic outline' of the World War, a general but adequate programme for the study of and research into all wars and a review of measures to put all this into practical effect.[13] On 13 August, 1918 the People's Commissariat for Military Affairs approved this proposal and forthwith set up a formal 'Military-Historical Commission' (*Voenno-istoricheskii komissiya: VIK*) which was in the first instance an expansion and elaboration of the 'military-historical unit' attached to *Vserosglavshtab*: the new Commission was charged initially with a study of those lessons which might be derived from the World War, though Soviet Russia had withdrawn unilaterally from that war with the Treaty of Brest-Litovsk and now the 'big' civil war was expanding with ferocious speed.[14] For the moment, however, the VIK occupied pride of place as the central 'scientific' body for the study of military history, while in November 1918 the Naval Commission for Research into and Utilisation of Experience of War at Sea (*Voenno-morskaya Komissiya po issledovaniyu i ispol'zovaniyu opyta voiny na more*) was set up within the Naval Academy, in which form it existed until 1923.[15]

Chairmanship of the newly created VIK went to a very senior *voenspets*, General of Infantry V. N. Klembovskii, with General of Infantry N. P. Miknevich – a famous name in Russian military publishing – and General V. A. Apushkin, yet another accomplished publicist in military matters, as assistants to Klembovskii. It is hard to over-estimate the contribution of these *voenspets* in setting up a professional framework for what was to follow and Professor Polikarpov is fully justified in complaining that so far no proper treatment of the *voenspets* has yet appeared: indeed, *Nachal'nyi etap* can be regarded as part fulfilment of this task, disclosing as it does much new material on the role and influence of these ex-Imperial officers. It fell to yet another senior *voenspets*, General A. A. Svechin – who was to make a major contribution to the formulation of strategic views in the 1920s[16] – to take over from Klembovskii when VIK was reorganised and expanded in December 1918, emerging as the 'Commission for Research into and Utilisation of Experience of War 1914–1918', a frame of reference which proved to be too constricting as the 'big' civil war raged on. In June 1919, a session of the editorial collegiate of the Commission, following the lead of the Republic *Revvoensovet*, recognised the need to exploit *Red Army* archives and duly approached *Vserosglavshtab* to draw into the Commission's work qualified personnel – fit and trained in 'military-historical work', a prescription which could only apply to ex-Imperial staff officers and generals. Not surprisingly, a whole cluster of senior *voenspets* took up positions with the Commission, among them the distinguished military historian General A. M. Zaionchkovskii (who had been serving as chief of staff to the 13th Red Army on the Southern Front), though scarcely less eminent were ex-Imperial senior officers such as Svechin, Bonch-Bruevich, A. A. Neznamov, E. I. Martynov, D. P. Parskii, D. K. Lebedev, V. N. Klembovskii and A. S. Grishinskii.[17]

In January 1920 the Commission reverted to its original designation – Military-Historical Commission – but this was more than a nominal change, for 'military history' was now coming to include the history of the Red Army and the course of the civil war. The ex-Imperial senior officers developed their weekly specialised seminars on military history, touching somewhat gingerly on civil war operations,[18] though the time had almost come when the history of the Red Army had to be considered as a theme in its own right. That situation was recognised in the draft plan for the reorganisation of the Commission, with an investigation into the history of the Red Army predicated on researching the 'spontaneous disintegration of the old/Imperial/army' with its dual aspect – the healthy elements forming the kernel of a new army, the diseased elements providing a baleful example of indiscipline, dissipated authority and contempt for specialists.[19]

This approach at once illustrated the limitations, or the limited horizons of the senior *voenspets*: if they could only see in the 'democratisation' of the Imperial army an example of discipline and much else gone to pot, then it was hard to believe that they would understand the nature of the Red Guard or the gigantic social upheavals which produced the Red Army with its class composition, rather interpreting the Red Army as the 'reconstitution' of Russian military power. The draft plan for a history of the Red Army and civil war operations was conceived along lines similar to those applied to writing the history of the late world war, resulting in an ambitious workplan for a 'strategic outline' of the civil war, supplemented by a whole range of monographs.[20] Once again *Vserosglavshtab* took a hand and on 7 January, 1921 ordered the Commission in a matter of two days to look into the most important aspects of the World War and the Civil War, paying particular attention to mobilisation, organisation, manning and supply and taking account of both positive and negative features.

General A. A. Neznamov went to work with a will, displaying in the process a certain disregard for political factors, laying about him right and left (in both the military and political sense). More pertinently, in stressing the need for a regular army with all its appurtenances, General Neznamov became entangled in the raging controversy over the merits (or deficiencies) of the militia system to replace the standing Red Army, the 9th Party Congress on 4 April, 1920 having already adopted its own resolution on a militia system, '*O perekhode k militisionnoi sisteme*'.[21] Nor did the senior *voenspets* grasp the political and ideological essence of the prevailing mood which looked to internationalism and world revolution, seeing in all this more or less a return to good old power politics and an expression of state sovereignty. The ripples spread, reaching into the Higher Academic Military-Pedagogic Soviet (VAVPS), where a conference was held on 16 January, 1921 to investigate the problem of studying the civil war experience and training 'Red commanders'. The head of the Main Administration for Military-Educational Establishments, D. A. Petrovskii, stressed the urgency of the problem and rather than leaving this to odd individuals and 'various historical commissions' it might be better to copy the example of the staff of the Western Front who sent questionnaires to actual civil war participants seeking information on their combat experience: General A. I. Verkhovskii, a senior *voenspets*, suggested gathering together select civil war participants who would be able to formulate what was required. VAVPS should, therefore, approach *Vserosglavshtab* with a proposal to set up a 'central circle' or a commission to evaluate the experience of the civil war.

General A. E. Snesarev, head of the General Staff Academy, General A. A. Samoilo from *Vserosglavshtab* and M. N. Tukhachevskii – commander of the Western Front – considered this matter with other officers, though Tukhachevskii pointed out from his own experience that it was no easy matter with civil war veterans to get all this down on paper. However, Petrovskii's initiative paid off and yet another commission was brought into being, one designed to evaluate civil war experience but to develop studies and materials which could be used for training the Red Army. The Red Army C-in-C S. S. Kamenev was appointed president, with Snesarev and V. F. Novitskii (a professor at the General Staff Academy) as members, committed to finishing their work within two months. Most significantly the senior members of the commission were seconded to the Supreme Editorial Soviet (*Vysshyii redaksionnyi sovet*) which was supervised by the Section for Military Literature attached to the Republic *Revvoensovet* – the highest reaches: the staffs of fronts, armies, divisions and brigades, even down to regiment, would publish non-secret material bearing on their civil war experiences and the military section of State Publishing (*Gosudarstvennoe izdatel'stvo*) would handle the actual published editions.[22]

The first session of the newly-minted commission lasted three days, at which Kamenev assigned other officers, including Boris Shaposhnikov, to assemble material which could be used for tactical instruction, based on civil war experience. The study of the civil war *per se* was gathering speed with the entry of V. P. Polonskii, head of the Section of Military Literature from the Republic *Revvoensovet*, upon the scene, who recalled at once that for the past year or so the editorial board of '*Krasnaya Armiya i Krasnyi Flot v revolyutsionnoi voine Sovetskoi Rossii 1917–1920*' (a group attached to the General Staff Academy and supervised by N. I. Podvoiskii) had been engaged on the collection of relevant materials.

Polonskii wasted no time. It would be more purposeful to concentrate all these activities under the umbrella of the Military-Scientific Society (*Voenno-nauchnoe obshchestvo: VNO*) attached to the General Staff Academy, which had already begun to build up its own Red Army archive, but Polonskii's ideas reached far beyond working over the material in order to provide tactical lessons and tactical instruction. The interests of world revolution and those of comrades in the west required that the hard lessons learned by the Red Army should be noised abroad, mistakes avoided and that these same western comrades should learn about the right road to build their own Red Army. To this end Polonskii proposed the publication – within six months – of a key handbook, *Kratkii ocherk istorii grazhdanskoi voiny i stroitel'stva Krasnoi Armii* and he went on to propose a grandiose, not to say a wild and woolly plan for further investigation of Red strategy and the civil war. The historian V. P. Koz'min proceeded to shoot all this down in flames: Koz'min wanted a specific answer to the question – who and which institution was to take on the work of studying the history of the Red Army?[23] Though he supported the idea of a 'managerial editorship for the handling of original materials' and the establishment of a central archive, why then should this be centred on the Military-Scientific Society rather than in an independent institution? A more positive approach would be to disassociate the whole enterprise from the General Staff Academy and from the Main Administration for Military Educational Establishments, putting it rather under the auspices of the Republic *Revvoensovet* and linking up with *Istpart*,[24] the commission studying Party history and the history of the October revolution at large. This would facilitate setting up a central archive for the study of the history of the civil war: Podvoiskii's editorial group would have no difficulty in making local contacts, collecting material and could constitute itself that '*sole* institution committed *exclusively* to the history of the civil war'.

Amidst this welter of argument the Military Historical Commission was disbanded on 29 May, 1921 and then re-formed, charged with the study of both the World War and the civil war (duly affirmed on 2 September, 1921), placed this time under the chairmanship of S. I. Gusev (head of the Political Administration of the Republic *Revvoensovet*) and with M. N. Tukhachevskii, newly emplaced as head of the Red Army Military Academy, as his deputy. One of the first steps of the new Commission was to develop a programme for a short history of the civil war, a task assigned to I. I. Vatsetis (one-time C-in-C of the Red Army), a distinguished *voenspets* in his own right.[25]

Not that this settled matters, though Vatsetis produced a very competent draft outline of a history of the Red Army, the first real attempt to assemble a history in its true sense.[26] This was challenged, in turn, by the proponents of the Academy's *VNO*, pointing to what had been achieved during the military academic year 1921–22, but the real battle was being waged between the 'oldsters' and the 'youngsters', with opinion hardening against the *voenspets*. In 1921 Tukhachevskii led the attack, castigating the 'metaphysics and pure scholasticism' which reigned supreme in 'Military-scientific circles', all in the search for the immutable and unchanging laws of war, ignoring the meaning of the class struggle and leaving out entirely Marxist theory as a tool to study military questions.

The young 'Red commanders' took the greatest exception to the 'academic' approach to military history, objecting in particular to the *voenspets* of the 'old school' who held sway in the Military-Scientific Society (VNO), though not all were as diehard as the *kraskomy*, the Red commanders nurtured in the civil war, would have them.

Nevertheless, this differentiation affected the work of both the Military Historical Commission and the Military-Scientific Society, wherein the problem of the 'study of the civil war' became (in Professor Polikarpov's words) a litmus test all its own and whose effects made themselves felt in other matters, such as the study of the Great War.

In any event, the 'Red commanders' trampled all over the Military-Scientific Society, the VNO, when in October 1921 Tukhachevskii became president of the board, with L. L. Klyuev (ex-lieutenant colonel) taking over the section dealing with military art and the historical section V. G. Sharmanov, military commissar to *Vserosglavshtab* – in short, the new board and its representatives were formed from students from the Military Academy, from 'Red commanders' military commissars and staff officers from the old ex-Imperial army and navy. As for the 'collective authorship' of the proposed *Ocherki istorii Krasnoi Armii za 1917–1922 gg.*, this also fell largely into the hands of students from the Military Academy, S. I. Ventsov, V. G. Sharmanov, I. M. Podzhivalov and others drawn from military–academic circles.[27]

If the question of *who* was to undertake this military-historical research had been decided, initially by default, what was not so clear was what should be used, or what was available in the way of actual source material. Even as late as 1922, relatively speaking, V. P. Polonskii was reporting to the Republic *Revvoensovet* that the work of the Commission for the Study of the Civil War could not make any significant progress until the Red Army Archive was put into some kind of order: it was not only a question of utilising these archives, it was a matter of actually rescuing them. In June 1918 the Council of People's Commissars had centralised all archives under the Unified State Archive Holdings (EGAF), closing down separate archives and thus eliminating access for 'bourgeois–aristocratic historians' and saboteurs. EGAF set up eight sections, No. 3 of which included naval archives: the two Petrograd sections housed the War Ministry archives, the Naval Ministry records and those of the Petrograd Military district, while Moscow held the so-called Lefortovskii archive, holdings covering the pre-revolutionary *Glavnyi Shtab* (Main Staff), and the Moscow section of the Military-Educational Archive with much material covering the Great War. War records (1914–18) were scattered through what had been frontline areas and rear echelons, while Red Army front commands had embarked on collecting records for transmission to a central collection, a process which caused the Military-Historical Commission in August 1919 to set up its own 'Section for the Collection of Historical Materials relating to the Combat Actions of the Red Army'.

To avoid further dispersion and dislocation at the end of 1920 the Republic *Revvoensovet* agreed to merge the Red Army Archive with the centralised holding, EGAF, while only months later (15 July, 1921) the Main Archival Administration (*Glavarkhiv*) decided to remove the Red Army Archive from the Military-Naval Section of EGAF and merge it with the newly established Archive of the October Revolution.[28] But troubles did not come singly: in March 1922 Professor A. M. Zaionchkovskii chaired a special meeting to investigate the problem of the archives, though hopes of speedy progress were dashed by the report submitted by the Commission to *Glavarkhiv*, disclosing a state of disorder and such 'scanty' holdings, with the situation not much better outside Moscow: lack of space and shortage of qualified archivists hardly helped to improve the situation. Years were to pass before order was finally established – even in January 1927 the central archival administration was reporting that there were still 400 tons of documents awaiting shipment from the various republics (twice the actual holdings of the Red Army Archive which amounted to only 200 tons) – though with the publication by Gosizdat in 1920 of a collection of studies and papers, *Fronty Krasnoi Armii Flota* (edited by the Soviet C-in-C S. S. Kamenev) covering the period 1918–19 a definite start had been made on writing up the history of the civil war. The problem of archival sources, however, continued to bedevil plans for more ambitious works and now the fifth anniversary of the founding of the Red Army was rapidly approaching, causing the Higher Military Editorial Board (*Vysshyi voennyi redaktsionnyi sovet: VVRS*) with S. S. Kamenev, V. A. Antonov-Ovseenko, D. A. Petrovskii and B. M. Shaposhnikov among others to convene a special group (an 'almanac editorial commission') with Antonov-Ovseenko at its head, assisted by A. M. Zaionchkovskii, M. G. Rafes (head of the military-political publication section of VVRS) and I. A. Troitskii to prepare this new publication.[29]

In the autumn of 1922 the Political Administration (*Politupravlenie*) of the *Revvoensovet* appealed to former members of the Red Guard (*Krasnaya Gvardiya*), the armed workers military organisation[30] and Red Army men for material – memoirs, papers, original material. Much to the gratification of the Political Administration, the material flooded in, 'whole monographs' included. The result was not unworthy of the effort expended, the volume appearing in 1923 under the title of *Grazdanskaya voina. Materialy po istorii Krasnoi Armii. Tom 1.* (*The Civil War: Material relating to the history of the Red Army. Vol. 1*), materials bearing on the initial period of the civil war embracing the period of the 'triumphal sweep of Soviet power' to April 1918.[31] Remaining to this day a unique and invaluable collection, *Grazhdanskaya voina* was a compendium of documentary material, memoirs (S. M. Pugachevskii and E. I. Kovtyukh) and a 'historical outline' on the 'Armed Forces of October' furnished by S. A. Spilnichenko. Published in an edition of 3,000 copies, the volume advertised itself not so much as a 'history' in the formal sense but rather a collection (*sbor*) of relevant materials, a fuller, more formal history having to wait on the better ordering of the Red Army archives.[32]

Volumes II and III followed in short order, in 1923 and 1924 respectively, covering the civil war in the Ukraine, two major studies on the civil war in Turkestan (by N. E. Kakurin and D. D. Zuev) but there was a lack of actual documentation, leaving Volume I as the undisputed leader as an actual source for the 'organisation of the armed struggle against counter-revolution': equally important, this was a demonstration of the rapprochement between the young historians of the civil war and the military historians of the 'old school', overcoming a certain 'infantile sickness' of Soviet historiography. *Istpart* had meanwhile plans of its own, having published in 1921 *Dva goda Krasnoi Armii i Flota: Istpart* had also established a military section, a section for the history of the Red Army under N. I. Podvoiskii, which was contemplating grandiose plans for 'a survey' of Red Army operations in the civil and revolutionary wars, but in 1921 it had to pull in its horns with the admission that a scheme on such a scale was not feasible. In 1923 Antonov-Ovseenko concluded his own concordat with *Istpart*, whereby the latter and its military section handed over its material relating to the post-October period, material which was used in the first volume of *Grazhdanskaya voina*. Nevertheless, *Istpart* made its own singular contribution through its provincial organs, one of the most significant works dealing with the initial period of the civil war being G. Lelevich's *Oktyabr v Stavke*, recognised in contemporary reviews and assessments as the first attempt to evaluate the role of the *Stavka* (GHQ) in the October revolution, a work which used the press and memoir material as its basis.[33]

There were also individual contributions which left a very distinctive mark on the historiography of the 'initial period' of the civil war, such as that developed by Dmitrii Furmanov with his distinctive 'historiographical/bibliographical' survey of the civil war, which also took account of the writings of the opposing side – assembled in his study 'Kratkii obzor literatury (neperiodicheskoi). O grazhdanskoi voine (1918–1920 gg.)', printed in that primary journal *Proletarskaya revolyutsiya*,[34] a study which bemoaned the fact that even at that date no 'major work' – *kapital'nyi trud* – on the civil war existed, in spite of attempts to manage this enterprise, citing works such as G. P. Georgievskii's *Ocherki po istorii Krasnoi gvardii* (on the Red Guard) or even the Red Army Staff compilation 'Otchet ob operatsiyakh Krasnoi Armii s l/XII 1919 po 25/XI 1920'.

There is more to be learned of Furmanov's overall contribution to the history of the early days of the civil war, a view pressed with some vigour and much justification by Professor Polikarpov. However, Dmitrii Furmanov was not a voice crying in the archival wilderness. In 1923, at the time of the publication of his study, two other works appeared dealing with the civil war, *Boevaya rabota Krasnoi Armii i Flota 1918–1923*, edited by V. A. Antonov-Ovseenko and B. M. Shaposhnikov (the ex-Imperial colonel who became subsequently a Marshal of the Soviet Union), a work put together by the military specialists of the Red Army Staff and the more modest study compiled by Antonov-Ovseenko himself, *Stroitel'stvo Krasnoi Armii v revolyutsii*, meant as a sketch to introduce a Marxist interpretation of the history of the Red Army and the civil war. Moreover, as head of both the Military-Historical Commission and the military section of *Istpart* Antonov-Ovseenko was no doubt intent on building a few bridges rather than furnishing a definitive methodological work, a task which two young lecturers at the Red Army Military Academy,[35] S. I. Ventsov and S. M. Belitskii, undertook with the reproduction of their course 'Kratkii strategicheskii ocherk grazhdanskoi voiny 1918–1922 gg.', a complete overview of the civil war as stipulated by the Military Academy itself, though one for which the authors supplied their own demarcation – to furnish the 'broad mass of command staff with the possibility of studying the birth of the Red Army and the *first stage of the civil war*'.[36]

Their first book on the Red Guard, *Krasnaya Gvardiya* published in 1924, dealt with the initial period of the civil war, which the authors considered to have run from the October revolution to the first days in May 1918 when the 'revolutionary detachments' fighting the German incursion were pulled back to man the 'screens' (*zavesy*), the holding positions on the Soviet frontiers.[37] The book considered the class composition of the warring parties, the foundation which enabled the authors to review the course of the fighting and the determinants of the 'triumphal sweep of Soviet power'. The analysis of the armed forces of the proletariat (and its opponents), Red Guard detachments, revolutionary elements of the old Imperial army and partisan detachments could establish the nature of the armed struggle at that time and, being successful, could provide guidelines for the further development of the armed forces and the military policy of the Soviet Republic. The main contrast was with the new elements introduced in comparison with the regular Imperial army, all of which required thinking over and illumination. It was also a war of movement, which could justify the term 'the railway war' – *eshelonnaya voina* – during this period, an assertion supported by V. M. Primakov in his study of the development of Soviet power in the Ukraine.

Though both authors of *Krasnaya Gvardiya* freely admitted the constraints imposed by the prevailing paucity of archival material, others continued the investigation into the course of the civil war, particularly the problem of periodisation and the nature of the 'initial period'. At the Institute of Red Professors M. N. Pokrovskii pressed the case for further study of the civil war, setting out his own idea of periodisation in an article in the journal *Bolshevik*, though it failed to satisfy several critics (including the editorial board of *Bolshevik* itself). Among the doubters was A. Anishev, a senior wartime military commissar (*voenkom*) and latterly a lecturer in the Red Army/Red Navy Military-Political Academy and author of a major work on the civil war, *Ocherki istorii grazhdanskoi voiny 1917–1920 gg.*, published in Leningrad in 1925. Indeed, Anishev's criticisms of Pokrovskii formed the basis of his own periodisation of the civil war employed in his monograph, setting out four main periods – October 1917–March 1918, April–May 1918, June–November 1918 and November 1918 to the spring of 1920.

Anishev's contribution consisted not only in covering the whole span of the civil war but also looking at the political context of the armed struggle together with the social processes which accompanied the continued fighting, the class struggle in its armed guise. Between them Ventsov-Belitskii and Anishev established two routes to the investigation of the civil war, the one operational-strategic (limited, in the case of Ventsov and Belitskii to the 'initial period'), the other more a military-political interpretation. Pride of place, however, must go to the work of Antonov-Ovseenko and his *Oktyabr' v pokhode*, published in July 1924, forming the first volume of the monumental, multi-volume history *Zapiski o grazhdanskoi voine* with its hoard of first-hand information and documentary material,[38] coming as it did from one of the leaders of the struggle of the Soviet forces against 'armed counter-revolution' and remaining as it has done an indispensable source for historians. Antonov-Ovseenko was able to draw on his documents, particularly those pertaining to the operations of the 'Southern revolutionary front', while N. V. Krylenko, writing on the demise of the old (Imperial) army – a text which did not see the light of day until 1964 – fell back on a more personalised account, thus placing it more or less within the framework of other memoir material dealing with the 'initial period'.[39]

In his essay on early research into the civil war Professor I. Sherman, writing in *Voenno-istoricheskii Zhurnal* in 1964, divides the publications of the late 1920s into four categories – research essays, monographs, memoirs and popular historical outlines. Throughout the 1920s some 257 items dealing with the civil war made their appearance, 87 of them involving full-scale publication as books or monographs, with 1928 (the tenth anniversary of the October revolution and founding of the Red Army) marking a rather special climax.[40] But statistics apart, it must be conceded that the work of N. E. Kakurin has to be accorded a very special place, not least by virtue of his major two-volume history of the civil war, *Kak srazhalas' revolutsiya* which appeared in 1925–26, accompanied by a shorter handbook, *Strategicheskii ocherk grazhdanskoi voiny. Kratkii uchebnik* (Moscow, 1926) designed for students of the Military Academy (a work which Professor Sherman castigates for its major errors).[41]

Kakurin's military experience and expertise was considerable, reflected in his association with Frunze and Tukhachevskii, his appointment as a senior instructor in tactics in the Red Army Military Academy and later as section chief with the Red Army Staff for the history of the civil war. His first serious work, *Strategiya proletarskogo gosudarstva . . .* (1921), on the strategy of the proletarian state, carried the imprint of the ideas expressed by Tukhachevskii in his radical essay, 'Strategiya natsional'naya i klassovaya' with its stress on new forms of armed struggle embracing political and economic factors.[42] Kakurin's periodisation set the first stage of the civil war in the winter of 1917–18 in the Ukraine and the Don as the organic continuation of the revolutionary process which had placed power in the hands of the proletariat as a result of the October revolution, with the second stage opening in May 1918 with the revolt of the Czechoslovak Legion and the 'activation' of foreign intervention and the third period stretching from November 1918 to the spring of 1920, bringing about the defeat of Kolchak and Denikin.

This signalled the 'end' of the civil war but it remained to account for the Soviet–Polish war of 1920, to which Kakurin devoted a prodigious effort (producing a major work in co-operation with V. A. Melikov):[43] as Professor Sherman points out, the acrimonious, embittered dispute over the course of Soviet operations and the cause of the Red Army's débâcle before Warsaw in August 1920 began to overshadow many other issues, resulting in a rash of 29 books, 76 substantial essays and a whole cluster of popular booklets and articles, the whole controversy fuelled by the growing antagonism between Stalin and his military cronies and the 'Tukhachevskii camp, long-standing rivals engaged in a deadly feud. However, the approach of the tenth anniversary of the October revolution and the creation of the Red Army concentrated attention upon a suitable commemoration, a theme taken up by the conference of the heads of political administrations in military districts and fleets in mid-January 1927. On this occasion A. S. Bubnov, head of the Red Army Political Administration, pointed to the significance of the civil war experience but went on to assert that, as yet, no work existed which set out the main features of civil war strategy. In his formal speech Bubnov intimated that a commission to commemorate the tenth anniversary had been set up, drawing in the plan for a three-volume history of the civil war which would involve the Military Academy, the Red Army Staff and participants themselves. R. P. Eideman, head of the Military Academy, had already organised an editorial board which had drawn up a preliminary synopsis – Volume 1 presenting a 'strategic outline', Volume 2 covering 'the main themes of the evolution of our Soviet operational art' based on civil war experiences and Volume 3 illuminating 'the most striking, characteristic episodes from wartime practice'.[44]

A formidable galaxy of talent was assembled to complete this task – senior and distinguished commanders (I. I. Vatsetis, S. S. Kamenev, M. N. Tukhachevskii, R. P. Eideman, A. I. Yegorov), experienced historians (S. I. Ventsov, S. M. Belitskii, N. E. Kakurin, V. A. Melikov), the Party's 'military workers' (A. S. Bubnov, V. P. Zatonskii, N. N. Kuz'min) and, not least, the military theoreticians (A. A. Svechin, V. K. Triandafillov, N. E. Varfomoleyev, F. V. Blumental). The finished product diverged quite markedly from the original plan: Volume 1 consisted of memoir material and episodic treatment of aspects of the civil war, Volume 2 (on the Red Army's military art), furnished a series of papers on Red Army organisation, mobilisation, logistics, Party-political work, considerations of strategy and tactics, while Volume 3 reversed the order of the original plan, being devoted to an 'operational-strategic outline'.

The publication of the third and final volume in 1930 marked not only the completion of this ambitious enterprise but also the culmination of the work of a decade or more to unravel the processes of the civil war. While not breaking new ground with respect to the periodisation of the civil war, in his preface to Volume 1 Bubnov stressed the organic connection between the October revolution and the civil war, 'a war in a new context and attended by a new correlation of class forces', a theme which had been elaborated over the years and which retains its relevance even today. Pointing to the distribution of material in the volumes, Professor Sherman emphasises its unevenness, with six chapters out of a total of 21 devoted to the Soviet–Polish war of 1920, three to the destruction of Denikin and three to the defeat of Wrangel: less space was devoted to the 'initial period' of the civil war and to the defeat of Kolchak, among other subjects. Professor Sherman also notes that publication of Volume 3 coincided with the onset of the Stalinist taint of the 'cult of personality', which was ultimately to wrench both history and historiography wholly out of shape and consign many a historian to his death.[45] But the truly grim days were not yet come and it wanted a further 17 years before Stalin would personally denigrate the significance of the 'Leninist legacy'.[46]

Yet another configuration, one also prompted by the onset of the tenth anniversary of the October revolution, was the initiative launched in February 1928 by the Society of Marxist-Historians which set up its own commission to investigate armed insurrection and revolutionary war, including civil war. The commission was charged with ensuring the close contact between military and civilian historians, in order to bring military-technical and military-operational issues to the attentiion of the civilian historians, while the military historians were to be urged to intensify social-economic analysis in their military histories. Throughout the 1920s, intertwined with the discussion of the scope and nature of the Russian civil war had been a turbulent series of exchanges on the problem of formulating military doctrine, a specific Soviet military doctrine: academics, soldiers and ideologues joined in this fray, where historical analysis of the Great War and the Civil War played a prominent role, not to mention the legacy of military theoretical writing from the days of Tsarist Russia. But a fresh twist was given to these deliberations with the establishment in 1929 of the 'Section for the Study of the Problems of War' under the auspices of the Communist Academy (*Komakad*) with A. S. Bubnov as its chairman and M. N. Pokrovskii, R. P. Eideman, Yan Gamarnik and I. P. Uborevich on the board: Bubnov also chaired a sub-section on general military affairs, Eideman the historical subsection. Plans were also afoot, in co-operation with the Red Army Staff, to produce an eight-volume history of the Russian civil war, covering all stages of the war and embracing aspects of military organisation and wartime military economics.[47]

The eight volumes never materialised, but the work of the Section for the Study of the Problems of War got off to a flying start. In December 1929 Tukhachevskii presented his paper on 'The character of modern wars in the light of the decisions of the VI Congress of the *Komintern*', Bubnov addressed the tasks facing the 'military section', S. M. Belitskii discussed Frunze's views of Marxism and Leninism in military affairs, B. I. Gorev took 'military-historical thought in the USSR and Marxism' as his theme – and thereby sparked off a controversy which rumbles on even today.[49]

'We ourselves have now succeeded in forgetting a mass of important facts concerning the breakthrough of Soviet power, the first steps of its institutions and so on . . .' This remark made by Lenin himself is reflected to a large degree in Professor Polikarpov's work on the 'history of historical studies' in the 1920s and the early 1930s, particularly the investigation of those 'first steps' which so speedily turned into the strides of civil war. In the view of Professor Polikarpov those 'first steps', or that 'first stage' is of such fundamental importance, retaining all its significance even for the present situation, that due attention should be paid to those who laboured both painfully and painstakingly to record, reconstruct and remember. Back to your own half-forgotten history books, comrades.

Notes

1 Professor Polikarpov, *Prolog* . . ., Moscow, 'Nauka', 1976, 415 pp. (9,000 copies): *Nachal'nyi etap* . . ., Moscow, 'Nauka', 1980, 371 pp. (2,850 copies). In 1963 Lt. Col. V. D. Polikarpov published an article on the destruction of the 'White Guard shock battalions', Belograd, 1917, *Voenno-istoricheskii Zhurnal* (hereafter *VIZh*), 1963, No. 1, pp. 103–09: He was also the editor of the important collection of memoirs by Civil War participants, *Etapy bol'shovo puti*, Moscow, Voenizdat, 1963, 528 pp. (40,000 copies): also as Colonel Polikarpov, article 'Nekotorye voprosy istoriografii grazhdanskoi voiny', *VIZh*, 1966, No. 7, pp. 75–84: see also V. Polikarpov, 'Nekotorye voprosy Leninskoi kontseptsii istorii grazhdanskoi voiny v Rossii' in *Zaschita Velikovo Oktyabrya*, Mocow, 'Nauka', 1982, pp. 81–93: see also V. D. Polikarpov in *Boevoe sodruzhestvo sovetskikh respublik 1919–1922 gg.*, Moscow, 'Nauka', 1982, pp. 177–89, on the Leninist concept of the history of the Civil War.

2 See *Nachal'nyi etap* . . ., p. 7: also *Zashchita Velikovo Oktyabrya*, op. cit., p. 84.

3 *Zashchita Velikovo Oktyabrya*, ibid., pp. 84–85.

4 See *Boevoe sodruzhestvo* . . ., op. cit., p. 178; also E. N. Gorodetskii, *Lenin – osnovopolozhnik sovetskoi istoricheskoi nauki*, Moscow, 1970, p. 216; also J. Erickson, 'Lenin as a Civil War Leader' in *Lenin. The Man, The Theorist, The Leader* (Eds. L. Schapiro and P. Reddaway), London, Pall Mall, 1967, pp. 160–62. Also N. N. Azovtsev, *Voennye voprosy v trudakh V. I. Lenina*, Moscow, Voenizdat, 1972 (2nd Edn.): also V. G. Tsvetkov (Ed.), *O voenno-teoretichesko nasledii V. I. Lenina*, Moscow, Voenizdat, 1964: also S. V. Lipitskii, *Leninskoe rukovodstvo oborony strany*, Moscow, Politizdat, 1979, esp. pp. 15–73.

5 Polikarpov, loc. cit., *VIZh*, 1966, No. 7, p. 79: see also bibliographical listing, *Istoriya istoricheskoi nauki v SSSR. Sovetskii period (1917–1967 g.)*, Moscow, 'Nauka', 1980, pp. 123–26.

6 For a list of Red Army commanders (Fronts, Armies, Divisions, also Far Eastern Republic forces), Front designations, Army/Division identification, see Section 6, *Direktivy komandovaniya frontov Krasnoi Armii (1917–1922)*, Vol. IV, Moscow, Voenizdat, 1978, p. 529ff.: divisional histories dating from the 1920/30s include 9th, 27th, 26th, 5th, 15th, 44th, 1st Kazan.

7 See review note, *VIZh*, 1977, No. 10, p. 127.

8 *Prolog*, op. cit., p. 26, on *Oktyabr' v Stavke* (83 pp.): I found this catalogued under *Kalmanson* rather than Lelevich.

9 Polikarpov, *Prolog*, ibid., pp. 16–17, esp. comments on the multi-volume *Triumfal'noe shestvie Sovetskoi vlasti*, and note on the publications '*Velikaya Oktyabr'skaya sotsialisticheskaya revolyutsiya*'.

10 *Prolog*, ibid., pp. 18–20, notes on early documentary collections, also (p. 19) on Collections 8415, Central State Archive of the October Revolution (TsGAOR SSSR), re Antonov-Ovseenko: on memoir material (Antonov-Ovseenko, R. I. Berzin, N. V. Krylenko . . .), ibid., pp. 21–26: see also an interesting study on

early memoir material, N. F. Sementsova, *Stanovlenie sovetskoi voennoi memuaristiki*, Moscow University, 1981, 131 pp. (2, 425 copies). For early publications also G. D. Alekseyeva, *Oktyabr'skaya revolyutsiya i istoricheskaya nauka v Rossii (1917–1923 gg.)*, Moscow, 'Nauka', 1968, and not forgetting Istpart, established September 1920: useful bibliographical essay by M. S. Volin in *Velikii Oktyabr'. Istoriya, Istoriografiya, Istochnikovedenie*, Moscow, 'Nauka', 1978, pp. 189–218.

11 See *Nachal'nyi etap*, Ch. 1, pp. 38–81.

12 For a relatively recent, useful narrative and analysis see S. M. Klyatskin, *Na zashchite Oktyabr.* Organizatsiya regulyarnoi armii ... 1917–1920. Moscow, 'Nauka', 1965, here Ch. 1, pp. 45–140; compare with R. I. Berzin, 'Etapy v stroitel'stve Krasnoi Armii (orig. 1920) republished *Etapy bol'shovo puti*, op. cit., pp. 100–135.

13 For details see Colonel I. Rostunov, 'U istokov sovetskoi voennoi istoriografii' *VIZh*, 1967, No. 8, pp. 85–86 (also diagram, organisation and manning VIK 1920–21): Professor Polikarpov corrects one or two points in Colonel Rostunov's article.

14 Rostunov, loc. cit., pp. 86–87: Polikarpov, *Nachal'nyi etap*, p. 84 on *Order No. 688*, 13 August, 1918, signed by E. M. Sklyanskii and V. A. Antonov-Ovseenko: change in designation, *Order No. 355*, 10 December, 1918, RVSR.

15 Rostunov, loc. cit., p. 87.

16 A. A. Svechin (1878–1938), 1917 Major-General Imperial Army joined Red Army, March 1918: leading military historian/theoretician, historical works plus *Strategiya* (*Strategy*) published 1926 and 1927, his 'reactionary' views denounced 1930/31 (Komakad stenogram, 25 April, 1931) – 'Protiv reaktsionnykh teorii na voennonauchnom fronte...' (Gosvoenizdat, 1931), 103 pp. See Col. A. Ageyev, *VIZh*, 1978, No. 8, pp. 126–28: also *Nachal'nyi etap*, note 59 to pp. 28–29 on Svechin.

17 *Nachal'nyi etap*, pp. 84–85.

18 Ibid., p. 86, papers by I. I. Vatsetis, A. A. Neznamov, A. F. Stepanov.

19 Ibid., pp. 88–89, on Neznamov's work, pp. 94–97.

20 Details ibid., p. 90, plan for monographs p. 91, assignments to Commission members, pp. 92–94.

21 For a summary of these discussions and controversies, utilising the indispensable materials collected by Trotskii in his *Kak vooruzhalas' revolyutsiya*, see J. Erickson, 'Some Military and Political Aspects of the "Militia Army" Controversy, 1919–1920' in *Essays in Honour of E. H. Carr*, Macmillan 1974, pp. 204–28.

22 For details, *Nachal'nyi etap*, pp. 100–103: on the organisation and work of *Gosizdat*, see *Istoriya knigi v SSSR 1917–1921*, Tom 1. Moscow, 'Kniga', 1983, pp. 172–207.

23 *Nachal'nyi etap*, pp. 108–110.

24 Further to *Istpart*, see M. S. Volin, *Velikaya Oktyabr*, op. cit., esp. pp. 194–95 (citing V. V. Maksakov, *Arkhivnoe delo v pervye gody Sovetskoi vlasti*, 1959) on the loss and destruction of archives: the State Paper administration (*Glavbum*) was even pulping them for the paper alone. ... Also *Nachal'nyi etap*, on *Istpart* plans for a history of the civil war in its entirety, here pp. 212–13.

25 For a recent work on I. I. Vatsetis, see *Glavnokomanduyuschii vsemi vooruzhennymi silami Respubliki I. I. Vatsetis*, Sbornik dokumentov. Riga, 'Zinatne', 1978, 363 pp. (English summary, pp. 358–63): also V. Polikarpov, introducing a

posthumous set of observations by A. V. Golubev, 'Pervyi sovetskii Glavkom I. I. Vatsetis', *VIZh*, 1972, No. 2, pp. 72–83 (with note on publications by Vatsetis).

26 For details, *Nachal'nyi etap*, pp. 122–24.

27 Ibid., p. 154.

28 Ibid., under 'Problema istochnikov', on the organisation of archives, pp. 156–64, also pp. 170–72.

29 Ibid., text of protocol, 22 October 1922, p. 178.

30 The Red Guard, *Krasnaya Gvardiya*, is a subject in its own right, though Professor V. I. Startsev has subjected the Petrograd RG to exhaustive study in *Ocherki po istorii Petrogradskoi Krasnoi Gvardii i Rabochei Militsii*, Moscow–Leningrad, 'Nauka', 1965, cited in *Prolog*, p. 15 as an example of paucity of archival materials even now: see also V. I. Startsev, 'Ustavy Rabochei Krasnoi Gvardii Petrograda' in *Voprosy istoriografii i istochnikovedeniya istoriya SSSR*, Sbornik statei. Moscow-Lèningrad, AN SSSR, 1963, pp. 176–221.

31 *Grazhdanskaya voina* consists of three main chapters – on the Red Guard, on the old Imperial army, on the creation of the Red Army – followed by the material supplied by Spilnichenko, Pugachevskii, Kovtyukh. My own copy is showing its age but I find it an invaluable collection.

32 Ibid., pp. 3–4.

33 See especially *Prolog*, Ch. 2, 'Voina protiv kontrrevolyutsionnovo generaliteta', pp. 131–259: also *Nachal'nyi etap*, pp. 214–18 (also *Krasnyi Arkhiv*, 1925, Nos. 8–9, pp. 132–52 and pp. 156–70).

34 Polikarpov on Furmanov, *Nachal'nyi etap*, pp. 222–28 (also on Furmanov's investigations of 'White Guard émigré' literature).

35 For a general view of these programmes, see, for example *Akademiya imeni M. V. Frunze* (Ed. General A. I. Radzievskii), Moscow, Voenizdat, 1973 Edn., Ch. 2, 'V gody mirnovo sotsialisticheskovo stroitel'stva', pp. 51–69.

36 See *Nachal'nyi etap*, p. 243 (my italics).

37 The Western and Northern 'screens' were directed from Moscow and Petrograd respectively: on the Western 'screen', see V. N. Yegor'ev, 'Iz zhizni zapadnoi zavesy' in *Grazhdanskaya voina 1918–1921*, Tom 1, Moscow, 1928, pp. 231–45 (reprinted in *Etapy bol'shovo puti*, op. cit., pp. 136–50).

38 See *Prolog*, pp. 21–24 on Antonov-Ovseenko (1883–1939): he remained a supporter of Trotskii until 1928, for which he was replaced by Bubnov, was sent abroad on diplomatic duties, executed in 1939. The three-volume work, *Zapiski o grazhdanskoi voine*, was published between 1924 and 1932.

39 N. V. Krylenko's memoir-manuscript 'Smert' staroi armii' was finally published in *VIZh*, 1964, Nos. 11–12: for other archival material, see E. N. Gorodetskii and S. M. Klyatskin, 'Iz istorii voennovo stroitel'stva sovetskoi respubliki...', *Istoricheskii Arkhiv*, 1962, No. 1, pp. 83–93: also E. N. Gorodetskii, *Rozhdenie sovetskovo gosudarstva 1917–1918 gg.*, Moscow, 'Nauka', 1965, pp. 399–412 on this early stage, early materials (Potopov, Krylenko, Podvoiskii): General N. M. Potapov's material has also been disinterred from the archives (see *VIZh*, 1968, No. 1). (I utilised much of this material – documentary, archival, memoir – in 'The Origins of the Red Army', *Revolutionary Russia*, Ed. R. Pipes, Harvard UP, 1968, pp. 224–56, not forgetting White records).

40 See I. Sherman, 'Pervye issledovaniya po istorii grazhdanskoi voiny', *VIZh*,

1964, No. 2, p. 99. Professor Polikarpov frequently takes issue with Professor Sherman, particularly the latter's monograph, *Sovetskaya istoriografiya grazhdanskoi voiny v SSSR (1920–1931)*, Kharkov, 1964. There are useful bibliographical references in *Ocherki po istografii sovetskovo obshchestva*, Moscow, 'Mysl', 1965, pp. 137–219.

41 I. L. Sherman, *VIZh*, 1964, loc. cit., p. 101. This could not fail to displease Professor Polikarpov (see *Nachal'nyi etap*, pp. 258–74 on Kakurin): see also the detailed essay by Professor A. Nenarokov, 'Istorik grazhdanskoi voiny' (on Kakurin), *VIZh*, 1965, No. 11, pp. 42–49, which also disputes Sherman's point.

42 A regular officer in the Imperial Army, Kakurin joined the Red Army in 1920, becoming closely associated with Tukhachevskii (in the Soviet–Polish war and the Tambov insurgency): for the Tukhachevskii-Kakurin connection and further to Kakurin's writings, see A. Nenarokov, *VIZh*, 1965, loc. cit., pp. 43–44.

43 See I. L. Sherman, *VIZh*, 1964, loc. cit., p. 102 (in all, 270 titles were devoted to the Soviet–Polish War): Tukhachevskii, Shaposhnikov, Klyuev, Putna, Yegorov, Gai, Mezheninov, published personal/command narratives, with N. E. Kakurin and V. A. Melikov producing their magnum opus, *Voina s belopolyakimi*, Moscow, 1925, (V. Polikarpov, *Nachal'nyi etap*, p. 269 points out that much material, 'published for the first time' in Vol. 3, *Direktivy Glavnovo komandovaniya Krasnoi Armii*, 1974, was actually published in Kakurin-Melikov).

44 For details, *Nachal'nyi etap*, pp. 290–98.

45 I. L. Sherman, *VIZh*, 1964, loc. cit., p. 195, reference Voroshilov's study 'Stalin i Krasnaya Armiya'.

46 See the famous (or infamous) publication, 'Comrade Stalin's Answer to a Letter from Comrade Razin', in *Bol'shevik*, 1947, No. 3, dismissing the idea that Lenin left any 'heritage', guiding theses on military questions . . .

47 See *Kommunisticheskaya Akademiya*. Sektsiya po izucheniyu problem voin. Zapiski. Tom pervyi. Izd. Komakad. 1930, here p. 217, Minutes of Commission on the History of the Civil War – plan of the proposed eight volumes. (Also *Istoriya Grazhdanskoi voiny. Plan . . ., utverzhdennyi glavnoi redaktsii*, Moscow, 1932, 127 pp.)

48 See *Komakad* papers, *Zapiski*, Tom pervyi (1930), loc cit., Tukhachevskii (pp. 6–32), Bubnov (pp. 3–5), Belitskii (pp. 34–36), Gorev (pp. 37–61, with discussion): see also Colonel I. Korotkov, 'K istorii stanovleniya sovetskoi voennoi nauki', in *Vestnik voennoi istorii*, 1971, No. 2, pp. 54–56, also Korotkov, *Istoriya sovetskoi voennoi mysli. Kratkii ocherk 1917–iyun 1941*. Moscow, 'Nauka', 1980, pp. 86–89 (on both Svechin and Gorev).

Zarozhdenie i razvitie sovetskoi voennoi istoriografii 1917–1941. (Ed. P. A. Zhilin), Moscow 'Nauka', 1985 (2,100 copies).
M. M. Kir'yan, *Problemy voennoi teorii v sovetskikh nauchnospravochnykh izdaniyakh*. Moscow 'Nauka', 1985 (1,650 copies).

Civilization and 'Frightfulness': Air Control in the Middle East Between the Wars

Charles Townshend

At the end of the great war between Western civilization and German barbarism, Britain found its global responsibilities vastly enlarged. The extension of its burdens was most noticeable in the increasingly vital strategic zone between north-east Africa and north-west India. India, liberally showered with good intentions through Morley-Minto and Montagu-Chelmsford reforms, remained disappointingly slow-footed on the road to political maturity. Later Viceroys were to fear that Indianization had done so little to bring Indian public life up to British standards that Imperial tutelage might have to continue indefinitely.[1] Likewise the Arabs, who had been promised freedom as their reward for joining the struggle against the Turkish oppressor, proved on closer inspection to be sorely in need of firm guidance. Instinctual obedience to government was absent in Arab lands like Mesopotamia. Open defiance was common. The civilizing mission, if it rested on universal principles, must impact on friends as well as foes.[2]

In the circumstances the establishment of straightforward colonial authority over the former Ottoman dominions was out of the question. This not only for political, but still more for financial reasons. The dramatic enlargement of British power coincided with equally dramatic pecuniary embarrassment. The control of such extensive lands by traditional military means was an unattractive, if not unthinkable prospect. Already, in the Sudan and on the North-West Frontier of India, the Empire had all but limitless commitments to 'pacification'. In the Sudan, conquered in the last years of the nineteenth century, the process of establishing control was still at an elementary stage. On the North-West Frontier, whose inhabitants were the most recalcitrant of all the Empire's ungrateful subjects, the no-man's-land between India and Afghanistan was in a state of perpetual war, and British policy perpetually veered from the 'forward' urge to exert complete control (on the model of the 'Sandemanization' of Baluchistan) back to the instinct of disengagement from an untenable situation. The former would be appallingly costly; the latter seemed humiliating and dishonourable, and perhaps strategically dangerous.[3]

The idea of entering into new commitments on a similar or even greater scale would have met political opposition. But of course the extension of imperial power occurred through reflex actions rather than opposable decisions. Syria and Mesopotamia became Occupied Enemy Territory, and a military administration (OETA) had to be created. A political policy, the Balfour Declaration, was adopted in London, but OETA was given no instructions to implement it. The failure of OETA to cope with the fierce Arab reaction to the threatened Jewish 'national home' led to its supersession by a civil High Commissioner in 1920, long before the legal basis of British rule was established. Only in 1923 was a novel framework of authority set up when Britain 'accepted' from the League of Nations a mandate to implement the Balfour Declaration in Palestine (an initially vague segment of southern Syria), and to take both Palestine and Mesopotamia (Iraq) forward to self-government.

The bloody riots in Palestine in 1920 and 1921, the full-blown insurrection in Mesopotomia in 1920, and the endemic *jihad* of fundamentalist groups such as the Ikhwan of the Nejd, were alarming indications of the nature of these new commitments. But, by the luck of the righteous, the war that had given Britain these problems also brought it the means of coping with them. The development of the military aircraft created a weapon with the near-miraculous property of lengthening the arm of government whilst shortening its purse. Air power offered the possibility of controlling vast inhospitable territories at a fraction of the cost of traditional military forces. And, although the substitution of air for land forces had not yet been proved to work, it was the perfect vehicle for the apostles of air power. The use of aircraft for internal control would rest, as military aviation in the European war had not, exclusively on their central contention that the impact of air action was moral rather than physical. More fundamental still, it would depend on (and validate) the existence of an independent air service.

Given the largely untried capacity of their weapons, the exponents of air power were astonishingly confident that they would succeed in establishing and maintaining internal security. This confidence stemmed from the simple logic of their ideas, expressed in the stark slogans favoured by Sir Hugh Trenchard. That the aeroplane was a weapon of attack, and not a defence against the aeroplane; that the bomber would always get through; that bombing could destroy the enemy's will to fight and that in a bombing duel the enemy would 'squeal before we did', were themes sounded as early as 1916.[4] The subsequent elaboration of these basic conceptions was minimal, usually little more than rephrasing. At the heart of the air idea was the conviction that the moral effect of bombing would be out of all proportion to its physical effect. This doctrine was perfectly adapted to internal security aims, where the principle of 'minimum force' was politically vital.

Belief in the unique psychological properties of air action also reinforced Trenchard's governing slogan, 'the air is one and indivisible'. Those who had penetrated the mystery of air power were a new breed of warriors, airmen, not merely flyers or (in the soldiers' derogatory term) 'chauffeurs'.[5] Only they could direct air forces and use air action to its full effect. The struggle to preserve a separate air service was powerfully, perhaps decisively, assisted by the discovery of a sphere of action in which the air force could secure primacy. All schemes of air control or air policing were to hinge on the assertion that the special logic of air power must determine the nature and sequence of all operations, and that it must be freed from the influence of traditional military ideas.

But how effective could air control be? Could it really replace traditional military methods? At its simplest, the substitution claim was that the air force could do the army's old job at much smaller cost. Here lay its primary appeal to the Imperial Government. But because the two arms were so different they could not do exactly the same thing. In practice the substitution claim was modified according to the territory involved. In some areas, the RAF claimed that it could actually do better than the army; in others it admitted that air action alone was inadequate and that air forces must act in cooperation with land forces. (This admission tended to be muted: in the case of Palestine, for instance, it was entirely lost on the outside world.) The spectrum was in part geophysical – wide open spaces, especially deserts, were more suited to air control, mountain or forest land less so. In part it was socio-economic – air action might be effective against primitive peoples, but might be too destructive for urbanized societies. (Yet the original contention about the moral impact of air attack was premised upon the vulnerable infrastructure of a modern society.)[6]

There was some inconsistency here. An early theorist of air control later conceded that in bidding for control of West and East Africa 'we overcalled our hand'.[7] But the implication seems to be that air control – defined as 'control without occupation' – was suited only to territories which were (a) administered rather than colonized, (b) markedly underdeveloped, (c) so marginal to British public perceptions that exemplary violence was politically tolerable. The RAF certainly did not admit this at the time.

In effect the potential application of air control was confined to the Sudan, Arabia and the North-West Frontier. But, since these provided the Empire's biggest problems, the significance of the idea was still considerable. The potential of aircraft for the maintenance of internal security had been grasped by military officers in various parts of the Empire during the war, but in the climate of postwar retrenchment the army quickly abandoned such thoughts. The first, and as the RAF saw it definitive, triumph of air control was the eviction of the 'Mad Mullah' from Somaliland in the winter of 1919–20. But the army accused the RAF of grossly exaggerating the psychological impact of air attack on the dervishes, and some officers even contended that the air operations had been prejudicial to the campaign as a whole.[8] Inevitable professional hostility towards a competing institution was heightened by the wild talk of the air publicists about the 'degradation of the infantrymen from being the first line of attack to the position of a mere "mopper up"'.[9] The air substitution idea would scarcely have taken practical shape without external intervention. As in so many other developments, the intervention was that of Winston Churchill.

As Secretary of State for War and Air, Churchill made the crucial connection between the infant air service and the vast desert expanses of the middle east. If Britain was to control these expanses it could not be by traditional means. In mid-February 1920 he asked the Chief of the Air Staff, Trenchard, whether he was prepared to 'take on' Mesopotamia, which the General Staff professed themselves unable to garrison.[10] When Trenchard, laid out by influenza, was slow to respond, Churchill pushed on alone. Springing fully armed from his head came a scheme for controlling the country with

> a series of defended areas in which air bases could be securely established. In these air bases, strong aerial forces could be maintained in safety and efficiency. An ample system of landing grounds judiciously selected would enable these air forces to operate in every part of the protectorate [*sic*] and to enforce control, now here, now there, without the need of maintaining long lines of communication eating up troops and money.[11]

Even at this early stage, Churchill's imagination conjured up the barracks to be built for the nucleus of officers and mechanics, the defence of the airfields by Moir pillboxes, the construction of special aircraft for purposes such as the movement of small military forces, and the development of specialised airborne weapons.

The Air Staff soon responded with the required assurances. It followed up Churchill's line in pointing out that air forces were especially suited to desert lands which had in the past undermined the health and efficiency of European troops. It claimed that 'the "long arm" of the new weapon renders it ubiquitous', or somewhat less rhetorically that 'the speed and range of aircraft makes it practicable to keep a whole country under more or less constant surveillance'. Insurrection could be nipped in the bud by prompt action, and patrolling and leaflet-dropping might be expected to prevent 'the seeds of unrest from being sown'. 'It must be remembered that from the ground every inhabitant of a village is under the impression that the occupant of an aeroplane is acutally looking at *him*.' Should this perceptual quirk not suffice, unrest could be countered by action mounted rapidly and maintained indefinitely.

> The Air Staff are convinced that strong and continuous action of this nature must in time inevitably compel the submission of the most recalcitrant tribes without the use of punitive measures by ground troops . . .
> With certain stubborn races time is essential to prove to them the futility of resistance to aerial attack by a people who possess no aircraft, but it is held that the dislocation of living conditions and the material destruction caused by heavy and persistent aerial action must infallibly achieve the desired result.[11]

The ambivalence underlying the surface confidence of the last sentence was to mar the theory throughout its life.

The translation of air control from an article of faith into a practical programme was to be a more erratic process than the airmen's early assurances suggested. It was also, along the way, to raise questions not merely of operating techniques or of service status, but, more seriously, of the nature of British government, and indeed of 'civilization'.

But the first problems were technical ones. The fact of being airborne obviously meant that aircraft could not utilize familiar forms of threat and force. The novel forms they employed were regarded by many critics with suspicion or dislike. Air action had an impersonal quality, and its opponents were inclined to move quickly from 'impersonal' to 'indiscriminate' and 'inhuman'. The RAF was to find it impossible to convince 'that curious alliance of sentimentalists and die-hards who chose to make out that air control consisted solely of "indiscriminate bombing"'[13] that it could employ very subtle gradations of force. In particular its contention that far from being impersonal, air power permitted a much more intimate contact between administrators and people, by dramatically enlarging the mobility of Political Officers, made no impression on its opponents.[14] Its argument that the speed with which aircraft could arrive at an incipient disturbance, coupled with their moral effect, would usually obviate the need for severe destructive force was rudely thrust aside. The War Office went straight to the core of the matter by saying that there would have to be times when weapons would be used, and 'the only weapons which can be used by the Air Force are bombs and machine guns'. If punitive measures had to be taken, 'the only means at the disposal of the Air Force . . . are the bombing of the women and children in the villages'. The Secretary of State for War (Churchill's successor Worthington-Evans) suggested icily that

> If the Arab population realize that the peaceful control of Mesopotamia depends on our intention of bombing women and children, I am very doubtful if we shall gain that acquiescence of the fathers and husbands of Mesopotamia as a whole to which the Secretary of State for the Colonies [Churchill] looks forward.[15]

The RAF had ways of countering such attacks. It could point out that military punitive columns shelled villages, and that the total of human misery caused by a column was much greater than would be caused by air bombing. Columns were not only expensive, but they themselves suffered major casualties, and often encouraged the tribesmen by offering a target perfectly suited to their fighting methods. The aircraft, by contrast, was invulnerable – in this lay a large part of its capacity to demoralize. This invulnerability was perhaps exaggerated. Aircraft, especially the slower-flying sort most useful for policing, could be brought down by small arms fire, and in some areas captured pilots were tortured and killed. The credibility of Sir John Slessor's assertion that overall 'the casualties on either side were negligible' depends on one's point of reference. No doubt the totals were small by contrast with those of conventional war, but there is equally no doubt that the RAF doctored its reports to make them look much smaller than they were.[16]

What the RAF found most difficult was to demonstrate that not only could it hit without suffering retaliation, but that it could hit without causing excessive damage. Its initial hope, again pioneered by Churchill, was that chemistry would provide the answer. Churchill's first sketch of air control involved the use of gas bombs 'which are not destructive of human life but which inflict various degrees of minor annoyance', at least in preliminary operations against 'turbulent tribes'.[17] But this beneficent vision foundered on technical difficulties. The gas shells which were available for conversion to air bombs were, the Air Staff found, 'non-lethal, but were not innocuous. They may have an injurious effect on the eyes, and possibly cause death'.[18] The Colonial Office functionaries, baffled by a non-lethal agent which could cause death, decided that the League of Nations would forbid its Mandatory to use such weapons. Britain was not a free agent in the middle east, and would have to defer to the universal prejudice against all forms of gas. In vain did the Air Ministry stress that lethal concentrations were most unlikely to be reached under air bombardment (because – though this point was not stressed – of its low accuracy). In vain did they point out that the army had used SK gas shells in quantity against the Mesopotamian rebels in 1920 with 'excellent moral effect'.

Denied its wonder weapon, the RAF returned to the counterpoint between 'dislocation' and 'destruction' outlined in its initial appreciation. Out of these twin threads it gradually wove a novel and subtle technique of persuasion, which it called 'air blockade'. By the 1930s this technique was to be so prominent in air doctrine that it was often mistakenly identified with the general concept of air control. It had, in isolation, a beautiful simplicity. Air action could impose an inverted blockade, keeping recalcitrant groups out of, rather than within, their settlements. The resulting disruption of economic and social life would eventually induce submission. In theory this could be done without any human casualties and with the minimum of material damage. It depended, obviously, on having sufficiently accurate information to locate precisely the villages from which the offenders came. But this would be the responsibility of the Political Officers.

The essence of air blockade was so simple that it scarcely admitted of refinement over the years. Herein lay its power as an interdepartmental weapon. The means by which the blockade was to be effected, however, were less beautifully simple. The earliest formulation of the process was made by Air Vice-Marshal Sir John Salmond, the rising star of the RAF. Salmond was sent on a mission to India in 1922 to spread the gospel of air control, and then took command in Iraq to pioneer its application. He reported back that

> It is a commonplace here that aircraft achieve their result by their effect on morale, and by the material damage they do, and by the interference they cause to the daily routine of life, and not through the infliction of casualties.

But in what, exactly, did the 'damage' and 'interference' consist? Salmond went on to note that air action

> can knock the roofs of huts about and prevent their repair, a considerable inconvenience in winter-time. It can seriously interfere with ploughing or harvesting – a vital matter; or burn up the stores of fuel laboriously piled up and garnered for the winter; by attack on livestock, which is the main form of capital and source of wealth to the less settled tribes, it can impose in effect a considerable fine, or seriously interfere with the actual food source of the tribe – and in the end the tribesman finds it is much the best to obey the Government.[19]

This paean to the advancement of civilization was greeted as a literary masterpiece by the Air Staff, especially its tongue-tied Chief.[20] 'If only India would agree!' Trenchard wistfully noted in the margin. The success of air control in Iraq was incontrovertible: it easily fulfilled Churchill's promise to Lloyd George to 'save millions'.[21] But Iraq was remote, turbulent, and threatened by Turkish invasion. Would the RAF's rough-and-ready methods be usable anywhere else?

Even Trenchard jibbed at Salmond's reference to 'attacks on livestock'. Yet the destruction of animals, however repugnant to English opinion, was unavoidable. Often they offered the only viable targets for aircraft, and the only way of putting pressure on their elusive owners. The spectacular success of Patrol S.9 in the Sudan, for instance, was measured by the unheard-of fact that 'the Nuer men in many cases left their cattle to their fate and herds were found subsequently abandoned'. The patrol's report was peppered with accounts of the slaughter and capture of cattle.[22] Salmond's essay, for all its easy-going talk of 'knocking huts about' and 'inconvenience', in fact hinted at great severity of action – in the last analysis of starving people into submission. This was the less acceptable face of blockade.

Even so, it was not the full extent of severity. Salmond still placed 'effect on morale' first in his list of functions. At the outset the RAF assumed that aircraft by their very nature had this effect. Soldiers disputed this, saying that in France troops had learnt how to shelter from air attack, and that primitive tribesmen would have even less difficulty in doing this, since their fighting formations were loose and their lands were rich in natural cover. Arguing the point with Rawlinson (then C-in-C India) in 1920, Trenchard countered by simply declaring that he had

> no fear that the Arabs will get accustomed to bombing. The troops in France did not get accustomed to it – in fact they felt it more and

the moral effect increased as the war went on. This is the case in all countries where bombing has taken place.[23]

Here was a straightforward opposition of beliefs. Trenchard's assertion was fundamental to his conception of air power, as was his proviso – 'it means going on and on with [air action] for it to have its full effect' – which posited the primacy of air over military logic.

Still, it was obvious to everyone thinking about air blockade that the moral ascendancy of aircraft would have to be cemented at the outset by exemplary violence – in fact, terror. Could this be done without loss of life? Trenchard declared that 'when punishment is intended, the punishment must be severe, continuous, and even prolonged'. His biographer holds that 'such severity was not to be misconstrued as "frightfulness"'.[24] He points out that Trenchard insisted that no settlement should be bombed until its inhabitants had received at least twenty-four hours' warning. On paper at least the RAF's minatory repertoire was much more extensive, and the final twenty-four-hour warning was only used after a sequence of other threats. Leafleting, loudspeaker warnings, and 'demonstration flights' were often all that was necessary to bring about a submission.[25] But, for these warnings to be heeded, there had to be a real fear of what air attack would entail. This fear could not be established by dropping leaflets.

In fact the RAF candidly accepted – at least internally – that the key to the moral ascendancy of aircraft would be 'frightfulness'. Towards the end of 1922, the Deputy Director of Operations prepared for the Air Staff a memorandum on 'Forms of frightfulness' which took as its point of departure Salmond's views on the undermining of morale by 'making life a burden': 'In other words,' he noted, 'we rely on "frightfulness" in a more or less severe form.' After discussion with Salmond it had been agreed that 'the efficacy of such a policy would be much increased if we were in a position to vary our methods so that the form of attack should have the impressiveness of novelty for as long a period as possible' (a remarkable, if unintentional, concession to the arguments of soldiers like Rawlinson).[26] A list of methods was thus drawn up.

The list ran from delayed-action bombs, essential if villagers were to be kept out of their settlements by night, since the RAF had no night bombing capacity, through phosphorus bombs ('No one who saw the "umbrella" of some 200 yards in diameter and rain of burning phosphorus pellets caused by one of these bombs at Hendon in 1921 would deny that this is a most alarming bomb, which should produce great moral results if sparingly used'); crows' feet, by which 'great numbers of cattle would be lamed and great numbers of people incommoded' (and discouraged from lying down on the approach of aircraft); aerial darts with whistling holes to magnify their psychological effect; 'throwdowns', or fireworks, which should 'keep the tribesmen on the jump and give them the impression that our bombing capacity is very large'; to crude oil, which could poison water supplies. Some of the methods, such as 'liquid fire', the ancestor of napalm, were abandoned as impracticable in the present state of technology. In the long run, high explosive bombs (albeit consistently defective) were found more useful than most of these fancy ideas. But the overall intention was clear. There was no sign of discomfort at the adoption of an approach to warfare which had so recently caused the Germans to be branded as barbarians.

In theory, and in the pictures sketched by the RAF for political and public consumption, the balance between punitive and demonstrative action lay markedly on the side of the latter. A reassuring note on 'Methods of air action against underdeveloped peoples' prepared for Arthur Henderson in 1930 re-emphasized Salmond's early contention that the short, sharp shock administered by air action was the most humane form of pacification. (Although, as we have seen, the RAF also held that air pacification would often be a lengthy process: the two arguments were not entirely harmonized.) An 'exaggerated idea of the slaughter and suffering involved by bombing leads to a very natural reluctance to authorize its use, and to all sorts of restrictions', the note gently chided. As a result

> the Air Force – on which we rely for the control of so much of the vast areas of undeveloped territory which we administer in the middle east – is denied the use of its primary weapon, or at least the swiftness of decision and promptitude of action which is so essential to the effective operation of air power is seriously prejudiced.[27]

Yet the force needed, as the airmen constantly reiterated, was quite small. In the operations against Feisal ed Dawish, 'only a few light bombs were dropped, yet it is reported that the countryside of Koweit was covered with panic-stricken persons out of control and in terror . . .' The curbing of the threat posed by the ferocious Ikhwan of the Nejd was seen by the RAF as proof that air action could force even the hardiest tribes to submit. Trenchard minuted savagely on one file of reports dealing with Ikhwan raids in 1928 that if the RAF were only

> allowed to use air power as it is intended to be used, by hitting back and going to Artawiyah and Ryadh etc. by air as soon as our own tribes were raided . . . all the nonsense talked in this copious correspondence would be totally unnecessary.[28]

They were dealing not with a European war but with a few thousand 'scallywags'.

In 1936 the accumulated rhetoric of air blockade was incorporated into a ten-page memorandum of guidance. The theory was 'that the tribes in the inaccessible parts of the Empire depend almost entirely on their villages and the amenities which are directly connected with them'; so that if 'a means can be found to prevent them from occupying their homes . . . they have no option but to submit'. If they took refuge in caves – which 'become foul and infested with parasites as time proceeds' – they would 'pass a most uncomfortable existence'. Lack of sleep, caused by continual explosions, was 'a potent factor in wearing down morale'. It might be necessary to continue operations for several months before a 'particularly stiff-necked' tribe gave in, but this required 'no particular effort on the part of the air forces'. Bombing would be on a small scale; 'one feature of our policy is very definitely the avoidance of casualties' so as to avoid generating resentment. (Yet another tacit concession to opponents of bombing.) In sum, air control was 'far from inhumane at least in conception'.[29]

Indeed, so velvet-gloved were the measures recommended that the reader might well wonder how they could have the overwhelming effects projected. The same question might arise from the official conclusions drawn up after the operations against the Mohmands on the North-West Frontier in 1935. Minimum force was to be used; the destruction even of property and crops was 'definitely not desired'; night flying was to be used instead of the indiscriminate delayed-action bombs; 'incendiary bombs and such weapons as rely for their effect entirely upon destruction' should only be used 'if it becomes necessary to superimpose upon the blockade itself definite punitive measures' – the implication being that this was unlikely.[30]

Operational realities may have been rather different. Even in Iraq, which the RAF saw as the unequivocal vindication of air control, doubts remained about its effectiveness. The RAF's claim to have reduced expenditure from 10 to 1.5 million between 1920 and 1930 was disputed on several grounds; but perhaps more importantly its claims to have achieved effective control (or, as critics put it, to give value for money) was also disputed. Aircraft were impotent in heavily-wooded Kurdistan, and there were too many indiscriminate punitive attacks.[31] Aden, transferred to RAF control in 1927, was seen by Trenchard as a natural sphere for air policing because it was 'an awful country, an impossible country' for European troops. Warlike operations against a Yemeni invasion were brilliantly successful: conducted by a single squadron at a cost of £8,000 instead of the estimated 6–10 million for conventional military methods. But the subsequent maintenance of control did not really resemble policing.

The AOC remarked in 1939 that numerous murders and 'road incidents' took place 'on our doorstep' – at least in the eastern part of the protectorate – without any interference or threat of bombing. Ingrams, the Resident in the western protectorate, was 'expecting too much even in normal times from air control'.[32]

When action was taken in Aden it was evidently often punitive. Ingrams, organizer of the legendary (if fragile) 'Ingrams' Peace' in the Hadhramaut, thought it 'little enough to have a few days' air operations in these outlying areas when one can be fairly confident that . . . lasting peace and content follows after them'. When in 1936 the Air Ministry found it necessary to remind the AOC Aden, Air Commodore McClaughry, that air blockade should be applied as strictly in Aden as elsewhere, and pointed out the 'untoward political results' of using incendiary bombs, it was told that in McClaughry's view air blockade was a 'very misleading term'.[33] 'Even though it may sound well in theory,' he later added, 'it is not a true definition of any air operation which has yet taken place so far as I am aware.'[34] The Quteibi operations, for instance, publicised by the RAF as a textbook example of air blockade, had employed punitive destruction. The sort of long-drawn-out campaign envisaged in the doctrine could be just as damaging – by preventing the sowing of crops or tending of flocks – as more overtly destructive action, and was certainly a serious strain on the forces involved. After the Quteibi campaign, McClaughry said, there was 'a decided reluctance on the part of the RAF to become involved in any further operations'.

McClaughry's correspondent at the Air Ministry admitted that the memorandum on air blockade had resulted from 'the extremely humanitarian phase through which we passed some months ago' because of 'one of those periodical attacks by India on the alleged inhumanity of the air method of control'. He regretted that the Air Ministry had not yet 'receded' from this phase, but conveyed the comforting news that Air Vice-Marshal Peirse, smarting from his recent experience of rebellion in Palestine, had now become DCAS and would 'support you fully if you and the Resident feel, during any operation, that a severe lesson is needed'.[35] Thus encouraged, the local commander went on to declare, three months later, that he was 'less impressed than ever' by the air blockade method. The Aden tribesman 'requires definite proof that we can hit him hard'.[36]

It seems obvious that the gentle vision of air blockade was a self-deception, if not a conscious fraud. Airmen really saw no reason why they should not 'hit hard': that was the essence of air power. Their outlook remained unchanged by the tremendous increase in the destructive capacity and accuracy of airborne weapons during the Second World War. Between 23 February and 4 March, 1948 the Bal

Harith tribe, a 'semi-nomadic people to whom bombing and rocket attacks on the scale of this operation are quite new', were subjected to 52 sorties by Lincoln bombers and Tempest fighter-bombers. Analysing the effect of the 87.4 tons of bombs and rockets and the 3,420 rounds of 20mm cannon ammunition delivered, the RAF noted that

> Nomadic tribesmen regard the camel as their most prized possession, as it provides them with virtually all the necessities of their frugal existence. The 'ilb tree provides fodder for the camel and shade for the man. Although great destruction was caused to the Bal Harith village, it is considered that an even greater factor in influencing the Bal Harith to capitulate was the destruction of their camels and 'ilb trees.[37]

Airmen were unable to understand why such clinical professionalism was regarded with abhorrence by so many observers, civilian and military alike. This did not stem, to be sure, from any sympathy for these frugal peoples' attempted rejection of the blessings of government. But there was an idea that air attack was in some sense wrong, in a way that traditional forms of land and sea attack were not. Against this irrational instinct the RAF battled persistently, and with little reward.

In this battle the RAF's primary mode of defence, in harmony with its fundamental principles, was offence. Alongside its extensive claims about the positive effects of air action went a withering denunciation of the failings of traditional methods. Time and again the RAF pressed the point that military occupation was not only expensive, but futile and even, in some cases, counter-productive. On the North-West Frontier, for instance, great garrisons like Razmak, 'very strong and theoretically mobile forces' occupying 'enormously expensive cantonments', did not 'dominate' Waziristan as the army claimed, but were imprisoned by it. Punitive columns aggravated conflicts and led to bloody resolution, as when the Darfur rebellion of 1916 was allowed so much time to grow that it could only be crushed by a full-scale battle. 'There were about 400 dead or dying within 500 yards of our zariba, many of them blown almost to bits by dum-dum bullets.'[38] This, in the airmen's view, was real inhumanity.

Trenchard pressed the offensive right through to his 'swan-song' as CAS, his final memorandum urging much wider substitution of air control for ground forces, and his most eloquent public statement of his ideas, his maiden speech in the House of Lords in April 1930. Here he put the air psychology quite picturesquely:

> The natives of a lot of these tribes love fighting for fighting's sake, and for the sake of glory and loot. They have no objection to being killed, some of them, if they can kill you and take your rifle, and, it may be, some domestic article like your boots, but they do not like fighting if they may only lose their boots and have no chance of getting yours.[39]

The implication that aircraft could remove people's boots (in fact most of the tribesmen he was referring to went barefoot) without harming a hair of their heads was not questioned by his peers, but it was questionable. So was his line that in seeking substitution the air force was merely offering to relieve the other services, especially the army, of burdensome, 'humdrum' chores. The army chose to interpret substitution not as an altruistic gesture but as a direct threat to its own status and funds. The RAF saw this reaction, publicly, as a regrettable misunderstanding; privately, as part of a ruthless campaign against the independent air service.[40]

It was not exactly either of these. There were certainly misunderstandings, some of them so persistent as to have been surely wilful. But the army's case, at both technical and ethical levels, was better than the airmen could admit. The dogma, 'the air is one and indivisible', was a dangerous misconception, as became clear in the struggle for control of naval aviation, where Trenchard's blinkered vision took him to the length of declaring that aircraft carriers were useless. If it were possible to be more wrong than this, Trenchard almost managed it in his handling of ground-support aviation. The Navy eventually succeeded in regaining control of its aircraft, but the army was less fortunate. This was not for lack of trying. The army did not, as airmen suggested, underrate air power: it was conscious of the need for specialised aircraft, formations and weapons for close cooperation with ground forces.

This technique, which was to be the basis of German military ascendancy in the first years of the next war, remained the neglected victim of the RAF's drive to secure the primacy of air logic. Yet air control, a major vehicle for this drive, always required ground forces. Substitution did not mean the removal of all troops, but the replacement of British infantry by cheaper local levies or gendarmerie. These were stiffened by armoured car squadrons. Since the army refused to supply these in Mesopotamia, the RAF raised its own, and developed its own vehicles. It saw the army's obstructiveness, not altogether unjustly, as the result of jealousy. Less justly, it treated the military counter-argument, that the ground was also 'one and indivisible', with derision. Yet its logic was as sound – or unsound – as the airmen's own.

Military criticism of air control started from the contention that it was less effective than action combining ground forces with air support, or indeed that it was ineffective. Initially it was simply dismissed as absurd. Henry Wilson's famous characterization of Churchill's scheme as a 'fantastic salad of hot air, aeroplanes, and Arabs' was followed by the less irresponsible but more desperate incomprehension of the GOC-in-C Western Command, India: 'I don't know what these Air people are at. Their schemes really sound so mad that either those responsible are mad, or else the rest of us are entirely wrong . . .'[41] A similar view was taken not only by arch-traditionalists like the recipient of this letter (General Montgomery-Massingberd), but also by a modernizer such as J. F. C. Fuller, who thought it self-evident that as people lived on the earth 'they must be controlled on the earth'. 'Pacification', he said, was different from the 'obliteration' caused by air action.[42] To this rather disingenuous dualism was added a belief that the 'inhumanity' of air power would rebound on the heads of its users.

The resulting compound was applied by Lord Plumer in the House of Lords debate initiated by Trenchard. Plumer declared unequivocally that 'the character and nature of the Air Force does not render them the most suitable force' to implement 'measures for public security and the maintenance of order and the prevention or repression of disorder'. The reason was that as 'essentially an offensive force' the RAF 'cannot possibly maintain [the] daily contact and association' that was the basis of imperial administration. Here Plumer deployed the army's favourite idea, that the distant parts of the Empire

> have been and are being consolidated and pacified by a constant daily association and contact with the officers and men of our forces. The inhabitants of those countries have taken our officers and men, quite rightly, as samples of British citizens, and, in consequence of their constant association with them, they have realised that British rule and British administration stands for integrity, justice and humanity.[43]

The appearance of aircraft, by contrast, was 'taken by the inhabitants as a threat'. It might produce a 'passive acquiescence in our authority', but could not inspire them with the 'higher and deeper feeling' that Plumer took to be the basis of 'true pacification'.

Not only did air power lack this positive quality, it had a negative quality. Plumer described bombing as a 'mischievous power' whose indiscriminate action would stir up 'feelings of bitter hatred and resentment' that would endure for many years – though he made no effort to answer the airmen's contention that punitive columns had just the same effect. His potent cocktail of pragmatic and ethical arguments was topped up by an experienced colonial administrator, Lord Lloyd, who confirmed that the policy of 'control from within' on the North-West Frontier since 1919 – manifested in the penetration of Waziristan by great military roads – had produced 'civilization and pacification'. Air substitution, Lloyd warned, threatened a return to the old indirect control. He was convinced that 'whatever air control can do, it can never civilize people nor pacify people'. As 'an impersonal and inhuman agency' capable only of intimidation and punishment, it would have 'a most damaging effect upon our repute all through the East'.[44]

The impact of this indictment was not weakened by the evident fallibility of Lloyd's judgement about the success of military control. Within weeks of his speech Waziristan had again erupted into *jihad*, and the imbroglio deepened as the decade went on. To the fury of the airmen, the use of air control, though supported by the Government of India's Tribal Control and Defence Committee in 1931, was reduced rather than expanded.[45] The air blockade method was rejected, or, if initially accepted, was instantly wrecked by the intrusion of ground forces: 'the troops marched about without ceasing, and the lashkars came and went . . .'[46]

The RAF's efforts to dispel the idea that air action was inhuman became increasingly Sisyphyean. Trenchard had pleaded with the Lords to recognize that all warfare was inherently brutal, and air action was no more brutal than any other form of military action. The AOC India suggested in 1931 'the tribesman has been compelled to accept aircraft as . . . Government's proper and powerful instrument for enforcing its just demands'. He maintained that

> The application of pressure directly on the life and property of the offending section or people . . . is a well accepted principle of civilized warfare. The tribe that has received a proper warning has only itself to blame for any casualties that may ensue from the bombing of a village. A fact now appreciated by all tribes that have had experience of bombing.[47]

(He added that the reduction in casualties to British forces meant that 'the dictates of humanity are being served with, in addition, a vast financial saving on the score of treatment and pensions alone'.) In the same vein as the Indian memorandum, the report on the two-month operation against the Quteibi tribe of Aden held that a 'sense of corporate responsibility' could be 'induced' by air action. The Quteibis had received some 28 tons of bombs and 40,000 bullets, and had at last made a 'good humoured submission'.[48] Lord Lloyd's idea that air attack could not get at the dervishes and magicians who were the centres of disturbance in the Sudan was countered by Slessor's pithy observation that 'no magic survives a good bombing'.[49]

The charm of these ideas, so irresistible in Iraq, had no power over the Government of India. The Commander-in-Chief told the Viceroy in 1935

> I loathe bombing and never agree to it without a guilty conscience. That, in order that 2,000 or 3,000 young ruffians should be discouraged from their activities, dozens of villages inhabited by many thousand women, children and old men, to say nothing of many who have refused to join the lashkars, should be bombed, and their inhabitants driven into the wildnerness, while the Air Force conduct a leisurely 'month or more' bombing . . . is to me a revolting method of making war, especially by a great power against tribesmen.[50]

This fierce outburst gives the measure of the gulf between the airmen and those who clung to a sense of propriety – albeit irrational or even hypocritical (the army had talked happily enough in 1919, before air control had been dreamed up, of using 'every modern convenience of war' against their infuriating Pathan antagonists).[51] Soldiers thought that, because they themselves viewed air attack as inhuman, tribesmen would take the same view. Airmen derided this sentimentalism. When the GOC-in-C Northern Command worried whether 'general reprisals with the bomb' would not generate 'collective hatred of the British race and all it stands for', and asked

> Is it fantastic to suggest that the psychology of the tribesman is not very dissimilar to that of the Britisher, and from that to deduce that their reactions will not be very dissimilar to those of the people of the British Isles during the war?[52]

the RAF's reply could scarcely be in doubt. 'It is of course fantastic to suggest that the psychology of the tribesmen, who spend half their lives shooting at each other, is similar to that of an English villager.'[53]

This gulf could not be quickly bridged. Progress required time to prevail. Not long after the Great War the airmen had foreseen the problem of reconciling the new arm with traditional restraints on war. War crimes proceedings against German bomber crews who had attacked London were dropped at the insistence of the Air Ministry. Such trials 'would be placing a noose round the necks of our airmen in future wars'.[54] Since the object of British air bombing during the war had avowedly been

> to bomb German towns . . . to weaken the morale of the civilian inhabitants (and thereby their 'will to win') by persistent bomb attacks which would both destroy life (civilian and otherwise) and if possible originate a conflagration which should reduce to ashes the whole town . . .[55]

the extension of the Hague Convention restrictions on naval bombardment to air bombing would destroy its whole essence.

The airmen were visionaries. They conjured up the infernos of Hamburg and Dresden while the technical means of delivering sufficient explosives were quite absent. The future, they were certain – until the advent of the ballistic missile – was theirs. The Air Staff's conclusion in 1921 was that

> it may be thought better, in view of the allegations of the 'barbarity' of air attacks, to preserve appearances by formulating milder rules and by still nominally confining bombardment to targets which are strictly military in character . . . to avoid emphasizing the truth that air warfare has made such restrictions obsolete and impossible. It may be some time until another war occurs and meanwhile the public may become educated as to the meaning of air power.[56]

The air control idea was a way of furthering such education without impinging too sharply on civilized sensibilities. In this it was only a partial success. The RAF assumed rightly that there would be less hostility to the use of air attack on the margins of the Empire than in, say, Ireland. But the persistent belief in a civilizing mission inherent in tribal pacification sorted ill with the visceral fear of air attack, and produced unexpectedly sustained resistance. Only total war could finally shoulder aside deep-rooted preconceptions of British honour, and curb the luxury of indulgence in 'fair play'.

Notes

1 Sir M. O'Dwyer, *India as I Knew It*, London 1925, ch. xxi. Linlithgow to Amery, 3 Sept., 1942. N. Mansergh and E. W. R. Lumby (eds.), *Constitutional Relations between Britain and India. The Transfer of Power 1942–7*. Vol. ii, London, 1971, no. 401.

2 Sir A. T. Wilson, *Loyalties: Mesopotamia, 1914–17*, and *Mesopotamia 1917–20: A Clash of Loyalties*. London 1931. P. Sluglett, *Britain and Iraq*, London, 1976, ch. 1.

3 Lecture, 'The Army in India', n.d. (?1930). PRO. WO. 106 5444.

4 Trenchard to Haig, Sept. 1916. H. A. Jones, *The War in the Air*, Oxford, 1923, Vol. ii, App. IX.

5 A. Boyle, *Trenchard, Man of Vision*, London, 1962, pp. 342–3, 345.

6 CID, ARP Sub-Cttee., 1st report, Oct. 1925.

7 Sir J. Slessor, *The Central Blue*, London, 1956, p. 72.

8 There is a good short account in D. Killingray, '"A Swift Agent of Government": Air Power in British Colonial Africa, 1916–1939', *Journal of African History*, Vol. 25, 1984, pp. 433–5.

9 *The Aeroplane*, 25 Feb., 1920; D. J. P. Waldie, 'Relations Between the Army and the Royal Air Force 1918–1939', Ph.D. thesis, University of London, 1980.

10 Memo. to CAS, 19 Feb., 1920. RAF Museum, Trenchard papers, MFC 76/1/36.

11 Sec. of State for War to CAS, 29 Feb., 1920. PRO. AIR 5 224. This was clearly a very personal proposal: the War Office later disclaimed all knowledge of the note.

12 Air Staff Memo. for Cabinet, 'On the Power of the Air Force and the application of this power to hold and police Mesopotamia', March, 1920. PRO. AIR 5 224.

13 Slessor, op. cit., p. 63.

14 Memo., 'The Use of Air Force in Iraq', 1923. PRO. AIR 5 338; Statement by Sir J. Salmond, 1924. AIR 5 476.

15 Memo., 'Policy and Finance in Mesopotamia', 17 Aug., 1921. PRO. CAB 24 127.

16 R. A. Beaumont, 'A New Lease on Empire: Air Policing, 1919–1939', *Aerospace Historian*, Summer 1979, p. 88.

17 Memo. for CAS, 19 Feb., 1920. Trenchard papers, MFC 76/1/36.

18 Air Council to Colonial Office, 15 Sept., 1921. PRO. CO 537 825. Notes on Air Ministry Conference, same day, AIR 5 476.

19 Statement by ACM Sir J. Salmond of his views upon the principles governing the use of Air Power in Iraq, 1924. AIR 5 476.

20 Boyle, op. cit., p. 509; Slessor, op. cit., p. 50.

21 M. Gilbert, *Winston S. Churchill*, Vol. iv, London, 1975, ch. 30.

22 Notes for CAS on CID paper 904.B., July 1929, Air Ministry, Slessor papers, 75/28/26.

23 Trenchard to Rawlinson, 18 Oct., 1920. Trenchard papers, MFC 76/1/136.

24 Boyle, op. cit., p. 390.

25 Air Staff (India), Memo. No. 1, April 1935. PRO. AIR 5 1323.

26 DDOI, Memo. for DCAS [Draft], 16 Dec., 1922, and Encl.2(a), 'Forms of Frightfulness'. PRO. AIR 5 264.

27 Slessor papers, AC 75/28/36.

28 Iraq: Operations, 1928, file V. AIR 5 460.

29 Notes on Air Blockade, and Questionnaire by No. 1 Indian Group RAF, 1936. AIR 23 708.

30 Ibid., and Air Ministry to AOC Aden, 17 Oct., 1936, loc. cit.

31 Nuri Said (Minister of Defence) to High Commissioner, Iraq, 27 Oct., 1928. Trenchard papers, MFC 76/1/36.

32 Note [draft] by AOC Aden, (?May) 1939. AIR 23 704.

33 Air Council to AOC Aden, 24 Oct., and replay, 11 Nov., 1936. AIR 23 708.

34 AOC Aden (McClaughry) to Air Ministry (Pirie), 12 Jan., 1937. AIR 23 708.

35 Pirie to McClaughry, 4 Feb., 1937. AIR 23 708.

36 McClaughry to Pirie, 12 May, 1937. AIR 23 708.

37 Aden: Operations against Bal Harith Tribe, 23, 24, 28, 29 Feb., 1–4 Mar., 1948. CO 537 3980.

38 Notes for CAS on Sir J. Maffey's CID paper 904.B, and AS Memo. 911.B. Slessor papers, AC 75/28/26.

39 HL Deb., 9 April, 1930, cols. 24–5.

40 It noted in 1921 that the 'real crux of the matter' was that regardless of the effectiveness of air policing, the General Staff 'cannot reconcile themselves to the prospect of this new service bursting the bonds of subordination to its older sisters.' Notes on Sec. of State of War's Memo., 24 August, 1921. AIR 5 476.

41 Lt. Gen. Braithwaite to Gen. Montgomery-Massingberd, 24 April., 1922. Waldie, op. cit., p. 174.

42 J. F. C. Fuller, 'Problems of Mechanical Warfare', *Army Quarterly*, Vol. III, 1922, p. 295.

43 H. L. Deb., 9 April., 1930, col. 37.

44 Ibid., col. 44.

45 GI, Foreign and Political Dept., to Sec. of State for India, 15 Oct., 1925; Narrative of Operations on NWF, Apr.–Sept., 1930, AIR 5 1324. India: Report of the Tribal Control and Defence Committee 1931, AIR 23 684.

46 Note for DCAS, 14 Oct., 1938. AIR 5 1323.

47 Comments of AOC RAF India on Report of Tribal Control and Defence Cttee., 10 June, 1931. AIR 23 685. Cf. 'Instructions regarding the Control of Operations, including the Employment of Air Forces, on the North-West Frontier of India', GI Army Dept., 7 April., 1932. AIR 5 1323.

48 Air Ministry Report, Feb., 1935. AIR 2 1385.

49 Note, 'Air Control in the Sudan', 1930. Slessor papers, AC 75/28/26.

50 FM Sir P. Chetwode to Viceroy, 20 Aug., 1935. (The note was 'withdrawn by C-in-C after strong protest by AOC'.) AIR 23 687.

51 Gen. Staff., India, Note on military policy towards the tribes on the NWF, 1919. AIR 5 1323.

52 Gen. Wigram to Chief Sec. NWFP, 26 Feb., 1936. AIR 23 687.
53 Air Staff note, loc. cit.
54 S.12847, AIR 5 192.
55 Rules as to Bombardment by Aircraft, loc. cit.
56 Ibid.

The 'Moscow Line' and international communist policy, 1933–47

E. J. Hobsbawm

The spectacular reversals in the official policies of the international communist movement, and especially that between the Sixth and Seventh Congresses of the Communist International, raise fundamental questions for any historian of that movement. They arise out of the complete centralisation of power in Moscow, together with the obligations of party discipline accepted by all communist parties. 'The line' was mandatory. It came from above, that is to say, by the early 1930s, it was either formulated by or for Stalin or had to be acceptable to him. 'Deviations' led out of the party, or during the purges, out of life. The theory of 'democratic centralism' implied full and free debate until a decision had been taken, but in practice by this time people knew perfectly well, at all events at the top of Communist parties, that 'democratic debate' served to endorse and ratify 'the line' rather than to form it.

It is therefore tempting to regard the Comintern, and through it the parties, simply as agents of Moscow, and their policy entirely as the reflection of Moscow's interests – that is to say, *de facto* of the state interests of the USSR as interpreted by Stalin. If this is so, then an autonomous history of the communist movement and its policy and aspirations is both unnecessary and impossible, at all events from the early 1930s on. To quote Borkenau:

> At first the Comintern had aimed at being an instrument of international revolution. With revolution receding into the dim future, first in the West and then in the East, it had increasingly

> become a card to be played in Russian factional fights, an instrument without any importance of its own. Now for the first time it became essentially an instrument of Russian foreign policy.[1]

And so, inevitably, did all its constituent parties.

This view is not only *prima facie* plausible, but has considerable political appeal. It was first systematically formulated by opposition communists or ex-communists – a rapidly growing body in the years between 1927 and 1934 – and notably by those who, after 1934, saw the Comintern as betraying the old aim of world revolution. For the policy turn of 1934–35 unquestionably marked 'a change of policy deeper than any the Comintern had undergone before',[2] and the abandonment of the belief that the only way to socialism was insurrectionary. Could there be any other explanation than that Stalin no longer wanted revolution outside the USSR, or was prepared to sacrifice it for the Soviet state's interests? 'As always' wrote a brilliant young black Trotskyite, with his accustomed verve, 'it is Stalin's foreign policy and not the workers' revolution that guides these paid agents.'[3] In fact, the most powerful historical attacks on communist policy after 1934 have come from the left, notably (among the more recent) Claudin's critique.[4] They are variants on the theme 'world revolution betrayed'. We shall have to consider its validity below. Paradoxically, the same theme of Communist parties as Soviet agents could be played in the anti-revolutionary key. Since Conservatives believed that Soviet Russia was committed to world revolution or conquest anyway, they hardly bothered to enquire into possible divergences between Soviet and revolutionary interests. However, it was clearly convenient for domestic as well as international purposes, to treat local communists exclusively as Moscow-activated zombies. In the extremer versions of paranoia even patent conflicts, such as that between the USSR and China, or between Soviet loyalists and Eurocommunists, are presented as Moscow-planned manoeuvres for purposes of disinformation. This is not a view which will detain even the most anti-red scholars, but it is well suited for the history of communism in the period before 1948, when it was, or seemed to be, both solidly monolithic and unquestionably Soviet-controlled.

This is the view challenged here, both in the light of a substantial if patchy body of research, and because it is based on a lack of understanding of the relations between USSR and the communist movement, and a short-circuiting of the actual history of the 1930s and 1940s. To take a simple example: it is a mistake to read the Comintern of 1939–43 back into the earlier thirties. The Comintern's

Executive Committee after August 1935 contained, as it had never done before, two direct representatives of the Soviet secret police (Yezhov and Trilisser/Moskvin).[5] From early 1937 it was the victim of Stalin's purges. While a case for the change of line in 1933–35 could have been made irrespective of the state interests of the USSR, the line-changes from September 1939 on were clearly only a function of Soviet foreign policy, not apparently preceded by any internal discussion – the highest functionaries of Comintern were, it seems, taken by surprise by the German-Soviet pact[6] – and imposed from outside. Indeed, the dissolution of Comintern was quite clearly decided by Stalin.[7] Moreover, this is not surprising. It looks as though Stalin's sense of uneasiness grew with every setback in danger and weakness at home. On the principle of 'how many divisions has the Pope?', the international communist movement could not provide the USSR with any effective help from, at the latest, mid-1937, when the French Popular Front was in disintegration and the Spanish Republic evidently doomed. Alone and weak, the USSR could rely on itself – and its concessions to capitalist powers could not but be in flat contradiction with the policy interests of non-Soviet communists, as had not necessarily been the case before. Thus in 1939–41 Stalin plainly felt that the need to keep the USSR out of the war, which implied friendly and cooperative relations with Hitler's Germany, meant the ruin of the Comintern's antifascist policies. Left to themselves, neither Comintern nor the leading western parties, had felt that these had necessarily to be abandoned.[8]

Again, from 1943 – perhaps before – the maintenance of friendship and alliance with the USA, extending indefinitely into the postwar future, had absolute priority for the USSR. This so-called 'Teheran line', intended as mandatory for all communist parties and felt to be such,[9] and supported by the dissolution of the Comintern and, early in 1944, of the CPUSA, frankly accepted that the extension of the Soviet system to western Europe would have to be sacrificed to winning the confidence of the capitalist USA, which, it was hoped, would permanently cooperate with a socialist USSR.[10] Consequently, no case is known in which, during this period, the USSR did not actively discourage communist parties from establishing communist power, even though revolutionary and pre-revolutionary situations clearly arose in several regions out of the victory against the Axis.

Memory is the great anachroniser. It is easy to reconstruct 1935 in the light of 1939, or 1949 or 1959, especially for those who have lived through the entire period. But anachronism, with lying and plagiarism, is among the three deadly sins of history.

However, reconstructing the history of the Comintern is unusually difficult, not only because much of the documentation remains inaccessible* but because of the peculiar *modus operandi* of the International, at all events by the early 1930s. In fact, the view of international communist parties as mere glove-puppets of Moscow derives its plausibility largely from the fact that it is usually almost impossible for the historian to discover firm evidence of proceedings which did *not* reflect orders from above.

In a sense Communist parties, the Comintern advisers attached to them and the central apparatus of the International itself faced something like a Catch 22. Until a change of line had been authorised from above – and by the early 1930s this meant by Stalin or his private office – any divergence from it was a 'deviation', for which the penalties could be severe; though before 1935 probably not yet mortal. To suggest that the line needed basic revision was thus a possible 'deviation'. Changes therefore could not be publicly prepared. Officially they had to be sudden. The official apparatus of Comintern and parties continued, for more than a year after Hitler's coming to power, to repeat the slogans of 'class against class', in spite of the evident absurdity of claiming that, especially in Germany and Italy, social-democracy ('social-fascism') constituted the main prop of the bourgeoisie and the main danger to the revolutionary working class movement.[11] And yet it is quite patent that a reorientation of policy as profound as that ratified by the Seventh Congress needed extensive preparation, preliminary discussion and reflection, even if we assume that in the last analysis it had to be taken or approved by Stalin. Moreover, it is perfectly clear that there *was* some process of debate during the almost eighteen months between Hitler's accession to power and the official change of the line, and that preparation for a Congress took even longer. It had first been planned for sometime in the second half of 1934, but eventually did not take place until July-August 1935.[12] It is the nature of this process, or even the mechanism which allowed it to take place, which remains in the dark.

All that is visible, therefore, is the 'official' time-table, which runs as follows. At the end of February 1934 Georgi Dimitrov, free from a German prison by the gallantry of his own behaviour at the Reichstag fire trial in December 1933, by an international campaign and a Soviet offer of citizenship, arrived in Moscow, where he immediately became a major figure in the Comintern, of whose West European

* The organisation's archives have been used, since the 1960s, by Soviet scholars, but in general without giving precise references or allowing the reader to put their citations into context. By far the most important body of communist historiography concerns the Italian Communist Party, and much of it throws light on the international scene. The memoir literature is ample, almost invariably axe-grinding, and often unreliable. The stand-by of earlier historiography, the official publications of the International and its periodicals, dries up after 1935.

Bureau (located in Berlin) he had been the chief until his arrest. We do not know exactly how his appointment came about but, given his enormous public prestige as the hero of the Reichstag fire trial, it was hardly surprising. But, as it happens, we know that Dimitrov's appointment had political implications. He had been the chief target of criticism by the leftist section which had taken over his own Bulgarian Communist Party in the name of the official 'class against class' line of the International. Indeed, somewhat against his will, he had been pushed into the West European Bureau, in order to remove him from active influence in his own party, which continued its vendetta against him and views he presumably represented.[13] Moreover, the line which he had so brilliantly and bravely defended in public (at his trial) was – as anyone in Moscow must have been aware – at some variance with the official line of 'class against class' which stressed opposition to the Weimar Republic and social democracy equally with opposition to fascism. Dimitrov concentrated his fire exclusively against *fascism*, no doubt for perfectly understandable reasons, but which did not make him any the less divergent from official orthodoxy, as he unquestionably knew.* In short, Dimitrov's promotion hinted at possible changes.

He was officially entrusted on 28 May with the preparation of the Report which he subsequently gave at the 7th World Congress, while at the same time the other main rapporteurs were appointed (Wilhelm Pieck, Manuilsky and Palmiro Togliatti/Ercoli, who had re-emerged as a substantial figure in the International at the XIII Plenum (November 1933) and was to join Dimitrov in Moscow). Perhaps even more significantly, the Comintern leaders most systematically associated with the old course, Béla Kun of Hungary, O. Piatnitsky and W. Knorin of the USSR, were not also associated with the preparations for a new Congress, at which they were not to be re-elected to their former leading positions.[15] On the same date there appeared an article in *Pravda* which, reproduced in *Humanité* a few days later, gave the official green light to the policy of united action between the French Communist and Socialist parties.[16] We may take it that the switch of Comintern policy was formally made or sanctioned not later than mid-May 1934. But why the surprising delay, given that Hitler's accession to power, which was plainly the decisive reason for it, had occurred at the end of January 1933?

It is argued that Soviet reasons of state alone determined the

* 'The political situation at that time was governed by two factors: the first was the effort of the National Socialists to attain power, the second, the counter-factor, was the efforts of the German Communist Party to build up a united working class front against fascism'.[14]

dating.[17] Stalin was not prepared to commit the international movement to an actively anti-Nazi policy until it became clear that Germany had definitely abandoned the Rapallo policy of German-Soviet cooperation across the ideologies. Indeed, during the 17th Congress of the CPSU at the end of January, Stalin himself – long silent on international affairs – specifically warned Germany against abandoning the Rapallo line. But that very day Germany and Poland signed a non-aggression treaty visibly directed against the USSR, which in turn led the French, threatened by the collapse of their old system of post-1919 eastern alliances against Germany, to revert to the old perspective of a Franco-Russian understanding.[18] In fact, early in May Barthou proposed a Franco-Soviet pact. Stalin therefore (the argument concludes) took the decision to swing the Comintern against the Nazis and in defence of bourgeois-democratic regimes prepared to resist them. It may also be added that, after the tempests of the First Five Year Plan, the USSR needed a breathing-space – ten years of peace, in Stalin's view.[19]

That Soviet reasons of state played an important part in the reversal of Comintern policy is undeniable, given that Stalin, who had to make or approve even rather less dramatic changes in international policy, was clearly concerned about the real and immediate prospects of the USSR rather than the hypothetical and remote ones of world revolution. But, of course, the priority of defending and strengthening the USSR over all other tasks was accepted throughout the communist movement, which took it for granted – reasonably enough – that the prospects of establishing proletarian power elsewhere depended on the existence, support and help of the first and only, but fortunately very large and powerful, workers' state. Never can this argument have looked more unanswerable than in 1933–4 when with one exception, for practical purposes, no Communist Party of major significance remained in being anywhere in the world outside the USSR, for even the Chinese CP was about to become a harried and heroic caravan in search of some remote area of refuge. The major exception was France, though even there the 'class against class' line had reduced communist representation in parliament to 9. (Hence the central role of France in the Comintern policy switch is hardly surprising.) Nothing could seem more reasonable to revolutionaries in the 1930s than that any sacrifice was justified to maintain the USSR in being.

And yet it is quite clear that the suicidal effects on the 6th World Congress line, which reached its peak of lunacy between 1930 and 1933, had long met with more or less muffled opposition within both the parties and the International. Examples (for instance, from Humbert-Droz, from the Czech delegates to the XII Plenum of EKKI in 1932 and elsewhere) are cited by Hajek.[20] It has been persistently suggested that, among the top leadership of Comintern, Manuilsky at least had reservations about the line of the early 'thirties, used his influence to eliminate elements of the ultra-left and to bring forward others, waiting for a moment when change might be suggested. There is no reason to disbelieve this suggestion.[21] And there seems to be no serious doubt that a sharp difference on policy developed at the highest levels of Comintern from the beginning of 1934, and particularly after the events of February 1934 in Austria and, above all, France, on the need for a changed strategy and on its nature and application.[22] This clearly led to the official turn of May 1934, and, equally clearly, was entangled with the urgent problems of what common action to organise between socialists and communists in France, where opinions in the French CP were also divided. The role of the Comintern representative with the French CP at this time, a former ultra-left Czech communist Evzhen Fried (known as 'Clément')* is generally regarded as important in helping to move that party on to anti-fascist lines. His own former views[24] would seem to suggest that there was at least some strong hint from Moscow that such a line would be supported. Fried's own views have never been ascertained by historians, since he was killed by the Germans in Belgium in 1943; the suggestion by Robrieux that he was killed on Soviet initiative has been shown to be baseless.[25] The fullest account of the turn, by two Soviet scholars, Leibson and Shirinya, argues that Stalin, as General Secretary of the CPSU(b), did not personally take the initiative in this change, but accepted the arguments of the reformers in this debate, notably Manuilsky and above all Dimitrov. This appears to be supported by Bulgarian accounts.[26]

This is not unlikely. The argument that the anti-German and pro-French shift in Soviet policy necessarily implied a total reversal of the Comintern line is not wholly convincing. In the first place, it was Comintern which, even in 1933, stressed the aggressive imperialism of German policy, at a time when Soviet foreign policy still kept its options open.[27] If the initiative for anti-Hitlerism came from anywhere, it was from these quarters. In the second place, the French partisans of a Franco-Soviet front were to be found not only on the left, but, as Borkenau long ago pointed out[28] also among moderates

* Comintern agents abroad were recruited, disproportionately, from a) the large colonies of communist refugees from countries where revolution or insurrection had been defeated, notably the Hungarians and Bulgarians, b) from peoples of cosmopolitan experience, such as Jews and those from the Baltic countries, c) from small CPs whose marginal role in their own countries left them with cadres to spare, such as the Swiss, but also d) from cadres representing tendencies which had been defeated in their own national parties – e.g. Dimitrov, Gerhart Eisler, Fried.[23]

and on the right. Rather than a Popular Front, Soviet alignment with France ought therefore, logically, to have implied a policy compatible with any suitably anti-German French administration; it is anachronism to read the subsequent pro-Germanism of the French right ('better Hitler than Blum') back into 1934. Nonetheless, a Kremlin initiative cannot be excluded. After all, almost a year elapsed before the debates within Comintern were allowed to emerge into the open; a year during which the consequences of Hitler's accession to power were plain enough, during which the socialists of different countries and the Second International made clear overtures of unity to the communists, which the International spurned.

However, the events of February 1934 in France and Austria are quite sufficient to account for the decision of the Comintern to initiate a change of line without more Kremlin action than an indication that discussion could proceed. Admittedly these events could be used to reinforce the positions of the left, since it could be argued they proved that the left wing of the social democrats, faced with the collapse of their leaderships' policies, was being driven to join the Communists (the 'United Front from below'), or even, as in Austria, out of the Social Democratic and into the Communist Party. Such action by scattered and leaderless German Social Democrats in the darkness of illegality for both parties was actually used by the ruined German C.P., sectarian unto death, to deny its evident defeat.[29] But if the capacity of *homo politicus* to rationalize any position is virtually unlimited, the lunacy of a line which prohibited any agreement between the leadership of two working-class parties, equally threatened with annihilation, was even more evident, at least in France where the situation was not yet lost.

The handling of the Doriot affair demonstrates that change was in the air. Jacques Doriot, a leading member of the French Political Bureau and of ECCI, publicly opposed the party leadership and signed an official socialist-communist pact in his fief in Saint-Denis. There was no love lost between him and the official leader Thorez, nor, presumably, had the party any illusions about Doriot, who himself clearly expected to be expelled and was preparing for a break with the party: he refused to attend Politbureau meetings and to go to Moscow. Yet it was not until mid-April that the word 'deviation' fell in the French Party and the Comintern, which had actually invited *both* Doriot and the French party to desist from controversy at the end of April, did not formally 'withdraw its protection' from him until mid-May.[30] The problem lay not in expelling a dissident. It lay in expelling a 'deviationist' who had publicly nailed his colours to the mast of an obviously sensible policy, towards which the French CP and the Comintern themselves were plainly moving after the February riots, though in a crabwise manner. In fact Doriot was expelled on 27 June, one month before the formal signing of the pact between the two French working class parties. Paradoxically, Doriot was probably a victim of his belief in the rigidity of the old Comintern line and consequently the inevitability of defeat for the French left. He clearly believed that Hitler was the winning side. Within two years this able and ambitious working-class politican had founded the only French party which can be legitimately called Fascist, which was to become a pillar of collaboration after 1940.

Whatever the antecedents, it was evident from June 1934 that socialist-communist unity (the 'United Front from Above') was the official line. One would, in the light of later experiences such as the 1939 turn, have expected the parties and the International to fall immediately into line. Yet it is clear that during July and August resistance to the new line in ECCI continued. While it was supported by Dimitrov, Manuilsky, Togliatti, Kuusinen (a good man at detecting which way the winds were blowing) and representatives of the French, Czech, Polish and other parties, it had not yet been accepted by Knorin, Béla Kun, Lozovsky and Varga.[31] The decision to put off the Congress in September was presumably due to the time needed to bring all the parties into line. Resistance certainly continued in the KPD: as late as 3 December, 1934 Togliatti wrote to Manuilsky that he could not understand why the KPD was so hesitant in applying the united front line.[32] Other parties which visibly lacked zeal for the new line, such as the Bulgarians and Hungarians, can readily be found. In short, the military metaphor of orders given and carried out is plainly out of place.

The United Front was both official policy, and had adequate precedents in Communist strategy, going back to 1921. The Popular Front, that is to say the extension of the anti-fascist alliance to 'bourgeois' and 'petit-bourgeois' parties, including Communist support for, or even participation in, coalition governments of such Popular Fronts, was certainly not yet official Comintern policy in the summer of 1934. Moreover, while it is possible that the abandonment of 'class against class' was due to specific initiative by Moscow, there is no evidence that Moscow led the way into the Popular Front, though it would naturally have to approve it. The most convincing piece of evidence against a Moscow initiative is that Togliatti, Dimitrov's right-hand man since the summer of 1934, and resident in Paris in the last months of the year, actually advised the French CP against extending the United Front to the Radical Party.[33] At all events it is clear from Togliatti's lengthy letter to Manuilsky of 19 November[34] that the Italian leader himself was as yet far from sure that the French communists were not making too many concessions to the allies to the right of them. It still seems best to see the French CP as making the running in broadening the Socialist-Communist front into a Socialist-Communist-Radical front, no doubt encouraged by the resident Comintern representative (Clément) who, in turn, felt that this was a logical extension of the general anti-fascist line which would get Moscow support.[35] It is perhaps significant that the preparatory reports of the International for the VII World Congress mention the 'people's front' (as distinct from the omnipresent 'united front') only in the report on France – and then in notably brief and vague terms.[36] Though the materials in this volume are dated July 1935, they are modified versions of reports prepared for the original date of the Congress, and therefore represent, by and large, the state of Comintern thinking as of autumn 1934. The 'popular front' was clearly not yet central to it.

And yet the 'people's front' is what marks the Seventh World Congress and constitutes a turning-point in international Communist expectations, because there was no adequate precedent for it in official doctrine. The 'united front' had been initiated in Lenin's lifetime, and indeed pushed through the Third World Congress of the Comintern in 1921 largely by the weight of Lenin's personal prestige, supported (more tactlessly) by Trotsky. *De facto*, as Trotsky pointed out, the world revolution, expected in 1919 'within months', had not taken place; now 'perhaps it is a question of years'. Put more mildly, the Communist vanguard had isolated itself from the mass of the working-class, and it was essential to gain the support of the masses. So far, as Lenin pointed out, no western CP had succeeded in gaining majority working class support. In other words the 'United Front' could be presented as a necessary preliminary to the detachment of social-democratic workers from their reformist loyalties, as indeed was the object of the tactics of affiliating to the Labour Party in Britain.[37] (Lenin's phrase about supporting British Labour leaders as the rope supports the hanged man, was to be endlessly quoted against British Communists by Labour leaders.) Nevertheless, nobody doubted that it marked a retreat from the hope of immediate Soviet revolutions. When these were once again believed (or at least alleged) to be on the agenda, as after 1928, unity, as in 1919–20, was seen as a brake on action, the social democrats, and especially the left social democrats, as diversionary forces. Still, winning majority support in the working-class movement hardly seemed incompatible with revolution.

The 'people's front', being an alliance with frankly bourgeois parties, which envisaged the actual support of, even the participation in, coalition government with them, was a much greater shock for revolutionaries. The very fact of participating in, or even supporting, non-socialist governments, had always been a sign of class treason for revolutionaries – for most socialists of the Second International before 1914, and *a fortiori* for Communists of the Third International. Indeed, the transformation of social-democratic parties after 1914 (for the most part) parties of unwavering opposition to parties of potential or actual government in bourgeois democracies was one of the strongest arguments of the revolutionary left against them. (Taking office in local government raised no such problems, but autonomous regional administrations did, as witness the impassioned debates in Comintern and the German CP over the governments in Central Germany, a bastion of radical socialism and communism.) There was no doubt that in revolutionary situations coalition governments with the non-communist left were legitimate. As immediate preliminaries to the dictatorship of the proletariat, the Bolshevik had, after all, formed such a government temporarily with the Left Social Revolutionaries after October. In colonial or semi-colonial countries, where anti-imperialist parties led by the local bourgeoisie or petit-bourgeoisie might be objectively revolutionary, and the working class was small, there was no *a priori* objection to joining in governments of anti-imperialist liberation, since these could themselves be important phases in the revolutionary process. (However, Chiang-Kai-Shek's 1927 break with the Communists made the idea of such governments somewhat less popular.)

The Fourth World Congress (1922) had considered the problem of such 'broad' governments seriously, not only because they were relevant to burning controversies within the German and Czech CPs, but also because, given that a European October was not immediately probable, other ways to revolution had to be envisaged. Radek, with his usual political perspicacity, had already recommended the undoctrinaire approach to the German CP, but (in spite of Lenin's approval) only as 'my personal opinion'. He argued, sensibly, that a soviet government might be forced on the bourgeoisie by revolution, but it might also arise out of the struggles of the workers in defence of a democratically elected socialist government. Whether to support a non-communist government was therefore a matter for judgment in the light of concrete circumstances. Indeed (following a line of thought in Marx and Engels), he did not exclude a workers' government elected democratically, which would be forced into the revolutionary road by the resistance of the bourgeoisie to it.[38] The Fourth Congress (where the 'broad' line met with some resistance) recognized various types of acceptable 'broad' goverments: 1) a Liberal government – which, in the best of cases, Communists could do no more than support with their votes; 2) a pure Social-Democratic government which, under some circumstances, might be a stage on the way to accentuating the revolutionary character of a situation; 3) a

Social-Democratic-Communist government and 4) a workers-and-peasants government formed by the democratic workers' and peasants' parties. The first two could not be regarded as true socialist and workers' governments, but the last two could represent serious points of departure for the dictatorship of the proletariat, i.e. a communist government.[39]

This was the precedent to which Dimitrov referred in 1935. It is strong enough to discredit the thesis that the 'popular front' had no antecedents in Comintern history,[40] but the difference between the situations envisaged in 1921–23 and those in the 1930s was nevertheless substantial. The only thing that clearly linked the two situations was that the workers or worker-peasant government, now the 'government of the united front', specifically extended to include 'the anti-fascist people's front', was envisaged as 'possibly constituting, in a number of countries, *one* of the most important transitional forms' or approaches to proletarian victory.[41]

It was seen, not merely as possibly necessary defensive tactics to hold up and defeat the otherwise unstoppable advance of fascism, a temporary coalition with one demon against a more threatening devil, but as a way to turn defensive into advance. And this implied a far more drastic revision of previous Comintern strategy than had hitherto been envisaged, namely an alternative to proletarian revolution.

That such an alternative was now envisaged appears clear, though the line publicly adopted by both Comintern and the USSR, that there was no discontinuity of policy, but only an adjustment to a changed situation, rather inhibited frank analysis. At all events private statements of a new perspective for the transition to power, now came from the most authoritative source of all. According to Thorez,[42] some time after October 1934, Stalin congratulated the French CP on its policy, remarking: 'You have found a new key to open the gates of the future.' No autobiography of a politician is on oath, but Stalin's letter of 1 December, 1936 to Largo Caballero specifically stated that 'it is quite possible that in Spain the parliamentary way will prove more appropriate for revolutionary development than was the case in Russia.'[43] No doubt for Stalin the only 'appropriate' way would have eventually to lead to total control by a Communist Party directly dependent on, and preferably under the direct orders of, Moscow, but this does not diminish the significance of doctrinal innovations for a leader who, after all, unquestionably saw himself as a guardian and teacher of the 'correct' theory.

What precisely the new perspective meant was by no means evident, partly because no communist dreamed in 1935 of publicly admitting, or even privately envisaging, any other way of overthrowing the exploiters than soviet power, partly because the actual interpretation of the new slogans floated and shifted, as the situation changed after the Congress.[44] Some peoples' front governments, or other governments including parties with which the communists wanted to form a united front – for instance social democratic ones, alone or in coalition – were clearly not seen as the ante-chamber of socialist transition. The French Communists did not actually join the People's Front government of 1936, though Thorez claims to have personally been in favour of doing so.[45] The situation in which such governments could be envisaged as governments of transition were essentially pre-revolutionary or revolutionary situations. Quite clearly, however, such governments were *not* envisaged as mere euphemisms for the 'dictatorship of the proletariat', as a resolution of ECCI had held the 'worker-peasant government' to be as recently as late November 1934. Dimitrov quite specifically condemned this view as 'left' doctrinairism and out of line with Lenin.[46] And when, after 1947, the new 'people's democracies' of eastern Europe were officially once again assimilated to the 'dictatorship of the proletariat', it meant the burial of the international line of 1935.

Nevertheless, the new line did imply a way forward to socialist power which was quite distinct from the October Revolution's road to it. This emerges clearly from an early, and obviously extremely official, public analysis of 'the peculiarities of the Spanish revolution' written by Togliatti in early October 1936, which both fits in with, and amplifies, Stalin's slightly later letter to Largo Caballero.[47] Here the Spanish revolution was described as the greatest event, after the October Revolution, in the history of the struggles for the liberation of the popular masses in the countries of capitalism. Its international significance lay in the fact that it was 'an integral part of the anti-fascist struggle which is developing on a world scale, it is a revolution which rests on the widest social base. It is a popular revolution. It is a national revolution. It is an anti-fascist revolution.' That is to say, it was not a mere bourgeois-democratic revolution like 1905 (with which it could no more be identified than with 1917), because it developed in the specific conditions of an armed struggle against military insurrection. It was obliged to confiscate the property of landlords and industrialists 'who had raised the banner of rebellion'; it was in a position to utilise the experience of the Russian revolution and, furthermore, it provided the Spanish working class with the chance to turn itself, so far as it was able, into the leading force of the revolution and to imbue that revolution with the character, forms and methods of proletarian revolution.

Nevertheless, it was more than the classic struggle of workers united with peasants, because the Spanish people's front had a much wider range of social support. Moreover, it was more than that 'revolutionary-democratic dictatorship of workers and peasants' which Lenin had seen as a possible 'next step' in 1905, because the logic of civil war pushed the Spanish government beyond the limits of the programme Lenin had envisaged for the 'revolutionary democratic dictatorship'. In fact, the war obliged it to take over control of the economy. Consequently, if victorious, 'such a democracy of a new type cannot but be the enemy of the conservative spirit. All the conditions which permit further development are present. It provides a guarantee for all the further economic and political conquests of the Spanish working people.'

The phrasing is deliberately vague and cloudy. The last thing Stalin or Comintern wanted was to advertise the possible Bolshevik transformation of Spain. And, indeed, it was quite clear that (as distinct from the anarchists) the Comintern did not envisage an immediate seizure of power and social revolution. What it did envisage was a sort of organic growth of the broadest possible front of anti-fascist forces, in conditions of armed resistance and by the logic of such a situation, into a 'democracy of a new type', which would have expropriated a large part of the country's landlords and capitalists (but as rebels rather than as exploiters), which would have established a high degree of control and direction of the economy, and which would therefore provide a springboard for a further leap forward. It need hardly be added that, in the course of the struggle, the leading role of the 'working class' would have been decisively enhanced. Any communist reader would have no difficulty in reading Togliatti's document. But even non-communist readers, looking at it with hindsight, cannot but be struck by how much of the policy, and even the reality, of the next ten years the Comintern document anticipated.

For, though the Spanish republic was defeated, Togliatti's pamphlet describes, with some accuracy, the shape of politics in the anti-fascist war of 1939–45: a war which was waged in Europe by 'people's front' governments or resistance coalitions (except in the USA and USSR), which in 1945–7 produced more governments including the Communist party in Europe than ever before or since, and which was waged by state-managed economies and ended with massive advances of the public sector, due to the expropriation of capitalists not as such but as Germans or collaborators. And indeed in several countries of central and eastern Europe the road had led directly from anti-fascism to socialist power; mainly, it is true, by virtue of Soviet occupation, but in some cases, of which Yugoslavia is the most prominent, through autochthonous development. All this strongly suggests that the new line was envisaged as a way – and self-evidently one unlike the October Revolution – to socialist power.

This has been denied, mainly by critics on the left.[48] (Critics of the right have not let themselves be embarrassed by the utter absence of any evidence that the USSR encouraged *any* communist party to establish soviet power.) It has often been pointed out that the CPs failed, and indeed refused, to make use of two allegedly revolutionary situations, in 1936 and again in 1943–45. But the two situations are quite different.

As for France in 1936, it cannot be seriously held that the situation was revolutionary or pre-revolutionary, or even that it seriously looked as though it was. The election victory of the Popular Front represented a minimal voting shift to the left – from 44.48% in 1932 to 45.94 for the combined Radical, Socialist and Communist parties,[49] but one greatly magnified in the public eye by the electoral system, which favoured the majority alignment, and by the dramatic shift to the left within it, which raised Communist representation from 9 to 72. This aroused an enormous and spontaneous surge of mass enthusiasm and mass militancy among workers. The CP can be criticised for not recognizing this surge and underestimating its force – as it was to do again in 1968. It can also be justly observed that before 1934 it would certainly have considered the insurrectionary potential of such an upsurge, and in 1936 it clearly did not. But it can not be criticised for failing to plunge into an almost certainly doomed second edition of the Paris Commune. Leftist adventurism certainly would not have suited the USSR, but neither would it have suited the French movement.

In Spain, unlike France, the CP was not a major factor in politics or the labour movement. The electoral system in February 1936 also produced a triumph for the Popular Front disproportionate to its actual support, though this was greater than in France: the Left polled about 50.5%, the right – somewhat strengthened since 1933 – about 49.5%.[50] Here, however, a pre-revolutionary situation was transformed into a revolutionary one by the insurrection of the generals. As we have seen, the Comintern recognised the Spanish events as a revolution, and threw its full resources into the struggle for the victory of the Republic. The view that a 'bourgeois' revolution in Spain could not be transformed into a socialist revolution, at least to the satisfaction of Communists, was put forward by the old hard-liner Knorin (in *Pravda*) against Dimitrov, but was clearly rejected.[51] But so also was the attempt to transform it immediately. Stalin's letter to Caballero specifically warned the Spanish government against policies alienating the peasantry and the 'petty and middle bourgeoisie' who might otherwise follow the Fascists, and to conciliate the moderate Republicans 'in order to prevent the enemies of Spain from regarding it as a communist republic, and to forestall their intervention, which would constitute the greatest danger to the republic'.[52] This moderate line undoubtedly suited USSR foreign policy, but is entirely defensible on other grounds. Without victory in the war, to which the Communists subordinated all else, all talk of a revolutionary socialist Spain was idle, as subsequent history demonstrates. Whether and how the war might have been won, and what may be said against the Spanish Communists' policy, are interesting questions. However, the suggestion that the war would have been more successfully waged along anarchist lines is based on neither evidence nor probability, but only on wishful thinking.

The debate about 1943–45 is much more interesting and relevant to our problem, for there can be no doubt that the situation in many parts of the world encouraged revolutionary hopes. The communist attitude to them was not uniform, in spite of the fact that Moscow quite unambiguously discouraged any attempt to use the favourable position established by communists in the anti-fascist resistance movements to establish communist power anywhere. Even in the areas liberated by the Red Army, or assigned by international agreement to the Soviet sphere of influence, the USSR went to some trouble to avoid the *appearance* of communist power, even though Stalin frankly told Djilas that 'this war is not as in the past. Whoever occupies a territory, also imposes on it his own social system. Everyone imposes his own social system as far as his army has power to do so. It cannot be otherwise.'[53] However, this very adoption of the principle *cuius regio, eius religio* plainly recognised the permanence of capitalism outside the minority of countries occupied by the USSR. As we have seen, after 1943 Stalin put his money on the maintenance of a peacetime partnership with the USA, and any suggestion that non-Soviet communist parties aimed at establishing red power was unwelcome. The Soviet line was, consistently, that the war should be fought by national coalitions of all anti-fascist or non-fascist parties, including but not (outside the Soviet sphere) dominated by the communists, and that these national coalitions should become governments after the war, or, if already in government, should be maintained after the war.[54]

A number of Communist parties refused to follow this line, notably the Chinese, the Yugoslavs, the Greeks and the Albanians. All were unshakably loyal to the USSR and to Stalin; indeed, China and Albania are the last remaining Stalin loyalists to this day. None, for various reasons, would accept the Soviet case that communist power was not an immediate perspective, insofar as it was put to them. (It is unlikely that Moscow thought much about Albania, which was then regarded by all except the Albanians as a sort of appendage to Yugoslavia, with which it was destined to be merged.)

The Yugoslav case is in some ways the most illuminating since, unlike the Chinese, who had been recognised as subject to advice rather than instructions since the middle 1930s, the Yugoslav CP was directly under Moscow which had indeed purged it and imposed Tito on it as a reliable leader. The Yugoslav party flatly refused to follow the repeated Comintern warnings, during 1942, against giving the partisan movement 'a communist character and aiming at the sovietization of Yugoslavia' (Dimitrov).[55] What is more, it argued its case. It clearly seemed inconceivable to them that a party which had, *de facto*, mobilised the peoples of its country single-handed to defeat Germany should not try to achieve what a communist party was in business for. It remained entirely loyal to the USSR, and indeed, when the mild line gave way to a hard line in 1947, it was the Yugoslav party which formulated the Russians' condemnation of the French and Italian CPs, and Belgrade which became – briefly – the headquarters of the new Cominform.[56]

It is therefore undeniable that Communist parties did not necessarily act in blind loyalty to orders from Moscow. How then are we to explain that no other communist parties in Europe tried a bid for power at the end of the war? The question is one about France and Italy, whose special position in the western communist movement was to be recognised by their association, alone of all parties in the capitalist world, with the new Communist Information Bureau. The parties in Soviet Europe were in power. The only question facing them was, how and how soon it would become indistinguishable from Soviet power. The parties in Britain, and the small Nazi-occupied countries of western Europe, were in no position even to dream of power. They had to be content with being stronger and more influential in a minor way than ever before and, for the most part, with being in their countries' governments. The situation in Germany depended entirely on the occupation authorities. But in France and Italy, it was argued at the time and has been held since, an overthrow of the old system was possible, and in neither state was it attempted. This lack of insurrectionary spirit was in 1947 condemned by the Yugoslavs, who claimed to have suggested insurrection to the Italians during the war and to have been rebuffed.[57]

The French case may be quickly dismissed. There is no doubt that, apart from possible scattered local initiatives, no seizure of power was made or intended.[58] But even if we suppose it had been, that is to say if the Communists had been willing to jeopardize victory over the Germans, which had been far from won, or risk a separate western peace with Germany directed against the USSR, which they feared, the political and military configuration of France in 1944–45 was such as to make any unilateral communist insurrection pretty hopeless. Indeed, not even the sharpest critics of the PCF suggest that 'the problem for a truly revolutionary party was . . . an abstract project of the conquest of power by the proletariat'.[59] What they are criticised for is failing to outmanoeuvre De Gaulle, who was rightly afraid that they might appear at the head of the insurrection which actually liberated most of French territory while awaiting the arrival of the allied armies 'as a sort of Commune which would proclaim the Republic, take the responsibility for public order, and dispense justice while taking care to sing only the Marseillaise and fly only the tricolour'.[60] The critique is legitimate. The Communists could probably have established a rather stronger position in the government of liberated France than they actually did. Whether this would have constituted 'the first steps towards the socialist revolution in the France of 1944' (Claudin) is another question. Given the restricted support for the resistance movement in France (until the last moment), the relatively modest scale of its armed operations, the anti-communism of the Allied governments and the presence of their armies, the odds were against it.[61]

In the northern part of Italy the chances of insurrection were unquestionably excellent, and improved by the long period during which the Allied armies were held on their way north, and a massively supported resistance movement with a considerable (and mainly communist) guerrilla force faced an enfeebled fascist state maintained only by the German army. In fact insurrection was the party's policy, and was carried out. However, from Togliatti's return to Italy it was understood that communist power was *not* its objective.[62] The question why the party did not try for at least regional power was discussed at the time, and has since been taken up in inner-party discussions.[63] The 'Greek argument', which emerged in late 1944, was certainly not primary, though it was evidently used in wartime discussions with the Yugoslavs.[64] While it was quite realistic to expect Allied military intervention against a left-wing attempt to take power, as in Greece, Togliatti's line had been determined before this occurred. Pietro Secchia, a hard-line opponent of Togliatti's, did not believe in the chances of a communist insurrection, given the weakness of the party's military forces. As he was in charge of these in the North, his evidence must carry weight.[65] Probably more decisive was the argument that a communist take-over in the North, even though it might be practicable, would mean the end of Italian unity. Certainly the southern half of the peninsula and the islands, where the left was feeble and the Allied military forces unshakeable, would secede from a red North if they could not destroy it. Equally strong, of course, was the argument that it would be suicidal to break Allied unity while the war was still not won – and Italians, who had expected the Allied breakthrough in 1944, knew well enough that it was not yet won.[66]

Nevertheless, anyone who follows Togliatti's statements from his return to Italy on, is likely to be convinced that he rejected a communist siezure of power not simply because it would have been inexpedient or impracticable, or because – obviously – it went against Soviet policy, but also because he envisaged a different road to socialism. How far Togliatti had evolved from the subtle, intelligent but convinced Stalinism of 1934 is a matter for debate. Moreover, the 'Italian road to socialism' which became part of the PCI's discourse later was perhaps not quite the linear prolongation of the Seventh World Congress as some of its champions were to claim. It was rather a graft of Gramsci (unknown as a theorist before his death) on Dimitrov, *via* the political reflection on his rather extensive experience by Dimitrov's number two, who was at this time the only man to have access to Gramsci's writings.[67] Still, the 'Italian road' was implicit in Togliatti's thinking during the resistance period. It is very improbable that he continued to see the transition to socialism as a simple seizure of power followed by a soviet Italy, or even that he thought of the 'new democracy' he had announced in 1936 simply as a more prolonged ante-chamber to such a system. Behind the policy of Stalin, which he loyally represented in public – in private he increasingly kept his distance* – there was an Italian political perspective.

To point this out is not, of course, to exempt the French and Italian Communist parties from criticism, and even less to exculpate Moscow, whose treatment of the international communist movement is indefensible. About the best that can be said in its favour (from a communist point of view) is that Stalin consistently acted out of a justified sense of weakness and vulnerability, which imposed policies of extreme caution. This meant that he felt he could neither extend communist influence beyond the zone occupied by the Red Army, nor let himself be drawn into open-ended commitments to militant regimes of foreign revolutionaries like the Yugoslavs, which could not be controlled. Stalin was also correct in writing off most foreign communist parties which had demonstrated, especially in the 1930s, that with all their devotion to the USSR they could not deliver what he actually needed. And it must also be said that, when the occasional CP went against Moscow's line and actually made a revolution, the USSR, in spite of Stalin's evident suspicions, welcomed its achievement. But if they had listened to the USSR there

* Togliatti did not attend the founding conference of Cominform in 1947 and tactfully refused the invitation to leave his Italian base for an eminent and honorific position close to Stalin.[68]

would have been no such achievement anywhere, for there can be no doubt that Moscow discouraged Mao and Tito, as it discouraged the French and the Italians.[69]

But why did some Communist parties go against Moscow in this matter while others – most – did not? That is the crucial question. There can be no conclusive answer, but by far the most likely hypothesis is that with all their fidelity to party discipline, and with all their, quite defensible, belief that the future of world socialism depended on the survival and success of the Soviet Union, most Communist parties of any significance did indeed think in terms of their own national situation. No doubt there were in each party a few men and women, generally in influential positions, who saw themselves as the Comintern's and Stalin's soldiers, theirs not to reason why, theirs but to carry out orders. No doubt there were some among them who realised that promotion came from Moscow rather than local success. And certainly all parties learned that the Moscow line was obligatory, however mistaken it seemed or was. But, despite much literature to the contrary, this did not mean that British or French communists did not think primarily in terms of Britain and France. A local perspective can, as students of the British Labour Party in the early 1980s know, be one of suicidal sectarianism as well as politically realistic. There was plenty of genuine support for 'class against class' in 1928–1935 – even, as we have seen, against what was clearly favoured in Moscow. On the other hand parties or leaders with genuine political assets likely to be dissipated by a Moscow line defended them as best they could. Either they looked for support in Moscow – and sometimes found it, as Arthur Horner did for his work in the South Wales Miners' Federation,[70] and, presumably, the Colombian CP for its guerrilla activities at a period when the general line for Latin America was not favourable to armed struggle – or they quietly dragged their feet. Neither the British nor the French CPs after September 1939 actually carried out the policy of 'revolutionary defeatism', or even of equating their own governments with Hitler's, which was implicit in the Comintern line of 1939–41.* Perhaps this was not due to deliberation, but merely to the natural desire of militants not to lose touch with 'the masses' whom, after all, they had to influence. But that is precisely the point. For parties which were genuinely in touch with their own working class, or significant

* It may be true, as Spriano points out, that the official documents of Comintern did not actually call for such a policy – they could hardly have done so without calling on German workers to overthrow Hitler also, which would have conflicted with the essential object of the new line, conciliating Hitler. However, for any student of Lenin, the implication of characterising the war as an 'imperialist war' were clear and did not have to be spelled out.[71]

sections of it, keeping in touch came naturally. It did not require deliberation. Following the Moscow line when it went directly against what they knew to make political sense: that was what required the effort which as disciplined communist cadres they were prepared to make, knowing what it cost them. Conversely, it is hardly surprising that the parties which actually believed themselves to be in a position to make a revolution wanted to do so, whatever Moscow said, or even found it inconceivable that Moscow might want to discourage them, except out of sheer ignorance.

There is thus no real difficulty in understanding why most 'capitalist' CPs followed the Moscow line and refused to make a bid for power. They were in no position to, and knew it. This is not to deny the undeniable, namely that almost without exception communist parties and their members, from top to bottom were utterly committed to the Soviet Union in general and Stalin in particular – those who were not did not remain CP members – and that Moscow often committed them to policies which damaged the political prospects of a CP in its own country.* But, by the standards of the October Revolution, the damage so done was minor. What, taking the most optimistic (or pessimistic) view, did the CPGB lose by its disastrous change into reverse gear in 1939, and again in 1941? Let us say, the chance to win affiliation to the Labour Party sometime during the war (it was defeated by 2 million to 700,000 at the 1943 Labour Party Conference), which would certainly have dramatically improved its political prospects. Thus it might have had more than its 1945 score of 2 Communist MPs and a handful of others regarded as underground CP members or sympathisers, and soon purged from the Labour Party as such. To put it at its highest, the CP might have established a greater permanent presence on the British national political scene and a position of substantial influence within the political labour movement. But it would not and could not have exchanged the prospects of a long and uncertain 'British road to socialism' for what most of its members had joined the Party for, namely the glorious prospect of working class power in Britain soon. It was one thing to sacrifice the chance to affiliation and a parliamentary seat for Harry Pollitt, but quite another for a party like the Yugoslav, on the verge of actually taking power, to sacrifice *that* chance.

In fact, the communist parties which were genuinely sacrificed to Soviet interests, it may be argued, were among those which actually

* This does not mean that these policies were always wrong. If Moscow jeopardised the chances of its parties in the West by advocating conciliation with Germany in 1939–41, it jeopardised them in the East after 1941 by putting the defeat of the Axis before everything else, including national liberation.

took power in the east-european zone of Soviet influence. These were the parties which had the equivalent of the Soviet purges and show trials of the 1930s imposed on them in 1948–52 by direct Soviet coercion. Soviet orders or prohibitions forced them to abandon policies which they believed to be in the interests of their countries – for instance, in the case of Czechoslovakia, to accept Marshall Aid in 1947, at least as a tactical ploy – and some which had long been part of their countries' communist party policy, such as a Balkan federation between Yugoslavia and Bulgaria.[72] Probably all had benefited in 1944–5 from the Soviet insistence that socialism was not on the immediate agenda, for some at least (one thinks of the Hungarian CP) would probably, left to themselves, have made a politically unjustifiable dash for all-out socialisation and soviet power. On the other hand some had clearly recognized the benefits of a slow and pluralist road forward which would allow local communist parties enjoying genuine mass support (e.g. the Czech and Bulgarian) to lead rather than coerce their allies in the right direction. The Soviet *Gleichschaltung* of 1947–48 cost them much. At the very inaugural conference of the Cominform in 1947, the Bulgarian representative continued to repeat that the dictatorship of the proletariat was no longer necessary under present conditions.[73] He was behind the times. Henceforth 'people's democracy' and 'dictatorship of the proletariat' were identical and all 'national roads to socialism' had to follow the Soviet pattern.

There remains one interesting case: a party which might conceivably have made a bid for power and refrained. Was there any other such case than that of the Italian CP in 1943–45? Probably not. Paradoxically it may be argued that the apparent Moscow loyalism of Togliatti concealed a far more profound rethinking of the model of socialism via soviet power,[74] than the insistence of the Yugoslavs and the Chinese on making their revolution without the approval of, or even against, Stalin. The subsequent history of the Italian Communist Party shows that, whatever determined its policy in the post-war period, it was not blind and automatic loyalty to Moscow alone.

The historiography of international communism will probably remain steeped in ideological polemic for the foreseeable future. All the more reason for historians to insist that one familiar ideological myth is unacceptable: the image of communist parties as no more than 'agents of Moscow'. That myth cannot survive a serious study of the period of anti-fascism.

Notes

1 Franz Borkenau, *The Communist International* (London, 1938), p. 388. For a similar view of a CP as primarily tied to Moscow, cf. Theodore Draper 'American Communism Revisited' and 'The Popular Front Revisited' (*New York Review of Books*, 9 May, 1985, pp. 32 ff; May 30 1985, pp. 42 ff).

2 Borkenau, p. 386.

3 C. L. R. James, *World Revolution 1917–36: The Rise and Fall of the Communist International* (London, 1937), p. 377–78.

4 Fernando Claudin, *La crise du mouvement communiste* (2 vols), Paris, 1972. Originally published in Spanish, Paris, 1970.

5 F. Svátek, 'The Governing Organs of the Communist International; Their Growth and Composition, 1919–43' (*History of Socialism Year Book 1968* (Prague 1969, roneo), pp. 257–259).

6 Aldo Agosti, *La Terza Internazionale: storia documentaria*, 3 vols. (Rome, 1979) III**, pp. 1162, 1164–5.

7 P. Spriano, *I comunisti europei e Stalin* (Turin, 1983), pp. 182–186 and in general cap 16.

8 Agosti 3** 1161–1165 for immediate communist reactions to German-Soviet pact and war. In its survey of 'One Year of Imperialist War' the *Communist International* (No. 9 Sept. 1940, pp. 571–584) did not so much mention the word 'fascism' or the German conquests . F. Fürnberg's 'The Question of Working Class Unity' (ibid., No. 10 Oct. 1940) did mention fascism, but only to point out the errors of Social Democracy, at the service of British imperialism, which claimed that the war was 'anti-fascist'.

9 The present writer can state this from personal memories for the CPGB.

10 Earl Browder, *Teheran and America: Perspectives and Tasks* (New York, 1944), pp. 13–14.

11 Cf. P. Spriano, *Storia del PCI* (Turin, 1969), vol. II, p. 384.

12 *Die Kommunistische Internationale: Kurzer historischer Abriss* (Berlin-East, 1970), p. 437).

13 Cf. Cde Krumov (Bulgaria) at the 7th World Congress: 'As to the damaging consequences of the factional line of the sectarian leadership group, it is indicated by the incredible fact that the campaign in connexion with the Leipzig Trial was conducted with extraordinary feebleness in Bulgaria, although Cde Dimitrov provided the Party with irreplaceable weapons for the fight against fascism.' *Protokoll des VII Weltkongresses der Kommunistischen Internationale (Ungerkürzte Ausgabe)*. Verlag Neuer Weg, Stuttgart, 1976, vol. I, pp. 229–230.

14 Cf. 'The Reichstag Fire Trial: Dimitrov's final speech' in Georgi Dimitrov: *Selected Speeches and Articles* (London, 1951), pp. 26, 30.

15 Miloš Hajek, *Storia dell 'Internationale Comunista (1921–35)* (Rome, 1969), p. 254.

16 J. Fauvet, *Histoire du Parti Communiste Français* (2 vols, Paris, 1900), I, p. 143.

17 This is the view taken in Claudin op. cit. See also Leo Valiani, 'Fronti popolari e politica sovietica' and F. Claudin, 'La politica di fronte popolare nell'Internazionale Comunista', in A. Agosti ed. *Problemi di Storia dell 'Internazionale Comunista' (1919–39): relazioni tenute al Seminario di studi dalla Fondazione Luigi Einaudi* (Turin, 1974).

18 Claudin in Agosti ed., pp. 219–221.

19 G. Amendola, *Storia del partito comunista italiano* (Rome, 1978), p. 230.

20 Hajek, *op cit.*, pp. 204–238, passim.

21 Franz Borkenau, *European Communism* (London, 1953), p. 71; A. Agosti, *Terza Internazionale* III**, p. 722.

22 Agosti, 'L'historiographie de l'Internationale Communiste' (*Cahiers d'Histoire de l'Institut de Recherches Marxistes* 2(36) 1980), pp. 35–6.

23 See Aldo Agosti, 'Il mondo della Terza Internazionale: i stati maggiori' in *Storia del Marxismo* (Turin, 1980), III, p. i, 379–437).

24 Hajek, op. cit. 217. For Fried see B. Lazitch and M. Drachkovich, *Biographical Dictionary of the Comintern* (Stanford, 1973).

25 Claude Coussement-José Gotovitch, 'Qui a tué Clément?' (*Cahiers Marxistes* N.S.XIV, Jan. 1983 (Bruxelles), pp. 38–40).

26 V. M. Lejbzon-K. K. Sirinja, *Il septimo congresso dell'Internazionale Comunista* (Rome, 1975). This is confirmed, on the basis of Bulgarian sources in J. Mérot, *Dimitrov, un révolutionnaire de notre temps* (Paris, 1972), pp. 184–7.

27 Th. Weingartner, *Stalin und der Aufstieg, Hitlers: die Deutschlandspolitik der Sowjetunion und der Kommunistischen Internationale (1929–34)*, (Berlin, 1970) 203ff. The USSR actually kept its diplomatic options open until well into 1935 (cf. Marta Dassú, 'Fronte unico e fronte popolare' in *Storia del Marxismo*, III, ii, 597).

28 *European Communism*, pp. 117–18.

29 Hajek, p. 267.

30 Fauvet, I., pp. 139–40.

31 Lejbzon & Sirinja, *op cit.*, 77ff.

32 Ernesto Ragionieri, Introduction to Palmiro Togliatti, *Opere*, III, p. 1 (1929–35), CXCVIII.

33 Ibid., CLXXXIX-CXC.

34 Ibid., CXCI-CXCIII.

35 The Soviet Institute of Marxism-Leninism's official '*Die Kommunistische Internationale: Kurzer historischer Abriss*' (Berlin, 1970), p. 439 quite specifically states that the initiative for the 'popular front' came from the French Communist Party. So does Tito (*Yugoslav Communists and the International Workers' Movement*, Belgrade, n.d. 13) who was then in Moscow.

36 *Die Kommunistische Internationale vor dem VII Weltkongress* (Moscow-Leningrad, 1935), pp. 241–42.

37 Protokoll des III Kongresses der Kommunistischen Internationale (Hamburg, 1921), pp. 89–90 (Trotsky), pp. 508–18 (Lenin), esp. pp. 510, 517; Hajek *op. cit.*, pp. 20–22.

38 Hajek, op. cit., pp. 46–47.

39 *Resolutions and Theses of the Fourth Congress of the Communist International* (London, 1923), pp. 31–34 ('The Workers' Government'). Labour governments as in

Australia and Britain were seen as 'Liberal governments'. Hajek op cit., pp. 50–52.

40 Claudin, *La crise*, I, p. 207.

41 *Protokoll des VII Weltkongresses der Kommunistischen Internationale* (*Ungekürzte Ausgabe*) (Stuttgart, 1976), I, pp. 363, 367 (Dimitrov's Report). This is a reprint of the special issues on the Congress published in *Rundschau über Politik, Wirtschaft u. Arbeiterbewegung* (Basel), 1935. The only report of the Congress published as such was late and incomplete (*VII Weltkongress der Kommunistischen Internationale. Gekürztes stenographisches Protokoll.* Moscow, 1939). Cf. G. Procacci, 'L'Internazionale Comunista dal I al VII Congresso 1919–35' (Istituto Giangiacomo Feltrinelli, *Annali*, I, 1958, pp. 283–315).

42 Maurice Thorez, *Fils du Peuple* (Paris, 1960 ed.), p. 102.

43 The letter is reprinted in E. H. Carr, *The Comintern and the Spanish Civil War* (N.Y., 1984), Note A., pp. 86–87.

44 Marta Dassú, *loc. cit.*, pp. 621–26; Agosti, *Terza Internazionale*, 3**, pp. 905–12.

45 Fauvet, *op cit.*, pp. 193–97.

46 Dassú *loc. cit.*, p. 603. For Dimitrov's condemnation – which appears to refer to this actual resolution – cf. *Protokoll des VII Weltkongresses*, I, p. 367.

47 Reprinted in E. Ragionieri ed. *Palmiro Togliatti, Opere*, IV, pp. i, 139–54. For Dimitrov's views, elaborated by Togliatti, see Agosti, *Terza Internazionale* 3**, pp. 953–54.

48 For general criticisms in this sense, see Claudin, *La crise*. For France 1936, Pierre Broué et Nicole Dorey, 'Critiques de gauche et opposition révolutionnaire au Front Populaire (1936–38)' (*Le Mouvement Social* 54, Jan.-Marsh 1966, pp. 91–134). For Italy, Renzo del Carria, *Proletari senza rivoluzione: Storia delle classi subalterne italiane dal 1860 al 1950* (Milan, 1970), vol. II, cap XX.

49 G. Dupeux, *Le Front Populaire et les Elections de 1936* (Paris, 1959), p. 126.

50

51 E. H. Carr, op. cit., p. 21.

52 E. H. Carr, op. cit., p. 87.

53 M. Djilas, *Conversations with Stalin* (Harmondsworth, 1963), p. 90.

54 F. Fejtöx, *Storia delle Democrazie Popolari* (Florence, 1955), pp. 64–65.

55 Agosti, Terza Internazionale 3**, pp. 1186–87. Immediately after the German attack on the USSR, Dimitrov told the Yugoslavs to bear in mind that 'in the present phase, the issue is liberation from Fascist oppression and not the socialist revolution.' Stephen Clissold, *Yugoslavia and the Soviet Union, 1939–73. A documentary survey* (Oxford, 1975), pp. 145–46.

56 Claudin, *La crise*, II, pp. 443–48.

57 Kardelj, as reported in E. Reale, *Avec Jacques Duclos Au Banc des Accusés* (Paris, 1958), pp. 34, 135.

58 Alfred J. Rieber, *Stalin and the French Communist Party, 1941–47* (New York and London, 1962), cap VI.

59 Claudin, *La crise*, II, p. 383.

60 Ch. de Gaulle, *Mémoires de guerre*, II (Paris, 1956), pp. 291–92.

61 The total of resistance combatants in the Forces Françaises de l'Interieur in April 1944 was 4200. Annex I, *Cahiers d'histoire, de l'Institut Maurice Thorez*, pp. 8–9, 1974, La Liberation de la France.

62 P. Spriano, *Storia del Partito Comunista Italiano V: La Resistenza. Togliatti e il partito nuovo* (Turin, 1975), p. 366 for Togliatti's directive to the Communists of Northern and Central Italy in June 1944.

63 Spriano, ibid., pp. 446–50.

64 Reale, op. cit., pp. 34, 136.

65 P. Secchia, 'La Resistenza: grandezza e limiti oggetivi' (*Rinascita*, 19 Feb. 1971, pp. 20–21). S. points out that no northern Communist leaders 'considered the non-existent possibility of fighting for the socialist revolution', and that the Resistance was incapable of winning any kind of power, even democratic power, because it never had the force to do more than liberate scattered and generally small zones for more than a month or two: 'we (the antifascists) never had effective power . . . because we always lacked the men and means to win it.'

66 E. Sereni, 'La scelta del 1943–45' (*Rinascita*, 29 Jan. 1971, pp. 23–34), who doubts that allied armed intervention against a communist seizure of power in North Italy was unavoidable, regards the question of national unity as the decisive consideration. This also appears to have been the impression of the (disapproving) Yugoslavs (Reale, p. 134).

67 G. Amendola, *Un'Isola* (Milan, 1980), pp. 31–34 for Togliatti's reception of Gramsci's manuscripts (*via* Piero Sraffa) about which he maintained extreme discretion.

68 For Stalin's attempt in 1950 to remove Togliatti from the effective leadership of the PCI, see G. Bocca, *Palmiro Togliatti* (Bari, 1973), pp. 543–54.

69 P. Spriano, *I comunisti europei e Stalin*, pp. 216–17. There is virtually no direct evidence for western Europe. Spriano cites what he rightly calls a 'sibylline' passage from Sereni in the article cited above ('If we are not mistaken, there was at the time occasion to discover the views on this matter of our Soviet comrades, even if in the form which can hardly even be described as oblique'). However, Longo in 1947 justified the Italian line to the Yugoslavs in private conversation as having followed Soviet instructions (V. Dedijer, *Tito Speaks* (London, 1953)), p. 305.

70 For 'Hornerism' see Noreen Branson, *History of the Communist Party of Great Britain 1927–41* (London, 1985), pp. 85–88.

71 Spriano, *I comunisti europei*, cap 10, pp. 106–16; Agosti, *Terza Internazionale* 3★★, p. 1170.

72 Fejtö, op. cit., cap IV, pp. 262–68. For the tradition of a Balkan Federation on the left, see E. H. Carr, *Socialism in One Country* I (London, 1964), pp. 203–7. More generally, L. S. Stavrianos, *Balkan Federation*. A History of the Movement toward Balkan Unity in Modern Times (Northampton, Mass., 1944). For the Czech attitude to the Marshall Plan (including the Czech Communists), see Josef Belda, 'Some Problems Regarding the Czechoslovak Road to Socialism' in *History of Socialism Year Book 1968* (Prague, 1969), pp. 113–54, esp. pp. 133–35.

73 Reale, pp. 75–76. For the reformuation of 'People's Democracy' see *On People's Democracy in Eastern Europe and China: A Selection of Articles and Speeches*. London 1951.

74 Cf. Donald Sassoon, *The Strategy of the Italian Communist Party from the Resistance to the Historic Compromise* (London, 1981) for a careful analysis of Togliatti's thinking, esp. pp. 32–33. See also G. Vacca, *Saggio su Togliatti* (Bari, 1974), esp. caps IV, V.

British Imperialism and the Partitions of India and Palestine

Wm. Roger Louis

The year Lord Linlithgow became Viceroy of India, 1936, was also the year of the Arab revolt in Palestine. 'With my Indian experience', he reflected on one of his visits to the Middle East, '[I] gained the feeling that I was witnessing an example of the dangers of alienating a peasant people from their lands.' A year later, in 1937, writing in response to the conclusion drawn by the Peel Commission that Palestine should be partitioned (yet retaining economic links and providing British strategic facilities), Linlithgow observed that 'Willie Peel' and his colleagues appeared to have made the best of a bad situation.[1] A separate state might prove to be a good solution after all – a thought that found an echo in most British official circles in 1947 perhaps more in regard to Pakistan than Palestine.

Both problems had their immediate origins a decade earlier, and events in Palestine were much on the minds of those in India. 'I fear that in certain parts of the country, e.g. NW India,' Mohammed Iqbal wrote to Mohammed Ali Jinnah in May 1937, 'Palestine may be repeated.'[2] In this critical year moderate Zionists took heart at the recommendations of the Peel Commission ('Today we laid the basis for the Jewish state' were the words of Chaim Weizmann, the President of the World Zionist Organization, after a conversation with the principal architect of the scheme, Professor Reginald Coupland of Oxford).[3] In Palestine itself the partition proposal signified to the Arabs an attempt at colonization comparable to that of the French in Algeria or the Italians in Libya – 'Hebrewstan,' as it was called by some Indian newspapers. In India, as Penderel Moon and many others have argued, the crucial point was the Muslim League's response to the implementation of the provincial autonomy of the India Act of 1935 and the electoral successes of the Indian National Congress in February 1937.[4] The ten-year ring to Indian and Palestinian developments – with 1937 and 1947 as the critical years – also had a resonance over three decades. If one were to pursue a Whiggish comparison, with the Montagu Declaration of 1917 as the Indian point of departure, and the Balfour Declaration of 1917 for the Zionist, then the story would end with only one year difference between Indian and Israeli freedom.[5]

Reginald Coupland (for the present discussion a central figure because of his involvement in both Palestinian and Indian affairs) stated in 1946 that 'the Indian problem . . . with all its obvious differences, is similar at root to that of Palestine. Muslim minority like the Jewish is fired with consciousness of "nationhood" which will not submit to a majority rule by another "nation".'[6] Coupland was increasingly apprehensive about the consequences of full-scale civil war in Palestine. Full political sovereignty imposed by the Jews on their own terms would lead to economic catastrophe, at least for the Arabs. If Palestine were to have been partitioned, it would have been best done quickly and decisively in 1937 with political as well as economic provisions (Haifa as a 'free port,' for example) to ensure stability. Here perhaps was the lesson for India. 'Partition', Coupland had written in his exhaustive study of *The Indian Problem* during the war, 'means that the Moslem State or States would be relatively weak and poor,' the same point he had emphasized about Arab Palestine. 'Will not Moslem Patriots say what those Arabs said: "What does it matter how weak and poor our homelands are if only we are masters in them"?'[7] Could not rationality yet prevail over the fanaticism of partition? As late as the spring of 1946 Coupland, and, as will be seen, many officials within the British government, refused to give up hope that outright partition in both Palestine and India might be averted.

The two cases are so dissimilar that analogies can be little more than tangential; but it is nevertheless possible to explain, from the British vantage point, why the Palestine episode ended so disastrously and why the accession to the Commonwealth by both India and Pakistan appeared at the time to be one of the great achievements of the Labour government. An examination of the two cases helps to explain the changing character of British imperialism in its response to nationalism, the Labour intitiative, and the circumstances of possible American intervention. The two situations developed so differently in part because of the attitude of the United States government. The possibility of American support for Indian nationalists appeared as a shaft of light in 1942 but flickered only intermittently thereafter. By contrast, the spotlight turned on the Palestine issue by the American Zionists, at least from the time of the Biltmore resolution calling for an independent 'Jewish Commonwealth' in May 1942, illuminates a main theme down to the time of Israeli independence in May 1948. The Indian and Jewish struggle against the British sustains the analogy, yet the intensity of the Palestine issue in Anglo-American relations was beyond parallel. One of Churchill's frequent complaints in the postwar period was that Palestine, a territory the size of Wales, held down four to five British divisions, nearly 100,000 men or roughly the equivalent of one-tenth of the Indian Army in 1947 of one million (coincidentally the figure 100,000 was the estimated size of the non-military European population in India). Viewed from the 'Imperial' perspective of India as the centre of the British Empire, Palestine was a disruptive element out of all proportion to its size or significance.

In 1946 the *Hindustan Times* (a newspaper of interest for present purposes because its editor, Gandhi's son, Devadas, appeared to have had a keen appreciation of Palestinian affairs) denied that there could be any comparison between Palestine and India simply because of difference in demographic scale: 'Except in the one respect that both are creations of British imperialism, there is no parallel between them . . . The total population of Arabs and Jews in Palestine is less than the number of Indians officially acknowledged to have died in the Bengal famine of 1943.'[8] The conventional British figure was three million. It is a point worth bearing in mind. In 1945 the respective Jewish and Arab populations of Palestine were 560,000 and 1,200,000. In the Punjab alone, a province over seventeen times the size of the Palestine mandate (minus Trans-Jordan), there were some 16,000,000 Muslims and 7,500,000 Hindus plus an almost solid block of 4,500,000 Sikhs. Nor was the demographic difference the only striking contrast. Bearing in mind Churchill's comparison of the size of Palestine and Wales, if one superimposes an Indian map over one of the British Isles and Europe, with Wales in the western part of Baluchistan (a province itself some sixteen times larger than Palestine), then Peshawar will be in northern Norway, Calcutta will be east of Moscow, and the southern tip of India will fall somewhere between Greece and Cyrenaica. Such comparisons would not have impressed the Zionists. The Jewish nationalists were driven by the messianic aspiration to return to 'Eretz-Yisrael' and they were above all obsessed with the six million Jews murdered by the Nazis, a unique event in human history surpassing all other considerations.

If the Holocaust provided the main postwar drive of Jewish nationalism, it was the immigration question that distinguished the Palestine problem from the one of India. Immigration in the interwar years increased the Jewish community from 83,000 to 444,000 – to some thirty percent of the total inhabitants. Part of the British purpose behind the 1939 White Paper was to stabilize the population at about one-third Jewish and two-thirds Arab.[9] Jewish immigration would be limited to 75,000 in the next five years, and thereafter would depend on Arab consent. The White Paper also prohibited land sales in some areas and placed further restrictions in others. To the Jews of course the White Paper represented appeasement of the Arabs as well as a betrayal of the Zionist cause, an abandonment of the Balfour Declaration of 1917 promising the Jews a national home in Palestine. Like the Jews, the Indian Princes in 1947 also detected British willingness to sacrifice historic commitment. British pledges were reinterpreted according to prevailing circumstances. In 1939 the White Paper aimed not only to secure Arab goodwill necessary to hold the eastern Mediterranean but also to avert partition. To the Foreign Office, at least, the positive purpose was the creation of a binational state with political and economic guarantees for the Jewish minority. The White Paper drew inspiration from the historical experiences of Canada and South Africa, and it anticipated the formulas which the Cabinet Mission in 1946 attempted to devise in order to keep the Muslims within a unified India. The wartime response of David Ben-Gurion reveals a profound difference between the Jewish struggle and the Indian, whether Hindu or Muslim. 'We shall fight the War as if there were no White Paper, and the White Paper as if there were no War.'[10] To the Jews a Nazi victory would be the ultimate catastrophe. It was not at all the same for the Indians, or for the Arabs.

There is another Middle Eastern parallel besides the one of Palestine which is significant for the issue of British power and the question of loss of 'Imperial' nerve. In 1942 the British held firm in Egypt as well as India. In the spring of that year German forces opened a campaign against Egypt. Had it been successful it might have snapped the 'spinal cord' connecting Britain and the short route to India, and it might have led to preponderant German influence in the Middle East. The protagonist of this episode was Sir Miles Lampson, the Ambassador in Cairo. Lampson was soon to be raised to the peerage as Lord Killearn in part because of his decisive stand. He is a figure of considerable interest in the Britain-Middle East-India connection because in 1943 Churchill attempted, unsuccessfully, to make him Linlithgow's successor as Viceroy. In February 1942 Lampson had surrounded the Egyptian Royal Palace with British tanks. He presented an ultimatum to King Farouk to abdicate or to purge his court of Axis influences and install a pro-British Wafd regime.[11] The successful intervention, like Linlithgow's clampdown on the 'Quit

India' movement a few months later, had far-reaching consequences. At the time, at least to the diehard Tories, it seemed to prove that Egypt could be ruled indefinitely, if necessary, by bayonets. The British Empire could endure if there was the political will power combined with adequate military force. Lampson in short personified Britain's dominant position in the Middle East. The younger generation of Egyptian nationalists, who rankled at the humilation of 1942, proved to be exceedingly sceptical whether the Labour government after the war would end the unequal relationship. The mystique as well as the reality of British determination and ruthlessness left a permanent imprint on Egyptian nationalism at a critical time.

It is helpful in getting a bearing on Linlithgow's response to the emergency in India to know that he regarded Killearn as well as Churchill as a reactionary.[12] Linlithgow is a much misjudged Viceroy, in part because he is seldom assessed according to his own goals and Tory code of conduct. '[H]eavy of body and slow of mind, solid as a rock and with almost a rock's lack of awareness,' was Nehru's judgement.[13] H. V. Hodson made a shrewd comment when he observed that Linlithgow's heaviness of style belied a decisiveness and vigour of mind.[14] Like Killearn, Linlithgow sought to preserve British supremacy, but he believed that the British in India could remain dominant only by adjusting to changing circumstances and keeping the game constantly in play. He was more vigorous than Killearn in attempting to align 'collaborators' of all political colours, Hindu, Muslim, Sikh, or 'Untouchable,' and just as determined to prevent any anti-British extremist from gaining the upper hand. In holding the balance in Indian politics, the Congress leaders were his main adversaries, of whom, before the war, he regarded Gandhi as distinctly more reasonable and pragmatic than the doctrinaire and 'radical' Jawaharlal Nehru. Linlithgow's political lodestar was the India Act of 1935, to which he had contributed substantially as chairman of the Joint Select Committee that guided it through Parliament despite the opposition of Churchill and other diehards. Linlithgow had an unrivalled knowledge of the Act's details and implications. Its purpose was a federal structure for a united India in which the Princely States would be integrated. In John Gallagher's words, it signified an adjustment in the method of keeping the Indian connection 'while retaining intact most of its fundamental advantages'.[15] Linlithgow believed in self-government, provided the British retained control over such areas as defence and foreign affairs, and perhaps he genuinely subscribed to the idea of Dominion status – but in the remote future, probably the twenty-first century. In the 1936–39 period he concentrated much of his efforts on persuading the Princes to accept the 1935 Act. He was not unduly dismayed when it had to be shelved because of the war.

Percival Spear has written that in 1939 'Pakistan was in the air.'[16] The Linlithgow Papers substantially confirm the details of the drift in Indian politics more than the atmosphere, in part because of the Viceroy's wariness in dealing directly with Indian politicians. 'I feel no doubt', Linlithgow wrote in March 1939, 'that the Muslims are beginning to feel increasingly uneasy at what Jinnah described as "Hindu arrogance", and increasingly apprehensive of the fate of a minority – even a minority of 90 million people – under the scheme of the [India 1935] Act.'[17] Linlithgow did not believe that the Muslim League or the Princes had the power to block the Act. His basic strategy was to play the Muslim League and the Princes off against the Congress. He made a serious misjudgment in underestimating Muslim sentiment before the outbreak of the war. He did not take the idea of 'Pakistan' seriously. He wrote after the adoption of the March 1940 Lahore resolution calling for the creation of a separate state or states of Pakistan: 'My first reaction is, I confess, that silly as the Muslim scheme for partition is, it would be a pity to throw too much cold water on it at the moment . . .'[18] What Jinnah feared, Linlithgow surmised, was a federal India dominated by Hindus. Part of the purpose of the famous British 'August offer' of 1940 was to assure the Muslims that they would be protected against a 'Hindu Raj' as well as to hold over the discussion of the 1935 Act and a 'new constitution' until after the war. The game of politics continued, in Linlithgow's judgment, with Jinnah and Gandhi as the principals and 'no other leaders in sight'.[19] Nehru he had written off as a hopeless Anglophobe extremist bent on Marxist revolution. Of the principal danger the Viceroy had no doubt: 'Congress will I fear have to be beaten in the present trial of strength before we can get forward.'[20] Such was Linlithgow's outlook in 1940, the year Churchill became Prime Minister.

Both Churchill and his Secretary of State for India, Leopold Amery, were Zionists.[21] By contrast with their attitude towards Palestine, they both rejected outright the idea of a separate Muslim state in India. Even Linlithgow responded less rigidly. Though contemptuous of the plan, he could nevertheless use it as a card to keep Jinnah in play. To Amery partition would be 'disastrous', 'fatal', the prelude to civil war and anarchy (though he rationalized it in 1942 as being compatible with Dominion status). Linlithgow and Amery's ideas in general must be distinguished from Churchill's. Both the Viceroy and the Secretary of State in contrast with the Prime Minister were enlightened Tories. Linlithgow had more of a commitment to the general development of India than any Viceroy since Curzon.

Amery was truly dedicated to the long-range Dominion status of a unified India and willing eventually to accept *two* Dominions. Churchill's celebrated denunciation of the India Act of 1935 reveals his general attitude: 'a gigantic quilt of jumbled crochet work, a monstrous monument of shame built by pigmies.'[22] As for Indian leadership, Churchill believed that it consisted of no more than a clique of the 'Hindoo priesthood' who were opposed by the peasant masses, the untouchables, the Princes, the Muslims, and other minorities. The Indian peoples therefore depended on British guardianship. 'When you learn to think of a race as inferior beings it is difficult to get rid of that way of thinking,' he later reflected. He applauded the 'Hindu-Muslim feud' as 'the bulwark of British rule.'[24] Despite the chasm in outlook that separated him from Amery and Linlithgow, Churchill could rely on both of them to defend the Raj against all comers, Americans as well as Japanese.

As Robin Moore has written, one way of viewing the Cripps mission of March 1942 is as the attempt by British Labour, at one stage with American assistance, to break the Churchill-Amery-Linlithgow throttlehold on India.[25] Clement Attlee, at this time Lord Privy Seal in the coalition government, once called Linlithgow a 'defeatist'. It was a perceptive remark. He saw that Linlithgow merely intended to uphold the status quo rather than to make political progress. 'We need a man to do in India what Durham did in Canada,' Attlee wrote to his colleagues in the War Cabinet.[26] Sir Stafford Cripps, a patriot as well as a Labour statesman committed to Indian independence, hoped to hold Indian loyalty by offering *de facto* Dominion status (or in other words self-determination and the possibility of Pakistan) and the Indianization of the Executive Council of the Indian government in all areas except the critical one of defence. He arrived in India after the fall of Singapore and the loss of Britain's Far Eastern Empire, the conquest of most of Burma by the Japanese, and at the time of possible invasion of the Orissa coast and southern India – and at the same time, roughly, to keep the Middle Eastern parallel in mind, that Rommel was advancing towards Egypt and Killearn had clamped down on Farouk. For present purposes Cripps made two critical errors: the first was his underestimating of Linlithgow's ability to block a settlement with the Congress leaders, and the other was his misguided hope of decisive support by President Roosevelt's representative in India, Colonel Louis Johnson.

Churchill, Amery, and Linlithgow of course saw a propaganda purpose in the Cripps mission. In Amery's words to Churchill, the aim was to provide something that would satisfy 'Moslems and *just possibly* some of the Congress, as well as Americans and Left Wing here'.[27] By the phrase 'just possibly' Amery expressed the doubt that

Congress would accept a formula in which the military command of the war would remain firmly in British hands. This was the principal point on which the Cripps mission broke down, despite Cripps's gamble that he could pull the Americans with him (through Colonel Johnson) in a proposal to admit Indian participation in the running of the war. Churchill supported the Viceroy and the Commander-in-Chief, General Wavell, in refusing to admit Indian influence in the command of the war. The Churchill-Amery-Linlithgow 'plus Wavell' axis thus blocked the Cripps-Johnson initiative to create an Indian national government which might have had the support of Jinnah as well as the Congress leaders. The significance was profound. One of the premises of the 1942 offer was that India might be held together by the Congress and the Muslim League fighting against the Japanese.[28] The collapse of the Cripps mission meant that Jinnah could pursue the alternative option of not joining a unified India after the war. It is arguable that if Roosevelt had leaned on Churchill, and Churchill in turn had been obliged to tone down Linlithgow and Wavell's objections, then Congress might have been able to participate in a 'national' government and Pakistan might not have become a mass issue.

Two Indian historians, M. S. Venkataramani and B. K. Shrivastava, have dealt at length with the American dimension of the problem.[29] As they point out, Roosevelt was getting advice from not only Louis Johnson in Delhi but also Harry Hopkins in London. As usual F.D.R. was hedging his bets. From my own rereading of the Roosevelt Papers at Hyde Park, he genuinely apprehended not only Japanese invasion of India but also possible revolution.[30] This was the gist of some of the warnings he received from Louis Johnson. But Harry Hopkins had his ear, and the voice was the echo of Churchill. Churchill was well aware that F.D.R. suspected that the British were unwilling to grant the equivalent of self-government and that a compromise might be found on the issue of control of defence affairs. F.D.R. was no doubt moved by Churchill's passionate eloquence. But he also made decisions that corresponded with his highest priorities in winning the war. By insisting on Indian self-government (about which Roosevelt himself had doubts) at this stage of the war – four months after Pearl Harbour – he would not only have caused dismay among his own military advisers such as Henry L. Stimson but he would also have driven a wedge into the Anglo-American alliance. It was better to keep on good terms with Churchill than Gandhi. No one can say for certain whether F.D.R.'s support of Johnson and Cripps might have won the allegiance of the Indian National Congress and thus might have helped to defeat the Japanese. What can be said is that Roosevelt's intervention in the

Indian issue would have had drastic repercussions in Anglo-American relations.

After the collapse of the Cripps mission, the next juncture was the 'Quit India' movement of August 1942. Linlithgow, from a Tory vantage point, rose to the occasion. The day after the fall of Singapore (15 February, 1942), he had written that 'the key to success in this war is now very largely in my hands'.[31] After the fall of Rangoon on 8 March he apprehended that Gandhi was organizing an all-out effort to undermine the authority of the government. He feared the danger of the Mahatma's 'Pétainism'. He had taken all precaution against the 'open rebellion' of the Congress. The day after the All India Congress Committee's demand for immediate departure of the British, Gandhi and other prominent Congress leaders were arrested. The rebellion was quelled within six weeks. By the end of the year there had been 1,000 killed, 3,000 injured, and more than 60,000 interned (the conventional British figures). '[If] we had [not] struck as swiftly and as decisively as we did,' Linlithgow wrote to Amery, 'we might have found ourselves faced with an extremely awkward situation, wholly revolutionary in character, well organised by people working underground and deterred by no considerations of non-violence or the like.'[32] Linlithgow felt that he was entirely entitled to claim that he was suppressing the most serious rebellion since 1857, indeed since the American revolution.[33]

At no time, of course, could the High Commissioner for Palestine have made such a claim. The comparison would be the crackdown on the Jewish nationalists in mid-1946, with some 2,700 interned, and the explosion at the King David Hotel in Jerusalem in July of the same year, with some 90 British, Arabs, and Jews killed. Yet, as long as the Palestine issue festered, Britain's security was threatened throughout the Middle East. There lies the reason why the Palestine emergency is comparable on a large scale to that of India. In India the key to British resolution of the problem lay in part in the success of Churchill, Amery, and Linlithgow in preventing the internationalization of the issue. The quelling of the 1942 disturbances proved to most Americans, including Roosevelt, that in India the British could manage their own affairs, and would resist to the bitter end any American interference. By contrast after 1945 the British had to rely on American assistance in dealing with Palestine. This assessment is not to minimize the place held by India in American calculations during the war itself. Auchinleck's biographer, John Connell, has written:

> Their stand-point was one of cold, vigilant, businesslike and rather naive detachment; but above all they were concerned with the sub-continent's strategic and logistical utility. By contrast the

British . . . knew India . . . and the Americans did not; and for the time being they ruled India.[34]

One may rightly infer that most Americans believed that the British Empire was in an impending state of dissolution in India and at least parts of the Middle East.

Roosevelt did not change his mind on not intervening in India, and he was kept well informed. Louis Johnson's successor was William Phillips, a former Under-Secretary of State who is a figure of considerable interest in the India-Palestine analogy because he later served on the Anglo-American Committee of Inquiry in Palestine in 1946. Phillips regarded Linlithgow as a chip off the old block of a figure well known in American revolutionary history, George III. Phillips was appalled at the pomp, extravagance, and arrogance of the Raj. He believed it a serious mistake on the part of Linlithgow not to keep open the channels of communication with the Congress leaders and not to seek a course of conciliation. Yet Phillips remained a 'perfect gentleman' (Amery's phrase) and acquiesced in Linlithgow's dictum to 'keep off the grass'. Phillips did so because this was Roosevelt's policy, not out of sympathy with British rule in India. As long as the war lasted, Roosevelt was content with the British upholding the status quo. Changes would come later. In his last despatch from Delhi in May 1943 Phillips ruefully reported that the British were 'sitting "pretty" . . . [and] have been completely successful in their policy of "keeping the lid on" . . . There is to be no change' – at least so long as Linlithgow remained Viceroy.[35]

When Lord Wavell became Viceroy in October 1943, his outlook in some ways resembled Linlithgow's. Wavell was not anti-Hindu but he was profoundly mistrustful of Gandhi and the Congress leaders. In his view Gandhi was a purely negative force, incapable of imposing or inventing a positive solution. Wavell was sensitive to Muslim sentiment. It is his Middle Eastern background which I wish to stress in order to sustain the Palestine theme, and here it is useful to contrast Wavell's general outlook with Cripps's.

Despite Cripps's intellectual arrogance, there was a rapport between him and the Congress leaders that never existed to the same degree with any other British statesman, certainly not Attlee and definitely not Wavell. Cripps believed that it was of transcendent importance for Britain to remain on good terms with the 400 million Indians – one-fifth of humanity – and therefore with its majority, the Hindus, and the 'Hindu leadership', led by Nehru and Patel (with of course Gandhi as the spiritual if not the guiding political figure). Cripps in other words pursued a line of conciliation, which in the eyes of his critics was one of appeasement.

Before his Viceroyalty, Wavell had become Commander-in-Chief in India after a lifetime of military service mainly in the Middle East. He certainly did not minimize the importance of keeping on good terms with the Hindus, but he attached just as much significance to maintaining good relations with the ninety-million Muslim minority in India, which was more than the combined population of the Arab states of the Middle East. Wavell regarded the 'Muslim world' as stretching in a loose sense all the way from Morocco to Indonesia. From this angle of vision the Muslim minority in India could be regarded as part of the overall majority; and the Hindu majority in India as a minority in the predominant majority. All of this had grave implications for the British Empire and Commonwealth unless the majorities and minorities (regardless how one looked at the problem) could somehow be reconciled. It was by no means clear that an 'even-handed' policy would work. Cripps believed that the British should tilt towards the Hindus, while Wavell's inclinations propelled him towards the Muslims.

'[T]he really fatal thing for us,' Wavell wrote in regard to the analogy between the Middle East and India, 'would be to hang on to responsibility when we had lost the power to exercise it, and possibly to involve ourselves in a large-scale Palestine.'[36] By late 1946, if not earlier, Britain stood on the verge of being drawn into civil war not only in Palestine but also Greece. In Palestine, Britain and the United States would find themselves on opposite sides. In India the British could count on American support, even in the event of partition, provided they worked to prevent further 'balkanization' and attempted to ensure stability by a peaceful transfer of power. It was imperative for the British to maintain American goodwill in the eastern Mediterranean and throughout the world. Attlee's phrase 'world-wide commitments' helps to explain both Palestinian and Indian dilemmas.

Are there further common denominators? This is not the place to analyze the details of the Simla conference of 1945 and the Cabinet Mission of 1946, on the one hand, or, on the other, of the Anglo-American Committee of Inquiry of 1945–46 and the conferences held by the British and the Jews and Arabs in 1946–47. One may however put forward two generalizations about the policy of the Labour government:

1 the goal was to avoid partition in both India and Palestine;
2 if the goal proved to be unobtainable and if, after every possible effort had been made at reconciliation, then the aim would be to cut losses strictly in terms of British self-interest.

It was on the latter point, as will be seen, that Wavell found himself out of step with the Labour government's method of doing business. His pessimistic outlook on Indian politics contributed to his sacking as Viceroy.

The Palestinian and Indian issues were handled entirely separately, the former by Ernest Bevin as Secretary of State for Foreign Affairs, and the latter by a Cabinet Committee on India and Burma with Attlee and Cripps as the driving forces within it. Significantly enough, Bevin was not on the India and Burma committee. It was commonly alleged that he knew little of the Jewish mentality, and it may be added that he probably knew even less of the Hindu. Richard Crossman once stated that it was a Godsend that Bevin had no hand in India because he would have mucked it up as well.[37] Bevin wished to keep India within the British Empire, though with a shift towards an 'equal relationship' (in his view synonymous with Dominion status) similar to the one he was attempting to bring about in Egypt. He entirely dominated the Palestine question. His solution was essentially the one of the 1939 White Paper in which there would be Jewish autonomy within a larger Arab federation. Like Wavell and Mountbatten in India, he was willing to negotiate the terms of the federation (or its variations of 'provincial autonomy' along the lines of Swiss cantons), but his goal was to create a binational society with Palestine remaining essentially an Arab country. He encountered the stone wall not only of Jewish nationalism but also of the President of the United States and his advisers. The Zionists, notably Weizmann, had managed to win President Truman over to their side, and the President, not the State Department officials sympathetic to the Arabs, determined American policy. Truman once candidly stated that his pro-Zionist attitude could be explained by his having no Arab constituents.[38] He also had few Indian constituents, which perhaps explains his relative indifference to the question of India. When Bevin visited America in late 1946 he was astonished at the extent to which Palestine had become an issue in American politics. The Zionists were able to wage a successful crusade not only because they captured the President but also because they won a substantial amount of public sentiment. The struggle against the British struck a responsive chord in America's own revolutionary history as well as with other ethnic groups, notably the Irish.[39]

Despite the powerful Zionist and American opposition to his policy, Bevin nevertheless hoped to form a common front with the Arabs, who after all were the dominant majority in the neighbouring Middle Eastern states as well as Palestine. It was the failure to carry the Arabs with them – a breakdown of the 'collaborative mechanism', in Ronald Robinson's phrase – that led Bevin and Attlee in late 1946 and early 1947 to refer the issue to the United Nations, where they still hoped that the aim of creating a binational state, in other words an unpartitioned Palestine, would carry the majority.[40] It lost by only a few votes on 29 November 1947. The British had already decided to cut losses, but only after all options had been tried and all possibilities exhausted. In the end Palestine was judged to be a drain on the British economy and a military liability. In the Cabinet deliberations on how best to minimize American and Arab antagonism, the case for an 'even-handed' withdrawal was overwhelming.

When the British evacuated Palestine in the spring of 1948, the withdrawal was remarkably similar to the 'breakdown plan' drawn up by Wavell two years earlier in India. By 'breakdown' Wavell did not necessarily mean to imply defeat but rather the possibilities and probabilities of British withdrawal as a result of unwavering Indian opposition. He foresaw prolonged stalemate between the Congress and the Muslim League which might paralyze the administration and eventually lead to mass disturbances. One of the lessons of the 1942 'Quit India' movement was the possibility that it might happen again. This time the British might not be able successfully to contain it. As an administrative and military precaution Wavell's plan for possible withdrawal was a rational and necessary measure. As a matter of policy for the Labour government, it was unacceptable. It seemed to Attlee, not to mention Bevin and others who denounced Wavell as a defeatist, to be prejudging or moving towards the most undesirable outcome without finally exhausting the possibilities of a political settlement. Until the constitutional negotiations had proved to be futile, Attlee refused to despair.[41] There was an element of the Major Attlee of the First World War who was contemptuous of military officers' capacity for political judgment. Attlee and Cripps became increasingly intent on a political settlement with the leaders of the Congress and the Muslim League, even if it meant the upheaval of partition. The scepticism whether Wavell could salvage the situation led to Lord Mountbatten's succession in March 1947. By late 1946 India, as Wavell himself admitted, seemed to be going the way of Palestine, but without the determined effort to turn the tide.

In 1946 there were certain turning points in both India and Palestine, perhaps points of no return. In February sailors of the Royal Indian Navy mutinied in Bombay. The mutiny had critical implications for British security throughout India. In March the Cabinet Mission failed to produce agreement on a sophisticated 'three tier' system of government which attempted to strike a communal balance in part by groupings of Hindu and Muslim majority provinces (a scheme not dissimilar to some of the variants of the 'provincial autonomy' plan in Palestine). After the Muslim League's

'Direct Action' and the Calcutta massacre of 6,000 in August, all hope was lost (in the consensus of British historical opinion) for a united India. The comparable turning points on the Palestine side may also be briefly stated. The report of the Anglo-American Committee of Inquiry in April recommended that Palestine be neither a Jewish nor an Arab state (in other words the implicit premise was that of a binational state) and called for the immediate admission of 100,000 Jewish refugees. There followed a concerted military effort by the Zionists aiming to force Britain into a political settlement; but there was also the explosion at the King David Hotel in July caused by the extremists. Ernest Bevin continued to hold out hope for a binational solution, but the extreme Zionists were on their way to proving that a campaign of terrorism might be successful.

Even though terrorism might be successfully combatted (as some British military officers believed it could), prolonged conflict would turn Palestine into an immense 'Bevingrad', in other words, a territory under harsh military occupation with troops bivouacked behind barbed wire. British forces would be compelled to wage guerrilla warfare in an urban setting against the survivors of Nazi Germany (as in fact proved to be the case). Quite apart from the demand on the manpower of the British Army, the strain on morale would be severe, even in a territory the size of Wales. According to one calculation there was one British soldier for every city block.[42] If the Jews could do it why not the Hindus or the Muslims, where the chances for success were far greater? Lord Wavell thus had good reason to be apprehensive of a 'large-scale Palestine' in India. Even if the willpower of a Killearn or a Linlithgow could be reasserted, where could the manpower be found?

'Up to now,' Field-Marshal Sir Claude Auchinleck (Commander-in-Chief, India) stated in June 1946, 'it had been possible to rely on the loyalty of the Indian Army.' The Hindu-Muslim rift now cast doubt on the reliability of Indian units even outside India itself. 'This even applies to Gurkha units', according to the Chiefs of Staff.[43] Should the Indian armed forces be disaffected, it would require no less than four to five additional British divisions to restore the situation. Where were the additional troops to come from? No British troops would remain in Greece. British forces in Germany would be halved. The reserve division in Italy would be removed. And the entire question of Indian forces in Indonesia would have to be reviewed. Not least there would be insufficient troops to keep the peace in Palestine.[44] Nor was there complete agreement on priority. According to Field-Marshal Lord Montgomery, who became Chief of the Imperial General Staff in July 1946, 'the provision of the divisions would be impossible in view of the present situation in Palestine and Venezia

Giulia'.[45] If there was one particular year when the sun never appeared to set on the troubles of the British Empire, it was probably the year 1946.[46]

If that year in some respects seemed to represent an 'Imperial' nadir, the one of 1947, Palestine aside, was Britain's year for a miracle (hyperbole was not restricted to the creation of the state of Israel). India and Pakistan agreed to Commonwealth membership. In Palestine all talk of a Jewish 'Dominion' had stopped in 1939, if not before. India and Pakistan resembled a phoenix arising from the ashes of the British Empire of a past age. 'This does not look like quitting', wrote J. C. Smuts, the Prime Minister of South Africa.[47] Indeed at one stage it appeared as if the British might more or less preserve the unity of India, with two Dominions but with one Governor-General who would coordinate defence issues and thus preserve Britain's status as a great 'world power'. Pakistan and India would continue to link the Empire and Dominions in the East in defence affairs as well as on the map, which would continue to be painted British red. As Professor Partha Gupta has argued, for the British the defence issue was at the heart of the matter.[48] When Mountbatten learned that Patel and Nehru would be prepared to accept, as an interim measure at least, Dominion status (and to muffle the Congress battlecry of an 'independent sovereign Republic') in return for an early transfer of power, Churchill and the Tories as well as the Labour government leapt at 'the greatest opportunity', in Mountbatten's ringing words, 'ever offered to the Empire'.[49] The terminal date of British rule, which Wavell had insisted upon and the British Cabinet had fixed at no later than June 1948, would be moved forward, eventually to 15 August – a date Mountbatten chose, in his precipitous effort to move as quickly as possible, not merely on grounds that it signified the anniversary of the end of the Second World War, but also because he apprehended the collapse of British authority.

These concluding comments will approach the actual transfer of power by viewing it in a Middle Eastern and American context, and finally by drawing a comparison between the territorial partitions of Palestine and India. One of the key decisions was taken by Attlee and Bevin after Christmas 1946 when they decided to withdraw troops from Greece and, almost simultaneously, as has been mentioned, to refer the Palestine question to the United Nations. A study of this juncture is rewarding because it indicates the common motive in both Palestine and India: the refusal to be drawn into civil war. In early 1947 the United States acquired a commitment to defend the eastern Mediterranean, thereby relieving the British of immense economic and military burdens and enabling them to concentrate on the 'British' Middle East. The sudden expansion of American power worked to British advantage in India. The Congress leaders were suspicious, in the words of Krishna Menon, of 'American absorption' – the Americans 'wished to capture all the markets, to step in and take the place of the British'.[50] Mountbatten played on those anxieties, just as he emphasized to Jinnah that Commonwealth membership could not be taken for granted. The accession to membership by India and Pakistan has to be seen, in other words, against the background of the developing cold war as well as a result of Mountbatten's ingenuity and the calculations of self-interest on the part of the Indians. The grandiose ambitions of the British to remain a 'world power' with the support of India and Pakistan were soon dispelled by Jinnah's insistence on becoming Governor-General of Pakistan (thus dashing Mountbatten's hope of coordinating defence affairs from a central position), and by the crisis in Kashmir; but could anyone else have 'bounced' (a word used in Whitehall) India and Pakistan into the Commonwealth? His achievement is not easy to compare in the other colonial emergencies of the era. One Colonial Office official – to take a random example – lamented in 1950 that there was no one comparable to 'bounce' the Cypriots into position in Mountbatten style.[51] Who was the Mountbatten of the transfers of power in Africa? The answer in short is that there was none.

The British decision to withdraw from Palestine was made on 20 September, 1947 (little over a month after the transfer of power in India) in the wake of the sterling convertibility crisis and, more directly, the majority report of the United Nations Special Committee on Palestine recommending partition. According to the minutes of the British Cabinet:

> *The Prime Minister* said that in his view there was a close parallel between the position in Palestine and the recent situation in India. He did not think it reasonable to ask the British administration to continue in present conditions, and he hoped that salutary results would be produced by a clear announcement that His Majesty's Government intended to relinquish the Mandate and, failing a peaceful settlement, to withdraw the British administration and British forces.[52]

As in India, the pace was quickened and the final date for the termination of the mandate finally set at 15 May, 1948. Once the evacuation (and its concomitant of partition) had been decided upon, then it would be, the British hoped, quick and decisive, with most of Arab Palestine absorbed by Transjordan. The principal calculation was that the Jews might be held to the coastal plain and contained in the areas allocated to them by the United Nations Special Committee on Palestine (which included the desert area of the Negev). The UN map, in the phrase used at the time, resembled a 'portrait by Picasso'. During the war of 1948 the Israelis were able to paint it mainly in their own colour by force of arms. The Jewish state was won on the field of battle. The frontiers were so determined. The Israeli triumph was curtailed only by an American ultimatum in January 1949. In contrast to the partition of India, there was no division of assets, no problem of dividing an army, and no dissolution of the civil service. Much of the Israeli success may be attributed to careful administrative as well as military planning. From the British vantage point in 1949, nothing was left 'but the dismal wreck of Arab Palestine'.[53]

The boundary award in India at least had the continuity of one pen and one man's effort to delimit Muslim and Hindu majority areas. Sir Cyril (later Lord) Radcliffe, by having himself to adjudicate among the boundary commissioners as Chairman, ruthlessly applied the geographical principles of Mountbatten's political maxim of equal self-determination, in Radcliffe's phrase, 'the fundamental principle of contiguous areas'.[54] Radcliffe himself remains somewhat of an enigma, but Mountbatten's aim in the partition is quite clear. He wished to avoid the impression of having anything to do with the boundary award, thereby ensuring his reputation for impartiality, and he hoped to postpone the announcement of the award until after the independence ceremonies. This he managed to do, and he later defended to the hilt his decisions about the pace, though he seems to have had pangs of conscience about the consequences. 'To be thoroughly candid and callous and brutal,' Mountbatten states in his final set of oral memoirs published in 1984, only 0.01 percent of the total population of 400 million were killed: 'That's the first thing to realize.' To reiterate his central explanation: 'I was afraid of not, 200,000 people, but two or three million dead which could easily have happened with civil war, easily.'[55]

If there is one point more than any other that emerges emphatically in Mountbatten's oral testimony, it is his determination in the summer and autumn of 1947 not to engage units of the British army. At any cost he was determined not to be drawn into civil war, which would risk not only the reputation of impartiality but would inevitably lose the goodwill of one side or the other and probably both. There lies the contrast with Palestine, where the British left with the ill will of the Jews and only with the cold comfort of knowing that the Arabs at least held the Americans to be in large part responsible for the creation of the state of Israel. There is at least one remarkable feature of these massive British disengagements from India, Palestine, and, it should be added, Greece. This is perhaps best established in relation to the bald statistics of the end of British tutelage in Palestine and India. There were over 1,000,000 Arab refugees. In India some six to seven million Hindus and Muslims changed sides, and at least 200,000 were killed.[56] With the exception of the disastrous RAF incident in January 1949 (in which four Spitfires on reconnaissance in the Negev were shot down by the Israelis), British forces emerged from these upheavals virtually unscathed. In India Mountbatten proved himself to be a consummate practitioner of disengagement. He was also quite right about the implications of Indian independence. If the British could avoid being drawn into civil war and manage to bring India and Pakistan into the Commonwealth, it would immensely enhance Britain's 'prestige' (at least among the other western powers). Walter Lippmann, for one (and he was perhaps the most influential of the postwar journalists), confirmed that judgment when he wrote a few weeks before the actual transfer of power that for the British this was indeed their 'finest hour'.[57]

Notes

1 Linlithgow to Zetland, 'Private and Personal', 24 September, 1936; and 2 August, 1937, Linlithgow Papers (India Office Library). There is a helpful biography of Linlithgow by his son John Glendevon, *The Viceroy at Bay: Lord Linlithgow in India, 1936–1943* (London, 1971). The best scholarly study of Linlithgow as Viceroy is Gowher Rizvi, *Linlithgow and India: a Study of British Policy and the Political Impasse in India, 1936–1943* (London, 1978). For discussion of trends in interpretation with which the present essay is concerned see C. H. Philips and M. D. Wainwright, eds., *The Partition of India: Policies and Perspectives, 1935–1947* (London, 1970); and A. K. Majumdar, 'Writings on the Transfer of Power, 1945–47,' in B. R. Nanda, ed., *Essays in Modern Indian History* (New Delhi, 1980). For historiographical comment on the Palestine literature, see the essay by Robert W. Stookey in W. R. Louis and R. W. Stookey, eds., *The End of the Palestine Mandate* (University of Texas Press, 1985).

2 In a letter of 28 May, 1937, in Syed Sharifuddin Pirzadi, ed., *Quaid-e-Azam Jinnah's Correspondence* (Karachi, 1977), p. 139. For this crucial period in Jinnah's life see especially Stanley Wolpert, *Jinnah of Pakistan* (New York, 1984), chap. 11; and Ayesha Jalal, *The Sole Spokesman: Jinnah, the Muslim League and the Demand for Pakistan* (Cambridge University Press, 1985), chap. 1.

3 N. A. Rose, *The Gentile Zionists* (London, 1937), p. 128; Aaron Klieman, ed., *Letters and Papers of Chaim Weizmann*, XVIII, A (Israel Universities Press, 1979), p. x.

4 Penderel Moon, *Divide and Quit* (Berkeley, 1962), pp. 13–14. See however the sophisticated challenges to various of Moon's arguments by Ayesha Jalal and Anil Seal, 'Alternative to Partition: Muslim Politics between the Wars,' *Modern Asian Studies*, 15, 3 (1981). For the India Act of 1935 see especially R. J. Moore, *The Crisis of Indian Unity 1917–1940* (Oxford, 1974).

5 For the Montagu Declaration see especially Richard Danzig, 'The Announcement of August 20th, 1917,' *Journal of Asian Studies*, XVIII, 1 (November 1968); for the Balfour Declaration, Mayir Vereté, 'The Balfour Declaration and its Makers,' *Middle Eastern Studies*, 6, 1 (January 1970); and for a rigorous analysis applicable to both, Conor Cruise O'Brien, 'Israel in Embryo,' *New York Review of Books*, 15 March, 1984.

6 As reported in the *Hindustan Times*, 6 May 1946. Coupland was writing shortly after the publication of the report of the Anglo-American Committee of Inquiry on Palestine. He feared, as did the Viceroy, Lord Wavell, that the Muslims and Hindus might find common cause against the British as they had after the First World War when the terms of peace with Turkey had abolished the Khilafat (see Gail Minault, *The Khilafat Movement*, New York, 1981). Coupland had served on the Palestine Royal Commission of 1936–37 and had assisted the Cripps mission to India in 1942. His Indian diary at Rhodes House, Oxford (MSS. Brit. Emp. S.15), is an invaluable background source for the themes of the present essay.

7 R. Coupland, *The Indian Problem: Report on the Constitutional Problem in India* (Oxford University Press, 1944), III, p. 99.

8 7 May, 1946. See M. S. Venkataramani, *Bengal Famine of 1943* (Delhi, 1973).

9 For the 1939 White Paper see especially Michael J. Cohen, *Palestine: Retreat from the Mandate* (New York, 1978); and Walid Khalidi, *From Haven to Conquest* (Beirut, 1971).

10 Barnet Litvinoff, *Ben-Gurion of Israel* (London, 1954), p. 132.

11 See Gabriel Warburg, 'Lampson's Ultimatum to Faruq, 4 February, 1942,' *Middle Eastern Studies*, 11, 1 (January 1975).

12 'I regard him as a very unsuitable choice,' Linlithgow wrote, though he opposed Lampson at least as much on grounds of inability to change with the times as on political outlook. Linlithgow to Amery, 3 December, 1942, Nicholas Mansergh and others, eds., *The Transfer of Power 1942–1947* (12 vols., London, 1970–83), III, p. 329.

13 Sarvepalli Gopal, *Jawaharlal Nehru, 1889–1947* (Oxford University Press, 1975), p. 255.

14 H. V. Hodson, *The Great Divide* (New York, 1971), p. 110.

15 Quoted in J. F. C. Watts, 'The Viceroyalty of Lord Irwin, 1926–31,' (Oxford, D.Phil. thesis, 1973), p. iii.

16 Percival Spear, *India: A Modern History* (Ann Arbor, 1961), p. 394.

17 Linlithgow to Zetland, 'Private & Personal,' 28 March, 1939, Linlithgow Papers F125/7.

18 Quoted in Uma Kaura, *Muslims and Indian Nationalism: the Emergence of the Demand for India's Partition 1928–40* (New Delhi, 1977), p. 170.

19 Minute by Linlithgow on Amery to Linlithgow, 'Private', 27 August, 1941, Linlithgow Papers F125/10.

20 Minute by Linlithgow on Amery to Linlithgow, 13 December, 1940, Linlithgow Papers F125/9.

21 By 1943 however Amery had retreated to the position that there should be an autonomous Jewish state only within a larger Arab confederation. Churchill was much less pro-Zionist than has been commonly believed. See the historical revision by Michael J. Cohen, *Churchill and the Jews* (London, 1985).

22 The best treatment of Churchill and the India Act of 1935 is Martin Gilbert, *Winston S. Churchill Volume V 1922–1939* (London, 1976), chap. 31.

23 Lord Moran, *Winston Churchill: The Struggle for Survival* (London, 1966), p. 394.

24 On this point see especially M. S. Venkataramani and B. K. Shrivastava, *Quit India: the American Response to the 1942 Struggle* (New Delhi, 1979), pp. 20–23.

25 See R. J. Moore, *Churchill, Cripps, and India 1939–1945* (Oxford, 1979).

26 W. P. (42) 59, 2 February, 1942, *Transfer of Power*, I, p. 112; quoted in R. J. Moore, *Escape from Empire: the Attlee Government and the Indian Problem* (Oxford, 1983), p. 10.

27 Amery to Churchill, 5 March, 1942, *Transfer of Power*, I, p. 324.

28 See Gopal, *Nehru*, chap. 17; and Moore, *Churchill, Cripps, and India*.

29 See *Quit India: the American Response to the 1942 Struggle*.

30 E.g.: the prominent journalist Louis Fischer noted after a confidential conversation with Sumner Welles (Under Secretary of State) that if 'things get much worse', in other words, if India appeared to be moving toward revolution, 'we might have reason to deal with the matter'. Memorandum by Fischer, 25 September, 1942, Fischer Papers, Franklin D. Roosevelt Library, Hyde Park, New York.

31 Linlithgow to Amery, 16 February, 1942, *Transfer of Power*, I, p. 186.

32 Linlithgow to Amery, 17 August, 1942, *Transfer of Power*, II, p. 740.

33 For the analogy of 1857 and 1942, see Francis G. Hutchings, *India's Revolution: Gandhi and the Quit India Movement* (Cambridge, Mass., 1973).

34 John Connell, *Auchinleck* (London, 1959), p. 727.

35 Quoted in M. S. Venkataramani and B. K. Shrivastava, *Roosevelt, Gandhi, Churchill: America and the Last Phase of India's Freedom Struggle* (New Delhi, 1983), p. 149.

36 Wavell to H.M. King George VI, 24 February, 1947, *Transfer of Power*, IX, p. 807.

37 See the New York tabloid, *P.M.*, 26 October, 1947.

38 See Evan M. Wilson, *Decision on Palestine: How the U.S. Came to Recognize Israel* (Stanford, 1979), p. 58.

39 See e.g. Isaiah Berlin, *Personal Impression* (New York, 1981).

40 See e.g. David Horowitz, *State in the Making* (New York, 1953), p. 143.

41 See 'Notes by Mr Attlee,' [November 1946], *Transfer of Power*, IX, pp. 68–69.

42 The classic indictment of the British administration in Palestine as a 'police state' is Jorge García-Granados, *The Birth of Israel* (New York, 1948).

43 Chiefs of Staff report, 12 June, 1946, *Transfer of Power*, VII, p. 892; Cabinet Minutes, 5 June, 1946, ibid., p. 815.

44 See *Transfer of Power*, VII, pp. 894–95.

45 Ibid., p. 965, n. 11.

46 See John Gallagher, *The Decline, Revival and Fall of the British Empire* (Cambridge, 1982), e.g. pp. 145–50.

47 *Transfer of Power*, X, p. 988.

48 Partha Sarathi Gupta, 'British strategic and economic priorities during the negotiations for the transfer of power in South Asia, 1945–47,' *Bangladesh Historical Studies*, VII (1983).

49 *Transfer of Power*, X, p. 699.

50 Mountbatten's conversation with Menon, 22 April, 1947, *Transfer of Power*, X, p. 372.

51 See minute by Mary Fisher, 31 January, 1951, CO 531/7453.

52 Cabinet Minutes (47) 76, 20 September, 1947, CAB 128/10.

53 Michael Wright (Foreign Office) to Sir Ronald Campbell, 30 March, 1949, FO 371/75064.

54 For a detailed assessment of the 'specialist surgeon', see S. A. Akanda, 'The Bengal Boundary Commission and the Radcliffe Award 1947,' *Bangladesh Historical Studies*, VII (1983).

55 Larry Collins and Dominique Lapierre, *Mountbatten and Independent India 16 August 1947 – 18 June 1948* (New Delhi, 1984), pp. 19–20, 24.

56 'Plus or minus 50,000', in Mountbatten's final judgment. Ibid., p. 24.

57 *Washington Post*, 7 June 1947; see Philip Ziegler, *Mountbatten* (London, 1985), p. 428.

Britain and the Marshall Plan

Kathleen Burk

On the face of it, there are certain similarities between the periods after the First and Second World Wars. There is the same need to reconstruct Europe, the same pre-occupation with the German problem and the threat of Soviet communism, the same French fears and consequent attempts by France to safeguard herself by tying down Germany, the same strains in British policy between the ties of Empire and Commonwealth and the need to help Europe. Above all, there is the same brooding presence of the United States, the source of food and raw materials, of military strength, of dollars and of firm intent. But there lies an important difference between the two periods: in the earlier period, the intent of the U.S. was to stay out of Europe and not get involved officially with the problems of Europe, while the post-1945 period was dominated by American intentions to reconstruct the world in a way that would safeguard as much as possible of a democratic, capitalist Europe, and – hardly less important – to force the British Empire back into the virtuous path of free trade. It is a complex period, and one which can only be treated sketchily in a short essay. But, by isolating the episode of the Marshall Plan, one can see in stark relief some of the major problems of the period: it is especially interesting to those looking at Anglo-American relations, and in particular at the use of finance as a weapon in foreign policy.

The Marshall Plan was a suggestion – nothing so firm as a plan – made in June 1947 by the American Secretary of State, George C. Marshall, the purpose of which was to help all of the European countries to reconstruct their economies, since the Americans had become progressively alarmed at the evidence of hunger and increasing chaos, both social and political. Over the period 1948–51 the U.S. granted in the region of $14 billion to the sixteen participating countries, with $2,694.3 million going to Britain. The policy was born of fear out of altruism, but the altruism did not prevent American negotiators from taking the opportunity to try and force American conceptions of the world on to the Europeans. The Americans wanted the Europeans to integrate their economies as a first step towards political unity: a united Europe, it was thought, would constitute a bulwark against Soviet communism. In these plans, Britain had a special place: she was to lead the Europeans into the new dispensation, and, in effect, to act as the American surrogate in European matters. But, in these plans, the British Empire and Commonwealth stood in the way. The Americans had by this time mixed feelings about the Empire. On the one hand, they were growing to approve of it politically, since British withdrawal would create a vacuum which would ineluctably be filled by communists unless the U.S. stepped in to fill Britain's place. On the other hand, the U.S. most emphatically did not approve of the economic arrangements which tied the Empire and Commonwealth together, that is, the organisation of the Sterling Area and the system of tariffs known as Imperial Preference. For her part, Britain was well aware that she depended on the unity of the Commonwealth and Empire, and on her ability to draw on its strength, to support her position as a world power. Thus, during the negotiations for the Marshall Plan between the U.S. and Britain, this fundamental struggle for power and position was never far from the surface.

1947 was a crucial year in the development of the Cold War. The Soviet Union was clearly consolidating its Eastern European sphere of influence, which American policy-makers were now concerned to prevent from expanding further. Thus, the containment of the U.S.S.R. was the first policy consideration of the American Government. When Britain publicly announced in February 1947 that she could no longer afford to give aid to Greece, the American Government responded with millions in aid for Greece and Turkey, and the enunciation of the Truman Doctrine: 'It must be the policy of the United States,' President Truman declared to Congress on 12 March, 'to support free peoples who are resisting attempted subjugation by armed minorities or by outside pressure.'[1] This speech set the immediate context for Marshall aid, in that in its urgency it expressed the consensus of the American Government as to the threat posed by Soviet communism. Thus the American Government determined to help those threatened by communism, whether externally or internally, if it was possible to do so, and as long as they tried to help themselves. The second problem, but a connected one, was that of Germany. The question was, should Germany be allowed to exist, but little more, or encouraged and helped to recover some semblance of her former economic strength? France, of course, wanted to keep Germany weak, and continually obstructed the Four Power discussions in Germany over what to do. In this she was supported by the American State Department. The American Army, however, like Britain, wanted Germany to recover her rightful economic position, since the conviction was that Europe would never recover until there was a strong German economy to lead and help sustain recovery.[2] From this point of view, the Marshall Plan was a way of accommodating German recovery within the context of European recovery: in other words, the decision as to whether to help Germany recover before her victims did would not have to be taken, since they would all be helped together. And, finally, the third problem was what appeared to be the imminent collapse of the Western European economies. This had several dimensions. First, both France and Italy had strong communist parties, which were in fact part of the governmental coalitions, and the fear was that economic chaos would allow them to take over as had happened, and would continue to happen, in Eastern Europe. May 1947 saw a communist takeover in Hungary, and in fact the Czechoslovakian coup in February 1948 would be used by the American Government to win support for the Marshall Plan in Congress. Secondly, the U.S. 'had an export surplus of seven to one', and, unless the economies of Europe were built up, American officials feared that a recession would inexorably spread over the U.S.[3] But the overriding problem in the economic context was a dollar famine. That is, much that the European countries wanted to buy, whether food or machine tools, had to be paid for in dollars, either because the goods came from North America, or because the countries with goods to sell, such as Latin American countries, required that the goods be paid for in dollars.[4] 36.3% of British imports in 1947 were dollar area imports.[5] Clearly the most urgent requirement in order to shore up and reconstruct the European economies, including that of Germany, so that they could resist the expansion of the Soviet Union, was dollars and lots of them: hence the Marshall Plan.

Britain agreed in general terms with these three American positions; the problem was, what price was Britain going to be required to pay as her contribution to their solutions? Much, in fact, might be demanded of Britain; she was, after all, hardly in the position of Germany, where things had to begin at the beginning, or even of France, with an inflation rate of 80%.[6] On the contrary, the U.S. still saw Britain as, at worst, a rival, which had to be contended with, and at best as the country which could act as the U.S. partner in Europe.

What almost no one in Washington realised in early 1947 was just how weak Britain was. In part this was Britain's own fault. As Sir Alec Cairncross has written; 'For most of the war, they [the British] were reluctant to expose the weaknesses of their position too nakedly to the United States and so undermine Britain's claim to be still a great power'.[7] Britain had lost about a quarter of her pre-war wealth during the war.[8] Further, alone of the European countries, she had massive debts incurred in fighting the war. What was necessary, and what developed over the period 1945–48, was an American sense that it was in the U.S. interest to help Britain to maintain her position: withdrawal from the Empire would only lead to communists filling the vacuum, and it would be cheaper for the U.S. to support the British Empire than to man the ramparts around the world herself. Thus, Britain and the U.S. agreed by and large on the political problems, and in some measure on their solution; it was the economic component of these problems that caused Anglo-American contention and friction. One question is, did the American Government use Marshall aid as a lever to force Britain to develop a different relationship with her Empire and Commonwealth? That is, did the Americans set out to attack the existence of the Sterling Area and Imperial Preference, requiring their demise as a condition for badly-needed funds? Unfortunately, where Anglo-American relations are concerned, straightforward questions rarely elicit straightforward answers: there is seldom one foreign policy emerging from Washington, and the background in 1947 was a President who did not really know what was involved, recurring conflict between the State, Treasury and War Departments, and the apprehension all of the above felt towards Congress. On the British side as well, a consistent foreign economic policy was never really sorted out, and there was disagreement within the Treasury, between the Treasury and the Bank of England, and between both of these institutions and the Cabinet. But to the question, did the American Government use Marshall aid to transform Empire and Commonwealth relations, the answer is a qualified no. There are three reasons for this. First, the attempts to attack the Sterling Area and Imperial Preference had in fact been made earlier, during negotiations in the autumn of 1945 for the American Loan. Secondly, by the summer of 1947 the U.S. saw Britain as her only possible strong ally against the Soviet Union, and if the price of British strength was discrimination against the dollar, then that had to be accepted. And thirdly, by 1948 and 1949, the attack against Britain's position at the centre of an economic Commonwealth took a new form: rather than try and break down the barriers of the Sterling Area, the American policy now was to undermine their centrality in British foreign economic policy by forcing Britain to integrate with Europe.

The Sterling Area had emerged in the 1920s (the return to gold in 1925 had been a Sterling Area movement), and after Britain went off gold in 1931, most Empire and Commonwealth governments (although not Canada) and some foreign ones proceeded to stabilise their currencies vis-à-vis sterling. Further, by the Ottawa Agreements of 1932, extensive and significant tariff preferences within the Empire and Commonwealth were instituted, and although the difference made was little more than 10%, they did hit some non-Empire producers.[9] By 1939, the whole Sterling Area was seen by the American Government, exaggeratedly, as an economic unit ruled by London, and as one which acted to the detriment of the U.S. It was thus a firm policy of the American State Department, headed by Cordell Hull, somehow to force Britain to give up the links of the Sterling Area and in particular the discrimination of Imperial Preference, and to join what was called a multilateral trading world, one more closely approaching free trade.

The course of the Second World War gave the State Department its chance. Britain became an international bankrupt even more quickly during the Second World War than she had during the First, and by the time that Lend-Lease was instituted her reserves were down to £3 million. Now, during the war goods imported from the U.S. were paid for, by and large, by Lend-Lease, and at the end of the war these liabilities, totalling $20 billion, were largely forgiven by the U.S.[10] However, Britain had significant sterling debts. She owed large amounts to countries in the Empire and Commonwealth and other non-dollar countries for imports; furthermore, she owed large amounts to India and Egypt for the expense of fighting the war. She paid in sterling, and by and large these funds were banked in London; by the end of June 1945 these current account liabilities totalled $10,900 million.[11]

What was to be done with these huge sterling balances? The Treasury and the Bank of England worried about this during the war, the Treasury rather more than the Bank.[12] These balances were a threat in various ways. If they were removed precipitately from London, this would strike a dangerous blow at the reserves. If they were used to purchase British exports, as the Bank and the Board of Trade wanted,[13] this would mean that Britain would be making 'unrequited exports': in other words, part of her sterling debt would be reduced, but she would receive no foreign currency in payment. In particular, Britain would not earn any dollars, which was what she needed and wanted. If these other countries used their own sterling, held in London, to purchase non-sterling goods, that would still mean that the sterling would have to be turned into dollars, which would threaten the exchanges, and Britain's gold and dollar reserves.

How should Britain deal with this threat? J. M. Keynes and the Chancellor of the Exchequer, Sir Kingsley Wood, both thought that the balances should be blocked, and they suggested this in 1942; blocking the balances would mean that they could not be withdrawn and used by their rightful owners, and the Bank of England fought against this ferociously. As far as the Bank was concerned, Britain's only hope for recovery after the war was to reinstate sterling as a major trading and reserve currency, and blocking the sterling balances would strike such a blow at confidence in the pound that it would not recover its former position.[14] Another possibility was to fund the balances, the turning of what was essentially the equivalent of current account balances, able to be withdrawn at very short notice, into a long-term debt, which would have little or no interest paid on it and would be repaid over many years. By August 1945 the Treasury and a reluctant Bank of England had agreed that, during the dangerous transition period after the war, there should be some control over the sterling balances. After negotiations with the individual countries in the Sterling Area, the balances would be partially released, partially written off as a Sterling Area contribution to the war effort, and partially funded at no interest for gradual release over fifty years. The rough proportions would be one for immediate release, four for writing off, and eight for long-term funding. As well, all were agreed that sterling availability was in Britain's long-term interest. The transition period during which all this was to happen was to be five years. However, substantial financial support from the U.S. was thought to be crucial to the success of the plan.[15]

Negotiations for such American support took place in Washington from September to December 1945. Keynes, who was the Treasury's major negotiator with the American Government over financial matters during the war, and his companions wanted a $5 billion (or possibly $6 billion) grant from the U.S. to tide Britain over the transition period, and it is clear that the American negotiators used this opportunity to extract formal agreements from Britain with regard to sterling and tariffs. Keynes was in an unenviable position. He had convinced the British Cabinet that a generous American Government would, because of Britain's sufferings in the common cause, grant a huge sum to aid Britain. Unfortunately, the change in the White House, with an inexperienced Truman, meant that the sympathetic Rooseveltian spirit had evaporated. Not only did the British negotiators become subject to pressures in the U.S. which they had not expected, they had in addition to cope with a Cabinet in London which did not see why Britain had to give up traditional positions merely for a few dollars.[16] The Treasury was little better. The Chancellor, Hugh Dalton, was thought even by his friends not to understand overseas finance, nor to be aware of the links between domestic and international financial policies.[17] Sir Wilfrid Eady, the official in charge of the Overseas Finance Section of the Treasury, actually wrote to Keynes thanking him for the two years' instruction he had had from him during the war years. Keynes himself wrote to Lord Halifax, the British Ambassador to Washington, after it was all over, that 'The ignorance was all embracing . . . And as for the insiders, so dense a fog screen had been created that such as the Chancellor and the Governor of the Bank had only the dimmest idea of what we had given away and what we had not . . . Political trouble there will be, for the Cabinet is a poor, weak thing'.[18]

In the end, what was agreed? Britain was to receive, not a grant, not an interest-free loan, but a loan carrying 2% interest, although there was a waiver clause attached, so that if Britain was in dire straits the interest would be waived; the loan was for $3,750 million, which Keynes thought would be barely sufficient, if nothing went wrong. In exchange for this loan, Britain agreed to try to deal with the sterling balances as described above, and further, she agreed that sterling would be fully convertible into dollars and other currencies within one year after the Financial Agreement was ratified. Keynes had envisaged a limited convertibility, covering in effect the end of the Sterling Area dollar pool, so that discrimination from the Sterling Area against the dollar should end. However, this limited convertibility was unlikely to stop at the borders of the Sterling Area, so Keynes yielded on the larger issue of general convertibility.

Either Britain yielded, in fact, or there would be no loan. The Americans had determined to pin Britain down to convertibility, and further, to the elimination of restrictions to trade between the Sterling Area and the rest of the world. They also insisted that the transition period should be only one year, instead of the five requested by the British. Negotiations nearly broke down over this, and it was only the stark realities of the situation that convinced the British Cabinet to accept the Agreement. Acceptance was probably also made easier for some because they doubted whether the Agreement could be made to work. As Dalton wrote in his diary, 'My cynical and secret reflection on the American Loan is that we shall be able to make good use of the Dollars – though we wish there were more – but that it is quite certain that the conditions will have to be "revised" long before A.D. 2001 and that, even in the next year or two it may well be that circumstances will require a considerable variation, which might even be "unilateral".'[19] As far as the Treasury was concerned, there was 'real consternation . . ., acute disappointment and some resentment'.[20]

Now, the reason that the Agreement was acceptable to Keynes as negotiator was that he had worked on the assumption that there would be a comprehensive settlement of the problem of the sterling balances during the eighteen months before full convertibility was assumed. This was not done, partly because the Bank of England was able to impose its views on the Chancellor and the Treasury. The Bank felt that the only way to prevent a disaster over the sterling balances was to persuade the holders of these balances that it was to their benefit to keep them in London. The implication of this for the Bank, as noted above, was that Britain must not block these balances. The Bank believed that the owners of the balances would therefore continue to find it useful to hold sterling in such quantities; working on this assumption the Bank believed that the threat of the balances was probably containable. If there were any problems, it was assumed that they could be solved by 'gentlemen's agreements'. In short, both they and the Treasury believed, as a Treasury official wrote, that 'we might be the world's greatest debtors, instead of creditors as in days gone by, but we were still capable of guiding the course of international trade and deciding when and in what manner we should take the lead and restore to sterling its traditional role'.[21] However, the Treasury at least was aware that, in order to carry through safely, Britain would have to limit its imports, and here they ran into the economic policy of the Labour Government. The Chancellor repeatedly warned his colleagues of the dangers inherent in the 'reckless pace'[22] of their expenditure, and the dollars provided by the American loan drained away much more quickly than had been expected, a result hastened by the rapid rise in American prices. This meant that by the time the year was up on 15 July, 1947 and the pound became convertible, Britain did not have the funds to sustain for more than six weeks the run on the pound. Holders of pounds in other countries were getting rid of them as fast as possible, and convertibility had to be suspended on 20 August, 1947.[23]

This was a turning point for both Britain and the U.S. The British did not return to convertibility until 1958, and they immediately began to strengthen the barriers against the dollar and against American exports, barriers which they had agreed to lower in the Loan Agreement. The Commonwealth Foreign Ministers in September 1947 began the process which led to their countries combining to exclude dollar imports by rationing, to restrict capital transfers outside their group, and to foster dollar-saving trade between themselves – back to Imperial Preference, so to speak.[24] It was an even bigger milestone for the Americans. The convertibility crisis brought home to them both how necessary Britain was in their anti-Soviet scheme of things and how fundamentally weak Britain was. Therefore, they had a choice: they could have a multilaterally-trading, non-discriminatory, but weak Britain, of little use as an ally, or they could have as an ally a Britain who, as leader of the Sterling Area, was independently strong. The U.S. chose the latter, but still, during the period of Marshall aid, tried repeatedly to bend Britain more to her way of thinking.

Consequently, during the negotiations over the Marshall Plan, the U.S. did not try to force Britain to open up the Sterling Area to American penetration, or at least not directly. The approach, rather, was to force Britain and her Commonwealth to join an integrated European economy.[25] The real objection to Imperial Preference and tariff barriers, after all, had been that American business was denied access to raw materials and markets in much of the world, or at least denied access on equal terms. If the Commonwealth were integrated into Europe, presumably the U.S. would then have access. A threatening Soviet Union notwithstanding, it must not be forgotten that the *quid pro quo* of the Marshall Plan was a thriving European market for American exports and private investment. So, by the end of the period of Marshall aid, the U.S. had given up the attempt for the time being to create a multilateral trading world, and had settled for a world of regional blocs with the hope that links between them would be forged.

On 5 June, 1947 George C. Marshall spoke at the graduation ceremony at Harvard University; he described the state of collapse of the European countries, called for a programme of reconstruction, not of relief, asked the Europeans to take the initiative, and invited all nations to participate, which implicitly included the Soviet Union. Ernest Bevin, the Secretary of State for Foreign Affairs, took the initiative in calling together the European countries to a meeting in Paris to plan a European response. Bevin and the Foreign Office shared the view of the American Government as to the threat posed by the Soviet Union, although only reluctantly did Bevin give up the idea that some sort of agreement with the Soviet Union could be reached. His prime goal in foreign policy was so to involve the U.S. in European affairs that she would not again withdraw, and in fact the summit of his policy was the signing of the NATO Pact in April 1949. Thus the opportunity provided by Marshall's speech was immediately utilised by Bevin and he took the lead in organising the European response.[26] The Conference on European Economic Co-operation met in Paris from 17 July to 22 September, 1947, and with great difficulty the members prepared a plan based on increased production in each country; this plan was then submitted to the Americans. It was essentially a list of the separate country plans and the total requested, $29,200 million, was too high. The Americans insisted that the European countries integrate their independent submissions, and come up with a smaller sum; bilateral negotiations were then to take place on each country's separate plans.[27] President Truman submitted a draft European Recovery Program Bill on 19 December, 1947 and the Congress finally passed the bill in April 1948, under the impetus of the February 1948 Czechoslovakian coup. The appropriations were approved in June 1948.[28]

Meanwhile, during the spring, the European countries were engaged in setting up the Organisation for European Economic Co-operation, the duty of which would be to co-ordinate the European economies in order to fulfil an American condition to receive Marshall aid; Sir Edmund Hall-Patch became the Chairman of the Executive Committee.[29] At the same time, the bilateral negotiations over the Economic Co-operation Agreement between the U.S. and Britain took place. The Economic Policy Committee of the Cabinet kept a close watch on the negotiations, which during June 1948 became fraught and nerve-wracking. The reaction of the Cabinet to the U.S. draft was that it was unacceptable; not only was the whole tone of the draft unpleasant, but the U.S. was claiming the right to force Britain to give most favoured nation treatment to U.S. goods while leaving the U.S. free to revert to high tariffs; further, Article X would enable the U.S. to put pressure on Britain to change its exchange rate, if the U.S. felt that the current rate of the pound was increasing Britain's need for help from the U.S. In other words, elements of the American Government were continuing the fight against the position of the pound and against Britain's commercial policies. Anglophobia on the whole dominated the U.S. Treasury while the State Department was a bit more sympathetic to British needs, since it shared with the Foreign Office the overriding perception of the Soviet Union as the primary enemy, and saw Britain as the main European power in the fight to contain the Soviets. The negotiations over the agreement nearly broke down on 17 June, after six gruelling hours in Washington, and only by changing the venue and appealing to the American Ambassador in London, who was sympathetic to the British position, was the deadlock finally broken on 24 June. Both sides adjusted their positions, but the article giving the U.S. the right to attack the exchange rate of the pound was dropped entirely, and the others modified to such a degree that Britain could live with them.[30] In the negotiations for the Loan in 1945, Britain had had to give in as the price for the Loan; by 1948, the 1947 sterling crisis having brought home to the U.S. the weakness of the British economy, Britain was allowed to prevail over the U.S. on those points which she felt were vital to her well-being.

One of the first problems which the Americans had to contend with, once Congress had agreed to the appropriations in June 1948, was the form of the organisation which was to administer the aid. Was it to be part of an old-line organisation – specifically, part of the State Department – or was it to be a new agency? The latter was decided upon, and the Economic Cooperation Administration (ECA) was established. Secretary of State Marshall was later quoted as saying that he had never wanted the agency to be part of the State Department: he had only wanted State to have some control over the public policy statements which inevitably would be made by the ECA.[31] As it happened, conflict between the two was not as dire as it might have been; it is probable that State felt it had enough to do, what with NATO, the Soviet Union, China, Palestine and other geopolitical problems, without fighting with the ECA, and therefore except at specific times of crisis, State let the ECA get on with the economic areas of policy.

Each country which received Marshall aid had a resident ECA Country Mission; the purpose of the country missions was to work closely with the government of the recipient country on their programme, perhaps influence it, and at any rate to know as much about the economic situation and policy of the country as the host government itself knew. The amount of interference in the affairs of the host country by the country missions varied enormously: in Greece the country mission was practically a second government, while in Britain the interference was minimal.[32] Parenthetically, the ECA headquarters in Washington felt that there were special problems with its country mission in London: to be specific, Washington often felt that the mission was captured by the British, and was more likely to argue the British case against Washington than Washington's case in London.[33]

The third American component in the organisation of the ECA besides the Washington headquarters and the sixteen country missions was the Office of the Special Representative in Paris. The Special Representative for most of the period was Averell Harriman, whose primary duty was to liaise with the European organisation, the OEEC, and encourage it to follow the path of economic and then political integration. As it happened, the Paris office grew out of all proportion. It was also supposed to co-ordinate the country missions, but in addition it developed into a policy-making office itself, sometimes in line with and sometimes against ECA in Washington. In the end, policy negotiations for each country developed along triangular lines, with in this case paper flowing from London to Paris and Washington, from Paris to London and Washington, and from Washington to London and Paris.

At the same time, of course, each country had its own organisation to deal with Marshall aid matters. In Britain, the London Committee, headed by Leslie Rowan, was set up to coordinate the British submissions and negotiate with the Country Mission which had offices in the American Embassy. The London Committee's submissions were then passed to their Paris Committee, which fed the British material to the Organisation of European Economic Cooperation. This was the organisation whose remit was to coordinate all of the country plans and submit an integrated plan to the Office of the Special Representative, which would then pass on it and submit it to ECA in Washington. It was the OEEC which the Americans hoped would eventually develop into a vehicle for economic and then political integration, but this it stubbornly refused to do,[34] remaining during the period of its existence in comfortable and useful obscurity.

There were two main problems which cropped up between the U.S. and Britain with regard to Marshall aid. They were the question of the use of counterpart funds, and the question of Britain's role in European integration. How Britain was to utilise the counterpart funds was, in the opinion of John Kenney, the London Mission chief from July 1949 on, the main recurring problem. Certainly arguments over their use crop up regularly at least from 1948 through to mid-1950. Briefly, what were these funds? Each recipient country was required to deposit in a special account an amount in the local currency equal to the amount of basic dollar grants it received from the ECA. This local currency was then divided into two parts: 5% of it was allocated to the use of the American Government in the country; the other 95% was to be utilised within the recipient country as the ECA and the country agreed. The 5% allocated to the U.S. was the source of arguments within the ECA: part of it was intended to cover the expenses of the Country Mission in London; the question was, how to spend the rest? The British counterpart funds had a special attraction for Congress and the American military establishment because of the strategic raw materials controlled by the Empire and Commonwealth. Harriman (the Special Representative) in December 1948 strongly opposed the use of any ECA expenditure, including counterpart funds, for the purchase of military goods: he felt that once any such purchase was allowed, the demands would only grow. Nevertheless he was overruled, and the bulk of the 5% allocated to the use of the ECA in Britain was spent on strategic materials such as tin and rubber.

But it was the utilisation of the 95% which caused the recurring problems. The general purposes for which counterpart funds were to be used included the monetary and financial stabilisation of the country, the stimulation of productive activity and the exploration and development of new sources of wealth. Generally, the ECA hoped that in all countries the 95% would be used for investment. Britain, conversely, insisted that it be used to retire short-term debt. By January 1949, for example, Britain had used roughly 90% of her counterpart for debt reduction and less than 10% for promotion of production and technical assistance; France, on the other hand, had used 85% of her counterpart for investment and 15% for debt reduction. Throughout the period, Britain (and Norway) used virtually the whole of their counterpart to retire short-term debt.[35] This intensely frustrated Washington ECA people: Richard Bissell, the Assistant to the Deputy Administrator and the top technical person, wrote in January 1950 that: 'Specifically, I believe that the ECA should try to influence investment programs and, more generally, the use of resources by the participating countries . . . we have almost a moral duty to try to exercise more influence over the use of resources by the European countries than we have in the past.'[36] Nevertheless, in May 1950 John Kenney again, but fruitlessly, tried to talk Britain into using £100 million of the counterpart funds for investment, this time in the colonies. Over the use of these funds, however, Britain refused to budge.[37]

The major Anglo-American conflict in the Marshall aid context, however, was over the proposals for the integration of Britain and her dependencies into a European economic organisation. Britain fought this tooth and nail, and only gradually came to compromise over certain proposals as a result of American assurances or as a result of weighing their chances of fending off American threats. The establishment of the Intra-European Payments Plan in October 1948 was one example. A major concern of the U.S. was to encourage intra-European trade in a multilateral sense, rather than on the basis of bilateral arrangements. The creditor countries among the participating nations in the Payments Plan were to establish special accounts, called drawing rights, in their own currencies, equal to the amount of the anticipated surplus of their exports over imports with each separate country. The debtor country in each bilateral arrangement could then use these drawing rights to finance its trade deficits with the creditor countries. This satisfied a basic object of the Marshall Plan, which was that trade among these countries should be directly financed by local currencies and not by dollars. But a dollar famine had been a prime cause of the Marshall Plan's creation, and the European countries continued to need dollars. Britain in particular was concerned not so much with European trade as with exporting to the dollar area. To enable these creditor countries in Europe, of which Britain was one, to earn dollars to finance their purchases in the Western hemisphere, the OEEC proposed the following: if a creditor country established drawing rights in its own currency for the benefit of its European neighbours, this country in turn would receive an equivalent allotment of ECA aid funds, that is, dollars, to finance its own Western hemisphere purchases. But this ECA allotment would be conditional upon the establishment of the drawing rights. It was decided as well that, if a debtor country did not use up all of the drawing rights extended by a creditor country, it could transfer them to another country. Britain fought against this, on the grounds that the creditor country could unexpectedly lose the compensating dollars, but in this case Britain lost.[38]

The Intra-European Payment Plan eventually developed into the European Payments Union in 1950. The idea of this was that both trade and payments should be on a truly multi-lateral level, and that countries should settle at least part of their net imbalances in gold or dollars. Britain of course fought this. Eric Roll, part of the British delegation in Paris, told a member of the Office of the Special Representative over lunch in April 1950 that there was a firmer ministerial position on this than he had known on practically any other issue, for two main reasons: first was the fear that behind the American proposals lay a desire to obtain new British commitments to a premature restoration of pound/dollar convertibility, and ministers frankly had been seared by the 1947 convertibility crisis; the situation was not helped by such views being expressed in Washington by officials of the American Treasury and the International Monetary Fund. But secondly, Hugh Gaitskell, the Minister of State for Economic affairs, and Sir Stafford Cripps, the Chancellor of the Exchequer, were afraid that the operation of the European Payments Union might tend to be excessively deflationary and threaten the maintenance of full employment in Britain. Britain only agreed to the Payments Union when Dean Acheson, the Secretary of State, sent an undertaking to Bevin in May 1950 to the effect that if British dollar outflows under the Payments Union reached an agreed danger point, the U.S. would consider a special allotment of dollar aid to Britain for the purpose of funding Britain's Payments Union outgoings. In short, Britain held out until the U.S. met her main concerns.[39]

Britain was repeatedly to fight attempts by the U.S. to convince her to integrate with Europe. The above economic argument was one important reason for Britain's resistance; another was the fear that European economic weakness might drag Britain down. But beyond these was the fear of a further diminution of her world role. Britain's own power was not enough by itself to support that role, and this meant that she had, in a sense, to co-opt the power of the U.S. It was imperative that the U.S. consider her a partner, even if only a junior one, to be consulted and listened to, and this would be undermined if Britain was slotted as merely another European power. This was expressed quite openly in the minutes of a meeting between very high-ranking officials of the Treasury, the Foreign Office, the Dominions Office and the Board of Trade on 5 January, 1949:

> Since post-war planning began, our policy has been to secure close political, military and economic cooperation with the USA. This has been necessary to get economic aid. It will always be decisive for our security.
> We hope to secure a special relationship with USA and Canada . . . for in the last resort we cannot rely upon the European countries.[40]

It was this basic need of the U.S., for both economic and military support, that motivated the British in the negotiations for Marshall aid, and it was this basic distrust of Europe that, in the final analysis, made Britain unable to go as far as the U.S. desired, and nearly required, towards European integration.

The U.S. of course understood this. Even Bissell, quoted earlier on the U.S. moral right to put pressure on those governments receiving Marshall aid, wrote to Paul Hoffman, the Administrator of the ECA, in September 1948 that it was not to the U.S.'s benefit for Britain to abandon her overseas orientation in favour of a European orientation.[41] This was more generally recognised in the State Department and the Executive, and was one major reason why Britain was never pushed too far. The technicians in the ECA sometimes lost their sense of proportion, but the political heads tended not to – Harriman sometimes excepted.[42] The American sense of its need for Britain blunted the use of the Marshall aid leverage it felt it possessed.

But just how irresistible was the leverage provided to the U.S. by Marshall aid? On the one hand, the British Cabinet agreed to the Bilateral Treaty in June 1948 because without Marshall aid, they were told by the Treasury, the level of food rationing would be 10% lower than the prewar average.[43] On the other hand, what were the magnitude of the numbers, and what use was made of the aid? During the period 1 July, 1948 – 30 June, 1949 Britain received $1,239 million, or nearly 25% of the total ECA allocation for the year; for Britain, 2.4% of her national income was represented by net Marshall aid after the operation of drawing rights. Imports funded by Marshall aid were 11.3% of British imports in 1949 and 7.5% in 1950. In Britain food imports, a large proportion of which were funded by Marshall aid, comprised nearly 40% of all imports, and over the period of Marshall aid, steel, machinery and vehicles constituted 8.8% of Marshall aid-financed shipments.[44] These numbers are not insignificant, but it can be argued that they could have been foregone if the U.S. had tried to exact too high a price for the aid.

The third reason for the lack of leverage was tactical rather than strategic. Bluntly, the American Government frequently spoke with several voices, while the British Government pushed policies in a unified manner. Gaitskell was not the only British minister to find that he could play off the ECA against the American Treasury, for example.[45]

By 1950 British reserves had increased rapidly. In September 1949, at the time of sterling devaluation, they had totalled $1,340 million; a year later they had more than doubled and were continuing to rise. Gaitskell, now Chancellor, argued that conditions were abnormal: the increased sale of raw materials and the restraint on dollar imports had led to what he considered to be an extraordinary rise in the reserves. He argued repeatedly against the cessation of Marshall aid to Britain a year early. But the American officials decided that, with British reserves having risen so sharply, the ECA would not be able to convince Congress to accept a continuation of aid to Britain,[46] and Britain's share of Marshall aid came to an end by June 1951.

The Marshall Plan is a prime example of the combination of altruism and self-interest in foreign policy. The altruism cannot be denied: after all, over $12 billion of Marshall aid was made up of grants, and certainly many of the people involved in the whole enterprise in their attitudes and enthusiasm were not unlike those who were drawn to serve in the Peace Corps in the 1960s. But American self-interest was certainly involved as well, which should not surprise anyone but the most naive sentimentalist.

It must also be seen in its geopolitical context. First of all, what clearly happened on the American side during the period from 1945 to 1949 was a transformation in their view of Britain. The world in 1945 and thereafter was to be a peaceful world, and the U.S. would again be able to concentrate on business as its business. Within this context Britain traditionally had been, and still was, her major rival. The U.S. wanted access to raw materials and markets, and she used the financial negotiations in 1945 to make certain that Britain agreed to the necessary conditions. But Britain had not for a century been a military rival, and, when a real military rival rose ominously in the East, Britain was suddenly seen in her real colours – the U.S.'s good, true friend. In view of the military threat posed by the Soviet Union, Britain's economic threat was seen in true perspective. The major theme in Anglo-American relations during the period is Britain's development from rival to ally. Finally, the specifically Anglo-American experience of Marshall aid provided a continuing training ground for the U.S. on the limitations of power and on the non-transferability of that power. The U.S. had discovered during the Paris Peace Conference after the First World War that when it came to a vital British interest – the right to blockade during wartime – there was no offer or threat which could force the British to give in. This happened again after the Second World War. Britain did not see her long-term interests, rightly or wrongly, as lying exclusively or even primarily in Europe, and there was nothing the U.S. could reasonably offer or threaten which could have forced Britain to change her mind. But things should be kept in proportion: after all, the same period saw the signing of the North Atlantic Treaty, the Berlin airlift and the beginnings of close cooperation during the Korean War. Comparatively, the Anglo-American conflicts over Marshall aid were unimportant, and they did not prevent the American Government, and in particular those involved with the Marshall programme, from gaining over the period an heightened sense of the fundamental soundness and quality of the British political system and a renewed sense of Britain's supreme worth as an ally.

Notes

1 Printed as an Appendix in Joseph Marion Jones, *The Fifteen Weeks (February 21 – June 5, 1947). An Inside Account of the Genesis of the Marshall Plan* (New York: Harcourt, Brace & World, Inc., 1955), p. 272. Daniel Yergin, *Shattered Peace* (Harmondsworth: Penguin Books Ltd, 1980 ed.), pp. 282–95.

2 John Gimbel, *The Origins of the Marshall Plan* (Palo Alto: Stanford University Press, 1976), p. 274. Alan S. Milward, *The Reconstruction of Western Europe 1945–51* (London: Methuen & Co. Ltd, 1984), chap. 4.

3 W. L. Clayton, 'Memorandum', 5 March, 1947, and 'The European Crisis' (Confidential Memorandum), 31 May, 1947, both Box 60, File Marshall Plan Memos, 1947, Clayton Papers, Truman Presidential Library, Independence, Mo. Yergin, *Shattered Peace*, pp. 306–7, for the quotation.

4 Milward, *Reconstruction of Western Europe*, chap. 1.

5 Imports (f.o.b.) for 1947:

	£ million	%
Rest of Sterling Area	494	31.6
Dollar Area	567	36.3
Other Western Hemisphere	154	9.9
OEE Countries	239	15.3
Other non-£ Countries	106	6.8
Total	1,560	

Source: *The 'Pink Book' on the Balance of Payments 1946–1957* (HMSO, 1959), Table 9, p. 32 (percentages added). Other dollar payments would be included in the Western Hemisphere figure as well. I owe this reference to Professor L. S. Pressnell.

6 Yergin, *Shattered Peace*, p. 306.

7 Sir Alec Cairncross, ed., Sir Richard Clarke, *Anglo-American Economic Collaboration in War and Peace 1942–1949* (Oxford: Clarendon Press, 1982), pp. xv–xvi.

8 Richard Gardner, *Sterling-Dollar Diplomacy in Current Perspective* (New York: Columbia University Press, 1980), p. 178.

9 Ian M. Drummond, *British Economic Policy and the Empire 1919–1939* (London: George Allen and Unwin, 1972), pp. 103–19.

10 Gardner, *Sterling-Dollar Diplomacy*, p. 208.

11 J. M. Keynes, 'Sterling Area Arrangements', 5 Nov., 1945, in Donald Moggridge, ed., *The Collected Writings of John Maynard Keynes, Volume XXIV* (London: Macmillan Press Ltd, 1979), p. 573.

12 D. E. Moggridge, 'From War to Peace – the Sterling Balances', *The Banker*, Vol. 122 (Aug. 1972), pp. 1033–4.

13 Gardner, *Sterling-Dollar Diplomacy*, pp. 325–6.

14 Moggridge, 'Sterling Balances', pp. 1033–5. Sir Hugh Ellis-Rees, 'The Convertibility Crisis of 1947', Treasury Historical Memorandum No. 4 (December 1962),

pp. 51–3, Vol. 267, file 3, Treasury Papers, Public Record Office (PRO), London.

15 J. M. Keynes, 'Overseas Financial Policy in Stage III', May 1945, in Keynes, *Collected Writings, Vol. XXIV*, pp. 281–90. Moggridge, 'Sterling Balances', p. 1035. Gardner, *Sterling-Dollar Diplomacy*, pp. 325–7.

16 Keynes, *Collected Writings, Vol. XXIV*, pp. 420–628. Box 148, Vinson Papers, Library of the University of Kentucky (Vinson was Secretary of the Treasury). Douglas Jay, *Change and Fortune: A Political Record* (London: Hutchinson, 1980), pp. 136–9. Alan Bullock, *Ernest Bevin: Foreign Secretary 1945–51* (London: Heinemann, 1983), pp. 121–5.

17 Ben Pimlott, *Hugh Dalton* (London: Jonathan Cape, 1985), p. 489, for example.

18 Letter dated 1 January 1946, Keynes, *Collected Writings, Vol. XXIV*, p. 626.

19 Clarke, *Anglo-American Economic Collaboration*, pp. 61–3. Diary of Hugh Dalton, entry for 7 December 1945, Vol. 33, Dalton Papers, British Library of Political and Economic Science, London School of Economics, London. Bullock, *Bevin*, pp. 123–4.

20 Ellis-Rees, 'Convertibility Crisis', p. 4, T.267/3. Professor L. S. Pressnell has noted that the Bank was most apprehensive about convertibility, and watched helplessly while Keynes and the government drifted into that particular Loan commitment.

21 Ellis-Rees, 'Convertibility Crisis', p. 11, T.267/3.

22 For the quotation see Chancellor of the Exchequer, 'Import Programme 1947/48', p. 11, 28 May, 1947, Vol. 129, file 19, Cabinet Papers, PRO. Dalton Diary, 29 July, 1947, Vol. 35, the L.S.E.

23 Ellis-Rees, 'Convertibility Crisis', pp. 18–22, 28–32, T.267/3. Dalton Diary, 17 August, 1947, Vol. 35, the L.S.E.

24 Susan Strange, *Sterling and British Policy* (Oxford: Oxford University Press, 1971), p. 62.

25 This was not, however, a new idea, even in the U.S. See Michael J. Hogan, 'The Search for a "Creative Peace": The United States, Economic Unity and the Origins of the Marshall Plan', *Diplomatic History*, Vol. 6, no. 3 (Summer 1982), pp. 267–85.

26 Marshall's speech is printed as an Appendix in Jones, *The Fifteen Weeks*, pp. 281–4. Bullock, *Bevin*, pp. 404–8. Charles P. Kindleberger, however, who was in the State Department at the time, argues that the British hardly moved with alacrity. 'The Marshall Plan and the Cold War', *International Journal*, Vol. XXIII, no. 3 (Summer 1968), p. 377. V. H. Rothwell, *Britain and the Cold War 1941–1947* (London: Jonathan Cape, 1981), pp. 275–6, 441–3. Record of a conversation between Troutbeck, Makins, Hankey and Radice, 5 June, 1947, Series 371, vol. 62399, no. UE4781/168/53, Foreign Office Papers, PRO.

27 Note by the Chairman of the London Committee, R.W.B.C., on Marshall Aid, 22 December, 1947 [Section I], PREM 8/980. Milward, *Reconstruction of Western Europe*, p. 80.

28 Yergin, *Shattered Peace*, pp. 350, 357.

29 Milward, *Reconstruction of Western Europe*, pp. 172–85. '. . . by our occupation of the chair of the Executive Committee through Sir Edmund Hall-Patch we shall be able to exercise a guiding influence on the day to day work of the Organisation . . .' Ernest Bevin, 'Memorandum on European Economic Co-operation', 21

April, 1948, C.P. (48) 109, PREM 8/980, PRO. Transcript of interview with Sir Edmund Hall-Patch, conducted by P. C. Brooks on 8 June, 1964, pp. 14–15, Truman Library.

30 Chancellor's brief for discussion with Harriman, May 1948, T.232/126. 'The Foreign Secretary pointed out that . . . The U.S. draft in its present form was wholly unacceptable . . .' Minute 4, Cab. E.P.C. (48), 20th Meeting, 3 June, 1948; Cab. E.P.C. (48) 48, 2 June, 1948; Cab. E.P.C. (48), 21st meeting, 8 June, 1948 (the Chancellor called Article X 'exceedingly dangerous'); O. Franks, U.K. Ambassador to the U.S., to the Foreign Office, 17 June, 1948, no. 2898; and Franks to F.O., 19 June, 1948, no. 2940; Cab GEN 240/1st meeting, 24 June, 1948, all PREM 8/768.

31 Transcript of interview with Marshall, 18 February, 1953, conducted by H. B. Price, Box 1, File Jan.–June 1953, Price Papers, Truman Library.

32 Transcript of interview with Thomas K. Finletter (Chief of London Country Mission 1948–9), 25 February, 1953, Box 1, File Jan.–June 1953, Price Papers, Truman Library.

33 Bissell to Foster and Hoffman, 13 July, 1949, Box 24, Subject Files, File Countries-UK Jan.–July 1949, Files of the Assistant Administrator, Programs, Economic Co-operation Administration Papers, Record Group 286, National Archives, Washington, D.C.

34 Milward, *Reconstruction of Western Europe*, chap. 5.

35 Price interview with John Kenney, 18 Sept., 1952, Box 1, File Aug.–Oct. 1952, Price Papers, Truman Library. 'Local Currency Counterpart Funds'. 31 January, 1949, Box 1, File Counterpart Funds and Harriman to Hoffman, and Finletter, no. REPTO 2048, 27 Dec., 1949, Box 1, File Counterpart Funds, Use for Strategic Materials, both Policy Subject Files, Central Secretariat, E.C.A. Papers. Hoffman to London, no. ECATO 188, 1 Sept., 1948, Box 62, Country Files 1948–9, File UK Funds, ECA Papers. Professor L. S. Pressnell has pointed out that France had little private sector investment during this period compared to Britain.

36 Memorandum by Bissell to two Labour Advisers, 23 January, 1950, Box 4 (1950), Interoffice Memoranda, Office of the Administrator Files, E.C.A. Papers.

37 Katz to Hoffman, 10 May, 1950, and Harriman to Secretary of State, no. REPTO 2432, 4 May, 1950, both Box 11, County Files, File U.K. Counterpart, Central Secretariat, Office of the Special Representative Files, E.C.A. Papers. Henry Pelling, *The Labour Governments, 1945–51* (London: Macmillan Press Ltd, 1984), p. 206. It should be remembered, however, that January 1950 had seen the drawing up by British Commonwealth Foreign Ministers, led by Ernest Bevin, of the Colombo Plan, the goal of which was the co-operative development of the countries of South and South-East Asia.

38 U.K. Cabinet-level Memorandum on Conditional Aid and the Transfer of Drawing Rights, 17 September, 1948; Bissell Memorandum on British Agreement – European Trade and Payments Plan, 5 October, 1948; and Memorandum on Shifting of Drawing Rights against Britain, n.n., n.d., all Box 24, Subject Files, File Countries-UK, 1948, Files of the Assistant Administrator, Programs, E.C.A. Papers. Explanatory Memorandum on Intra-European Payments Plan, 15 October, 1948, Box 2, Policy Subject Files, File Intra-European Payments Plan, Central Secretariat Files, E.C.A. Papers.

39 Milward, *Reconstruction of Western Europe*, chap. 10. Gordon memorandum to Katz on talk with Eric Roll, 5 April, 1950, Box 87, Country Files 1949, File

Material to be Filed, Comm. and Rec. Section, Office of the Special Representative Files, E.C.A. Papers. Pelling, *Labour Governments*, p. 201.

40 Clarke, *Anglo-American Economic Collaboration*, p. 208.

41 Bissell Memorandum for Hoffman and Bruce, 22 September, 1948, Interoffice Memoranda (April 1948 – May 1950), Office of the Administrator Files, E.C.A. Papers.

42 See, e.g., Memorandum probably by Geiger and Cleveland, 1 September, 1949, for a proposal to bounce France, Italy and the Benelux countries into an economic union before their governments had 'time to think through in detail all of the consequences, dangers and repercussions.' Box 1, Copies of Outgoing Letters, Reading File 7 Oct. 1948–30 Sept. 1949, Assistant Administrator Programs, Special Assistant to Administrator Files, E.C.A. Papers. For Harriman, see repeated references to his activities in Milward, *Reconstruction of Western Europe*.

43 'Economic Consequences of Receiving No European Recovery Aid', 23 June, 1948, C.P. (48) 161, Cab 129/28.

44 Milward, *Reconstruction of Western Europe*, pp. 96, 100–2, 437.

45 Philip Williams, *Hugh Gaitskell* (London: Jonathan Cape, 1979), p. 221.

46 Memorandum on UK Gold and Dollar Reserves, 8 November, 1950, Box 11, Country Files, File UK 1951, Central Secretariat, Office of the Special Representative Files, E.C.A. Papers. Price interview with Hugh Gaitskell, 12 November, 1952, Box 1, File Nov. 11–20, 1952, Price Papers, Truman Library.

MICHAEL KÁROLYI: A friend

Éva Haraszti

A special friend of Alan Taylor was Michael Károlyi, the Hungarian socialist count, the President of the short lived Hungarian Republic in 1918, the great émigré of twentieth century Hungary. They met in 1940 in Oxford at the very moment when the historian wrote about this Republic when working on his book on The Habsburg Monarchy. There was a ring at the door. There stood a tall man with a limp and a cleft palate: none other than Michael Károlyi himself.[1] From this time on the two radicals became friends. They had many things in common. Both above all loved the truth, both hated fascism, both were socialists, both liked good jokes and both enjoyed the society of women. Both had been delicate children, both were modest in personal habits, both liked travelling (mainly in France) and both had the capacity to modify their views in public. It would be easy to draw up a much longer list of things which they had in common but there is one important thing which must be added. Both were critical of the official policy of their nation and both were very fond of their homeland.

They belonged to different generations. Károlyi was thirty-one years older than Taylor. It did not matter. Deep down they were still young men; though when they first met Michael was sixty-five years of age and Alan thirty-four.

Their friendship lasted as long as Károlyi lived. The last time that they met was in 1951 in Vence, in the South of France. Károlyi was in exile for the second time, having left Hungary because of the Rajk Trial in 1949.

Their friendship flourished in Oxford and in London during the Second World War. Later they met a couple of times, when Károlyi became Minister and later Ambassador of the Hungarian People's Democracy in Paris. They probably met fifteen to twenty times. Alan Taylor helped with Károlyi's autobiographical work, *Faith Without Illusion*, and wrote a preface to it when it appeared in London in 1956, after Károlyi's death. They did not need to meet often to maintain their friendship. They were always on the same wave length, they could always tease each other, they could make light hearted remarks about the most serious things and they found life extremely funny when others would have been hurt or sulky.

Alan Taylor, already expert on the Habsburg Monarchy, was able to discuss with Károlyi such matters as the dual monarchy, the First World War, István Tisza, Hungarian foreign and home policy; and his views were well respected and carried weight with Károlyi. However, Alan Taylor found it hard to get across to him the realities of British foreign policy or the nature of the leading personalities involved in decision making. Károlyi shared the shortcomings of many continental politicans in understanding British political decision making. He often believed to be policy what was just politely discussed or cautiously promised. He would have never believed that preconceptions could be held so inflexibly in a democratic society, and that there would be such hostility to his views because they were seen as being of the far left. He always thought that through his Labour and radical friends, such as George Trevelyan or Francesca Wilson, the quaker lady, or through Ernest Bevin, he would be able to influence the British Government. Alan Taylor tried and tried again to explain what to expect. Because, after the Second World War, Michael had such faith that he could influence British foreign policy if he could explain his views to Labour's Foreign Secretary, Alan did arrange through Ellen Wilkinson a private meeting between Bevin and Károlyi. This was against Foreign Office advice. What was the result? Nothing.

The story of Michael Károlyi in exile can be begun with an extract from a Foreign Office draft on Károlyi prepared in 1944, when the Hungarian Council was established by many Hungarian émigré groups:

> On the 31st October 1918, Emperor Charles, the King of Hungary nominated Count Michael Karolyi as Prime Minister of Hungary. On the 16th November 1918 Count Michael Karolyi became the President of the Hungarian Republic. This was the will of the people, as a result of his uncompromising anti German attitude and Entente friendship as well as his progressive ideas on social and

> national problems before and during the last war. The Hungarian Republic under his leadership instituted social reforms and passed the law for radical land reform which aimed at eliminating the feudal system. Count Michael Karolyi started the distribution of the land on his own estates in Kapolna. Ever since he has been known amongst the people of Hungary as the 'land distributor of Kapolna'. Breaking off the traditions of the feudal system, the Hungarian Republic worked for complete agreement amongst its minorities and with the neighbouring states. Since the establishment of the Counter Revolutionary Horthy Regime in 1919, Count Michael has been living abroad (in Czechoslovakia, Yugoslavia and since 1924 in France and in England). He went several times on a lecture tour to America. In 1931 and 1934 he spent several months in Soviet Russia. In 1932 his pamphlet 'The Land is yours' was illegally distributed in Hungary. In exile he remained faithful to his progressive ideas, and is known and respected as a courageous fighter for a new democratic order amongst the freedom loving peoples of the world. He is the President of the New Democratic Hungary Movement in London.[2]

This was a fair account of Károlyi's life and activities. It did not mention one often quoted sin of his: namely, that he paved the way during his presidency in 1918 for the ensuing proletarian dictatorship of Béla Kun. This question was and still is debated by historians who, until her death in 1985, occasionally got stern rebukes from the elderly Countess Károlyi, the talented writer Katinka. The truth is that Károlyi did not foresee the coming of the dictatorship of the proletariat. Even at that time he would not have approved of it. But the question in March 1919 was not a choice between proletarian-dictatorship or democracy but between proletarian-dictatorship and White terror. Certainly Károlyi would not have backed the latter at any price.[3]

There was, though, a slight distrust of Károlyi by the Foreign Office and British statesmen from the very beginning of his political career (which began when – as Károlyi used to say – he 'remade himself' at the age of thirty-four). Károlyi tried to establish regular contact with the Entente powers from November 1918 until spring 1919 and asked them through private and official channels to send a mission to Hungary. He wanted to meet Wilson or any one whom the Entente powers would nominate as their representative. But their policy was not helpful to him. As Lewis B. Namier so precisely drafted: 'It is not for us to stimulate revolution or to uphold Count Károlyi against his opponents of the right or of the left. Where our own interests are so doubtful and the situation so obscure, non-interference seems the only course to adopt. At least it saves us from unnecessary commitments.' Károlyi, unlike Oszkár Jászi, his Cultural Minister and the expert on nationality problems, was convinced that the Entente, and especially Wilson, would help him at the forthcoming peace conference and that principle and democracy would prevail. As a result the people of the late Habsburg Monarchy would achieve self-rule. When, at the Peace Conference, so many decisions were dictated by the French and Italian nationalism, Károlyi realised that Wilsonism and Leninism were irreconcilable. He had to choose between them. When he looked back to this period, in the spring of 1946, in a speech in the Hungarian Parliament, he said he was no longer a 'Károlyist'. 'I was already pro-Russian at the time the Czar abdicated,' he said. 'In Hungary I was a count . . . I felt Hungary needed the Russian orientation for geographic reasons and felt that the friendship with the Slavs was not possible to realise without Russian friendship. You can imagine how much I was thrilled when under Lenin the new Russia was created. And here I quote Napoleon, who said that geography is the basis of foreign policy and creating alliances. I love in vain – or we love in vain – China. An alliance of Hungary and China is impossible. And the same is true as regards the Western European countries. But all the same we must have inspiration from them. And because in the West there are many who are for peace but there are many who are against East-West peace, we Hungarians have to fight with all our means to ensure that the Russian and English-speaking world build up an easier, better relationship.'[5]

Károlyi's attitude to problems was always: Use commonsense. He tried to use commonsense and was taken aback when his words did not meet approval. In early 1919, when there were major economic and political setbacks arising from Hungary's catastrophic situation, his influence on the general public shrank from day to day. In this situation he tried to explain to the Allies, that their nightmare (i.e. the bolshevization of Hungary) was not the result of Moscow propaganda but the result of poverty, lack of coal, and unemployment. What Hungary needed was economic help. He gave a dinner party for Colonel Cuninghame who led the English mission in Vienna. At it Cuninghame explained that, if bolshevism was not suppressed in Hungary, the Entente would let the Roumanians, Czechs and Serbs occupy Hungary. On the other hand, if Hungary were strong enough to suppress bolshevism herself, he would personally ask President Masaryk to give coal to Hungary. Károlyi and the Social Democratic ministers present at the dinner party were shocked. All the same the Hungarian Council of Ministers on 18 and 20 February, 1919 decided that the Communist leaders should be arrested. The leader of the Communists, Béla Kun, and nearly a hundred other Communists were put in prison. This action should have shown clearly to the British that Károlyi himself was not a communist. All the same at this time and later the British Government did not trust and did not need Károlyi. He was too revolutionary, too pro-Soviet. When in Hungary the counterrevolutionary Admiral, Nicolaus Horthy rode into South-Hungary on his white horse and established his regency for more than twenty years, he became the favourite of the British Establishment so long as he did not become too close to Hitler. Indeed whilst Baldwin and Chamberlain were Prime Minister, the pro-German and pro-Italian sympathies of Horthy and his ministers were not seen as sins. Even after Count Teleki committed suicide in 1941 because he could not betray the Yugoslavs, Churchill still said that Hungary would have a seat preserved at the table of the future peace conferences. Half-feudal Hungary was always a partner for the British Foreign Office, but the reddish émigré Count Michael Károlyi was not.

The British Establishment was not against Károlyi as a person, but against his political ideas. Károlyi always opposed Horthy whereas the Foreign Office wanted to stabilize the Horthy regime. Whilst Britain permitted Károlyi to settle down in Britain in 1923 the British Government backed the Hungarian Prime Minister Count Bethlen who at this time made a successful visit to Britain asking for foreign loans to Hungary. The Hungarian Ambassador in London did everything he could to prevent Károlyi from being allowed to live in England, including providing muck-raking information to the Home Office. However at this time Károlyi had many influential friends in the Labour Party, including G. M. Trevelyan, Noel Buxton and H. N. Brailsford who stood by him. Others, notably Professor Seton-Watson, Wickham Steed and Eduard Beneš, who happened to be in London at that time, intervened on his behalf. Károlyi was permitted to stay in England. However the Foreign Office did not help him against the Hungarian judicial decision that condemned Károlyi as a traitor, for revolutionising his homeland in 1918–19 and disarming her defence system.

The Hungarian Embassy's main line against Károlyi was that he meant to spread Bolshevism in Britain. The Hungarian Prime Minister also made the accusation to the British ambassador in Budapest. Károlyi was followed by the police in London as, some sixty years before him, Louis Kossuth was. Károlyi's Labour friends asked him not to make political declarations. He was under surveillance, sometimes his letters were opened.[6] After a while, Károlyi got used to London, and radical London to him. He joined the '1917 Club'. From 1924 on, when the first Labour Government took office, Károlyi gave lectures on Hungary and hoped in vain that Ramsay

MacDonald would not give a loan to Horthy Hungary without political conditions. In this he was deluded. Though he made more and more friends amongst left-wing and radical intellectuals, people such as Bertrand Russell, the Webbs and H. G. Wells, his friendship with Ramsay ended abruptly. As Károlyi put it in a letter addressed to Jászi: 'The Labour Party and the League of Nations succeeded once again to save the rotting reaction in Hungary'.[7]

In the late twenties Michael Károlyi, coming back from Mexico, where he had studied the land-reform of the revolutionary Calles Government, foresaw the coming fascist rule in Europe. He was convinced that unless the peace treaties that followed the Great War were revised and eastern Europe organised under a federal and socialist system, there would be another major war within a decade. Károlyi also thought that Britain should give up flirtations with the small semi-fascist, reactionary regimes in Eastern Europe.

Károlyi, like other émigrés on the left, saw the clouds gathering over Europe. As an émigré, he was unable to influence European politics to any significant extent. There was one achievement which Károlyi was proud of. He saved the life of an eminent Hungarian Communist, Frigyes Karikás, who illegally returned to Hungary and was sentenced to be hanged.

Károlyi saved Karikás's life by travelling to London and for a whole week trying to convince members of the National Government to make approaches to the Hungarian government on this matter, warning them how much damage his execution would cause to the appreciation of the Horthy Government in Great Britain. Karikás's life was saved. Instead of being judged by martial law, he was judged by common law and he served three years in prison.

As an émigré Károlyi could not achieve much success fighting against fascism. In the mid-1930s, Károlyi had cause to complain of how difficult it was to publish in the British press data concerning German rearmament. He found it impossible to warn the British ruling class of the dangers of appeasement. They felt that warnings, such as those by Károlyi, would only bring about European conflict. 'We were looked at as warmongers and they let us know that the West was not prepared to risk a war on behalf of the émigrés.'[8] This sounded like Palmerston in mid-Victorian times. Then Palmerston tried to reassure the Austrian and French ambassadors that they should no longer be worried by Ledru-Rollin, Mazzini and Kossuth. They were less dangerous in England, as he wrote, than in their own country.

Károlyi and his family moved to England at the end of 1938. His daughter Éva married an Englishman, his second daughter Judit studied at Oxford though she became a French citizen and their only son Ádám became a test pilot. The family bought a house near Winchester, near where Ádám was based. Károlyi loved the quiet country life and made many friends amongst the local gentry. But he still spent much of his time among his political friends in Paris. The Károlyis were to suffer personal tragedies as well as political ones. His son died in a plane crash and his body was buried at the cemetery of St. Andrew's, Chale on the Isle of Wight. A decade and a half later Michael Károlyi was buried in the same tomb. Later both bodies were taken to a mausoleum in Hungary.

Károlyi was rejuvenated by his political activities from 1940 until his death in 1955. After the fall of the Chamberlain Government he immediately gave an interview to the Polish émigré journal, *Free Europe*, and in it called on all Danubian countries to unit. The Károlyis, who had lived in Oxford, now moved to London. There they were impressed by the courage of the people. Churchill united the nation, and the ordinary Londoner was confident that Hitler would be defeated. Károlyi was impressed by Churchill, a man of his own age. However he was critical of Churchill's continued faith in Horthy. The situation changed after Count Teleki's suicide and Hungary's entry into the war on the wrong side.

By the late 1930s there were Hungarian émigrés in London of all political shades. Some were pro-Horthy. Many old radical and left-wing émigrés wanted an anti-fascist united representation in London under the leadership of Károlyi, but he did not want to make compromises with those who had anything to do with Horthy, regardless of how disillusioned they had become. We need not go into any details of the Hungarian émigré movements in London which eventually did become united against fascism under the leadership of Károlyi. Michael Károlyi's biographer, the Hungarian historian Tibor Hajdu, makes it clear that this unit of the Hungarian émigrés representing some 4–5,000 people was really a parody of unity. It showed all the signs of the usual weaknesses of émigré political activities and Károlyi, knew this.[9] He never ceased to work in London, though, and published with his wife many anti-fascist articles in the radical, liberal and socialist newspapers (*Manchester Guardian*, *Reynolds News*, *Tribune*, *New Statesman*, etc.) and took part in activities to further the idea of a Danubian confederation. This included nearly forty lectures during the war. The Károlyis also made friends with many radicals and socialists, including the Taylors, the Spenders and Jan Masaryk.

The tone and attitude of the Foreign Office and BBC towards Károlyi was rather sceptical and critical until March 1944. Professor Aylmer Macartney, who sympathised with the Horthy régime and who was both a leading historian from Balliol College, Oxford, and who represented the Foreign Research and Press Service of the Foreign Office, urged that Britain should be cautious as to which groups she identified with in Hungary. He urged that Britain should avoid the following groups in Hungary:

> Legitimism,
> High Toryism and positive support of the 'feudal' idea, large landed interests, etc.
> Big business and capitalist interests
> The names of Liberalism and democracy. Each of these has been so twisted in Hungary as to bear today an unfortunate connotation: 'Liberalism', that of unrestricted Jewish exploitation of the peasant and worker: 'democracy', a mask for Czech hegemony in the Danube basin
> Jews in general
> Anything containing more than a cautious and qualified mention of the word international
> 'Octobrism', i.e. the Károlyi regime of 1918–19
> Communism or Bolshevism.

These warnings were written by Macartney in February, 1942.[10] But even when the Hungarian Council in London was formed with Károlyi as President, and Károlyi was permitted to carry out anti-fascist propaganda through the BBC, with some backing from the Foreign Office, he was still regarded 'out of date, out of touch and fanatical'.[11] All the same when Károlyi wanted to call on Anthony Eden or meet the Parliamentary Under Secretary, he was not turned down. Thus Károlyi discussed with government officials the aims of the newly-formed Hungarian Council in Britain which at the same time was 'in full accord with the Democratic Hungarian movements in the United States as well as with the cooperative groups in the Latin American countries'. It might reasonably be deemed, as Károlyi wrote, to represent the overwhelming majority of democratic Hungarians living abroad, irrespective of political party and opinion. 'The aims were to unite all Hungarians to fight German and Hungarian Fascism, to encourage our soldiers to surrender to the Red Army and to persuade Hungarians to join Marshal Tito's partisan armies . . . and to help in building up a democratic, progressive, Hungary which would be a barrier against future German aggression, would collaborate peacefully with our Slav neighbours and would base its foreign policy on the principles of the Teheran declaration.'[12]

Károlyi was duly received not by Eden, but by G. H. Hall from the Foreign Office. The attitude of the Foreign Office officials to Károlyi is clear from their minutes. Thus W. Allen observed on 5 June, 1944:

'The Hungarian Council was formed as a result of the fusion of Hungarian political groups in this country, Count Károlyi's own group, the Communists and the moderate group with which some former members of the Hungarian Legation in London are associated. None of these Hungarians except Count Károlyi himself is of any importance and Count Károlyi has been so long outside Hungary that it is most unlikely that he has any important part to play in future. He enjoys, however, the support of the Czechs and possibly through them of the Russians. From the point of view of many patriotic Hungarians this is a liability rather than an asset. I see no reason why the Secretary of State or the Parliamentary Under-Secretary should receive Count Károlyi but possibly he should be seen by Central Department or even by an Under-Secretary. It might be of some interest to hear what he has to say for himself.' And Frank Roberts added the same day: 'I think Count Károlyi should certainly be received. He has an idea that he is "persona non grata" to the FO, and never responded to earlier hints that our doors were open to him wherever he chose to call. As an ex-Prime Minister he should perhaps be received by Mr Hall, if he can spare the time or at least by an Under-Secretary.'[13] Hall received Károlyi and gave a fair account of Károlyi's views in a memorandum which ended, 'Lastly Count Károlyi expressed a strong desire that Great Britain should treat Hungary in the same friendly manner as Czechoslovakia is at present treated, and that she would continue to use her influence in all matters affecting the Eastern European nations'.[14]

Károlyi also made an approach to Brendan Bracken, the Minister of Information, sending him a copy of the Hungarian Council's programme. Bracken, however, declined to discuss Károlyi's plans, observing in a letter '[I doubt] whether I should be much help to you if we discussed the matter further. It is for the Foreign Office to speak for the Government on the questions you raise and I think that they would not be pleased if the Minister of Information interfered in their affairs.'[15] Károlyi naturally wished to impress Bracken. He not only wanted more facilities to broadcast to Hungary but also consideration to be given to the possibility of Hungarians resident in the UK joining Marshal Tito.

The Foreign Office frequently considered what attitude to take to Károlyi in mid-June. One minute stated: 'As regards contacts with Hungary and with Tito S.O.E. will I am sure prefer to steer clear of using Count Károlyi's organisation and they will certainly do best by relying upon their own selected agents. I do not think the time has yet come when Tito would be likely to welcome Hungarian recruits from this country; nor would the Károlyi-Tito combination seem likely to prove the ideal method of approach from the point of view of opinion inside Hungary.' Another by Roberts observed: 'Regular broadcasting and leaflet facilities would be a mistake, although an occasional bit of publicity might be all right. We must also bear in mind the fixed principle that the Hungarian Council is self-constituted and enjoys no degree of support or encouragement from H.M.G. P.W.E. (Political Warfare Executive) do not think that it would be a good idea for Count Károlyi to be given facilities for a regular weekly BBC broadcast to Hungary. Apart from the obvious political implications of such an arrangement, which might well be undesirable, Count Károlyi has an extremely bad voice for broadcasting and would never be passed by the BBC in any normal microphone test. Further, to judge by his past declarations, his broadcasts would be monotonous and repetitive, however excellent their political line might be, and the propaganda effect achieved would therefore be small. The BBC is already reporting any statements made by the Hungarian Council from time to time on special occasions, and is giving them a good deal of space. P.W.E. do not think that the BBC should be asked to go beyond this. If Count Károlyi should give an interview to a news-agency or the press in his personal capacity, not purely as President of the Council, this would of course also be reported by the BBC on its news value. On this basis the Count will be receiving parity or slightly more than parity of treatment with the dissident Hungarian ministers. P.W.E. now have fairly good facilities for leaflet dissemination over Hungary. They do not think, however, that the propaganda value of Count Károlyi's name, or of that of the Hungarian Council, is such that they would be justified in asking the Allied Air Forces to undertake sorties to disseminate proclamations made in the name of either the one or the other. If, on the other hand, it should become possible to produce a news sheet at Bari for dissemination over Hungary, statements made by the Council might well be reported briefly in these.'[16] By the autumn of 1944 Michael Károlyi was already thinking of returning home to Hungary. By this time he was seventy (a birthday celebrated by a gathering of friends, presided over by Seton-Watson). Károlyi's hopes for a Danubian confederation were dashed by the view of the post-war world which emerged from the meetings between Stalin, Churchill and Roosevelt at Teheran and between Stalin and Churchill in Moscow. At the latter conference (October 1944), it was decided that Hungary would be part of a zone of friendly, small nations around the Soviet Union.

Károlyi was elected one of the MPs for Budapest in April 1945. In June he wrote to Mr Matyas Rákosi, the leader of the Communist Party and – according to the leader of the British Political Mission in Hungary – 'an intimate friend', making it clear that he wished to return to Hungary. He later wrote to Rákosi offering to represent the new Hungary in London. However, time elapsed and Károlyi returned to Hungary in 1946. By this time a general election had been held in Hungary and the leader of the Smallholders Party, Z. Tildy, formed his government.

In Britain Ernest Bevin was unsympathetic to events in Hungary. If he saw a lengthy note prepared by Macartney on Károlyi's career, it would not have disposed him favourably to Károlyi. In it Macartney wrote: 'In his exile he has not ceased to attack with extreme bitterness all Hungarian Governments from that of the Counter-Revolution of 1919 onwards. They in their turn have vilified him most bitterly and unfairly making him responsible for all the misfortunes which fell on Hungary in 1919. The accusations of treachery are entirely unjust, for Károlyi was certainly a patriot, as he also certainly wished to effect democratic reforms which were long overdue in Hungary. But it is equally certain that this extreme vanity and dilettantism which led him to push himself into a position for which he was totally unfitted and in which he committed blunder after blunder, did in fact greatly aggravate Hungary's position. To this he is of course, entirely blind and his only version of his unpopularity in Hungary is that he is hated because he was a democrat; and all those who do not accept him as their heaven sent leader are fascists and reactionaries. This propaganda has had considerable effect among the more simple British, as well as among Hungarian émigrés who hope to make a career out of following him.'[18] Károlyi was enraged by Bevin's attitude to Hungary. Bevin increasingly made it clear that he did not wish to recognise the new Hungarian government unless they held free elections. To Károlyi this was hypocritical. For twenty five years the West had shown no great interest in democracy in Hungary when Horthy had been in power. Károlyi hoped that the West European governments would recognise that early elections in Hungary could be disastrous, given the deep roots of Horthyism; that time would need to be allowed if radical and socialist parties were to have a chance to put their policies over to the people.

After a general election had been held in Hungary in November 1945 Bevin agreed to see Károlyi. This was the meeting that Alan Taylor arranged. It lasted for twenty-five minutes and left Károlyi a disappointed man. After the meeting Károlyi told Taylor that Bevin let Károlyi do the talking. Bevin listened and made the occasional notes, and at the end said that he was in favour of trade connections with Hungary.

Károlyi failed to win positive support from Bevin. He resisted Károlyi's appeal, which was, as Alan Taylor recollects, 'Comrade, the Foreign Office people cheat you. They are all pro-Horthy. But I who am a real democrat can explain to you about the democratic forces in

Hungary'. Károlyi had wanted the backing of the Labour Party when he got back to Hungary. He failed to get this. Bevin was not interested in the Hungarian count. He was not interested in what Károlyi had to say. Bevin had firm preconceptions about Eastern Europe and the role of the Soviet Union in that area. The winds of the Cold War period had begun to blow.

Károlyi arrived in Budapest in May 1946. His spirits were low. He was afraid that fascism had not been eradicated with the liberation of Hungary. However when he arrived he was delighted by the enthusiasm in post-war Hungary.

Károlyi's attitude to Hungary's problems at this time are revealed in a letter to his friend Oszkár Jászi in August 1946, written when Károlyi was back in London winding up his affairs there. Károlyi had few illusions. He could see the problems in Hungarian politics – the briberies and the petty jealousies, the rampant nationalism and revisionism. He could also see the external problems– the blunders in Hungary of the Russian and English authorities and the faults of Stalinist foreign policy generally.[19]

Károlyi wanted to play a part in Hungary's recovery from the Second World War. He offered to help at the peace conference in Paris, but his offer was not accepted. He gave good advice on improving Czech-Hungarian relations, but on the whole it was not taken. He spent a lot of his time in late 1946, early 1947 quietly in his home in Buda.

This simple retired life did not last long. The Smallholders Party in Hungary became a haven for Hungarian right-wingers and anti-Soviet politicians. At the time when this party and its leader Ferenc Nagy was becoming regarded by the Left as the centre of counter-revolutionary activities and conspiracies, Károlyi became the head of the Hungarian delegation to the Interparliamentary Union Conference at Cairo. At the same time he became the president of the Hungarian UNO Society and his wife became the co-president of the Hungarian-English Friendship Society. As a result they became the focus of many expectations. When Ferenc Nagy defected (on the advice of Ràkosi) it was thought for a while that Károlyi would become the president of the Hungarian Republic.

Károlyi visited London again in June 1947. During this visit he gave an interview to the *Manchester Guardian* (published on 21 June), in which he discussed the political difficulties facing Hungary, the nature of the Smallholders Party and the Hungarian attitude to Marshall aid. Károlyi wanted to see Bevin, but he was not given such an opportunity again. Instead he sent an aide-mémoire to the Secretary of State. This was summarised by a Foreign Office official as follows '. . . the aide-mémoire emphasised the existence of "reactionary" elements in the Smallholders Party, which had found their way into the administration and the diplomatic service. It stated that Mr Nagy was fully aware of the conspiracy and was playing a double game, and that, had the conspiracy been successful, a Government would have been set up which would have been anti-Russian and anti-Socialist. This would have been detrimental to the interests of Hungary. He concluded by declaring that "the new Hungarian Democracy" does not wish to antagonise the West, but that Britain and the U.S. must attempt to understand the peculiar problems and difficulties with which Hungary is now faced'.[20]

Soon after this Károlyi was appointed Minister to Paris, where he stayed for two years from August 1947. At that time Duff Cooper was the British Ambassador in Paris. He sent a good account to Bevin of Károlyi's first visit to him. 'Such formal calls usually last a few minutes, but Count Károlyi stayed with me for nearly an hour, and expressed his opinions on any subjects.' Károlyi referred to the elections in Hungary and, while admitting that they had not been conducted quite as they would have been in England, 'he maintained that there had been very little undue influence used, which he said was proved by the success of the Catholic Party. This, he said, showed that the Russians were exercising far less pressure in Hungary than was generally supposed.'[21]

Károlyi maintained a critical atitude towards the new Hungarian Government, towards the dogmatic features of Rákosi's foreign policy, his pseudo nationalism and his methods. Károlyi was an internationalist, a broad minded European, who had fought consistently and strongly against Horthy and did not want silly mistakes to be made in the new Hungary. He wrote to Erik Molnár, the historian and the then Foreign Secretary, that he knew that the West-European methods of democracy would not do in Hungary as long as the Fascist poison was still there, but he was deeply worried that exactly because of this the principles of humanity could not be exercised.[22] When he made a visit to Budapest in January 1948, he met Rákosi and other leaders and asked permission to publish a review about the Danubian Confederation. He then went to Prague. The tragic death of Masaryk made him very depressed. Returning to the Embassy in Paris he could sense, from his official activities and his personal connections, the onset of the Cold War. The seventy-three-year-old experienced peace warrior tried to do what he could, but he was thinking about making a dignified retirement on his next birthday in March 1949. His determination to go back to Hungary and to retire was reinforced by the coming trial of Cardinal Mindszenthy.

The Cardinal was arrested at the end of 1948 and Károlyi did not feel that there was sufficient justification for this act. He wrote a long letter to the then Foreign Secretary, László Rajk, and made it clear that he felt it would have been much better to send the Cardinal to Rome. Károlyi clearly saw what an international scandal would be created by the trial of the Cardinal and he thought it could have been easily averted. He did not want to resign at that time as it would have been seen internationally as a protest against the government over their policy to the Cardinal.

How the Károlyis felt in connection with Mindszenthy is shown in a very secret and personal letter written by John Strachey, the Minister of Food, to Bevin. 'Dear Ernie, I asked you whether you would like a note on a recent conversation which I had with Countess Károlyi, the wife of the Hungarian Minister to France. You said that you would like such a note.' Then Strachey told Bevin that the Countess was an old friend of his and begged complete discretion. He continued: 'Countess Károlyi deplored the Mindszenthy Trial. She said that Cardinal Mindszenthy had undoubtedly been the leader of the Catholic Opposition to the Hungarian Government; that his programme was the restoration of the Habsburgs; he was not an intelligent man but he was strong, determined and courageous, a good orator and had a very great following amongst the pious Roman Catholic Hungarian peasants; he had deliberately played the role of martyr. She thought the Hungarian Government had been terribly ill-advised in making a martyr of him. She thought the Government would have been justified in expelling him from Hungary and that this would have been by far the better course.' The Countess had gone on to say that if the Hungarian people then took part in a free election, they would vote for the right wing parties and would restore a reactionary régime of the Horthy type. She and her husband felt that there 'was no longer any basis for moderate parties; there was a naked conflict of Right and Left, both of which intended to govern by dictatorial methods.' She also thought that the long persistence of Hungarian feudalism, right up to 1940, would give the Hungarian Communists a better position than they had in neighbouring countries.[23]

This was written on 1 March, 1949. Károlyi went home to Budapest in May, to arrange his retirement with the then Secretary of State, Rajk, whom he had found to be a plain straightforward man. Rajk saw Károlyi in the presence of the Ambassador of France, which was a very unusual procedure. Next day Károlyi was informed by his friends that the Secretary of State had been arrested. At the same time as Rajk was arrested, so was P. Mód, whom Károlyi respected and whom he knew to be a loyal Communist Party member. Károlyi immediately wrote a very excited letter to the Under-Secretary of State, A. Berei, asking for explanations. In July 1949 Károlyi received an insulting letter from Rákosi, the first Secretary of the Communist Party. Károlyi returned to Budapest in August and Rajk's confession was shown to him. Károlyi could not believe all the nonsense in this, and protested about it in letters and conversations with the Hungarian leaders, Rákosi and Gerő. Nobody could have convinced him that Rajk was a traitor to the Communist cause. Károlyi failed to convince those who prepared the trial which led to the executions of Rajk and his so called accomplices. Károlyi arrived back in Paris in mid September 1949. He made a desperate effort to save Rajk's life when he found out that the Blue Book about Rajk's trial contained what he knew to be a clear lie. Rajk in his trial confessed that he helped B. Sulyok to escape abroad when Rajk was Home Secretary. But Károlyi remembered Rákosi, the First Secretary of the Communist Party, telling Károlyi that he meant to give a passport to Sulyok with the knowledge of the Prime Minister to enable him to leave the country. Rajk, as Home Secretary, had not given him the passport. He left the country in secrecy.

Károlyi therefore sent a telegram to the Prime Minister on the 13 October, 1949 and urged that the Rajk trial should be reviewed. If he did not get an answer within twenty-four hours he would publish his telegram in the French papers. He did not get an answer. Rajk and his companions were executed and Michael Károlyi became an émigré for the second time in his life.[24]

Károlyi did not want that. He wished to end his life in Hungary. The spirit and zest went out of his life. He retired to Vence. With the help of his wife he wrote his memoirs. Alan Taylor visited him in the early fifties and later recalled 'Michael was still the same enchanting personality with the same curiosity about what was going to happen in the world.'[25] But some months later his health began to give way. He lost more than twenty-four pounds within a short period. His last political interview was with Radio Ujvidék at the time when Stalin died. He hoped for better policies from both the United States and from the new Soviet leadership. He also expressed his admiration for the people of Yugoslavia, especially for their ability to make socialism work, and hoped that the Cold War would soon end. He reminded the West of its part in bringing about the Cold War and, with the exception of the social democrats, he criticised the Hungarian émigrés in the West. It was notable that Károlyi did not speak about the possibility of him returning to Hungary.

Károlyi died in March 1955. The Hungarian Press marked his death with only one sentence. The *Times* obituary on 21 March, 1955 had the title 'Aristocratic Rebel'.

In Hungary Michael Károlyi was rehabilitated after the old Stalinist leaders were swept aside. In 1962 his body was exhumed and taken to

Hungary for a state funeral in Budapest, an honour previously accorded only to two great émigrés, one from the eighteenth century, Rákóczi, and one from the nineteenth, Kossuth. As Taylor wrote 'Michael surely deserved this honour as the First President of independent Hungary, though it would also have amused him.'[26]

Since then there has been much written and published in Budapest on Károlyi. Books by him and his wife (who lived on until June 1985) have been published, there have been biographies of him written by eminent Hungarian historians, and there was an academic conference to mark the centenary of his birth. His statue stands near the Danube next to the Hungarian Parliament.

Lord Curzon said once: 'The first rule in foreign policy is to make sure you understand your own mind. The second is to make sure the other fellow understands it.' Károlyi certainly understood his own mind and acted according to his understanding. It was a great pity that other people understood it only after his death.

Notes

1 A. J P. Taylor, *A Personal History*, Hamish Hamilton, 1983, p. 156.

2 PRO. FO. 371.39247. President and Members of the Hungarian Council in Great Britain.

3 Hajdu, T., *Károlyi, Mihály*, Budapest, 1978, p. 334. In Hungarian.

4 PRO. FO. 371.3134. Draft by L. B. Namier, 11 November, 1918. Quoted by Hajdu, p. 298.

5 Hungarian Parliamentary Papers, 10 May, 1946. Quoted by Hajdu, p. 298.

6 PRO. FO. 371.8859. Quoted by Hajdu, p. 500.

7 Michael Károlyi to O. Jászi, 14 April, 1924.

8 Károlyi, Mihály, *Hit illuziók nélkul* (Faith without Illusions). In Hungarian, Budapest, 1977, p. 364–5.

9 Hajdu, op. cit., p. 477.

10 PRO. FO. 898/58.

11 PRO. FO. 371.39247.148/129144. British Legation, Stockholm. Chancery to Central Department, FO.

12 PRO. FO. 371.39248. Count M. Károlyi to Eden, 2 June, 1944.

13 PRO. FO. 371.39248. C.7482/2/21.

14 PRO. FO. 371.39248 C.7826. G. H. Hall to Central Department, 9 June, 1944.

15 PRO. FO. 371. 39248. B. Bracken to Károlyi, 8 June, 1944.

16 The minute was written by Bowen on 22 June, 1944 and others in the department agreed with it. PRO.FO. 371.39248.

17 PRO. FO. 371.48462. R.6590/26/21. Sir A. D. F. Gascoigne to D. Howard, 14 March, 1945.

18 PRO. FO. 371.48465. R.14204/26/21.

19 On the activities of the English authorities in Hungary, a British All-Party Parliamentary Delegation in spring 1946 observed, in its unanimously agreed report, 'The British political mission appears to be out of touch with the reality of the political situation.'

20 PRO. FO. 371.67178. R.8710/11/21.

21 PRO. FO. 371.67184. RI.2207, 3 September, 1947.

22 Letter to E. Molnár. Quoted by Hajdu, p. 511.

23 PRO. FO. 371.78519. R.2664.

24 Ms. Michael Károlyi: The Rajk Trial and M. Károlyi, *História*, 2, 1983. In English in The New Hungarian Quarterly, 99, 1985.

25 Taylor, p. 200.

26 Ibid., p. 239.